BLOOD & BONES: SIG

Blood Fury MC®

Book 2

JEANNE ST. JAMES

———

Acknowledgements:

Photographer/Cover Artist: Golden Czermak at FuriousFotog
Cover Model: David Cook
Editor: Proofreading by the Page
Beta readers: Whitley Cox, Andi Babcock, Sharon Abrams & Alexandra Swab
Blood Fury MC Logo: Jennifer Edwards

———

www.jeannestjames.com

Sign up for my newsletter for insider information, author news, and new releases:
www.jeannestjames.com/newslettersignup

Author's Note

Welcome to Manning Grove, PA...

This is where my Brothers in Blue series was based. If you haven't met the Brysons yet, it's recommended (but not required) to read that series before this book. Matt and Carly Bryson from Brothers in Blue: Matt (Brothers in Blue, book 3) are a major part of this book. The Bryson brothers, Teddy and their family will be making appearances throughout the Blood Fury MC series. Thank you for coming along for the ride!

Please note: Blood & Bones: Sig is an intense story and might include triggers for some readers.

Character List

BFMC Members:

Trip Davis – *President* – Son of Buck Davis, half-brother to Sig, mother is Tammy, Runs Buck You Recovery

Sig Stevens – *Vice President* – Son of Buck Davis, mother is Silvia, three years younger than Trip, helps run Buck You Recovery

Judge (Judd Scott) – *Sgt at Arms* - Father (Ox) was an Original, bounty hunter/owns Justice Bail Bonds

Deacon Edwards – *Treasurer* – Judge's cousin, skip tracer/bounty hunter at Justice Bail Bonds

Cage (Chris Dietrich) – *Road Captain* – Dutch's youngest son, mechanic working at Dutch's Garage

Ozzy (Thomas Oswald) – *Secretary* – Original – manages club-owned The Grove Inn.

Rook (Randy Dietrich) – Dutch's oldest son

Dutch (David Dietrich) – *Original* – Owns Dutch's Garage, sons: Cage & Rook

Dodge – *Prospect* – Helps manage Crazy Pete's Bar

Sparky – *Prospect* – Mechanic at Dutch's Garage

Mouse (Mickey) – *Prospect* – Mechanic at Dutch's Garage

Shady – *Prospect*

Stella – *Trip's ol' lady* - Crazy Pete's daughter, owns Crazy Pete's Bar

Former Originals:

Buck Davis – *President* – Deceased
Razor Stevens – *VP* - Deceased
Ox – *Sgt at Arms* – Deceased
Crazy Pete – *Treasurer* – Deceased
Tin Man (Tinny) – Deceased

Others:

Silvia Stevens – Sig's mother, Razor's former ol' lady
Tammy Davis – Trip's mother, Buck's former ol' lady
Bebe Dietrich – Cage & Rook's mother, Dutch's former ol' lady
Clyde Davis – Buck's father, Trip & Sig's grandfather, deceased
Lizzy – Sweet butt
Max Bryson – *Chief of Police* – Manning Grove PD, Bryson brother
Marc Bryson – *Corporal* – Manning Grove PD, Bryson brother
Matt Bryson – *Officer* – Manning Grove PD, Bryson brother
Adam Bryson – *Officer* – Manning Grove PD, Bryson's cousin, Teddy Sullivan's fiancé
Leah Bryson – *Officer* – Manning Grove PD, Marc's wife
Tommy Dunn – *Officer* – Manning Grove PD
Teddy Sullivan – Owner Manes on Main, Adam Bryson's fiancé
Amanda Bryson – Max's wife, owner Boneyard Bakery
Carly Bryson – Matt's wife, OB/GYN doctor

Prologue

AWAKENING

Sig ground his teeth, hoping it would help drown out the noise. The bed squeaking. The thumping of the headboard against the wall. The deep, loud grunts of the man between his mother's legs.

Years.

He'd heard it for years. Ever since he could remember.

He'd peeked in on them a few times when he was too young to know better. Not understanding what was going on.

Curious.

He'd quietly open the door just a crack and put his eye to the sliver of space.

Watching.

Wondering why the man was on top of his mother. Why they were both making those noises.

Why this happened so often.

But it did. A lot.

Anytime his father wasn't around.

Which was also a lot.

But he knew his father would come home later, usually

after Sig was in bed, and do the same thing to his mother, too.

Only there wasn't as much noise. At least on his mother's part.

He'd also watched them a couple times.

Then one day he realized what they were doing.

What it all meant.

And for a while, he had a hard time looking his mother in the face.

A long time.

Eventually, he learned what they were doing because he'd watch the same type of thing happen in front of everyone at the warehouse, which was the Blood Fury's church, the clubhouse for his father's MC.

Other women. Other men. Lots of them.

He'd even seen his father do it right out in the open to women who weren't his mother.

Right there.

In front of everyone.

He wasn't the only one. In fact, sometimes there was a line-up. All his father's club brothers. Sticking their dicks into the same woman as she was held down on a table or over a barrel. And she'd be smiling and encouraging them.

At least most of them. Not all.

Some were awake, some weren't.

Some would leave after that and never return.

Others came back for more.

When he'd gotten older, his body began to react when watching it. And he wanted to stand in line, too.

Hell, he'd even watched his best friend get his cherry popped by one of those sweet butts. What he thought, at the time, was a nicer name for what he learned later was a club whore.

He'd been in the crowd that circled Trip and the sweet

butt as Buck ordered the woman to spread her legs and let Trip nut inside her.

Trip did. And he'd only been fourteen.

Sig had been eleven at the time and hoped his father, Razor, would order the sweet butt to do the same for his own son.

He hadn't.

So, when his body would react, he would have to hide for a while until his painful erection went back down, or he'd end up making a mess in his underwear because he couldn't control it.

Once, one of the other women in the warehouse had noticed his discomfort and blown him a kiss, saying, "Whenever your daddy says it's okay."

Razor never did.

Because Razor didn't give a shit about his boy.

Not one shit.

Not like Buck did for Trip.

While Trip was his best friend, he also never told him that his father was coming over and screwing his mother.

Because he couldn't.

Buck had always warned him to keep his "fuckin' mouth shut." To keep the Blood Fury's president's visits to his mother a secret.

"You tell anyone, I'll fuckin' kill her, boy. You hear me? She wants it. Begs for my dick. That's the only reason I'm here. You say somethin' an' if I don't kill her first, your pop will." He had grabbed Sig's long hair, fisted it painfully and ripped his head back. "You fuckin' hear me?"

Sig had struggled not to cry out or show his fear. Because that was what Buck wanted. Buck liked people to be afraid of him. "Y-yeah."

"Not a goddamn word, boy."

In truth, Sig was afraid of Buck. Most everyone was.

Except for Sig's mother, Silvia. And maybe Trip's mother, Tammy.

Buck had a nasty temper and you didn't want it focused on you. Otherwise, you'd be hurting and that hurt would last a while.

Like the time Buck caught Sig watching a couple weeks ago. He'd rolled off his mother and within a couple strides, had a frozen Sig by his throat and thrown to the floor at the foot of the bed.

Sig was just glad the man wasn't wearing his boots. Otherwise, he might have ended up dead.

Instead, a naked Buck stomped on him a few times. In places Razor would never see. Sig's back, his stomach, his ribs, even his junk.

Sig had curled into a tight ball, trying to protect himself. When that didn't work, he struggled to crawl back out the door, clawing his way across the dirty, worn carpet.

Luckily, Buck let him go, still kicking Sig as he did his best to escape. And once he got near the open door, Buck kicked his ass right out of it, slamming it behind him and just missing Sig's foot.

Sig had laid in the hallway for the longest time, simply trying to breathe, trying to think, trying not to cry out loud.

But then he'd heard it again. The bed squeaking, his mother moaning, Buck calling her really dirty names between his grunts.

His mother had said nothing while Buck had kicked him. Never begged Buck to stop.

She just let him do it.

Later on, when asked, she'd answered, "You did wrong, you deserved what you got."

That was it.

Sig was so mad about that, he'd done something stupid.

Last time Buck was screwing his mother, he'd snuck into the room while they were busy, took the knife the club prez kept in his boot and hid it under his dad's jeans that had been left in a pile on the floor.

That was a week ago. And he was disappointed nothing came of it.

Razor never confronted Silvia. Or Buck. Not that he knew of, anyway.

If his dad had found the knife, he must not have thought anything of it. Or only thought it was his own.

But either way, eventually Sig would give Buck what he deserved. Even if he had to wait until he was older.

He wouldn't always be twelve. One day he'd be big enough, strong enough, to teach Buck a damn lesson he wouldn't be able to forget.

And then he'd take the club's top spot from him.

But that would be years from now, so he had to wait.

He had to suffer through listening to the bastard screwing his mother.

He had to suffer through hearing that bed make noise, as well as the two occupants.

He grimaced and covered his ears.

He could still hear them.

Buck screwing his mother. His mother letting the bastard do it. Encouraging him to give "it" to her harder. Faster.

He squeezed his eyes shut, took a deep breath and rolled off his bed. He needed to get out of the house. Needed to get away from them.

That bastard got what he wanted, whenever he wanted.

It was like Buck was king of the club.

He ruled them all.

And no one was going to stop him.

Sig vowed it would be him someday. Buck would pay.

He tagged his jeans from the floor and yanked them up his legs, pulling on the first shirt he came across. He snagged his sneakers as he went and threw open his door, trying to ignore those noises as he passed his mother's bedroom door.

"Asshole," he muttered under his breath as he kept rolling.

His feet stopped moving as the front door of their tiny house was flung open and his father came barreling through.

Finally!

Finally, his dad was going to stop Buck. Take him down a peg or two.

Before Sig could say anything, his dad shoved him out of the way and into the wall, not saying a word to him.

Like he wasn't even there.

Like Sig didn't even exist.

Like he was only in the way.

His mouth dropped open as he saw his father pull his Sig Sauer from under the back of his cut, lift his boot up and kick in the bedroom door, even though it wasn't locked.

It wasn't locked. Why did he have to kick it in?

Sig's feet unfroze and he quickly followed his father, now scared to death for his mother. "Ma!"

All that got him was a big hand to his chest and a painful shove backward. "Get outta here, kid," Razor yelled, raising the gun.

"But—"

The room was so small the sound exploded around him. He squeezed his eyes shut and fell to the floor, hearing nothing for the longest time.

Nothing but the ringing in his ears.

The acrid burn in his nostrils.

His heart escaping out of his chest.

He was afraid to open his eyes.

His father had killed his mother.

That was what he'd done.

That wasn't what was supposed to happen.

He forced his eyes open and all he could see was his mother's open mouth and her wide eyes as she screamed.

But Sig couldn't hear it.

He couldn't hear anything.

But he could see it.

Razor's .40 pointed to Silvia's head. And his beet red face, the angriest Sig ever saw him. His father's finger twitching dangerously on the trigger.

His mother wasn't dead, but she was about to die.

Just like the lifeless man lying naked on top of her. A hole dead center in his back. A dark red puddle spreading quickly over the dirty sheets beneath them both.

Sig's throat was raw because he was screaming. He just couldn't hear it.

He still couldn't hear shit.

But he could see it.

He could see his father raise that gun and strike her in the head with it.

Not once.

Not twice.

Too many times to count.

That wasn't supposed to happen.

He could barely hear his father bellowing, "Knew you were a fuckin' whore! Never shoulda made a whore like you my ol' lady."

Razor was only supposed to kick Buck's ass. Teach the bastard a lesson.

That was it.

Nothing more.

"See your fuckin' whore mother?" The shouted question sounded muffled over the loud ringing still in his ears.

But he heard it.

And, yeah, Sig saw her. He'd never be able to un-see her.

Naked and bloody, her distorted face swollen and split. Sig wasn't sure if she was still breathing.

"Ain't nothin' but filthy snatch. Here's a lesson for ya, don't make a cunt like that your ol' lady, kid."

His father spun on his boot and Sig never saw him again.

It wasn't until a few days later, he discovered he had witnessed the man he thought was his father shoot the man who turned out to be his real father point-blank. That was also when he agreed with Razor's opinion his mother was no better than a lying, cheating whore.

It wasn't until a few days later, the whole club imploded. Just like his family.

Ox, the club's enforcer, shot Razor dead right between the eyes. Then another member tried to take out Ox and failed.

When they thought things couldn't get worse, they did.

Brothers became enemies. Family became strangers.

And his best friend became blood.

Only by then, once he found out Trip was his half-brother, his best friend was long gone.

Chapter One

THE GLOW of the lantern sitting on the ground created a small circle of light around them.

Sig gave Rebecca a smile while she coyly turned her eyes downward and only gave him a shy one back.

It was all a bullshit act.

But to get what he came for, he played the fucking game.

And in the end, it was always worth it.

The eighteen-year-old stood wringing her hands, while her dirty bare feet twisted nervously under her long, plain blue dress.

That dress did nothing for her curves. He knew because he'd seen those curves without that ugly-ass dress quite a few times. But the dress was necessary, not for their little game, but because she was required to wear it.

Dresses like that were all she owned.

Just like she was required to wear that fucking black "kapp" on her head, covering her blonde hair that, when he ripped the pins out, almost fell to her waist.

He also knew the carpet matched the drapes. And it was thick fucking carpet, too.

This two a.m. meet had become a regular thing. Him parking his sled off the road in a nearby field so his loud exhaust wouldn't wake her family, then hoofing it through the dark to the barn, using only the glow of his cell phone to make sure he didn't break his goddamn neck.

Because she was still in the midst of rumspringa, she also had a cell phone of her own. She hid it from her family but used it to text him whenever she was in the mood to play.

She was in the mood to play tonight.

He was in the mood to play with her.

Especially since rumspringa was almost over for her and she had to decide if she would stay in her community and marry the man her parents wanted her to, or leave. So right now, she was texting Sig often.

She had caught his eye when she accompanied her friends delivering their family's goods to The Barn, the Fury's new church. The local Amish families kept the MC supplied with a lot of shit. Eggs, milk and the like, along with keeping them flush with tobacco and hand-rolled cigarettes.

If they only grew pot like they did tobacco, the MC would be in pig fucking heaven.

But instead of growing weed, they grew women like Rebecca. Innocent looking on the outside, dirty little whores on the inside.

Rumspringa was their chance to go wild. Sow those fucking wild oats.

And Rebecca was a ho, not of the tool variety.

He didn't have to chase her because she chased him. And, without a fucking fight, he let himself get caught. Because pussy was pussy, whether it was Amish or "English." He wasn't that fucking picky as long as it was young and fresh.

And Becky couldn't get any more farm fresh. Only she wasn't giving up that ready-to-pick cherry. Not to Sig.

"When you gonna give me that pussy?"

She rolled her eyes at the question he asked every time they got together to play. "You know I'm saving it for my husband."

"Never thought you plain women would be such dirty 'lil sluts."

"I'm not a slut. I'm sweet and innocent." She flashed her big baby blues at him and gave him a smile that was far from fucking innocent.

That meant it was time to play.

"That fuckin' sin sifter on your head don't help keep you from lyin' or sinnin', does it?" Sig took a step closer, his palm sliding down the hard-on under his jeans.

"No. I've been *bad*."

Oh yeah. "What'd you do this time?"

"I talked back to my daddy."

"Your daddy don't like it when you talk back, now does he?"

"No," she answered with a slight shake.

It wasn't from fear, fuck no. It was from excitement. Her flawless ivory skin was now flushed, her eyes heated, her lips parted, her little slut tongue slipped over her plump bottom lip. Then she grabbed that lip between her teeth, biting down hard.

His balls tightened at that. "So, what does your daddy do when you talk back?"

She tipped her head down and glanced up at him from under heavy eyelids. "Sends me to bed without supper."

"Bet you're hungry, then."

"Yes," she hissed softly.

"Bet I know what that little whore mouth is hungry for. What it's always hungry for." Sig took another step closer until he was boot to bare toe with her. "Get on your knees for your punishment."

Grabbing her blue dress in both hands, she pulled it up

her sweet, thick thighs and dropped to her knees on the hard dirt.

"You know what to do."

Becky unbuckled his belt, unfastened his jeans and slowly unzipped them.

He could hear how ragged her breathing was. A slow grin spread across his face.

He yanked that black cap from her head and tossed it on a nearby straw bale. Then tore his fingers through her hair, the pins popping loose and falling to the ground. Her thick, long hair tumbled around her, hiding her pretty face.

He grabbed a fistful and jerked it hard until her face was lifted to his, then he ripped it back, arching her neck and making her cry out softly.

He stroked his fingers down the front of her throat where the skin was taut from the strain of her neck.

Her hands hadn't stopped working, and within seconds, his dick was throbbing within her fingers. She began to fist him, her eyes getting hotter as she was forced to meet his. Her mouth gaped and she panted.

"Your daddy needs to teach you a lesson on back-talkin', don't he?"

"I'm sorry. I didn't mean to speak fresh like that."

"Too fuckin' late for sorries," he mumbled.

He pulled his dick from her hands, slid the head slick with precum across her mouth and when she opened it wider, he plunged inside.

She gagged immediately, like she always did, until she got used to how deep he fucked her face.

Now grabbing two handfuls of hair, he dipped his head down to watch her as he began to thrust. Little whimpers escaped her every time he went deep. Tears began to form in her eyes and slip from the corners. Her mouth was stretched, her cheeks bellowed in and out with each thrust and her face turned almost purple. She gagged again as he drove deep between her lips, faster and harder, strings of spit beginning to cling to his dick.

When she reached up to grab the root, he pushed her hand away. They'd done this enough times, he knew her limit but he'd take her right to that very edge. Still, he allowed her to grip his balls, her fingers circling the base of them tight, her short nails digging into the delicate skin.

But, *fuck*, he got off on that, handing her that power when on the surface it seemed she had none. One good fucking squeeze to his sac from her and he'd be right next to her on his knees.

The more he pumped into her hot, wet mouth, the closer he was getting to popping one of those nuts, so he slowed, let her breathe a little bit, then stopped.

He slipped from her.

"Why did you stop?" she asked him, wiping off the spit clinging to her lips and chin and drying her cheeks with the hem of her ugly dress. At least it was good for something.

"You know why."

"Because I've been bad." Like the obedient bitch she was, she nodded and got to her feet as Sig slid his belt from the loops of his jeans which were now down around his ankles and gathered above his boots.

"What d'you do besides talk back?"

"I pushed my little sister and made her fall."

"Why'd you do that?"

"Because I like when Daddy punishes me," she whispered.

And, *Jesus fuck*, didn't that almost make him shoot his fucking load across the stall.

He folded the black leather strap in half, snapped the loop sharply together once, and waited.

"And how does your daddy punish you for hurtin' your sister?"

Her cheeks became even darker and her blue eyes glittered as she stared hungrily at the belt in his hands. "He spanks me with a leather strap."

This was one of the games they played. Only it wasn't a fucking game.

This was something Becky needed and Sig was more than willing to give it to her.

In fact, he more than liked giving it to her and needed it, too. Because sometimes the fire raging inside him could become so out-of-control that this was the only thing that helped contain it.

Too bad she was Amish and already spoken for to a man who would most likely never give Becky what she needed.

The only thing he'd give her was fucking brats and lots of them.

As soon as one popped out, he'd want her belly full with the next one. Her future husband had a large farm and needed help to work it.

Standardbreds pulling their buggies, draft horses working in the fields and a litter of kids doing all the farm labor and housework.

But for now, Becky was getting what she needed by using Sig.

And Sig was using her.

It was an agreement that benefitted them both.

So, until Becky changed her last name, Sig was getting what the fuck he could. And Becky was getting what she asked for.

"You know what the fuck to do," he growled.

She turned, her long blonde hair swinging, and went over to two straw bales stacked along one of the stall walls. She faced them, leaned over, and yanked her dress up and over her ass, exposing the fact she wore no underwear.

Exposing the fact the woman had never shaved that *ripe-for-the-picking* pussy.

Normally, he didn't like that. But knowing he couldn't go

there, it drove him fucking nuts, making his dick throb and leak like crazy.

Yeah, he couldn't go there, but she was willing to give him something else.

He yanked his jeans up slightly so he could follow her, then stood far enough away from her to give himself a good downswing.

He didn't even warn her or hesitate. Because ever since he got her text, his mind had been on nothing but what was about to happen.

Today had been one of those fucking days where he'd been ready to crack. Just like the sharp crack of the leather against her bare ass.

However, that noise, that sight, almost made him come. But this was only the beginning and he needed to hang on. It'd only get better.

His arm raised again and her ass twitched in anticipation. A red narrow welt instantly decorated her pale cheek.

Goddamn beautiful.

He let his arm fall as hard as he could and another crack of leather against flesh filled the air. A little whimper escaped her as a sharp breath escaped him.

But this, so far, was nothing for her.

How she discovered what she liked and needed, he had no fucking clue. But he only knew he was not the first one to do this to her.

Her rumspringa started when she was sixteen and from what she told him, her and her friends had gotten a bit wild.

He brought the belt back down hard across both cheeks and she jerked forward with a moan. She now had multiple raised welts, but he wasn't done.

She'd want more. And he needed to give her more.

Because every strike loosened up the tension deep in his gut.

Every strike helped his world stop spinning and curbed the urge to run.

Trip would be pissed if he bailed and left the Fury in the lurch. He did his best not to do that. At least not yet.

And this was one way he was handling it.

So, he gave Becky more of what she wanted and what he needed. Until both cheeks were a deep red, almost purple in some spots. Until she'd have a hard time sitting down.

Until he knew some of those welts would turn into bruises.

But not once had she ever told him to stop. She would've bitched at him if he had.

After a dozen or more strikes, when she finally reached back and put her hands on the inflamed skin of her ass, he knew she'd had enough.

He knew she was ready.

Fuck. So was he.

He dropped the belt to the ground, pulled a lubricated wrap from the front pocket of his jeans, ripped it open and rolled it down his throbbing length.

He shuffled forward and separated her burning hot, stripped and swollen cheeks, and brushed her tight, puckered hole with his thumb, making her groan into the straw.

Keeping her cheeks spread, he leaned over, spat on her anus and pushed his latex-covered cock against it.

Then closed his eyes as he slowly slid inside her.

She squeezed him tight and he had to stop to catch his breath. Because everything that had gone on before had him already teetering on the fucking edge.

It wouldn't take much for him to topple.

But she loved him taking her up the ass, and he needed to make it good for her. Because she made it good for him.

And he didn't want these secret meets to stop any time soon.

It was a perfect relationship.

He came over, he nutted, he went back to his apartment above the bunkhouse. No bitch to scrape off afterward. No clinging, no commitment.

No nagging cunt.

Even better, he got to burn off some of his pent-up rage using his belt. Or his hand. Or one of the buggy whips from the tack room. Whatever she was in the mood for.

When he left, they were both satisfied.

She got what she wanted, he got what he needed.

Fucking perfect.

Gritting his teeth, he dug his fingers into her full hips and began to pound her, watching the flesh of her marked ass ripple with each thrust.

After a few seconds, he reached around and played with her clit.

The only thing she didn't allow him was to fuck her pussy. With his dick or his fingers. Anything else went.

Sometimes they played a new game. Sometimes they played a game they've played before.

Like tonight.

Her soft whimpers became cries and she rocked her hips against him, encouraging him to fuck her harder.

He did his best without trying to bust a nut.

But he was close. So fucking close.

He'd been hard off and on most of the fucking day because she had texted him early this morning while he was still in bed. Which made him jack off in anticipation.

Then again in the shower.

Now this would be his third load of the day, but he was still struggling not to lose it too soon.

He was about to fail...

A noise, like a footstep, behind him had his hips stutter, then halt.

But before he could turn his head to look over his shoulder, something heavy was thrown over him, turning his world dark. A huge cloth blanket. And it smelled like horse shit.

Before he could find the edge to throw it off of him, something hit him hard.

Like a club to the ribs, making him lose all the oxygen in his lungs.

And again.

He gasped for air.

He couldn't find any.

Then another strike, this time against his head.

And another.

And one more.

As his knees crumpled, the darkness swept in.

———

SIG GROANED. His world was still dark, but it wasn't because his eyes were closed.

He carefully drew in the horse shit scented air.

As his lungs expanded, he groaned again.

Moving slowly—as if he had a fucking choice—he carefully felt around until he found the edge of the blanket and tugged it off his head.

He blinked. At least doing that didn't cause pain. Unlike breathing or moving.

He stared up into the night sky, slowly inhaling, exhaling, keeping his breaths shallow.

Even so, he winced at the shooting pain in his ribs.

His mind replayed the last few moments before everything went dark.

Wasn't the first time he'd had the shit beat out of him.

Probably wouldn't be the last.

He spat out a bit of mud, then wiped the back of his hand over his bleeding, throbbing lip, wincing again.

Damn.

He carefully pressed his fingers around his swollen right eye, checking to see if the socket was broken. It didn't seem to be, so maybe the blanket had cushioned some of the blows.

But still... He felt like he'd been kicked in the nuts by a fucking horse.

He had no fucking clue where he was. But wherever it was made him a sitting duck. He needed to move.

Somehow find his fucking sled.

Then somehow make it back to The Barn.

After a few more minutes, he cursed up into the night air. He patted the hidden pockets of his cut to see if he still had his cell phone.

Thank fuck he did. Hopefully, it wasn't broken. Otherwise, he might be hanging out in some field for the next day or so.

With as muddy as he was, he was most likely dragged to his current location, so that meant he probably wasn't too far from Rebecca's parents' farm.

That also meant he needed to get the fuck out of there before the sun rose. *Way* before the sun rose, since those fuckers woke up before the ass crack of dawn.

He pressed the button on the side of his phone and with another wince, lifted it in front of his face.

Thank fuck it was working.

He scrolled through his contacts and found the one he was looking for.

Definitely not Trip. Because if his brother found out what just happened, he had a feeling his ass would be kicked all over again.

And right now, he couldn't fight back.

Right now, he was as vulnerable as a goddamn newborn.

"Fuck!" he shouted to the sky, but that shout cost him.

"Goddamn it," he whispered, because that was much less painful.

Who could come get him and keep their fucking mouth shut?

Who could pick him up and take him somewhere other than The Barn?

He found the name he needed and hit Send.

Chapter Two

THE POUNDING on the motel room door had Sig groaning and trying to roll up to a seated position.

He finally accomplished that, but it had taken more time than he liked.

"Fuck," he muttered. "Door's open."

Ozzy pushed it open. "Your junk covered?"

Sig tipped his eyes down and considered his naked body. The one still sporting a hell of a lot of colorful bruises. "Has it been fuckin' covered the last dozen times you've been in here?"

"Fuck no, but I'm about sick of seein' it."

"Just jealous of my monster cock."

"Just to tell you, ain't a monster." Ozzy moved deeper into the room, but left the door wide open. "Not even close."

"Musta seen a lot of dick."

"Not by choice," Ozzy muttered.

Sig winced when he laughed. Even after three days of being holed up at the MC-owned Grove Inn, his ass was still hurting.

But it was improving.

"You find my sled?"

"Yeah."

"Was it in one piece?"

"Also yeah."

Sig glanced up at Ozzy. "So, now what?"

"Droppin' your ass off there to ride it home."

"That's gonna suck."

"Probably not as hard as that Amish snatch you got caught fuckin' up the ass."

Sig grunted. It was a fucking shame he'd never get that ass or mouth again. That had been some sweet addictive shit.

He tilted his head as he squinted up at the club's Secretary. "They didn't kill 'er, right?"

"How the fuck would I know? The fuck if I was knockin' on their door askin'."

Sig's lips thinned out. "Yeah."

"So, anyway, you gotta go. Got this room rented out for tonight. Need to get the housekeeper in here to clean up after your ass. You're a goddamn pig."

Sig groaned again as he carefully pushed himself to his feet. "At least I didn't shit the bed."

"Good thing, otherwise you woulda been layin' in it for three damn days."

"Trip wonderin' where I'm at?"

"Fuck yeah. He's got repo jobs lined up and you nowhere to be found. Wonderin' if you caught any charges. Didn't tell 'im you caught a beatin' instead."

"So much for them Amish bein' pacifists," Sig grumbled.

"Yeah, well, when you're fuckin' one of their virgins up the ass, that tends to piss 'em off. Let's fuckin' go. Don't got all day for your belly achin'."

"What'd you tell the prez?"

"Didn't tell him nothin'. You make up a fuckin' story.

Haven't seen or heard from you. Right now, I'm a deaf and blind motherfucker. That's your fuckin' mess, you clean it the fuck up."

Sig sighed. He had no clue what the fuck he was telling Trip. But his brother wasn't going to let his VP's disappearance go ignored. Trip was wound too fucking tight for that.

"How we gettin' to my sled? Ain't ridin' nut to butt with you."

"Still got Lizzy's cage."

Lizzy was one of the sweet butts who showed up one day at The Barn a couple months back, right before Sig did. She was great at sucking and fucking but was too old for Sig's tastes. She had to be at least thirty.

He liked his snatch fresh and Lizzy was hardly that.

But Ozzy tended to jump on her whenever he could. Which was often.

Lizzy probably hoped Ozzy would claim her as his ol' lady. He wasn't, and never would. But that still didn't mean he didn't take advantage of what Lizzy offered.

They all did.

Except for Trip. And Shady.

But then Shady was a weird fucking dude. Too goddamn quiet.

And the motherfucker was about to be patched in soon. As well as Dodge, Sparky and Mouse.

The club was growing faster than Trip expected, which made his brother happy. Not that Sig gave a shit about Trip's happiness. He didn't.

He used to when they were kids and best friends. But then shit changed.

He pulled on the clean jeans and shirt Ozzy had snuck out of Sig's apartment. The others had been covered in caked mud. He gingerly sat on the edge of the bed and slid on his socks and boots, then shrugged into his cut, grateful Ozzy had Lizzy clean it for him.

"Let's roll," Sig said as he forced his way vertical again.

They rolled.

———

Once Sig was dropped off at his sled, Ozzy headed one direction and Sig the other.

Luckily, there wasn't any more damage than there was already. His sled wasn't perfect. In fact, it was a piece of shit.

Cage, as Road Captain, told him he needed to do something about that.

And Sig would. When he fucking felt like it. Not because he was being ordered to by that douchebag motherfucker.

Sparky and Dodge had offered to work on it for him. But Dodge was busy helping run Crazy Pete's bar with Stella, and Sig figured Trip would be pissed if he pulled Dodge away from that, putting more pressure on Trip's ol' lady.

So, it was up to Sparky, and sometimes Mouse, but they could only do it after normal business hours at Dutch's garage. Because of that, it had been a slow fucking go since Sig had no other wheels. His rust bucket Ford truck had died not long after coming back to Manning Grove a couple of months ago.

He didn't have enough scratch to fix both.

Not yet, anyway.

He should've gotten half the farm from his so-called granddaddy, but his fucking half-brother got it all, instead.

Most likely because ol' Clyde had been embarrassed that Sig ended up being his grandson and then that unwanted grandson ended up living in and out of prison. More in than out.

Could've been the reason.

Even so, Trip owed him half. Which, if he ever got it, he'd sell off and put a shitload of scratch in his pocket.

But Trip's asshole was too tight, and he was never giving Sig half.

While Sig got a free place to stay, it was a small apartment in The Barn's bunkhouse and not the goddamn big farmhouse where Trip and Stella lived.

Once again, Sig got the shaft deep up his ass.

And he hated taking dick there. Never liked it, never would.

Now, as he rode along Copperhead Road, he debated whether to head back to The Barn and deal with Trip, or just keep riding.

If it wasn't for every damn bump he hit, making him grit his teeth and grumble a curse, he'd keep riding.

Maybe even roll past the farm and keep rolling out of Manning Grove to never come the fuck back since he no longer had Rebecca to help work out his temper when it boiled out of control.

Jesus fuck, he was going to miss her and their late-night sessions.

It was going to suck that his belt, which he had luckily found next to him in the field, would only be used to hold up his damn jeans.

Unless he found someone else.

Maybe one of those sweet butts. Didn't matter how old they were if all they had to do was bend over and give him their ass.

Yeah... Maybe...

A flash of color moved quickly through the woods to his right.

And again.

What the fuck?

Sig released the throttle, slowing down in case it was a deer or something. Because hitting a deer on his sled would fucking suck. Especially since he was still hurting from the last "collision" he had with some sort of object.

While having fresh venison would be great, becoming roadkill himself wouldn't.

Though, wrecking would give Sig a good excuse to give Trip on why he looked the way he did and hadn't come home.

But hitting anything with a sled would still suck donkey dick.

That flash of red and white kept moving quickly toward the road but awkwardly. Like whatever it was might be injured or, at least, limping.

And it was zig-zagging through and around trees and brush.

He hit the brakes and swerved to the narrow berm, squinting up through the thick woods.

No. Not a fucking deer.

Not a coyote.

Not a bear.

Human.

A fucking woman.

Holy fuck. A naked woman.

Long red hair. Pale as fuck skin. Too fucking thin.

Totally naked like a woodland nymph. Or some fairy.

Or a fucking ghost.

Or just a naked fucking woman.

One who was scared.

And running away from something.

Or someone.

Or maybe running toward something.

Or someone.

Him.

She was blindly running toward him.

What the fuck.

He kicked his stand down and jumped off his sled, then almost fell to his knees as the pain shot through him. He took a second to catch his breath, then straightened, trying to get a bead on this wild woman.

When she spotted him, her eyes went wide and she veered in a different direction. And when she turned, he spotted it.

Oh fuck.

She was thin everywhere. Skin and bones except for her belly, which was rounded. He guessed it could be a sign of malnutrition like those kids starving in Africa he'd seen in all those commercials.

Or...

"Hey!" he yelled, which hurt like fuck.

Where the fuck was she going?

He moved as quickly as he could down a small ditch and up a sharp incline until he was in the woods, heading in the direction she was.

"Hey!" he yelled again, but not as loudly this time, because his lungs were having a hard time keeping up.

She darted around a tree a few hundred feet from him.

Goddamn it.

He pushed past the searing pain and began to run, clenching his teeth as he did so. Biker boots were not made for running, especially not in the thick brush. *Fuck,* bikers weren't made for running, period.

Branches smacking him in the face and ribs did not help him keep moving, either.

Nor did it help her. Because he was about to give the fuck up and let her go.

Let her go back to the pack of wolves that raised her. Because the fuck if he needed to deal with some mental woman on the loose. He already had enough of his own issues.

But then she tripped and disappeared as she tumbled, a small cry hitting his ears, causing him to move faster in that direction.

When he got close enough, he saw she had ended up on her knees in a slight dip with one hand to her distended belly, and he tried not to fall himself. He picked his way over the slippery rocks hidden beneath the thick carpet of rotting leaves and downed branches to get even closer.

She was struggling to get to her feet, sobs coming from her open mouth, tears creating a path over her dirty cheeks.

Then he was there.

"No!" she screeched at the top of her lungs. "No!"

Jesus fuck. A shiver slid down his spine at the pure terror in her voice.

She got to her feet and before she could run, he hooked her around the waist, pulling her to him.

She shrieked so loudly he winced, then winced again as she clawed at his arms, fighting like a crazy woman. Pure panic in her hazel eyes. Nonstop tears.

Her body, nothing but skin, bones and belly, heaving with each sob.

He dodged her knee a couple of times, trying not to get nailed in the fucking nuts, and wrapped his arms tightly around her flailing arms, pinning them to her sides.

He pushed his own pain out of his head when he yelled, "Jesus fuck, woman. *Stop*... Stop. Only tryin' to help. Need my fuckin' nads."

She didn't stop, so he tightened his arms, making sure her teeth, which were snapping at him, didn't catch anything important.

With a hair-raising howl, she stomped on his foot, but her bare feet did nothing since he had his steel-toed boots on.

Then she cracked her heel into his shin. Twice.

"Fuck!" he yelled. "Stop it! Only tryin' to help you, you crazy bitch!"

When she suddenly went limp, he got really suspicious.

Her head dropped forward, her muscles went loose and it was only her breathing still out of control.

"You done?"

She didn't answer, which meant she wasn't done.

"Only tryin' to help," he whispered, afraid to loosen his hold. "If I let you go, you won't run?"

"I... need..." Her long, dark red hair was a total disaster. Knotted and dirty with twigs and pine needles stuck in the strands. It looked like it hadn't been washed or brushed in weeks, if not longer.

"You need to what?"

"To... run."

Fuck, if that didn't send another shiver shooting down his spine. "Gonna help you run."

Her head lifted. Her mouth was parted and she still panted.

She was way too thin. Her ribs were showing, her hip and shoulder bones protruding. Her skin almost transparent, especially over her belly where it was stretched tight. Her blue veins could be seen like a highway map under that pale skin. Purple half-moons discolored the skin under her haunted greenish-gold eyes.

Old and new marks circled her wrists and ankles. Her skin was bruised and raw in places. Bloodied in others.

An old yellowish bruise colored one cheek. A new purplish black one colored the other.

Marks in the shape of fingers decorated her throat.

A large bruise covered the right side of her ribs.

Multiple welts striped her back. Long and thin. Reminding him of the buggy whip marks left behind on Becky when he had used it.

Her feet were so filthy it appeared she wore dirt shoes.

Her nails were ragged and black, too. They were also bleeding like she had tried to claw her way out of something.

Sig's stomach turned. "Gonna help you."

"They... can't... find me."

"They won't." Whoever the fuck "they" were.

"They can't." Her voice was hoarse and raw, like she'd been screaming too much.

"They won't," he repeated more firmly.

"They can't."

"Okay," he whispered, bile starting to rise up his throat at the panic tinging her words.

"Can't go back."

"You won't. I'll make fuckin' sure of it." *Jesus*, his heart was pounding in his throat.

"N-never."

"What's your name?"

"I... can't."

"Okay. You don't have to. I'm Sig. Gonna take you somewhere safe."

She squeezed her eyes shut, her face twisting. "Nowhere is... safe."

"I got somewhere."

"They'll find me."

"No."

Her eyes went wide and she screamed, "Yes! They'll find me. I didn't give them what they wanted yet."

His blood froze at her panic.

"They're not... *done* with me."

"Who?"

"I have to... need to... leave... They're following me."

Was this woman totally off her rocker? Had she escaped some sort of mental institution? Were some white coats chasing her?

Jesus fuck. Maybe it was a bad idea to take her back to the farm.

"Who's followin' you?" he asked again, still not letting her go.

"Them."

Goddamn it! "Who?"

"Them up there."

Sig went solid and he slid his eyes up the mountain in the direction where she had come from.

Oh fuck.

Oh fuck, fuck, fuck.

They needed to move. Needed to go. Right now.

"We gotta go," he encouraged her, talking fast. "I have wheels. Can get you away from 'em faster. But you can't run if I let you go. Gotta fuckin' promise me."

She said nothing. Which to Sig meant she wasn't promising shit.

Which meant as soon as he let her go, she was going to run. And if she did, he was letting her. If she didn't want his help, then fuck her.

But he was not getting his ass shot or strung up. There were most likely booby traps in the woods. How she didn't get caught up in one, he had no fucking clue. He was surprised she didn't get a leg snapped off in a bear trap.

He had no idea what to call her but he needed to make some sort of connection. He picked the first thing he could think of. "Red, gonna give you my shirt, 'kay? And when we get to my bike, I got a flannel shirt in my bag. You can cover up with that. Then I'm gettin' you the fuck outta here. I promise. Now, you gotta promise me you won't fuckin' run."

She blinked, her hazel eyes unfocused, her face paler now than before. Her adrenaline spike was crashing. He wasn't even sure she'd be able to cling to him on the back of his sled. But they had no other way to jet, so maybe he'd tuck her in front of him. She was slender enough he should be able to steer his sled around her. As long as the pigs didn't see him.

If they were in the area, they were both fucked. Especially with how both of them looked.

Fuck. He should drop her off at the pig pen anyway. Let them deal with her crazy ass.

"Lettin' you go now." He slowly released his arms and hissed at the pain shooting along his own ribs. He pushed through it to slide his cut off and remove the T-shirt he wore over a long-sleeved thermal.

Once he was done, he was surprised to see her still standing there. But she was shivering like a newborn fawn with her arms crossed over her protruding stomach, not even trying to hide the rest of her nakedness from him.

At this point, she probably didn't fucking care. She was probably just glad to be alive and upright.

Sig worried about that upright part. She could collapse at any time.

He tugged his shirt over her head, pulling her mess of hair free. The shirt only fell to her hips, leaving her lower half uncovered.

Shit.

He'd wrap his flannel shirt around her waist to cover her better. It was better than nothing.

"Let's go," he said gently, after putting his cut back on. "Gonna help you." He held out his hand. She stared at it for a long moment. "Red, it's me," he jerked his chin up the mountain, "or them."

She didn't move.

He heard a clock ticking loudly in his brain. Or maybe that was his thumping heart. Either way, they needed to move.

"Red," he said more firmly, her panic starting to seep into his own skin. "Me... Or them."

More tears slid down her face as she continued to stare at his outstretched hand, which was now almost as dirty as hers.

He figured she needed to decide on the lesser of two evils. One known. One unknown.

Her mouth opened and a thick, raw, "You," escaped and she grabbed his hand.

Thank fuck.

He gave her a sharp nod and helped her out of the woods.

Maybe she wasn't the crazy one in all of this.

Maybe it was him.

Chapter Three

He steered his sled carefully down the rutted, rough lane toward The Barn. His teeth clenched the whole time as not only everything on his body screamed, but so did his mind.

He needed to get her somewhere where she wasn't exposed. Where she was safe.

He rode past the farmhouse, hoping not to run into Trip. He didn't have time to deal with his brother's bullshit right now.

The woman who was straddling the seat in front of him, leaning back against him and clinging onto his bare outstretched arms with her sharp, broken nails, was who he needed to focus on.

Hopefully, Trip was out on a repo job. And he hoped to fuck Stella was home.

If not, he'd be on his own dealing with Red.

He maneuvered his sled around the MC's clubhouse to the back of the bunkhouse, to the exterior stairs that took him to his apartment.

He parked it as close as he could to the bottom of the metal steps, shut his engine off and heeled his kickstand down.

Then he tried to breathe.

And still his spinning thoughts.

The woman's head which had been flopping forward for most of the ride, like she had fallen asleep, lifted just slightly. "Where…"

"Somewhere safe. None of 'em will know you're here. And if they find out, they won't be able to get to you. You'll be protected here."

Fuck, he hoped that was true.

Trip was going to have a problem with this.

Maybe even Judge.

But he needed more eyes on the lookout than just his own two.

At least until all of this was figured out.

At least until he had some better answers.

At least until he figured out where she needed to go. Who he could hand her off to, besides back to those hillbilly, in-bred, redneck motherfuckers on that mountain.

The Shirley Clan.

An extended family who declared themselves and their mountain one of those bullshit sovereign nations. They made up their own laws and didn't follow the same ones the rest of Americans had to.

Or at least, that was what they wanted. Law enforcement and federal agents didn't seem to agree. Unfortunately, Sig wanted nothing to do with law enforcement or the feds himself. So, bringing Red back to the farm might not be the smartest fucking idea.

But those marks on her body and those torn, bloody nails made him think she'd done her fucking best to escape some sort of confinement.

And he knew all about being confined. He knew all about having your damn freedom yanked from you. He knew all about being locked up against your fucking will.

And that shit twisted his gut.

Only difference was, Sig knew how and why he ended up in prison each time. He had no clue how Red ended up on that fucking mountain. Or why.

Or if she had gone voluntarily, why she was now trying to escape.

Especially if what he suspected was the reasoning behind why her stomach was the way it was.

He'd done pregnant women before, so he knew what a knocked up one looked like, but not one of them had been as thin as Red. How a baby could be growing in her belly like that, he had no fucking clue.

But again, it could be because she hadn't eaten in a very long time and her gut was just distended.

Maybe that was it.

Because if she was carrying a Shirley spawn, then shit just got even more fucked for them both.

He put one hand on her shoulder to make sure she didn't topple off his sled and he dismounted, then helped her to her feet. As she stood, she wobbled slightly.

Fuck.

He needed to get her upstairs fast before anyone saw them, before anyone fucking snitched to Trip.

He gritted his teeth, squatted with a searing curse due to the pain that shot through his body, and hooked her under the knees and curled an arm behind her back.

She hardly weighed a thing for being about five-foot-five. Even for possibly being knocked up.

But at the moment, his pain overrode his anger. His breath hissed and he ground his molars as he slowly and carefully made his way up the steps, gripping her securely to his chest.

"I can... walk."

The fuck she could. But he couldn't say a fucking word. Not yet. Not through the excruciating agony that wanted to take him to his knees.

When he got to the top landing, he hissed out another sharp breath and dropped her to her feet. He dug for his keys deep within his front pocket, plugged one into the lock and shoved the door open.

"Inside," he managed to get out.

She hesitated.

He got why.

She was wondering if she had escaped one nightmare to walk into another.

"Ain't gonna hurt you." When she didn't move, he added, "Swear it."

"'Ain't gonna hurt you... Just cooperate an' give us what we want. Don't fight an' you won't get hurt,'" she said on a broken whisper.

What the fuck? Another chill shot down Sig's spine. She was quoting someone.

"What'd they want?" he whispered.

She didn't answer, but, *thank fuck*, she stepped over the threshold into the dark interior of his apartment. She took a few more steps, then hesitated. He hurried in behind her, hit the lights and closed the door.

She suddenly collapsed to the floor, pulled her knees to her chest and curled into a ball like one of those wooly caterpillars when he poked at them as a kid.

"Fuck," he said under his breath as he heard her soft sobbing.

He hoped to fuck it was from relief of getting out of whatever fucked up situation she'd been in.

"Are you a Shirley?" *Fuck*, he should've asked that in the beginning, back in the woods. Because you did not take Shirley property from them. Not a car, not a woman, and definitely not one who could be carrying a Shirley spawn.

They protected their property like an MC protected theirs.

With everything they had.

She didn't answer him. She probably needed food and definitely a bath, most likely medical attention. But if she was a Shirley and he took her somewhere, nothing would stop them coming off that mountain to claim one of their own.

Nothing.

And he wasn't letting that happen. Not until he knew the whole story.

Most likely not even then.

It was one thing when a woman wanted welts and bruises because she asked for it, craved it, got off on it, it was another when it was forced on her against her will.

He had a feeling Red was not into being beaten for sexual pleasure.

It was those dirty, bloody, broken fingernails that gave it away. This woman had fought to escape the hell she'd been in. She had not volunteered to be tied up and beaten.

His jaw shifted and his fingers curled into fists.

He'd done a lot of stupid shit in his life. He'd done a lot of shit he'd gone to jail for. Abusing a woman was not fucking one.

He'd never done anything a woman didn't ask for. He enjoyed pussy. He didn't destroy it. He appreciated it when a woman knew what the fuck she wanted and wasn't afraid to ask for it.

He had no doubt Red hadn't asked for anything she'd been dished out.

But right now, he was over his head. He needed help with her. From someone maybe Red could trust.

Stella.

She was the only female that lived on the farm. None of the sweet butts or female hang-arounds were allowed to shack up in any of the rooms in the bunkhouse. Trip didn't want it turning into a whorehouse.

So, Stella was it.

Problem was, Stella didn't trust Sig. But if he could convince her to help with Red...

He hoped to fuck she was home.

"Gotta go up to the main house for a quick minute. You need to stay here. Be back as soon as I can." Trip's ol' lady could ignore a text, but she couldn't ignore Sig if he stood eye to eye with her.

Since Red was still curled into a ball, he wasn't sure if she heard him. He just had to make sure she didn't bolt when he ran up to the house. He dug his keys back out, thankful that the deadbolt was one that needed a key to lock or unlock it from the inside. When he stepped back outside, he locked Red in.

He moved as fast as he could in the distance between The Barn and the house, which was about two football fields, and cursed in relief when he made it to the back door without passing out in pain.

All the shit that happened in the woods, the ride on his sled and carrying Red upstairs had aggravated his cracked, and possibly broken, ribs and made every injury on his body throb.

He pounded on the back door and waited.

A few seconds later, Trip's ol' lady, wearing her long black hair with blue stripes loose around her shoulders and her normal rocker-style clothes, opened the door, her blue eyes narrowed on Sig.

Before she could say anything, he said, "Need your help, Stel."

If she wasn't suspicious of him showing up at the back door, she was now. "For what?" As she took him in, her lips took a deep downward turn. "Fuck. You look like hell."

"Yeah."

Her eyebrows pinned together. "*Yeah*? What happened? Where have you been?"

Christ. He wasn't getting into that right now. Especially with her. "Around."

Her face twisted with annoyance at his bullshit answer. "You look like you had a fight with a honey badger."

"I did."

"And he won."

"Yeah, Stel. Seriously. Need your help."

"For what?"

"Just need to show you."

She pressed a hand to her forehead, her frown deepening. "Sig..."

"Stella, goddamn it. Wouldn't ask if..." He wasn't going to fucking beg. His pulse began to hammer and his blood simmer. "You know what? Fuck it. Fuck you."

He turned and carefully made his way off the porch and into the uneven grass as he headed back to the bunkhouse.

Fuck her.

Fuck her.

Fuck her.

A few seconds later, the sound of flip-flops chasing him down made him slow.

"This causes issues with Trip, I'm giving you a black eye on the other side."

"Then you might as well swing now." Sig didn't hide his grin, though it quickly turned into a grimace.

"Oh fuck," she groaned.

"Yeah, *oh fuck* don't even cover it."

"What'd you do?" she asked, walking by his side. "Is whatever it is why you're all beat up?"

"Noooo," he dragged out. "That's a whole other fuckin' issue."

"Oh fuck. Trip's not going to be happy with that issue, either?"

"Thinkin' that's a big fuckin' no," Sig admitted.

"Jesus, Sig," she whispered. "He's got enough shit on his plate. He doesn't need you dragging more shit home."

"Didn't go lookin' for this shit. It found me."

"You could have left it where it found you."

Fuck no, he couldn't. Otherwise, he would've.

They got to the rear of the bunkhouse and Stella stopped, staring up the steps to the second level. "It's in your apartment."

Sig's jaw got tight. "Yeah, Stella, it's in my apartment." He turned on her. "You seriously fuckin' don't trust me that much?" He began up the stairs with another silent, "Fuck you."

As annoyed as he was with her distrust, he was still relieved when he heard her following on his heels.

"You haven't shown me anything yet to make me think I can trust you, Sig..."

"Whatever," he muttered under his breath. He swallowed the "bitch" on the end of it. Now was not the time to have it out with the Prez's ol' lady. Louder, he said, "Don't do it for me, then," as he unlocked the door.

"Then for who?"

He pushed it open and jerked his chin toward the interior. "Do it for her."

"What the fuck?" Stella whispered behind him. She pushed past him, knocking him aside and making him wince. She rushed up to the woman who was still curled in a ball on the floor right where he'd left her. Stella fell to her knees and glanced up at Sig. "You do this?"

Goddamn it. "Fuck no."

"Then who? Why is she just wearing a tee and flannel shirt? Why is she filthy? Why is she injured like that?"

"Stella," he began, trying hard to hold onto any patience he had left. "Had those fuckin' answers, I'd give 'em to you."

Stella brushed the knotted, caked hair away from Red's face. "Where did you find her?"

"Runnin' in the woods. Naked."

Stella's mouth dropped open as she stared at Sig. "What?"

"Runnin' down the mountain... Off Copperhead Road."

She blinked a couple times, then her blue eyes went wide. "The Shirleys?" she whispered.

When Stella said that name, Red jerked on the floor.

Sig just lifted his eyebrows in a silent answer to Stella.

"Oh fuck," Trip's woman muttered. Then when the significance hit her, she whispered, "*Ooooh* fuck," even louder. "We need to get the cops involved. I can call Max."

"No!" Sig shouted quickly, not wanting her to call the fucking local Chief of Pigs. "No. Don't know what the fuck's goin' on yet. If she's... If she belongs to... *them*, then we need to keep her location on the DL. Pigs find out... They'll go up there, tryin' to arrest someone... Those motherfuckers might figure out where she is. Even if they arrest the one that... Even if they do, there's a shitload more of 'em. Let's just do what we can first. Then figure it all out."

"Sig..."

"Goddamn it, Stel. She needs to get cleaned up an' dressed. I'd do it but..."

"But you shouldn't touch her," Stella finished, her eyes troubled. "Yeah... Okay... Let's get her to the house and I'll run her a bath and do what I can to help. But maybe she needs to go to the hospital." Stella raised her eyebrows at Sig. "For... you know... one of those kits..."

"What kit?" A pregnancy kit? He was thinking it was too late for that.

"For evidence." Stella tilted her head in a silent signal.

Sig picked up what she was putting down. But, *Jesus fuck*, it was way too late for that, too. Stella just hadn't seen the obvious evidence yet. Not with the way Red was curled around her own belly. "Know what fuckin' happened."

"Yes," Stella said carefully, "but to pinpoint who..."

"Sure as fuck she knows who."

"But... proof's needed for..."

"No. It's not. She may be carryin' the proof."

Stella's eyes went wide again and she stared at Red, who wasn't saying a word, just lying there with her eyes closed. Almost like she was wishing the floor would swallow her whole and she'd disappear.

He got it. There'd been plenty of days he felt like that, too.

"If she's... She definitely needs to go to the ER then... And get the—"

Sig finally exploded. All this jawing wasn't helping Red. "Stel, just need you to fuckin' help her. Goddamn it. That's it. No more. Ain't gettin' the fuckin' pigs involved yet. I'm gonna handle it."

"Sig..."

"Stella."

"You don't know what's all involved here, do you? Quite possibly..." She threw her hands up in frustration. "Are you going to risk going back to prison for a stranger if you decide to *handle* this on your own?"

Sig frowned at the silent woman on his floor. "She ain't a stranger."

"Wait. You know her?"

He paused and pressed his fingers to his temple, rubbing it. The pain shooting through his brain was killing him.

Hell, everything was killing him.

And Stella asking all of these questions he didn't have answers for was making it worse.

Until Red talked, they wouldn't know shit. But what he did know was he needed to get her cleaned up and food in her belly.

Stella sighed loudly, then asked, "You got food up in this pig sty?"

"Some. More downstairs, if we need it."

She nodded. "Okay, we won't move her to the house. Not until we can figure out what the hell happened. Go fill your tub. I'm going to stay with her, try getting her up. Once she's in the tub, I need you to cook something light. Nothing heavy. She needs fluids, too. More than water. Like Gatorade or something similar. You have some, or do the boys have some downstairs?"

"Downstairs, I think. For their fuckin' hangovers." And his, too, but he left that part out.

Stella's lips flattened out. "Go. Go get the tub running. Then go down and grab some and also grab whatever you can cook. You hear me?"

Sig stared at Red for a moment.

"Sig..."

He ripped his gaze from the woman who he had no doubt was broken inside and out and glanced at Stella. "Yeah."

Stella gave him a nod. "Go."

He nodded back and headed into the bathroom, now glad it had a tub, which he'd told Trip was useless in a bachelor's apartment. But Trip had said he got a good deal on it and to suck it up, it was only a fucking tub. "Just fuckin' live with it," was his final say on it.

Sig shook his head as he started the water, making sure it was hot and squeezed some body wash into it, making suds.

Red was probably going to need more than one long soak to get all the dirt off her. But he'd leave that to Stella.

While he'd handle the rest.

Chapter Four

Autumn blinked. Then blinked again.

All she saw was carpet that needed a good vacuuming. And a pair of dirty boots.

Those boots belonged to the man who captured her in the woods.

He'd caught her escaping.

She had finally been free and now she wasn't.

She was never going to get free.

Never again.

She just wanted to die. To get it all over with.

Those boots suddenly disappeared.

Then a hand brushed the hair away from her face again and it was surprisingly gentle. She hadn't been touched like that in a long time.

Every touch she received in the last year had been harsh. Painful. Unwanted.

Not soft or caring.

"Hey, I'm Stella. I'm going to help you, if you'd let me."

Stella.

Sig.

"What's your name?"

She turned her head barely enough to see the woman on her knees next to her.

"If you're not ready to tell me yet, that's okay." She got to her feet and Autumn heard flip-flops head in the same direction the boots went.

Autumn's gaze landed on the door. Freedom laid beyond it. It wasn't far. She could make it.

Planting her palm on the floor she pushed herself to a seat, her only focus that escape route.

She had no idea where she'd been taken, she just knew she was no longer on that hellhole of a mountain.

On the ride in, she'd noticed it was a farm of some sort. And she was above a barn. She had noticed some fields in the distance and a tree line. If she could get to that tree line, maybe she could disappear.

But she had no clothes, no money, no credit cards, nothing.

Even if she had a phone, she had no one to call.

Except for 911.

And like that Sig said, once the police saw her, they'd go up that mountain and arrest Vernon, if not more of them, doing more harm than good by tipping off the Shirleys to where she was.

Then they'd come find her.

To take back what they deemed as theirs.

She was not giving them that. Not ever.

Because what they thought was theirs, was also hers. And right now, she had full control of it.

Then the woman... Stella... was back, squatting beside her. "Red, the tub's almost full. I'm going to help you, okay? We'll get you cleaned up, feeling better. Sig will make you something to eat in the meantime. I'm sure you're hungry. And thirsty."

Hunger wasn't anything new. She was used to it now. The hollow ache in her stomach. The fuzziness in her brain.

Even when they brought her food, she had refused to eat it.

Food would keep her living longer. And the longer she lived, the longer her nightmare continued.

And she had just wanted it all to end.

But they had forced her...

"C'mon," Stella encouraged softly. "Let's get you to your feet and into the tub. You'll feel better once you soak in that warm water. I promise."

"Why?" Autumn got caught in her dry throat as the woman helped her to her feet. She tried again. "Why?"

"Why what?"

"Why are you helping me?" Her voice was so raw, it hurt.

"Why wouldn't I?"

"You don't know me."

"No, I don't. But I'd like to."

She was lying. Why would this woman want to get to know her?

Autumn closed her eyes for a second as dizziness made her sway.

"Sig!"

Heavy booted feet quickly approached her.

"Can you help me get her into the tub?"

Without a word, she was scooped up again. She lifted her eyes and met his. Brown.

They held pain. His face would be handsome if it wasn't so messed up. Like he'd gotten into a fight.

And the agony he was trying to hide also etched his face.

Within a few strides, he carried her into the bathroom and put her on her feet only long enough for Stella to pull the T-shirt over her head and untie the flannel shirt from around her waist.

She should care this Sig was seeing her naked again.

But she didn't.

She no longer cared anymore. Her body had no longer become her own a year ago. It was only a container for the organs that kept her alive and the seed they had planted inside her.

Sig picked her up once more and, with a grimace twisting that face, gently placed her into the warm water, getting the front of his shirt soaked.

She felt the need to thank him, but she couldn't push the words past her lips.

She forgot what it was like to be thankful.

It was a strange feeling.

And she wasn't sure why she was where she was. What their plans were for her.

Maybe she shouldn't be thankful at all.

But whatever their plans were, she was too tired to care at the moment.

The warm soapy water pulled at her, making her even more weary.

Even so, it was a thousand times better than the bucket of water and sponge she'd been occasionally given to use. Or the cold spray of the hose when she began to stink too badly.

"What do you need from me? Besides some clothes, shampoo and that kind of stuff."

"Anything that will make me feel human again and... and not like breeding stock."

Stella's face paled, her pretty blue eyes wide. "Breeding stock?" she whispered.

Autumn closed her eyes. She didn't know these people. She didn't know if she could trust them.

A clean washcloth appeared in front of her face.

"Do you want to do it yourself? Or I can help you, if you want."

Autumn grabbed the cloth between her fingers and stared at it. "I..."

"Do what you can while I run and grab you some things. I can help you get the spots you can't reach when I get back. Sig's out in the kitchen now, making you something to eat. I have no idea if he can cook. I hope so... I'll be back..."

With one last concerned look at Autumn, the woman rushed from the bathroom, leaving the door wide open.

Then *he* appeared in the doorway and the smell of something cooking followed him in.

"Got you some Powerade. Cherry. Need to drink this whole thing. Yeah?"

She stared at the bottle in his hand as he stood tall over her next to the tub. She lifted her eyes to his.

Brown.

Holding a different type of pain this time.

He cracked the lid on the bottle, removed it, and held it out to her. "Sorry. Don't got a straw."

She said nothing as she took it and put it to her lips. When she began to drink, she couldn't stop. She hadn't realized she'd been that thirsty. But she had no idea when was the last time she drank anything.

She tipped the bottle higher and some of the red liquid slid down her chin and discolored the already brown bathwater.

"Whoa," he said, pulling it from her fingers. "Not sure if you should be drinkin' it so fuckin' quickly."

"You kind of talk like them."

Them. Maybe this was all a trap and he was one of *them.*

He frowned and set the bottle down on the floor next to the tub. "Yeah, but the difference is I ain't a hillbilly, inbred, redneck, white trash motherfucker. Just a white trash motherfucker who rides a hog." His lips thinned for a few seconds, his fingers curled against his thighs and he blew out a soft breath. "Forgot to add ex-con. Anyway, gonna be all right in here? Gotta check the stove. Suck at cookin' but can make scrambled eggs and toast. Most stupid motherfuckers like me can."

Not waiting for an answer, he turned and walked out.

She scrubbed the washcloth down her face, then over her chest and arms. But the water was so dirty, it was only getting off the worst of it.

She leaned over, turned on the faucet full blast and partially opened the drain. She rinsed the washcloth under the warm water and continued to work on her crusty skin as best as she could.

But she quickly tired. Her muscles were weak and her brain still fuzzy. The seed inside her had begun to sap most of her energy a long time ago.

Then she was back. That Stella.

Shampoo, conditioner, a razor, lotion and more in a bucket. She dumped the contents onto the floor, and tucked the bucket under the running water. "Lean your head back," was all she said.

Autumn complied and a bucketful of warm water was poured over her mess of hair. It would be easier if the woman had brought along a pair of scissors and just cut it all off. She might need to dye it anyway when she escaped and went into hiding.

Everyone noticed her hair. The color was hard to miss.

But with a lot of patience, Stella wet her hair, shampooed it, rinsed and did it again. Four times it took to get it clean. And all the while the filthy water kept circling down the drain and clean water kept trying to keep up.

After massaging conditioner into her hair, Stella began to carefully undo the gnarls with her fingers and a wide-toothed comb.

Autumn closed her eyes again with how good that all felt. She hadn't been to a salon since... She couldn't remember when.

For a moment, she almost felt human again. Almost.

Until Stella asked, "How far along are you?"

The water in the tub was no longer high enough to hide the curve of her belly. "I don't know."

Stella shook her head and Autumn understood her confusion.

"I... I lost track of time." She had a good guess, but she wasn't sure. One day, one week, one month blurred into the next. She had been given no way to keep track of time, and, really, she hadn't wanted to. It might have been worse to know.

"You need to see a doctor."

She had no money. No way to pay a doctor.

"I have a great OB/GYN. Maybe—"

Autumn cut her off. "I just need to go..." Maybe this woman, this Stella, could help her escape.

Stella gently squeezed her bony shoulder. "Where?"

"I don't know."

"Do you have family somewhere?"

"I used to."

Stella's dark eyebrows knitted together. "What does that mean?"

"I... I can't go to them." No. It was because of them she ended up in Pennsylvania.

In the woods. Up a mountain. In a cage.

"Anyone else?"

"No. Everyone I know is in Ohio. If I go back there, word will get back..." Word would get back up that mountain where she was. And if she went back to Ohio, she'd be forced to return. Once again, against her will.

"Back?" Stella prodded.

"Just back... I... can't risk it. I just need to disappear. Will... Will you help me?"

"Do you have money somewhere? Clothes? A place to go?"

"No."

"How will you survive? You have nothing."

She knew that. She did. But hearing someone else say it made it so much more painfully clear. She had nothing.

No one.

Not even hope.

Stella stopped working on a knot when Autumn drew her knees in closer and dropped her forehead to them, curling up as much as the tub would allow. As much as her belly would allow.

Today was the first day in a long time that she cried. She didn't think it was possible anymore. She cried in the woods when she spotted Sig. She cried on his motorcycle. She cried on his floor.

Now she was crying in his tub.

But the bath was making her feel human again.

And that was the problem. It was making her remember what it was like to *feel* something.

"You're right. I have nothing," she said in a broken whisper. Not even the seed that had been planted inside her. She didn't even have that. Not really.

Stella squeezed Autumn's hand that was wrapped around her own shin. "No, I was wrong. You have something now. Us. And my ol' man loves to remind me that something is better than nothing. I swear it's his damn motto. That needs to be his next tattoo."

Autumn sniffled and wiped her nose on her own knee. "Old man? Your father?"

A small smile curled Stella's lips. "No. My *ol'* man. My future husband. He's a biker like Sig. They're half-brothers. Ol' man is just a term we use. Like husband or boyfriend."

Stella said nothing more as she finished getting the knots out of Autumn's hair, then took the washcloth and scrubbed her back until it was clean.

After a while, the water circling the tub became clear.

Her fingers and toes were wrinkled and she began to shiver since it was no longer warm.

Stella helped her up, wrapped a thick towel around her and used another one to towel-dry her hair. "I should've brought a hairdryer," she muttered more to herself than to Autumn.

When she was done, she helped Autumn sit on the closed toilet seat and handed her the Powerade bottle.

"Finish that. I brought a couple things you'll fit into and then you can eat whatever Sig made. Though, it might be cold now. I'll tell him to heat it back up."

She disappeared for a few moments, then was back with a T-shirt, black leggings and some socks.

Once Autumn was dressed, Stella said, "We can get the police involved, if you want. Take you to the ER first and then report what happened there. They can arrest whoever did this to you, you know."

She didn't want to do anything but disappear, to somewhere the Shirleys couldn't find her. "No. They'll want me back. They'll do whatever they can to get me back."

"For the baby?"

Autumn closed her eyes. She ignored that question. Just like she did her best to ignore the seed that grew inside her.

From the beginning, she knew it was better not to get attached. So, she didn't.

She was just the host until she was no longer needed. Because she never planned on going along with everything else they had wanted from her.

"Hey," Stella whispered, grabbing her elbow. "C'mon, let's see what Sig made you."

The woman with the long black hair with blue stripes assisted her out of the bathroom to the open kitchenette on the left at the end of the short hall.

And there he was, the man who'd caught her in the woods, who helped her off that mountain, standing behind a short counter with two stools. One had a plate sitting in front of it and a glass of what could be OJ and another glass with what looked like water.

His dark brown eyes followed her and Stella as they made their way to the stool. As she sat down, she stared at the plate half full with scrambled eggs, the other half two pieces of buttered toast.

She breathed deeply, inhaling what real food smelled like again. And the seed inside her moved. Surprised, she pressed her hand to her belly. And the seed moved again. Restless.

It hadn't died like she feared.

She had worried that if it died, she'd have to start the nightmare all over again until she gave them one that lived.

But this one was alive.

Fear shot through her. Now, they'd be determined to find her. To find it.

"Did the baby kick?" Stella asked, her face soft and a small smile curling her lips.

The baby.

"No," Autumn said quietly. "My stomach growled."

She didn't miss when Stella's eyes slid to Sig's and they gave each other a look.

She didn't like that look.

"Take your time eating. While you do that, I'll clean up the bathroom."

Stella disappeared and then it was just Autumn and Sig.

In that little kitchenette.

"Eat," he said. His voice was low and deep.

She stared at the plate again, then picked up the fork, stabbing at the chunks of eggs. She lifted it to her lips and stuck out her tongue to taste them.

The familiarity flooded her senses. She shoved the eggs into her mouth, swallowing them down before she even chewed them. Then she began to shovel the small yellow mountain into her mouth to fill her belly. When she was done with that, she began to take large bites of her toast, eating it quickly, chasing every mouthful with a gulp of OJ.

Filling that hollow.

Settling the movement of that seed.

When she was done, she sipped at the remaining sweet, but tangy OJ and noticed Sig hadn't moved an inch since before she began.

"You ate all that in like a couple minutes, Red. You want more?" He wasn't joking, his expression was serious, his eyes troubled as his gaze lifted from her empty plate to her face.

She nodded.

His nostrils flared and he nodded in return, giving her his back at the stove as he began to prepare her more eggs.

She studied that back. It was broad and covered in a leather vest. The same one he wore when on his motorcycle. It had various patches on it. The one on the top read, "Blood Fury," the bottom one said, "Pennsylvania," and a large center patch consisted of a bloody skull and crossbones. She remembered the three rectangular ones on the front. *Sig. Vice President. Manning Grove.*

Is that where they were? In Manning Grove? The only thing she knew after being blindfolded and tied up was she had been taken to Pennsylvania. And that was a big state.

When she left, she needed to go as far away from Ohio or Pennsylvania that she could.

Mexico. Canada. Or even Australia. She could get lost there.

Stella said Sig was a biker, so all of the tattoos and the vest made sense. He also said he was an ex-con. She wondered if he was a violent one. Bikers probably liked to get rowdy and into fights, which was most likely why he had a massive black eye.

"What happened to your face?"

"A mistake," was all he said.

"One you'll learn from?" She didn't know why she asked that.

He spun around, a scowl on his face and the spatula in his hand. "How'd you get up that fuckin' mountain?"

Autumn jumped and her heart stopped as the door crashed open behind her.

They found her.

Chapter Five

Autumn fell from the stool and curled up in a tight ball behind it, squeezing her eyes shut.

They found her.

They were there to take her back.

"What the fuck!" Sig bellowed, making her wince.

"What the fuck is right!" bellowed back another male voice, just as loud.

Heavy boots came at her from both directions. Sig from around the counter and the intruder from the front.

"What the hell, Sig!" the new voice yelled.

He was a Shirley, she knew it! It had been all a trap, like she suspected.

Just to capture her and hand her back over.

Stella's voice came from the side. "What the hell, Trip? Calm down."

"Why's there a fuckin' woman hidin' behind the stool? What did you fuckin' do, Sig?"

"Didn't fuckin' do anything, *brother*."

A big hand clasped her forearm, hauling her to her feet. She was going to be dragged out of there in a second. Her hair fell around her face becoming a curtain she could hide behind.

"Trip! Let her go!"

"Why the fuck you in here, Stel? Who the fuck is this?" The hand shook her.

"Let her go and we'll explain," Stella tried to reason with whoever it was.

An arm slipped around her shoulders and she was pulled from the hand that held her hostage.

"Why... She's... You got some teenager knocked up?"

No. No. This man had it all wrong. But Autumn couldn't catch her breath to explain.

She opened her eyes and lifted her face so she could see him. The man who was angry. The man who wanted answers. He wore the same kind of black leather vest as Sig and had almost just as many tattoos. And the two men looked slightly similar.

But then so did all the Shirleys.

"Is... this..."

Stella's arm tightened around her shoulders. "Yeah, this is my ol' man." Her lips were pressed into an angry slash and her blue eyes were on fire. "Trip, it isn't Sig's baby. And you need to calm the hell down. This isn't helping anything or anyone."

"How the fuck can I calm down when I just got news about why his ass got handed to him?" The man, this Trip... his eyes were also on fire.

No one said a word. Not Stella. Not Sig. Not one of them looked happy, either. Far from it.

The heavy tension in the room was making Autumn's chest tight and her heart was trying to beat right out of it.

A twinge in her stomach made her wince again. The seed wasn't happy, either.

"Who the hell is that?" this Trip asked again.

"Don't let him take me back," Autumn finally managed in a whisper, fisting Stella's shirt. "*Please.*"

"He's not taking you anywhere," Stella returned softly, squeezing Autumn's fist. "I'm taking you back to the bedroom to lie down. That's it. That's as far as you're going. You need some rest and that's what you're going to get while we deal with this."

"I don't want to go back."

"I promise. You are *never* going back."

Stella said they were bikers. Both of them. Brothers, too. Not Shirleys.

That's what she said. Autumn hoped the woman wasn't lying.

She couldn't take any more lies.

Stella snagged another bottle of Powerade off the end of the counter and with one arm still around Autumn, guided her down the hallway to a partially open door at the end.

She kept her voice low when she asked, "Why are they fighting? Is that who beat Sig up?"

"No. It wasn't him. They just..." Stella inhaled a loud breath, closing the door behind them. "They need to work a few things out, that's all."

"About me."

"No, Red. About a lot of things."

Red.

"My name isn't Red." Autumn stared at the big bed. It was messy, a thin quilt in a pile on the floor, the sheets tangled. The pillows not lined up neatly.

But it was a bed.

A bed.

And it looked as good as that plate of food, if not better.

She felt her eyes begin to burn.

Again.

"I know. Are you going to tell me what it is?"

That got Autumn's attention back on the woman, who had been nothing but kind and helpful to her.

"Do you want me to change the sheets? I don't know if he has another set. But he can be a pig."

"No... It's fine... I..." It was a million times better than where she'd been sleeping for the last year. She sat on the edge and ran her hand over the cool sheets. The mattress was so soft.

Her eyes got heavy and the thought of getting some sleep actually made her yawn.

"Get in. Do you want to wear your leggings? They don't look very comfortable since they don't fit over your... stomach. Maybe sleep in just the T-shirt." Stella lifted a finger. "Hang on... Let's see if Sig has any clean boxers." Stella went over to the dresser and began to pull open drawers. "Jesus. This man needs a keeper." She held up a pair of boxer briefs. "I don't think these will fit much better. I can grab you panties at Walmart later today. I didn't think you'd want to wear any of mine."

"I don't have any money."

"Yeah, you said that, Red. We can pay for a few essentials. Until we figure out... Until things get settled."

Autumn worried about telling Stella her real name, so she didn't know why she did it. Maybe because she really needed to trust someone. Anyone at this point. And the woman, a complete stranger, was being kinder than she needed to be. "Autumn. My name. I'm not a teenager like your ol' man said."

"Autumn," Stella repeated, gripping the underwear in her fist, then moving to the bed and putting them on the nightstand. "Just in case you want to try to wear them. Autumn," she repeated. "I like that. And I didn't think you were a teenager. But right now, you're so thin... You look really young."

Autumn had no idea what she looked like. She hadn't looked into a mirror in a long time. And while in the bathroom, she'd avoided it. But she wouldn't be able to avoid it forever. Especially since the seed had made her use the bucket in the corner a lot in the last few weeks.

"And Sig tends to like..." Stella didn't finish that sentence. "Doesn't matter. That's Sig's issue, not yours. Right now you just need to get some rest. I'm going to do my best to get one of my doctors over here to take a look at you. Just to make sure you and your... you are all right."

"I can't pay for a doctor, either."

"Don't worry about it. Just rest for now. We can worry about that later."

———

SIG PLANTED his boots wide apart, and faced off with his brother. "You scared the fuck outta her."

"I don't even know who the fuck she is. And what'd I say about keepin' women here in the bunkhouse?"

"First of all, this ain't the bunkhouse, it's my goddamn apartment—"

"Above the bunkhouse, which means part of the fuckin' bunkhouse, Sig."

Sig kept talking over his brother, "And I only found her this mornin', *brother*."

Trip's brown eyes went wide. "You *found* her? What d'you mean you fuckin' *found her*?"

Sig opened his mouth, but snapped it shut when Stella came rushing out to where they were standing. Trip's ol' lady was not wearing a happy face. Not at fucking all. None of them were. "Get outside, now. Autumn needs rest. You two go do what you need to do, but not in here."

"Autumn?" Trip spun back to Sig, his jaw tight. "She one of those fuckin' Amish girls?"

"Her name is Autumn?" Sig asked Stella.

"You didn't know her goddamn name and you're fuckin' her?" Trip's brows dropped low. "Also, still waitin' on a good answer why you're in Sig's apartment, Stel."

Stella rolled her eyes and shook her head. "Because she needed help."

"From what? Escapin' Sig? 'Cause it's certainly too late for her to get rid of that kid."

A muscle ticked in Sig's jaw.

"No..." Stella shook her head, getting just as pissed as Trip, and jerked her eyebrows up at Sig. Her temper was about to blow. "You take it from here, Sig. Just somewhere else. Not right outside, either. She needs sleep. Go downstairs into The Barn and do what you need to do, but get it done," she hissed. "And then leave it there. Don't you fucking dare bring that shit back up here." She jabbed her finger toward the floor.

Trip's jaw shifted as he stared at his ol' lady. After a second, he jerked his chin toward the door. "Let's fuckin' go. Can't wait to hear this fuckin' bullshit."

Sig remained where he stood as his brother stalked to the door and ripped it open. Then Trip disappeared and his heavy boots could be heard stomping down the metal steps at a fast clip.

Blowing out breath in an attempt to cool his simmering blood, Sig began to follow him and Stella stopped him by calling out his name. He paused and glanced over his shoulder at the woman who normally tried to be the peacemaker between him and Trip. She normally didn't encourage them to do what they needed to do and "get it done."

"Get this fixed between the two of you and soon," she ordered, her blue eyes narrowed on him. "You two are fucking blood whether you like it or not. So, act like it. I'm not going to live through a repeat of what happened twenty fucking years ago, do you understand that, Sig? Not again."

"Nobody wants to live through that shit again, Stel. Not one of us. That's why it was fuckin' stupid of him to resurrect the goddamn Fury." With that, Sig closed the door behind him, doing his best not to slam it and wake Red. *If* she was even sleeping.

He slowly and carefully made his way down the steps, into the backdoor of the bunkhouse, down the long, narrow corridor and finally through the door at the end of the hallway which led to the main area of The Barn.

The Blood Fury's church.

Thank fuck it was empty. No one playing pool. No one playing darts. No one getting drunk or high. Or getting their dick sucked or fucked by a sweet butt on one of the school bus bench seats that lined some of the walls.

Trip had gotten a good deal on them and they were easy to clean.

His brother was fucking way smarter than Sig. He had an eye for business and a Pitbull-like determination to make something out of nothing more than anyone else Sig knew.

Sig always admired him when they were kids and had been thrilled when Trip wanted to hang with him, even though Sig was three years younger.

They had been close like brothers before they even knew they were.

Now, things weren't the same. Things had changed for both of them because of that day. The day Razor shot Buck dead on top of Sig's mother.

Sig strode right past Trip, who stood waiting with his hands on his hips, his baseball cap thrown onto the bar and his hair hanging loose.

Was the fucker ready to go at it with him?

"Not fightin' with you, Prez. Would be unfair since I got

cracked ribs. Lemme heal up first and then if you wanna go a round, we can fuckin' do that." He ducked behind the bar, grabbed the Wild Turkey and a glass, pouring himself a healthy dose of medicine to dull the pain. He downed it, hissed and wiped the back of his hand across his mouth.

"Don't wanna fight with you, Sig. You're my VP, you're my partner in the repo biz, *you're my goddamn brother*. Wanted you here." Trip dropped his head and shook it, staring at his boots. "Gotta keep your shit clean."

"I am."

Trip's head popped up and he shot a glare in Sig's direction. "Are you fuckin' shittin' me? Let's break this shit down..."

Oh fuck. Sig lifted a palm. "Don't need to. I fucked up. Admit to it." He poured himself another double shot and downed that quickly with another hiss.

"You're damn right you fucked up. And also noticed you didn't say it won't happen again."

"Want me to lie?"

Trip ignored that. "You might've fucked up our relationship with the Amish. We fuckin' need them, Sig. They do a lot of work for us. Not only construction, but they provide shit from their farms, like meat, eggs, milk, fruit, veggies, even hand-rolleds. All which saves us a fuckton of money. If I had to buy all that shit from the store to feed everyone, the club coffers would be empty and we'd have to raise dues. Anyone livin' in the bunkhouse would also have to pay more a month to live here. You get that, right? Need to keep a good relationship with those Amish. All of 'em. They're one fuckin' close-knit community. Like we should be. But you stickin' your dick in their women creates a huge fuckin' issue."

"She came to me." Why the fuck did he feel the need to defend himself? Rebecca didn't get anything she hadn't asked for. In fact, she got *everything* she asked for. Even to keep her virginity. "Brother, she was fuckin' legal, which I know is one of your concerns."

"You think? That's a huge goddamn concern and rightly so. And don't care if she was forty. You don't fuck with 'em. Not one. Leave 'em all the fuck alone. You don't?" He jabbed his finger toward the back of the barn. "All those fields out there? All those fuckin' fields our granddaddy farmed? All those fields those Amish families are farmin' for us? And, in turn, providin' us with a shitload of food, tobacco and all the rest? You fuck that shit up and you're gonna be out there farmin' it all yourself. You. Give you a goddamn hoe. And not the kind of ho that's got a pussy. You got me?"

Sig stared at the empty glass in front of him. The whiskey hadn't kicked in yet. His blood was still humming, his ribs aching, his temples throbbing.

He didn't need any of this shit. He never should've come back. Knew it was a mistake to come back to this rinky-dink fucking town with nothing to do but beat off or find some available pussy to pass the fucking time.

Knew it was a mistake to promise Trip he'd stick around.

Knew it was a mistake to take that VP slot.

And a mistake to tell Trip he'd help with the repo business.

Also, knew it was a huge fucking mistake to come back to a place that had nothing but bad fucking memories.

Nothing could or would wipe that shit away.

Nothing.

And now upstairs was a woman living her own nightmare.

One that could be a million times worse than Sig's ever was.

"Know what the worst of it is? What Rebecca's brothers told me? You weren't just stickin' your dick in her ass, but beatin' it bloody with your goddamn belt!" Trip's face was now red and he was beginning to pace. Sig waited for the steam to come shooting out of his ears. "And if you continue fuckin' with 'em and knock one up? Fuck! Don't be surprised if those supposedly peaceful people suddenly find a loaded shotgun to borrow. Think you look bad now? Either you'll find your fuckin' ass full of buckshot or with a goddamn ring on your finger and workin' one of their farms, barefoot in cow pies and your calloused fingers pullin' on cows' titties. Which of those sound good to you?"

Neither. Because neither was going to happen. "Can't get 'em pregnant usin' the hole I'm usin'. They get what they want and save what they need to for their future husbands. Supposed to be virgins and they remain so that way. It's a fuckin' win-win."

"Christ," ripped from Trip. "Yeah, looks like a whole shitload of winnin' when you got a bad shiner, cracked ribs and who knows what else. Which I told 'em they had every right to give you 'cause you touched their damn property. It'd be like someone touchin' ours, Sig. Same fuckin' shit. Hope that snatch was worth what they doled out."

"You have no idea," Sig said under his breath. Now was not the time to think of Rebecca's red striped ass.

Red.

Fuck.

"Honestly, you deserve another fuckin' blanket party from us just like they gave you." Trip sucked in a sharp breath. "Did my best to smooth that shit over. Dutch is gonna help by talkin' to a couple of the elders, if it gets that far. Hopin' it don't, and her brothers keep that shit to themselves outta fear of Rebecca gettin' shunned. Already promised 'em you'll stay a million fuckin' yards away from any pussy wearin' one of those bonnets. You need somethin' to stick your dick into, find a fuckin' sweet butt or one of those silicone pocket pussies. No Amish, no underage. You get me?"

"She was eighteen," Sig reminded him.

Trip's eyebrows shot up his head and he yelled, "I don't give a fuck! You're almost thirty-three fuckin' years old. Find somethin' old enough to grow hair downstairs. And make sure she's not fuckin' Amish." Trip got suspiciously quiet, then pursed his lips and tilted his head, studying Sig a little longer. He wasn't as loud when he said, "Now we got that straight, let's move on to the next issue. What the fuck's goin' on with that redhead upstairs?"

Sig's mouth got tight. "Found her."

Trip's brow dropped low and he plugged his hands on his hips again. "She ain't a stray puppy, Sig. Don't just *find* some random woman."

He was so fucking wrong about that. "Found her on Copperhead Road in the woods."

Trip blinked, then muttered, "Fuck."

"Yeah. It wasn't 'til I caught her—"

"You *caught* her."

Sig ignored his interruption. "That it hit me where she was runnin' from. Soon as I did, got us both the fuck outta there. Had to convince her, though."

Trip rubbed a hand across his mouth. "You think..."

"Fuck yeah. No doubt, Trip."

"Those fuckers gonna come lookin' for her? 'Specially her bein' pregnant like that? Think it's one of theirs?"

"Yeah. Thinkin' it is and, right now, kinda hopin' they do."

"They do what? Come the fuck down here and try to get her back? Yeah, that's what we need, to keep makin' enemies. No," Trip held up a hand. "*You're* makin' us enemies all on your own. First the Amish, now the Shirleys, next you'll be havin' the pigs breathin' down our goddamn necks by harborin' some knocked up woman who does *not* belong to us. They'll be pissed we didn't report whatever the fuck happened to her right away. We need to keep shit smooth with them, too, Sig. Let's not fuckin' forget that. She tell you what happened to her? Why she's skinny, knocked up and on the run?"

"Nope. Got a good fuckin' guess, though."

Sig reached for the Wild Turkey again, but Trip snagged it first. "Gimme a glass."

Sig grabbed a glass from the shelf, set it on the bar, and Trip poured them both a healthy amount of whiskey. His brother stared at his for a long time before knocking it back. When he was done, he slammed the glass on the bar and said, "She's their property."

Normally, he'd say yeah, but... "Nope. Think they stole her from somewhere else. You see her shredded nails and those bruises? She was fightin' to get free."

Trip's eyes and expression went dark. "Then they kidnapped her and..."

"Yeah."

"For that baby?"

"Thinkin' so."

"Sick inbred motherfuckers," Trip barked, then poured himself another couple of fingers worth of the cheap whiskey. "Fuck," he muttered, scraping a hand down his beard. Then he shouted, "Fuck!" to the ceiling.

"Yeah," Sig breathed through the whiskey fumes.

"She shouldn't be here."

"Yeah." He wasn't going to argue that fact.

"Someone stole our property, we'd be out for blood."

"Yeah. Finders keepers, though, right? They stole her from wherever, we're stealin' her from them."

"Are you fuckin' crazy?" Trip bellowed. "You are goddamn crazy."

"Know you don't wanna hear this, brother, but *we're*

figurin' this shit out. Not gettin' the pigs involved. We're handlin' this. 'Cause we're gonna handle it right."

Trip squeezed his eyes shut and bit off a "Christ." He opened those brown eyes the same exact shade as Sig's. "Chief ain't gonna like it, us not givin' him a head's up if he catches wind."

"*If* he catches wind. But don't really give a fuck what the pigs like or don't goddamn like. They've known about these inbred mountain motherfuckers forever. What have they done about 'em?"

"Can't do nothin' if they don't break the law."

Sig didn't need to remind him that they broke the fucking law when he went up there to repo a car and the tow truck got all shot the fuck up. But there were plenty of other laws that clan broke. Those pussy motherfuckers just didn't want to deal with them.

"Fuckin' makin' meth and moonshine up there, Trip, and rapin' women. My guess? Maybe even usin' them for breedin' for fresh blood so all their babies don't turn out cross-eyed and three-legged." Damn toothless, banjo-playing, hillbilly, mountain goat fuckers.

Sig's blood was starting to scream through his veins at the thought of what might have happened to Red up there. And he wanted to know every goddamn thing. Because they were going to pay for every single one of those things.

"Yeah, can't imagine too many women voluntarily join their clan."

"Yeah, and you can only breed so much with your sister, mother and daughter."

"Fuck, fuck, *fuck*," Trip muttered. "She's carryin' one of their babies, they'll want her back. Or at least the kid once it's born. Doubt they're gonna stop until they get one or both." Trip took another deep breath.

He wasn't the only one struggling with all this. Sig was

having a hard time wrapping his head around someone who'd use another person just for breeding. In his lifetime, he'd met the dregs of the fucking Earth. So, he shouldn't be surprised.

Human trafficking was a real thing. And, *for fuck's sake*, he wouldn't be surprised if Red got caught up in something like that. Not willingly, of course. With the way she looked, there was no fucking way she volunteered for any of that shit.

And because of that, all those bastards on that mountain needed to die. Slowly, too. But that was something that would take a hell of a lot of planning. And right now, they didn't know the whole story yet. Sig was only making assumptions with what he saw and also Red's condition.

"Think there's more women up there bein' held against their will?"

Sig stared at his brother. "Dunno. She was naked, Trip. Fuckin' naked, running down the fuckin' mountain, bruised up and in a fuckin' panic. I caught her, told her I would help her and she still fought me, that's how out of her mind she was. She didn't ask me for help, had to force her to take it. That's not right." He tapped his temple. Something wasn't right upstairs with Red. But that shouldn't be surprising. If she had been locked up and used like he suspected, then that could break anyone's sanity. "She's skin and bones and I got no idea how that kid in her belly's still survivin'." Especially after the tumble she took when he was chasing her. Or the hits she took to get those bruises.

"Think it's still alive?" Trip asked, surprised.

"Yeah. It moved while she was eatin'. But she acts like it's some sort of alien in there. Like she doesn't want to admit to what it really is. Thinkin' it's just 'cause her mind's broken right now."

Trip sucked a breath in through his nose, then breathed out a long, "Fuck."

"Have a feelin' she's been up there a long time." And

that thought seared his gut. He'd done some long stints in prison. Some worse than others. But getting thrown in the hole was the worst. Being in a box by yourself could test your mind and your reality.

"Well, yeah, at least long enough to get knocked up. Unless they kidnap pregnant women. Which…" Trip's jaw shifted. "For fuck's sake."

"They could be doin' that, too. Who fuckin' knows with those hillbilly inbreds."

"Should get her to the hospital. We don't need this trouble, Sig. Drop her off there, outside their doors all anonymous-like and let 'em deal with her. It'd be better for her. Better for that kid she's bakin'. And better for us, too."

"She ain't goin' nowhere right now. Not 'til she tells us the whole fuckin' story. Not gonna drop her off somewhere only for the Shirleys to swoop in and fuckin' take her again. Ain't gonna happen. Not on my fuckin' watch."

Trip pursed his lips and studied Sig, who dropped his gaze to his empty glass again. "Why?"

Good question. Why? Why the fuck did he even care? Not once in his life had he given a real shit about any woman. Not once. They were all cheating whores like his mother. Why suddenly he needed to help Red, he had no fucking clue. "'Cause I know her."

Jesus fuck. He didn't know why he said that. The same that he said to Stella upstairs.

"What? How the fuck do you know her?"

"I just do."

"You didn't even know her name was fuckin' Autumn!"

"Yeah."

"You wanna explain what the fuck you mean?"

Sig shook his head. "Don't know how to explain it. I just do."

"Brother," Trip started softly.

Sig raised his gaze.

"If she's been through what we're thinkin' she's been through..."

"Yeah."

"That's a lot of shit to deal with," Trip finished.

"Yeah." Sig's mouth flattened out. "Just wanna help her and..." He drew in a breath. "I found her. I'm gonna help her." *Finders fuckin' keepers.*

"Brother, your head's fucked up right now. You got bashed upside it with a club or somethin' just a few days ago. You ain't thinkin' straight. And findin' out you get off on beatin' a woman like you beat that Amish girl... This chick up there?" He jerked his chin up toward the ceiling. "She ain't ever gonna be into that shit. She *lived* that shit for real."

"Yeah. Wanna help her, Trip. That's it. Figure out what the fuck went on up there and then help her get to where she needs to go. That's all. Swear it."

"Don't fuckin' swear to somethin' you won't be able to hold yourself to. Especially when it comes to a woman you just *found* a couple hours ago." Trip turned his back to Sig and stared out through the large open area of the barn. "Get 'er story. Figure out what the fuck went down. We ain't doin' shit 'til we know everythin'. Once we do, we'll take it to the table and discuss it. Got it?" He turned and glanced at Sig over his shoulder. "You get me?"

"Yeah."

"You don't go up that fuckin' mountain alone. If somethin's gotta be done, then we're plannin' it right and doin' it together. Like a brotherhood should. We all gotta stick together. Not just on this but everythin', Sig. You ain't alone anymore. None of us are. We're stronger together than apart. Remember that. Everythin's gotta be out on the table for this to work."

Sig wasn't sure if he believed all of that, but he nodded anyway even though Trip couldn't see it.

"But still wanna kick your fuckin' ass about that Amish chick. You let me know when your fuckin' ribs are healed so I can do that."

Sig grinned as he watched his brother snag his hat off the bar, slap it on his head and open the barn's front door.

"Tell my woman to get her ass back to the house, too," he threw over his shoulder. The door slammed shut.

Chapter Six

Sig opened the door and saw Stella cleaning up the kitchenette.

"Don't gotta do that."

She turned her head to glance at him over her shoulder. "Your place is a pig sty and I figured it would keep me busy while Autumn is resting and you two assholes were downstairs working shit out." She turned and began to wipe the counter down with a sponge. She paused and lifted her light blue eyes to him. "You don't have any new bruises, so I'm hoping you two did that."

"Yeah."

"Is he mad?"

"He's not happy."

"Didn't think he would be. But I need to know what I'm dealing with when I head back to the house."

Sig tilted his head and studied Stella, who was now finishing with the counter. His kitchen hadn't looked that good since the day he moved in. He could get one of the sweet butts to clean his apartment but then they'd want dick from him. And so far, he'd avoided any and all of them.

Maybe he needed to find a house mouse. They tended to be on the younger side and didn't spin on every brother's dick like a sweet butt.

Fuck. Now was not the time to be thinking about that shit. Now, he was staring at his brother's ol' lady and they were dealing with a pregnant woman in his bed. And right now, Stella was worried about what condition her ol' man was in and what she'd be walking into when she returned to the house.

"He got it honestly, Stel."

Her hand froze and she straightened. "I know."

"We both did."

Her face twisted and she rinsed the sponge off in the sink. "I know."

"He was a fuckin' bastard." He hated to say his father's name, but Stella picked up what he was putting down.

She placed the sponge on the corner of the sink to dry and took a deep breath. "I remember, Sig. I lived the same life you two did."

"Not the same."

"Close enough."

"You think he'd ever lose it enough to fuckin' hurt you?"

Stella quickly schooled her face. "Do you?"

"Only you can answer that."

She nodded, but looked troubled. "Have you ever taken your anger out on a woman?"

"Yeah."

Her eyes went wide.

"Not the way you're thinkin'. I..." *Fuck.* "I... find a volunteer."

Her eyebrows dropped low. "A volunteer? What do you mean?"

"Some women like—"

Stella's hand rose quickly. "Got it. No need to explain. Consenting adults and all that shit, right?"

Sig said nothing.

"Consenting, right?" Stella prodded.

"Right."

"And all *adults*, right?"

"S'far as I know."

Stella groaned and turned to dry her hands off with a paper towel from the half-kicked roll that was tucked into the corner of his counter. When she was done, she tossed it on top of the overflowing garbage. "You have to do better, Sig. You have to. For him. For you. For all of us. Please do better."

"Was startin' to 'cause I had Rebecca. Now I don't."

"I'm going to assume Rebecca was the Amish girl Trip was talking about. The one you got your ass kicked over?"

"Yeah."

"You liked her?"

"I... needed her."

"She liked... whatever you did to her?"

"Yeah."

"She was an outlet."

"Yeah."

"Just find yourself another outlet. One old enough to consent, Sig. If that's what it takes to keep you from spinning out of control, then that's what it takes. Trip does a counting thing with his breathing. My guess is Buck's was..." Her mouth remained opened but the words just stopped.

"My mother."

Stella nodded. "Just like a gun. There's a trigger and a safety. One does the damage, one prevents it. You just need to find the safety that works for you."

Sig stared at Trip's ol' lady. The queen of his brother's kingdom. The fucking woman was smart. And no-nonsense. They didn't always see eye to eye, but suddenly he realized what Trip saw in her, how she helped keep his life and his temper level. For the most part.

Sig no longer saw her as that pain in the ass little girl that followed her and Trip around, always trying to get Trip to kiss her. Always telling Trip he was going to marry her. Until the day it all stopped.

That day, out of anger, Trip pushed her hard enough to slam her head into a cinder block wall, splitting it open.

Looking back, that seemed to be the day where everything in their lives began to spin out of control.

Stella got hurt, then Buck and Pete kicked the shit out of Trip for doing it, saying it was so he learned to never put his hands on a female in anger. Though, that didn't make sense to Sig. He'd seen the other club brothers be violent with women and hurt them. Buck never said shit to them. Maybe it was only because Stella was Pete's daughter.

Because, in truth, Buck probably didn't give a fuck Trip cracked open Stella's head. Probably didn't give a shit she needed stitches.

But he had to save face with Pete.

He watched them beat the fuck out of him, to teach Trip a lesson. But in doing so, Sig learned that lesson, too, and he worried that the person he was closest to would die before it was over. Sig had hidden behind a barrel and watched the whole thing, terrified, trying to remain quiet so he didn't get caught. Because he did not want the same beating that Trip got.

His best friend could hardly move for days. Then Buck visited his mother a day or so later.

The day Razor came home and...

And everything that had been spiraling just imploded. No one was left untouched by the mess it created.

Not fucking one of them.

Fuck, he needed to get out of that head space right now. He couldn't visit the past. Instead, he needed to focus on the current problem. Which was a pregnant Red, who was currently sleeping in his bed.

"She tell you anythin' more than her name?"

"No. But I think that baby is one of the Shirleys'. I'm not sure, but I assume she didn't volunteer to get pregnant. Not with how she looks."

"Fuck no. D'you see her nails?"

"Yes. I..." Stella's mouth twisted. "We need to do somethin', Sig."

No shit. "We're gonna. Told your ol' man we're handlin' it. One reason he's not real happy right now. Just need to get the whole story from her first."

"And you think she's going to tell it to you?"

"Maybe. If not me, maybe you. Know you already helped, but need you to help make your ol' man see why we need to handle this ourselves. Not go to the fuckin' pigs."

"He wanted to go to the cops?"

Sig nodded. "He's worried about stirrin' up shit with them. Becomin' their focus. Creating bad blood between them and the Fury, like in the past."

She chewed on her bottom lip. "So am I. But in the past, the Fury would've handled this on their own. They never would've went to the cops, either."

"Right. He needs reminded of that. That we handle our own business."

"But, Sig, is she really our business? She doesn't belong to us. You said you know her. Do you really?"

He stared at Stella for a moment. "Know what it's like to be trapped, unable to escape, Stel. Know what it's like to fight to survive, to fight for my freedom. So, yeah, I know her."

"But, Sig, you had a choice to stay out of jail. I don't think she had a choice."

He hadn't only been talking about jail. "Maybe not. And, yeah, I fucked up."

"A lot."

Sig grimaced at her reminder. "Yeah, a lot."

His first of many major fuck ups was planting Buck's knife under Razor's jeans so he'd find it. That one action caused the complete annihilation of the Blood Fury.

The action of one stupid twelve-year-old fucking kid.

She jerked her chin up at his face. "You getting into fights isn't going to keep you out of jail."

"It wasn't a fight."

"What was it?"

He sighed. "I'm sure Trip will tell you everything."

"Oh great," she groaned with a frown.

"Yeah," was all he said.

She shook her head. "I need to get back up to the house." Stella headed toward the door but stopped right before it. "She needs to get looked at. She needs medical attention. Prenatal vitamins. We have no idea even how far along she is. Do you want me to call my doctor and see if I can get her an emergency appointment?"

"Yeah. Will need to take your Jeep, cover that red hair, sunglasses. Whatever. Just in case those fuckin' Shirleys are out lookin' for her."

Stella nodded. "I'll take care of all that. And I'll give the doctor the heads up on the situation. You just take care of her in the meantime. Small meals. Lots of fluids. Sleep. That's what she needs. Trip had a couple repos for you today with the rollback. I'll tell him he needs to find one of the prospects to handle them. Don't leave her alone, Sig. I have a feeling if she gets a chance, she'll try to run."

Sig had no doubt Red would try to run, too.

And he wouldn't blame her one fucking bit.

"Stel," he called out, making her pause with her hand on the knob. Then he said a word that felt foreign on his tongue. "Thanks."

Stella gave him a small smile and left.

The first thing Sig did was lock the deadbolt and tuck the key deep within the front pocket of his jeans.

The second thing he did was take off his boots and head straight back to his bedroom.

He quietly opened the door and walked as softly as he could through the dark. To the right was the only window in the room since to the left was Judge's apartment. Straight ahead, behind his king-sized bed, was the second level storage area for The Barn.

A spare sheet covered the large picture window, which he only used to filter out some of the morning sun since he wasn't worried about privacy up there, even though his window faced the courtyard. He didn't really give a fuck if anyone caught him walking around his room with his dick out. In fact, he'd mooned some of the prospects and hang-arounds a few times by shoving his ass against the window when they were out there partying all night. They'd all been drunk, including him.

He grinned. If he checked, he'd probably find several ass and nut sac smudges on the glass.

That grin quickly disappeared as he studied the woman in his messy bed. He couldn't remember the last time he washed the sheets, but at least they weren't full of cum stains since he hadn't brought a woman upstairs to his bed yet. And he was sure as fuck his bed was cleaner than the cage, or room, or wherever Red had been kept locked up.

She had probably slept directly on a concrete or dirt fucking floor.

A muscle in his jaw popped as that image flashed through his mind.

At least he had a great fucking mattress. When he moved in, that was the one thing he'd splurged on. Especially after sleeping for years on those shitty mattresses in prison that were nothing more than a thin pad. Worse, they'd be covered in *supposedly* "washed" sheets with dark pube hairs stuck throughout the rough fabric. Not his own pubes, of fucking course.

He carefully sat on the edge of his thick memory foam mattress and was glad it didn't shift, causing Red to wake.

Either she was dead asleep or was faking it.

But her breathing was slow and steady, her lips parted slightly, her fingers curled tightly around the sheet that had been tucked around her, most likely by Stella.

She was curled up on her side. Because she was so thin, when she was standing, from the front it was hard to see she was pregnant. From the side... there was no doubt. Her rounded stomach wasn't huge, but it was noticeable.

She was definitely a few months along. Maybe more.

The most pregnant chick he ever fucked had gone into labor right after, which is one reason the girl kept begging him to fuck her. He hadn't wanted to at first until, while she was sucking him off like a pro, she refused to let him finish in her mouth and insisted if he wanted to finish, he either needed to jerk himself off or fuck her.

So, he did the latter. Without a wrap, too, since there was no fear of knocking her up.

It was probably one of the best fucks he'd had before he'd turned eighteen. Her tits were huge and he'd taken her doggy style and came once, then she rode his dick and drained his nuts a second time.

He'd just been thankful for a free suck and fuck at the time, and also that it wasn't his brat in the bitch's belly. Or child support coming out of his wallet.

He pursed his lips as he studied the now clean and unknotted red hair spilled over one of his pillows. He reached out and captured a long, damp strand between his fingers, lifting it and sliding the silky length back and forth between his thumb and the pad of his index finger.

He'd never been into redheads. He never understood the appeal.

And she was a true redhead. It had been hard to miss

when she was running naked. The contrast of her red hair and her ghost white skin had been startling.

Almost like fire and ice.

He released her hair and ran a knuckle over one hollowed cheek, noticing how dark those purple half-moons were under her dark red lashes.

Her lips were chapped and the bruises ruined the perfection of what should be ivory skin. He hadn't noticed a freckle on her face earlier. Not one.

He matched his own fingers up to the bruises on her throat to compare the hand size. It was similar to his.

A man's.

What did she do to deserve someone choking her like that? Squeezing hard enough to leave marks?

Sig sucked a breath in through his nose and held it, counting to five in his head before releasing it softly from between his lips. It was a technique Trip used to keep from flipping the fuck out.

After Trip told him about it, Sig tried it. It didn't always work. It depended on what the issue was and how far gone he was.

Using a belt, a whip, or whatever the woman on the receiving end requested, always seemed to work the best.

But it wasn't practical. And he needed to find a backup since he now lost Rebecca or his ass might end up right back in fucking jail.

That would make Trip furious. And Sig would lose the little he had in Manning Grove.

His goal was to get his half of what his grandfather left behind, what was owed to him, and he couldn't do that if Trip cut him off from the MC, the repo business and the farm.

Right now he was sitting solid with a roof over his head, food in his gut, and a way to make some scratch. But that didn't mean he'd stick around forever. He'd never stuck in one place for very long unless he was forced to because of razor wire and an inmate number.

He let his fingers trail over her shoulder, which was covered in one of Stella's T-shirts, and down her bare arm to her clenched hand. He worked the sheet loose from her fist and gently smoothed out her fingers. Then he kept moving to the only place the woman was more than simply skin and bones...

He spread his palm over her belly and waited. He almost jerked his hand away when he felt the slight movement.

How that kid had survived, he'd never know.

One problem was, he didn't think Red would want anything to do with it.

Another one was, that baby was most likely fathered by one of those inbred motherfuckers.

He hoped he was fucking wrong. But he also hated hoping that Red was kidnapped when she was already pregnant.

Was one really worse than the other?

Yeah, it was. Having a baby fathered by one of those Shirleys would be a million times worse. To be used for breeding like a brood bitch would be a million times worse.

Fuck.

He needed to find out the truth. All of it.

Maybe she had a husband somewhere. A family. People who were panicked about her disappearance. People, other than that fucked up clan, searching for her.

People who loved and cared about her.

People who were missing her.

He followed the movement of the baby with his palm and when it finally stopped, he removed his hand, brushed the hair off her forehead and studied her for a few more minutes.

She needed to rest. And he needed some air.

Because suddenly, he couldn't breathe.

———

Autumn's eyes opened and, in the dark, the large numbers from digital clock next to the bed glowed bright.

Time. She had lost track of it for longer than she could remember.

Time had become immeasurable within those four walls that had contained her.

After the seed was planted, they began to track it for her, and sometimes they'd mention how long it had been and how long they had to wait.

But her mind hadn't held onto that information.

She didn't care.

She didn't want to know.

She just knew as the seed grew, so did her belly.

And that's all they wanted. The seed to grow.

However, now that seed was restless and had woken her up.

Plus, she needed to use the bathroom. A real toilet with toilet paper. And a sink with a bar of soap where she could wash her hands. A towel where she could dry them off, too.

She now appreciated those simple things.

You learned quickly to appreciate things you took for granted before but which had become no longer accessible.

Like a real bathroom instead of a bucket.

Or a real bed with sheets and a blanket without moth holes.

Or clothes.

Or awful slop that hadn't been forced down her throat.

She shifted to the edge of the bed and set her feet on the floor, staring at her now clean toes. She couldn't remember the last time she had a manicure or pedicure.

A lifetime ago.

She'd been tied down every once in a while so they could clip her nails so she wouldn't hurt them by using them as weapons.

Once, she had slashed Vernon across the face when he was trying to plant that seed.

He'd gotten so angry he'd punched her in the temple, knocking her out. When she came to, she was no longer tied over the breeding bench but was propped in a seated position in the corner of her "room" with semen sliding down the inside of her thighs.

She had wondered if it was only Vernon's. Because sometimes as punishment...

She squeezed her eyes shut.

Was it really only this morning that she had escaped? She must have slept all day and into the night.

Her belly seemed larger and the seed heavier already.

That was what happened when you watered and fed a planted seed.

It thrived.

She groaned as she pushed to her feet. The T-shirt Stella had given her only fell barely to the top of her hips due to her belly. Everything below was bare.

In the dark, she could see where Stella had placed Sig's boxer briefs on the nightstand. She snagged them and pulled them up her legs, the waistband just stretching far enough to circle her belly.

It would do, even though it felt weird to wear clothes. She hadn't worn any in so long.

She quietly moved through the bedroom to the door and opened it slowly. Listening. Waiting.

Nothing.

Silence.

The bathroom was two doors down and she was afraid to turn on the light, to see herself in the mirror. So, she didn't. Instead, she left the door open and did her thing in the semi-dark.

She had been forced to use a bucket and not only urinate in it but defecate, too. And not once did she have privacy when she'd done it.

Anyone could have walked in and watched her.

Watching was one thing. Touching another. Vernon normally didn't allow that. Only his wives or daughters were allowed in the shed. To bring her food, to empty her bucket. To hose her off. And in the beginning, when she was allowed one, to replace her ratty blanket.

To force her to eat.

To punish her when she didn't obey.

When she was done relieving her bladder, she didn't flush, afraid it would catch someone's attention. Whoever else was in the apartment. Because she knew she hadn't been left alone.

She wouldn't be allowed to escape.

She snuck down the short hallway to where the front room was. The open living area and the kitchenette.

A large screen TV on the wall was on, but muted, the glow from it flickering around the room. Colors from what-ever show was playing illuminated the man sprawled out on the couch.

Sig only wore a pair of jeans, the button open, the zipper partially undone, one hand tucked inside. His eyes were closed, his feet bare, his chest full of tattoos. The arm tucked behind his head had a full sleeve, which ran all the way up along his neck.

The man had a trimmed dark beard covering his lower face, the sides of his brown hair were clipped very short, almost shaved, only the top left longer. But still not long at all.

Not like his brother.

His lips were parted and he snored softly.

If she was going to leave, now was the time.

She could walk out the front door and disappear into the night. She could be far away before anyone would know.

She could disappear. Change her name. Dye her hair.

Become someone else. Someone no one was looking for.

She moved quietly and quickly toward the door and slowly turned the knob. When she pulled, it didn't budge.

She pulled again.

Nothing.

Closing her eyes, she pressed her forehead to the solid metal door and pressed her palm to it. On the other side was freedom.

She was so damn close.

She felt for a lock on the knob, but it wasn't turned. Then she felt around for a deadbolt.

There.

There it was.

But there was nothing to turn. Nothing to unlock. The pad of her index finger slid over the slot where a key would go. She blew out a breath.

She needed a key.

She pushed away from the object that kept her trapped and glanced around at every surface where a key could be tossed. The counters. The tables.

Nothing.

Her eyes slid back to Sig on the couch. Then they landed on the leather vest he wore, which was hung over the back of one of the kitchen stools.

She quickly moved to it and felt for pockets. She found plenty of things hidden in them. Condoms, what looked like hand-rolled cigarettes or joints, a small folded knife, but not a set of keys or even a single one.

He locked her in and held the key.

She'd gone from one captor to another.

She'll have to find another way, another time to escape. Tonight would not be it.

She moved back to the couch and studied the sleeping man.

He had helped her. He'd helped her escape that mountain.

Was he really locking her in, or was he only trying to keep her safe?

It didn't matter, she had no way to escape at the moment. She was two stories up and had no way to climb out of a window and land on the ground without serious injuries.

And, if she survived, there'd be no choice but to take her to a hospital where the Shirleys could find her and lie about who she was.

Once again, the sting in her eyes surprised her.

Maybe it was once again due to the loss of hope.

Running through the woods, she had it.

Riding away on the back of his motorcycle, she felt it.

But now that sliver of hope seemed out of reach. Once again.

She headed back down the hallway. Stella was right. She needed rest.

Sleep and food would make her stronger, more capable of escaping, of thinking more clearly. Right now her brain was still fuzzy and she was having a hard time concentrating.

She quietly closed the bedroom door behind her and checked for a lock on the knob. There wasn't one.

Of course.

The bed called her, but she ignored it to go to the large picture window, the only one in the room and she pulled the sheet away from it to peer outside into the night.

Her freedom was out there. Beyond this place. Beyond that mountain in the distance.

If the seed survived, she was sure she could bargain for her freedom in exchange. She would just need to hand over what grew inside her.

But as much as she didn't want the seed, she refused to give it to them, either.

She'd never hand it over to people like them.

Never.

She hadn't given them any part of her willingly and wasn't going to start. She'd rather die first because she'd never be able to live with herself.

Her gaze swept the area next to the building where a couple of fifty-gallon barrels had fires burning in them. The glow of one picked up some movement from under what looked like an open-sided pavilion.

Steady movement.

She tried to focus on what it was making it.

Her brows pinned together as everything became more clear, in her sight and in her mind.

A man.

His pants around his knees. Thrusting.

A woman. Naked from the waist down.

On her stomach, bent over the end of a picnic table.

His hand was fisted tightly in her hair, holding her down.

His other hand was smacking her.

On her ass. Her hips.

He was breeding her.

Trying to plant his seed.

Forcing her to produce a baby.

One for *them* to raise.

She couldn't pull her eyes away.

She couldn't fight the urge to watch. To witness what he was doing to her. To see if she also needed to escape.

He began to hit her harder and thrust faster.

Did Autumn hear her screaming?

Yes, barely.

She was crying out something.

And then his head was thrown back, and his pace stuttered before slowing to a stop.

Autumn still couldn't pull her eyes from them.

This was what happened to her.

This very thing.

What she was forced to submit to.

How the seed was planted.

The man stepped back.

And the woman moved.

She wasn't tied down.

She was free to stand. To escape.

Unlike Autumn had been.

The woman turned to face the man and went to her knees onto the concrete.

Autumn couldn't see what she was doing. His big body blocked her. But his hands were in front of him.

A couple minutes later, whatever she was forced to do was over and she stood up again.

The flame of the roaring fire nearest to them lit up her face.

She wasn't scared. She wasn't crying.

She was smiling as she wiped her mouth with her hand.

She liked what he had done. She liked what she had done, too.

He grabbed both sides of her head and pulled her into a kiss, then yanked up his jeans, while she wiggled a short skirt down over her hips.

She ran her hand gently down his face. And he threw an arm around her and steered her out of Autumn's view.

Her heart was pounding so loudly in her ears, she didn't hear the door open.

She didn't hear him approach.

But she jerked when she felt his presence.

Behind her. Close.

"She wanted it," Autumn said to the window as she continued to stare out at the emptiness.

Silence.

"She liked it."

"Who?"

"The woman." The sheet fell from her fingers.

"What woman?" A slight sharpness colored his question. Maybe suspicion? She didn't know him well enough to be sure.

"Out there."

Sig moved the sheet away from the window and looked out, scanning the area. "There's no woman out there."

"There was. With a man."

He didn't say anything for a few moments. Maybe he was waiting for her to explain her disjointed thoughts. And if she did, she'd reveal more than she wanted to.

Finally, he prodded softly, "What were they doin'?"

Autumn blinked and let what she witnessed run through her mind again. Like a movie. This time knowing the man and the woman were both willing participants. Both had enjoyed it.

Like she used to. In the past. When she was willing.

Something moved inside her and it wasn't the seed.

No, it was a weird sense of warmth that swirled through her. Something she hadn't felt in a long time.

"What were they doin', Red?"

Red.

His name for her.

"Not breeding."

More silence, but the air around them became heavy, thick. Like it was tangible and she could reach out and touch it.

"Having sex," she whispered. "They were having sex and they both were enjoying it."

"Happens a lot around here, Red. Most of my brothers ain't shy. They don't care who's watchin'. So, if you keep starin' out that window, you might see a lot of it. When you go downstairs into the main barn area you might see it out in the open there, too. You walk through the bunkhouse, you may hear it. Sometimes in stereo. May even hear it comin' through the wall when Judge has got a visitor. No one's forced here, Red. No one. So anythin' you see's okay with all parties involved. No one's bein' hurt unless they enjoy that type of shit. It's all good. And you don't have to do anythin' you don't want to here, either. No one will ever force you while you're here. You're safe. Trust me."

You're safe. Trust me.

Her new "stepfather" had said the same thing. *You'll be safe. Trust me. No one's going to hurt you if you cooperate.*

She didn't know him well enough to believe him, either. "I don't know you."

"But I know you."

What did he mean by that? She had no memory of the man standing behind her.

"You hungry?"

"It's the middle of the night."

"Yeah. Seein' as we're now both up, and you slept all day, I'm sure you need to eat somethin' again. Gotta get your strength back up, gotta fill out those bones. You've got a long way to go."

She turned to find him still so close. He was a lot taller than her and his head was tipped down.

She couldn't see the color of his eyes, but she knew what they were.

Brown.

Even though she couldn't see them clearly, she knew they were hard and troubled, held a lot of secrets and a lot of pain.

He'd lived a hard life.

She only lived a hard year.

He was still standing after whatever he went through.

She needed to do the same.

And to survive, to show the Shirleys they hadn't broken her, she needed to eat. She needed to find herself again.

To find that good life she lived over a year ago.

To find Autumn once more.

Or even a woman named Red.

Chapter Seven

Autumn sat on the examining table in one of those blue gowns. She had been told to tie it in the front.

A knock on the door preceded it opening and a female voice calling out, "Hello! I'm Dr. Bryson, but you can call me Carly." The doctor came around the curtain with a wide smile and stopped. The smile faltered as she took Autumn in. It wasn't hard to see that she had to force it back in place as she continued, "My office is very informal. Stella called and told me... Well, that you needed a checkup because you're pregnant and haven't had any proper prenatal care. Is that correct?" Her eyes fell to Autumn's stomach. "Well, that was easily answered. She didn't say over the phone you were that far along."

The doctor put her chart down on a nearby counter and stepped up to the examining table. "You can go ahead and lie back."

Autumn adjusted her position, the paper cover under her making a sharp crinkling sound as she did so.

"Do you know how far along you are, Autumn?"

"No."

"Oh... Uh... When was the last time you had sex?"

Autumn frowned up at one of the tiles in the drop ceiling. "I don't know. Months. He stopped once I stopped bleeding."

"Bleeding?"

"My period stopped and he stopped not long after that."

"He? The man outside in the waiting room?"

"No."

"Then who? Your boyfriend? Husband?"

How did she answer that? Should she lie?

"I don't know his name." She decided to lie, though she didn't know why since it would only make things messier.

"You didn't know him?"

Autumn squeezed her eyes shut and cursed. This doctor was going to examine her. She was going to figure out everything soon enough. And she wasn't sure how much Stella told her already.

"Just a man I know."

"A man you wanted to have a baby with?" The doctor grabbed a rolling stool and moved it to the end of the table, then pulled out the stirrups. "Slide down to the edge, please, and put your feet in the stirrups."

She didn't want to. She really didn't.

"I just want to check you to see if you're okay... To make sure everything is... okay."

Autumn already knew that answer. Nothing was okay.

She ground her molars as she slid her butt to the very edge of table and plugged her feet into the stirrups.

"Drop your knees and relax."

Relax. Right. She knew the deal, it just had been a while since she did it.

And now one more person would soon know what happened to her.

"I'm going to exam you now. I want to make sure nothing is... That everything looks normal. Okay?"

No, it wasn't okay. "Yes," she whispered. She promised Stella she'd do this.

"Have you had any spotting?"

"Sometimes."

"Cramps?"

"A few." She had figured most of them were from hunger.

When the doctor was done down between her thighs, she rolled back and removed her gloves with a snap. "I'm going to measure your stomach next and then call in the tech to do an ultrasound. Is that okay? This way we can try to figure out a due date and see if everything is on track."

Nothing was on track. "I can't pay for any of that."

"I... I think that's been covered, so don't worry about that right now. Let's just worry about you and the baby."

"Seed."

Suddenly, the doctor was standing at her side, peering down at her and wearing a confused expression. "Seed?"

"Yes. What he planted inside me."

Carly's surprised eyes flashed to Autumn's face and her frown deepened. "You mean when you got pregnant?"

"When he planted his seed."

Her brow dropped low and her eyebrows pinned together. She quickly grabbed her chart off the counter and glanced at it. "Autumn, how old are you? I just want to make sure my chart is correct and there wasn't a typo."

She had to be a year older than what she was before she was taken. "What month is it?"

"It's... uh, October... October third."

"I'm twenty-five." She had missed her birthday. Not that there had been anything to celebrate.

"Autumn," Dr. Carly said softly, like she was talking to a three-year-old. "What's the highest level of education you've completed? You marked college on your form."

College seemed a lifetime ago. When her future seemed

bright and shiny. But why would the doctor ask her that? "I finished my degree..." *Not long before...* "A while ago."

"So, you should understand how a baby is conceived."

Of course, she did. "Yes."

"And that the baby inside you shouldn't be... *isn't* considered a seed."

That stinging sensation in her eyes began again.

The tall, blonde doctor only hesitated a moment before saying, "You're definitely underweight. That's not good for you or the—"

"The seed."

"The... seed," Carly finished awkwardly. "Let me get the portable ultrasound machine in here. Sit tight." She squeezed Autumn's hand. "Then we'll get some answers, okay?"

She suddenly wished Stella had come along with her, so she wasn't so alone. But the woman had apologized because she was needed at her bar and said Sig would take good care of her, instead.

The door to the examining room opened again and another woman, shorter with dark hair, pushed a portable ultrasound machine into the room, followed closely by the doctor.

"The man out in the waiting room... He's not the father?"

"No." He did not plant the seed.

"Do you want him in here when we—"

"No."

After the ultrasound was set up and jelly was squirted onto her exposed rounded belly, the doctor stood by her head, staring at the screen as did the tech.

"Do you want to hear the heartbeat?"

The heartbeat. "No." Seeds didn't have heartbeats.

Autumn dropped her eyes and watched as the wand slid around her stomach. Back and forth, pause. Click. Back and forth. Pause. Click. It looked bigger today than yesterday.

The last couple of days, Sig had made her a big breakfast and made sure she ate it all. He did the same this morning before tucking her into an old Jeep and driving her to this office in a large medical building.

He had made her wear one of Stella's scarves around her hair, covering it completely, a big pair of dark sunglasses and more of Stella's clothes. As well as a pair of borrowed sneakers.

The doctor squeezed her hand again. "Do you want to know the sex?"

"No." Seeds didn't have a sex.

"Do you even want this baby, Autumn?"

Seeds didn't have a heartbeat or a gender... but babies did.

Her throat got tight and her own heartbeat began to speed up.

"Laura, can you step outside and give us a few minutes?" Dr. Carly said softly.

"Yes." The ultrasound tech quickly left, leaving Autumn and the doctor alone.

"Autumn," the doctor began softly. "The life—what you call the seed—in your womb is viable, even though very small for its age. I need you to understand it's not a thing. In a couple of months you're going to give birth to a living, breathing baby. As long as we can get you two back on track with nutrition and pre-natal vitamins. You realize that, right?"

A tear slipped from the corner of her eye and she quickly swiped at it. A burning started in her nose as a second tear escaped.

"It's too late to terminate this pregnancy, Autumn. You're too far along. You have no choice but to see it through. I'm assuming from the little Stella told me and from what you call this baby, you don't want it and having it wasn't your choice. Can you tell me why? Can you tell me why you're in this condition and why you call this baby a seed?"

Autumn tried to swallow but she couldn't.

The woman squeezed her hand again. "Autumn, if you were raped, I can help. I can notify the police—"

"No! No... No... I..." She licked her dry lips. "I can't go to the police."

"They can arrest whoever hurt you, if that's what happened. The bruises... Were they done by the man waiting for you?"

"No. He's done nothing but help me."

"Help you...?"

"Escape."

A small noise came from the doctor. "Let me help you sit up." She wiped the jelly off Autumn's stomach, tied her gown shut and powered the table until Autumn was sitting upright and looking right into the doctor's pretty, but very concerned and serious face. "You've clearly been abused. Your low weight, the marks on your body. The baby being undersized. Please talk to me. I can help. As a doctor, I'm obligated to help."

"I can't tell you, because if I do, they'll find me."

The doctor's face paled and she whispered, "Who will find you?"

"The one who planted the seed."

Dr. Carly rubbed at her forehead where it was wrinkled due to her frown. She opened her mouth, and nothing came out. It snapped shut and when she opened it again she said, "If you don't want this baby, Autumn... If you can't love or take care of it, there are plenty of couples who would love that chance. It's not a bad thing to want better for your child than what you can give it. It takes a lot of strength to recognize that fact. It's not easy, but sometimes it's for the best. You and the child would both be better off. The child would be loved unconditionally and you could get a chance to heal from your ordeal and you wouldn't live with a constant reminder of what happened."

She was right, the seed would be so much safer with someone else other than her. If she kept the seed, the Shirleys would never stop looking for it. Never stop trying to steal it back.

And they were never getting it.

"Yes... Yes, someone needs to take the seed and keep it safe. I can't. It would always be at risk with me."

"Does the person who," Dr. Carly grimaced, "planted the seed... Does he know you're pregnant?"

"Yes. That was the reason they took me."

"Took you."

"Brought me here to Pennsylvania."

"Did someone force you to come here?"

Autumn closed her eyes. She didn't want to talk about it. She just wanted to forget it all. Just go away somewhere and begin a new life. "I'm tired. I need to go back now."

"Autumn..."

"Please. I've had enough. I want to do what you said. Give it to someone who will love it and take care of it. That's not me."

"Autumn..." Carly said with a sigh.

The woman was getting frustrated. Well, so was Autumn. If she didn't want to talk about it, she wasn't going to talk about it.

"Do you give me permission to discuss my findings from your exam with the man who came with you?"

Yes, that would be good. Sig could explain things better than her. His thoughts would be clearer. His words would make more sense than hers.

Right now she was feeling exhausted, her mind was

scrambled and her thoughts tangled into knots. "Yes. Please talk to him."

Carly squeezed her shoulder. "Okay, get dressed. I'll come get you once I talk to him. And we'll figure some things out, okay? It'll be fine. You'll be fine."

Sure it would.

Everything would be just fine.

———

Sig spun on his boot heel when the door to the waiting room opened. He expected it to be Red, but it was a tall, leggy blonde wearing a white coat, instead.

"Are you the doc?"

She nodded as she approached. She jutted out her hand. "Dr. Carly Bryson."

Sig only stared at her outstretched hand, trying not to sneer at that last name. "Bryson?"

She dropped her offered hand, not seeming to take offense. "Are you willing to step into my office and have a few words? Autumn gave her consent to allow me to talk to you... about her... And the baby."

"Are you callin' the cops?"

Her eyebrows shot up her forehead. "What? No. I need more information first. That's why I need to talk to you. I'm not sure what..." She rubbed at her forehead, clearly agitated. "I need more answers than what I'm getting from her."

They all did.

"Your fuckin' last name is Bryson. Only Brysons I know are all... All wearin' badges."

Her lips curved up slightly but that small smile didn't reach her green eyes. "Yes, it seems to be a common theme in this town." Those lips fell flat. "Please, come this way."

She opened the door into the back and held out a hand, encouraging him to step through.

He followed and they both took a quick right turn down a short hallway and through another door into a small office. Once he stepped inside, she shut the door and settled behind the desk in a high-backed leather chair. "Please sit. Autumn is getting dressed. One of my physician assistants will escort her to the waiting area when she's done."

"Can't leave her alone, Doc."

"Why?"

"She'll run."

"In her condition?"

"Yeah. Trust me."

The doc pursed her lips and then pulled a cell phone out of her pocket. She quickly texted someone. "Okay, I'll have my PA keep her in the examining room until we're done."

"Someone needs to guard the door to the room she's in. She might try to sneak out."

"What?"

"Again, just trust me. She runs, it could be bad."

The doc's open mouth snapped shut. She sent another quick text, then set her phone down on the desk, concern etched on her face. "Talk to me. What the hell happened to her? Who got her pregnant? Do the police need to be involved? She's all bruised up. She's underweight. The pregnancy is much farther along than her size makes it appear. What the hell is going on?"

The last came out more of a demand than a question. The woman was no-nonsense and sounded like she could be pretty damn dominant if she wanted to be.

Sig sucked in a breath and said to the doctor sitting across from him, "I tell you everythin,' you don't go to the fuckin' cops, you get me? It's safer for her if you don't."

"Is it the mob or something?"

"No. Not the mob. Kinda worse, kinda not."

She shook her head. "Now I'm confused."

"And so is Red."

"Red?"

"Autumn," he corrected. But that name didn't sound right on his tongue. That was someone else's name for her. Not his. To him she was Red and always would be.

The doc's eyebrows dropped low. "Okay, so talk."

"Gotta promise me no cops."

"My husband is one so I don't know if I can do that if there was a crime involved. Which is what it sounds like."

Godfuckindamnit. "Fuckin' figures."

The doc lifted a hand. He supposed it was to soothe his worry. It didn't.

She spoke quickly. "It seems like Autumn wants nothing to do with this baby, so I talked to her about the option of adoption. It's a good solution for an unwanted child and she seemed open to it. Maybe my husband and I would be interested. The timing is finally right for us and we've been on a waiting list for a while now. Autumn doesn't have insurance and she needs a lot of care right now since Stella said she's had no prenatal care at all... And with the way she looks, I'm sure that's true. We..." The doc spread her hands flat on her desk. "We could help. Make this easier on her and us. It's a win-win. Especially if the baby is born with medical issues from being underweight since I'm a doctor. *And,* if she wanted, it could be an open adoption. We're not opposed to that."

Sig sat back in his chair and studied the doctor who had just spilled a lot of shit he needed to wrap his head around. He wasn't surprised Red didn't want to keep the baby. She called it a fucking *seed.* What woman did that?

He knew that answer.

One whose mind wouldn't allow it to admit to what it really was. Whose mind didn't want her to become attached to the result of trauma. Whose mind didn't want to admit to everything that happened to her.

She probably needed a crazy doctor in addition to a baby doctor.

No *probably* about it.

The woman had more issues than only being pregnant because of a rape. She might have permanent scarring of her mind.

All of this was over his head. He could quickly drown in it all. And he had enough of his own issues to deal with to try to take on Red's, too.

But, *for fuck's sake*, did a doctor and a local pig really want a baby sired by a Shirley? A Bryson pig, more than anyone, knew what those Shirleys were like and how fucked up they were.

That baby might never be normal and Sig had no clue how fucked up that kid could end up. It would have Shirley blood and wasn't even given a fighting chance to survive with the way Red looked. Skin and bones, beaten up, most likely forced to live like an animal. Her mental status questionable.

Sig's fingers curled against his thighs, his nails digging sharply into the denim of his jeans.

This whole thing was just plain fucked up. Why the fuck was he getting involved? Why didn't he just hand Red over to the doc to take care of? Let her husband deal with the Shirleys. Let them protect her and find her a safe place to stay until the kid was born.

It wasn't his kid, so he shouldn't care one fucking bit about it.

So, why was he taking any of this on his shoulders?

Why the fuck did he even care at all?

It was some fucked in the head woman who had a baby from some inbred motherfucker planted inside her. There was nothing even remotely normal about the whole thing.

He did not need this shit. Not at all.

He needed to concentrate on getting what was owed him and then getting the fuck out of town. He should be only looking out for himself. That was it.

Because if he took on Red's situation... He couldn't roll out any time soon.

He'd be stuck in this goddamn town for the next few months. Long enough to protect Red until her "seed" was born. Long enough to help her find a safe place to land afterward.

Damn, he did not need this shit.

He did *not* need this shit.

Goddamn it.

"Might rethink that fuckin' offer, Doc, once I tell you what I know. And believe me, I don't know everythin' yet. I'm sure it's much fuckin' worse than what little I do know."

Carly also sat back, pushed her glasses to the top of her head and crossed her arms over her very generous chest. "If you knew my husband, you'd know I can handle a lot of shit. So, fucking lay it on me."

Damn.

So, he did.

SIG STEPPED outside his apartment and watched as his brother and his woman hoofed it up the steps. He had one arm wrapped around his ribs because they were aching like fuck right now. He'd been doing too much shit and not giving them a chance to heal properly.

"Inside?" Trip asked as he jerked his chin toward the closed door behind Sig.

"She's sleepin'." She had been for the past couple of hours.

"How is she?" Stella asked and leaned her ass against the metal railing at the top of the steps.

The landing was a large rectangle, big enough to include both Sig and Judge's doors, but not to where it reached the large picture windows at the "front" of their apartments, which actually faced the fields behind the barn and bunkhouse. Trip had it designed that way for security reasons.

Both Sig and Judge agreed it was a good idea. Just like their front doors being metal, windowless and including a heavy-duty deadbolt.

"She's exhausted just from that trip to the doctor."

"Probably doesn't take much being that malnourished and pregnant at the same time," Stella murmured. "I always felt tired when I was pregnant."

"Say what?" Sig asked, his eyes automatically going to Stella's stomach. That was the first he'd heard of Stella having a kid. He wondered what happened to it.

"That's not what we're here to discuss," Trip said firmly, before Sig could ask.

His eyes slid to his brother's, picking up what Trip was putting down. "Right."

"Baby good?" Stella asked.

"For the most part. But even after that appointment, the kid's still an 'it' or 'the seed' to her."

Stella frowned, her eyes troubled as she nodded. "Might take a while for her to see it differently. Pregnancy messes with a woman's mind sometimes, but the way she got pregnant—if we're right in our assumptions—probably really screwed with her big time."

"No shit," Sig whispered.

"We need to decide what the fuck to do with her, Sig," Trip said. "She isn't ours. I still don't think it's a good idea we keep her here."

"We can move her to the house," Stella suggested.

Sig tried not to grin at Stella misunderstanding her ol' man on purpose.

"That's not what I fuckin' meant, Stel."

Stella shot Trip a look Sig was glad wasn't directed at him. "Where can she go? She has nowhere."

"That's not our fuckin' problem. She's not carryin' Sig's kid. She's not Fury blood. She's nothin' to us."

Sig avoided Stella's stare when she finally did look at him. "Speak for yourself," she whispered.

"She's better off stayin' in my apartment than the house, Stella. Got Judge next door with Jury, who'd scare the shit outta anyone. Got Deke downstairs with Justice. Both those dogs are protective when needed. Judge would kick anyone's ass who tried to break in here. There are more eyes and bodies at The Barn and bunkhouse than up at your place. 'Specially when you're at the bar and Trip's out doin' a repo or at the bar with you, or even at The Grove Inn checkin' in with Ozzy. She'd be alone. And I'm not just worried about them snaggin' her back, I'm worried about her runnin'."

"She'd be crazy to run," Trip said.

True, but... "You just said the reason she'd run."

"Because she's crazy?" Trip asked.

"Think shit's really broken up here." Sig tapped his temple. "It'll be awhile 'til she gets over it."

"If ever," Stella added. "We don't even know everything she went through, yet."

"And may never. Which is another reason maybe it's not best to keep her here. Hand her over to the pigs."

Jesus fuck, what was with his brother being such a fucking dick about it? "And then that opens up the possibility of the Shirleys gettin' her back. Might put her on those hillbillies' radar when the fuckin' pigs get their emergency response team, with all their big-ass military-grade toys and hard dicks, rushin' up that mountain to make a fuckin' arrest. It's better to take care of them quietly."

Judge's door opened and the big man stepped out, his American Bulldog by his side. "Go on," he commanded the dog, jerking his hand toward the stairs. "Go pop a squat and get the fuck back here." With a loud, excited bark, Jury rushed down the steps, her tail raised and waving like a flag, as she headed toward the field. As Judge kept an eye on his girl, he asked, "We havin' a fuckin' meetin' out here?" to the rest of them.

"Nope," Trip answered.

"Sure as fuck sounds like it. Any decisions made about us gettin' involved with that woman in Sig's bed needs to be brought to the table."

"Yeah," Trip agreed. "It's gonna have to happen since Sig won't see reason."

Sig's jaw tightened. "Didn't know you were such a cold fuckin' bastard, brother."

"And you're not?"

"Would also help to know the whole goddamn story before any of us vote on it," Judge added.

"But you might not get that for a while," Stella admitted. "You all might need to decide with only what we know at this point. And then decide on how much you all want to get involved. Trip's right. She doesn't belong to the Fury. She's not from Fury blood. We have no ties to her. There's no good reason for us to take her on. None." She lifted her hand to stop anyone else from talking. "But that doesn't mean we shouldn't. She's fucking alone, boys. Alone. If it was me? I'd be really fucking grateful for some heroes to step in right about now. Especially since she's struggling in more ways than one. Don't I remember you boys all wanting to be super heroes with capes growing up? Now," Stella turned her attention to Sig. "What happened at the doctor's? Let's at least hear that first."

Damn, the woman had some *cojones*. Not as big as Judge's but close. Sig bit back a grin. While that was amusing, what he was about to say wasn't. "Said the kid could come out with all kinds of birth defects. And not just 'cause he'd be related to a Shirley."

"He?" Stella asked.

"Yep. Red didn't want to know, but I asked. From what the doc could see, even though the kid's smaller than it should be, it's a boy."

Trip closed his eyes. "Damn."

"Don't even think about it, Trip," Stella warned.

"They might want the kid," Sig stated.

"Who?"

"The doc and her pig hubby," Sig answered his brother.

"What?" Trip almost shouted.

"Yeah, said they've been lookin' to adopt. Needs to run it by her rotten half first and, of course, Red would need to sign the kid over. She said she would."

"Autumn's willing to give up the baby?" Stella whispered.

"You really surprised?" Judge asked her. "Gotta be hard to keep a baby created from rape or... worse."

"But still..." Stella whispered again, her hand pressed to her lower belly. She shook her head. "I get what you're saying and it makes sense, but I'm having a hard time wrapping my head around it."

"She don't see it as a baby, Stel," Trip reminded her. "It's just a thing that she was forced to carry. For them. She probably has it in her head the kid wouldn't be hers afterward, anyway. Put yourself in her shoes. Would you get attached to a baby knowin' it's gonna be stolen from you the second it was born? Fuck no. You'd separate yourself from it. Not get attached."

Sig frowned at his brother. He was making too much fucking sense. And what he said did make sense and was a good reason why Red called the baby a "seed."

"Anyway," Sig said, "if Red will agree with the adoption

and the doc's pig hubby also agrees, she wants Red to come stay with them 'til the kid's born. Then they'd pay to send her wherever she wants to go from here. They'd help her get far away from that mountain and those inbred sister fuckers. But you all know what I fuckin' think about her goin' anywhere right now."

Judge pulled at his long beard and tilted his head. "Adoption's a damn good option, though. What's to avoid those brother fuckers from snaggin' the kid after he's born?"

Sig shrugged. "He'd have their last name. Doc said their names could be on the birth certificate. Everyone in town knows they're waitin' on a kid to adopt. Them gettin' one wouldn't cause a stir. It's kinda perfect. Also might help that the father on record's a fuckin' pig."

"Will the Brysons want the kid if he's born," Stella glanced at Sig's closed door and lowered her voice, "with problems?"

"If he's half Shirley, he's gonna have fuckin' problems," Trip muttered, then grinned. Until Stella whacked him in the stomach. The grin was long gone as he winced and rubbed his gut.

Sig continued, "She also stated that if Red eats right, keeps her stress low, takes the vitamins she gave us, the kid could be okay. If she refuses to do better and remains in the condition she's in, both could die when the kid's born. She needs to get her strength up."

"So, the Brysons want to take her in and make sure she's taken care of," Judge said simply.

Jury galloped back up the steps, her tongue hanging out and her tail wagging as she shoved her nose into everyone's junk—like she always did—before sitting by Judge's side, staring up at him like the sun rose and set on that giant motherfucker.

Judge always was spouting that dogs were more loyal than bitches. And Deacon always busted his balls by reminding his cousin, Jury *was* a bitch. Just of the four-legged variety.

"Yeah," Sig finally answered the big man, after double checking to make sure all his junk was still intact after being molested by the dog.

"Autumn want that?" Trip asked, looking way too hopeful.

Sig assumed Trip was referring to Red moving in with the doc. "Didn't ask her. I told the doc no."

"Fuckin' A," Trip muttered. "Not likin' this, Sig."

His blood pressure was beginning to spike at this bullshit of them wanting Red to go stay somewhere else. "What fuckin' part of she's stayin' on this fuckin' farm don't you understand? She can stay on my fuckin' half."

"Don't work like that, Sig—"

"Sure as fuck does 'cause I'm makin' it work like that." His fists clenched and unclenched as he tried to keep his shit packed tight. "Also told the fuckin' doc we'd be better at protectin' her and why."

"I'm sure she liked hearing that since her husband is a Bryson," Stella said dryly.

"She agreed."

Stella's mouth dropped open. "What?"

Trip and Judge also looked surprised at that answer.

He shrugged again. "He works, she works. Who's stayin' with Red when they're both workin'? Who's makin' sure she don't freak the fuck out and start runnin'? Who's makin' sure she eats and takes her vitamins?" He tipped his chin down and growled, "Who the fuck's makin' sure those goddamn inbred billy goat fuckers don't come kidnap her from right under their nose? Bryson's limited on what he can do legally."

"And we're not," Judge said softly, rubbing Jury's big blocky head.

"Yeah we are, brother," Trip reminded him. "We're just as limited as to what we can do *legally*."

Sig interrupted him. "And when the fuck have I ever kept shit legal?"

"When the fuck have you ever lived more than a few months not behind goddamn bars, Sig?" Trip reminded him, beginning to get just as pissed as Sig.

Once their two tempers flared things could go to shit quickly between them.

"Sayin' it again, it ain't smart harborin' her," Trip practically yelled, the tendons in his neck popping.

Sig watched his brother's chest rise visibly as he inhaled through flared nostrils, held it for five seconds, then blew it out. He wasn't the only one who noticed. Stella put a hand on Trip's arm afterward and their president visibly loosened a fraction at the touch.

Not a second later, Trip had Stella pulled into him, one arm securely under her tits and his face in her hair.

"Sig's right, Prez," Judge agreed, surprising the fuck out of him. "Got a lot of eyes here. And more are always comin' in. Club's grown and still growin'. Got more than enough people to keep an eye on her. To keep her safe."

"And what about the Shirleys?"

"We'll deal with them, too," Judge answered Trip.

Trip's eyebrows shot up his forehead. "How? Burn down that damn mountain?"

"Been thinkin' 'bout that," Sig started. "We're gonna deal with them real quiet-like. They won't report shit to the pigs since they refuse to follow any laws other than their own. Hell, they hate the pigs more than us. So, they start comin' up missin', you think they're makin' a missin' person's report?"

Judge grinned. "Fuck no."

"Right. They ain't runnin' their mouths to the pigs.

They handle shit themselves up there, just like we should down here."

Trip scraped a hand through his long hair while staring sightlessly past them all. "Again, don't want the Fury in the pigs' crosshairs. And the doc's husband bein' one complicates the fuck outta this."

"Brysons want her baby that bad?" Judge shrugged heavily. "Then that pig's gonna have to put on some blinders or look the other way. That could be part of the agreement. But it's best to try to keep him in the dark as much as fuckin' possible. Less he knows, the better for us."

"What if the baby's born with that red hair, Sig?" Stella asked, who was now pinned against Trip with both his arms wrapped around her, the one still under her tits and the other now across her hips, as if he was holding on.

Sig got it. Stella grounded him. Almost like an emotional support dog. His eyes dropped to Jury, whose ears were now getting scratched, and he lifted them to Judge, who was doing the mindless scratching. If the dog could smile, she would be.

Well, damn. Maybe Sig needed to get a fucking dog.

Stella continued, "I mean, if he comes out looking like a Shirley and sporting Autumn's red hair and hazel eyes, they might eventually realize who his birth mother is. It could be dangerous to keep him in Manning Grove."

Sig considered that, but he didn't have an answer. Red was in no shape to be a mother right now and the doc taking the baby couldn't be a better scenario. "Gonna cross that bridge when we come to it, Stel. She's gotta get to the end of this pregnancy and spit out that kid first. She signs the adoption papers? She's free. She can go on her way and never look back. Go live her life and forget about whatever the fuck happened to her."

"You find out what happened yet?" Trip asked, sounding a lot less ticked.

"It's been only three days, brother. She hasn't spilled it and I haven't pushed. And after today, I now know she don't want this kid, which means my guess was probably right. Someone on that fuckin' mountain 'planted' that 'seed' in her. That kid ain't just a product of rape, she was bred on purpose to get fresh blood up there."

Stella winced. "Sig, don't use that word."

"Might be true, though, Stella. And if they're breedin' women up there against their will, that shit's gotta stop."

"Right," Trip muttered. "But how the fuck did she get there? That's what I wanna know. Where the fuck did she come from?"

"She mentioned that everyone she knows is in Ohio, but she don't wanna go back there. That's all I know. Gonna try to get more info from her without diggin' too deep and breakin' her even more." Because forcing any info from her would make shit so much worse for her.

"I'll talk to her, too. I need to go pick up some clothes for her at Walmart or Target, anyway. Maybe some maternity wear. When I bring it back, I'll strike up a casual conversation with her," Stella said.

"If there are more women up there, Sig, we're givin' that info to the pigs. We are not goin' up there guns a-blazin' like some fuckin' special ops shit or somethin'."

"You Marines can't handle that kind of badass hero shit?" Sig teased Trip.

"Yeah, we can but we'd rather let those cocky-mouthed SEALS get their asses shot at first. We ain't fuckin' stupid."

"All right," Stella interrupted sharply. "Hey, did Carly say how far along Autumn is? I want to know how much bigger she's going to get when I go shopping for her."

"She wasn't a hundred percent certain yet since the baby's so small right now, but her best guess with the way things looked was thirty-one weeks."

Stella gasped. "Holy fuck. She doesn't look that far

along at all. I was guessing maybe four, five months at the most."

"Yeah, Stel, that's why she said it's important she get healthy and soon. The doc also wants to see her every week to make sure there ain't any complications and that they're both progressin' as good as possible. Maybe even do more bloodwork. Doc's really worried 'bout both of 'em survivin' the birth."

"I'm sure. Damn," Stella whispered. "I'll pick up some shit for her after I take care of some obligations at the bar and I know Dodge won't need help with anything. I'll also bring her back some food from Dino's. A big piece of that Death by Chocolate cake, too. No one can resist that."

"Yeah, Stel. Thanks."

Trip released his ol' lady and she approached Sig. "You don't have to thank me, Sig. I'm doin' it for her."

"Thankin' you, anyway."

Stella nodded, smiled softly, and reached out to squeeze his arm. Sig dropped his gaze to where her hand touched him and then he lifted it to his brother, who was watching their every move.

He trusted Stella. He just didn't trust Sig.

As their eyes met, Trip clapped his hands sharply together once. "'Kay, then. We need a meetin' and I'm callin' it. Tonight. Yeah?"

"Yeah," both Sig and Judge answered at once.

With a nod, Trip grabbed Stella and guided her down the steps.

Chapter Eight

Sig studied the Fury's insignia of a bloody skull and crossbones carved into the thick wood of the table top. He remembered this table—which the executive committee had used during their meetings—being in a back room at the warehouse. It was where all the important decisions had been made.

Also during weekend-long parties, a lot of DNA was left behind on that fucking table.

Blood, cum, spit. All of it.

He remembered one time when he, Judge and Trip had hidden under the table and waited.

They learned a lot that night. Including how to stay quiet as fuck so they didn't get caught and get their asses beat.

They also learned how deep of a pounding a woman's throat could take while face-fucking her before she puked all over herself.

It had been both fascinating and horrifying at the same time for all three of them. Especially when the brother made her use her own shirt to wipe the shit off her face and continue taking that pounding until he came down her throat. Then without a word, he left her there on her knees in her own filth, crying.

Judge and Trip were barely old enough for their dicks to get hard while watching, but they did. Unfortunately, Sig had been too young, so they had both shoved him and laughed, calling him a baby.

That memory had him shaking himself mentally as his gaze slid around the meeting table, wondering if the man sitting next to him and the other one sitting at the end of the table as the current club president remembered that night.

Now was not the fucking time to ask.

Actually, the time was never.

"Goddamn it, Jury, get your fuckin' nose outta my dick," Ozzy griped. "Your fuckin' dog's a perv, Judge."

"Maybe you should wash it after you stick it in Lizzy. Probably smells like roadkill," Judge said, then patted his thigh. "Jury, heel."

Ozzy hooked a thumb at the other white and brindle American Bulldog in the room. "How come Justice don't molest us like that?"

"'Cause he don't like dick. My dog ain't gay," Deacon answered.

"He ain't gay, then why's he lickin' his fuckin' balls?" Ozzy asked.

"You'd lick your own balls if you could."

Ozzy pursed his lips, then shrugged. "Yeah, true."

"Can we bring this fuckin' meetin' to order?" Trip barked, smacking the gavel on the table.

"'Stead of disorder?" Cage asked.

"Okay, you first, Road Captain," Trip said to him. "Set up another run. This Sunday."

Cage gave him a sloppy two-finger salute. "That it, Prez?"

"No. Dutch hear from any of the elders?"

Ah fuck. Sig was not looking forward to rehashing the Amish bullshit again.

"Nope. All's quiet on the *Sig-fuckin-the-virgin-Amish-girls-up-the-ass* front."

Sig leaned forward and planted both hands on the table. "Don't be a hater, asshole. Just jealous your fist don't even want you."

"Better my fuckin' fist than doin' time for fuckin' girls that ain't turned ripe yet."

"That's one thing not on my fuckin' sheet." He'd gotten caught doing a lot of stupid shit, but that wasn't one of them.

"Yet," Cage said with a smirk. "Better start cardin' them to make sure it stays off your record. That clan's law might be 'old enough to bleed, old enough to breed,' but that ain't true for the rest of us."

Sig dipped his chin as he considered Cage across the table. The asshole probably had no idea about Red yet, but Sig didn't give a fuck, he was an asshole all the same. "Can show you firsthand what's on my fuckin' sheet, if you're that interested. Can go down the list and demo—"

Trip smacked the gavel on the table hard, getting their attention. "Can we get the fuck back to business here and not turn this fuckin' meetin' into a brawl? Jesus fuck." He shook his head. "Any-fuckin-way, gotta keep things cool with 'em. Can't afford to fuck that up."

"Tell Sig that," Ozzy said, grinning at him. "Plenty of pussy startin' to show up at The Barn. No reason to go elsewhere. Not one of 'em has said no when I ask 'em to spread it and show me that shiny pink center."

"Christ," Judge muttered beside Sig.

"My point is—"

"Taken," Trip finished for Ozzy. "Your fuckin' point is taken. Sig's aware to stay the fuck away from those girls... women."

"Speakin' of women, we need to talk about the knocked up one sleepin' in his bed," Deacon said.

"That's last on the agenda," Trip muttered.

"What knocked up woman?" Cage asked.

Ozzy's head spun toward Sig. "You got a fuckin' kid on the way? Didn't think they'd get knocked up by doin' 'em up the ass. Musta slipped and went in the wrong hole."

"Fuck!" Trip yelled. "It ain't his kid. Let's table that right now and get the other business outta the way first. We'll circle back to that."

Deke laughed. "That's what he does. Circles 'round to the backdoor."

"Oh, this should be fuckin' good," Ozzy snickered.

"Will my Sergeant at Arms keep order at this fuckin' table?"

"Shut the fuck up, assholes, and let the prez speak," Judge growled, then went back to rubbing Jury's ears since her head was in his lap. Sig noted *not* sniffing the man's balls. "That good?" the enforcer asked Trip.

"Great." Trip sighed and shook his head. "Let's talk about somethin' other than pussy. Need to patch in Sparky and Mouse. It's time. Told 'em six months, it's been that."

"What about Dodge and Shady?" Sig asked. They were probably getting close to the end of their time, too. It'd be easier to patch them all over at once and get it done. Make room for more prospects in the bunkhouse.

"Dodge got another month to go. Shady at least two," Judge said.

"Two?" Ozzy asked, surprised.

"Yeah, he came later and still don't trust that motherfucker."

Sig asked Judge, "What's he done for you not to trust 'im?"

"Hardly says shit," the big man answered.

"And that's a plus right there. 'Specially with all the rest of you fuckers who got diarrhea of the fuckin' mouth," Sig grumbled.

"Bringin' Sparky and Mouse to a vote. Wanna do it now and surprise 'em later?" Trip asked.

Yeahs went up around the table.

"Anyone got a problem with either of 'em?" Trip asked.

A couple noes were heard.

"All in favor of Sparky and Mouse gettin' their full rockers and patches?"

A loud "Aye" rose from each of them.

Trip then asked the obligatory, "Anyone opposed?"

Silence filled the room except for Justice's loud snoring where he was curled up near Deacon's feet.

"'Kay. You heard it. Ozzy, let 'em know they're no longer considered dog shit and can get out of those shitty bunkbeds and pick an open room. We'll throw a little celebration downstairs and hand 'em their patches after the run Sunday. Sig, set that up. Deke, have 'em tell you whatever road name they want on their patches and get 'em ordered, yeah? Don't tell anyone what they chose, let 'em announce it at the party. Got it?"

"Yeah," Deacon answered.

Trip raised a palm and grimaced. "Unless the names are stupid as fuck. Then run 'em by me first."

Deacon grinned. "Got it."

"Means two more open spots for dog shit, Prez."

"Yep," Trip answered Ozzy. "Know anyone?"

"I'll keep an eye and ear out."

"Just like you let your dick hang out," Cage said.

Ozzy shoved him and then grabbed his junk, shaking it. "Know you want it, closet cocksucker."

"A cocktail weenie ain't a meal, Oz. Lizzy ain't told you that yet?"

Trip ignored them. "Ozzy, you know what I'm lookin'

for. Now, who else got business to bring up before we circle around back to that other subject."

"Me," said Deacon.

"The treasurer has been recognized and now has the table," Trip announced.

"Christ," Judge muttered.

Ozzy snorted.

And Cage just shook his head as he sat back in his chair and crossed his arms over his chest.

"Wanted me to keep an eye out for property for sale 'round town and in the area. Found two possibilities. Car wash at the other end of the lot where Justice Bail Bonds is, near the Walmart. And," Deacon lifted one brow and smiled, "a pet crematorium. The local vet built it. He's old as fuck now and wants to unload that part of his business. His kids don't want anythin' to do with it."

"Why the fuck would we wanna burn pets?" Judge asked, stroking Jury's head, which was still in his lap. The dog was asleep while sitting up.

Deacon shrugged. "It's a good business. Looked at the books and it's in the black."

"Yeah, plenty of good businesses out there. Like the car wash," Judge suggested.

"Not one like this."

"Yeah, there's a reason for it," Deacon's cousin grumbled. "It's creepy as fuck."

"You ain't gonna get her cremated when she dies, then spread her ashes?" Deacon asked Judge.

Judge's big body jerked. "Bite your goddamn tongue."

"Well, when my boy dies, I'm havin' his ashes put into somethin' I can display. A lot of people do. Dead pets are a big business."

"That didn't sound right," Cage said.

"Know what I fuckin' mean. People spend a lot of scratch on their fuckin' pets. They treat 'em like family.

Prolly spend more on their fuckin' pets than their own damn semen demons. And I'm sure after hearin' what we're gonna discuss next, thinkin' a crematorium would be fuckin' perfect for us."

The table went silent. Deacon's smile got even bigger.

"Jesus fuck," Trip muttered.

"Yeah. Think about it," Deacon said.

"How big are the furnaces?" Judge asked, suddenly looking a whole lot more interested.

"He's got two in the buildin'. One for smaller animals like cats and shit. And one," Deke paused dramatically, "big enough for full-sized hogs, even cows."

"Damn," Sig whispered, sitting back.

Deacon's eyes slid to Sig. "Damn right. That's a big fuckin' deal."

"Okay, I'm fuckin' lost here," Ozzy said. "Why the fuck do we wanna burn cows and not eat 'em? I love a good steak."

"Don't wanna burn fuckin' cows," Trip said, rubbing a hand over his eyes. "Wanna burn somethin' the size of a cow."

"What's the size of a cow?" Ozzy asked, his eyebrows pinned low. "A horse?"

"An inbred goat fucker," Sig whispered. His eyes met Trip's, whose lips were nothing but a slash since he was pressing them together so hard.

"Not sure we wanna get into that type of business," Sig's brother said. "Seems like there'd be a lot of rules we'd need to follow. You know, like EPA and shit. Could be a hassle."

"It's lock and key, brother," Deacon explained. "Just gotta maintain the equipment, the buildin' and the licensing. It's easy fuckin' peasy. Pick up the animal, put it in the Easy Bake Oven, set it to well-done and *poof*... got ashes. Shovel those into a bag. Throw that bag into whatever container they pay us a lot of scratch for, then deliver them to the grievin' owner."

"What about the cows and horses?" Ozzy asked.

"Those ashes can get spread in a field as fertilizer," Deke answered with a half shrug.

Sig's eyes held Trip's again as he murmured, "We got plenty of fields."

"We sure do." Deacon raised his eyebrows at Sig. "Lots of room to spread ashes of large animals."

"Goddamn genius, Deke."

The man sat back and shot Sig a smile. "*Nooo* shit."

"Fuckin' genius," Sig repeated, scraping his fingers down his beard.

"We got the scratch for it?" Trip asked Deacon.

The club's treasurer nodded. "Enough for the down payment. Gonna negotiate the sellin' price with the vet. Get it knocked down some. He wants us to offer his clients a discount. Told him no fuckin' problem. He's even gonna help train whatever dog shit prospects we get to run it. Also talked him into includin' the van he uses for pickup and delivery. *And...* best part... he's willin' to finance the balance with a super fuckin' low interest rate."

"Damn, Deke," Trip said, looking impressed. "How soon he wanna close on it?"

"Fuckin' yesterday. But I'll get with him and hammer it all out. Because of regulations and licensing, might take a little longer."

"What about the car wash?" Cage asked.

"We do the deal with the vet, ain't got the scratch for the car wash. That'd be a bank loan for the balance, if we did. And the banks are a major pain in the fuckin' ass to deal with for an *organization* like us. The crematorium's the best deal outta the two."

"Yeah," Sig said under his breath. It sure fucking was.

"Let's vote," Trip suggested, surprising Sig by suddenly being on board with the idea.

Within thirty seconds, the plans for the club to buy a pet crematorium were approved by everyone sitting at that damn table. The table where Judge, Trip, Sig and Stella's fathers sat around more than twenty years ago.

Now the current exec committee needed to talk about Red.

Sig needed to not only get his brothers at the table on board, but the rest of the brothers in the MC, too.

He needed everyone to do their part in protecting her. And they needed to do it like she was club property. For at least as long as she was living in his place. Until that kid was born and safe from the clan.

After that?

Hell, he had no fucking clue.

———

Sig sat out on the landing in a folding chair, his bare feet up on the metal railing, and an open beer on the floor next to him. He'd set up two chairs out there so Red could get some fresh air and sunshine when he wasn't out there smoking.

He didn't want to smoke anywhere near her, since seven days after finding her running through the woods, she was already starting to look better and not as much like a haunted skeleton. Her skin wasn't so translucent, her hazel eyes more focused, her speech a lot clearer, and her cheeks no longer hollow.

They shouldn't be. She was eating more often and now finishing every meal he put in front of her. She was even starting to putt around the kitchenette a little, sometimes making herself a snack. Once even making him a big pot of spaghetti.

She had eaten more of it than he had and was turning into a bottomless pit.

And he knew why.

The kid inside her was becoming a lot healthier, too. Her belly had popped out almost overnight and seemed almost twice as big as when he first found her. Though, she never talked about it. Never touched it when he saw it moving, even through the maternity tops Stella had picked up for her. He'd been tempted to reach out and feel a kick or two himself. But he didn't.

She didn't want to think about what was growing inside her. She still called it a seed and never called it a baby.

Not once.

Sleeping on the couch this last week really fucking sucked. His back was killing him, his neck was stiff and his ribs slow to heal.

It wasn't just Red holding him back from going on the club run that afternoon, it was the thought of hitting all those bumps in the road. He needed to finish up healing so he could get back to normal.

He lifted the joint pinched between his thumb and middle finger to his lips, took a long drag, tipped his head back as he held the smoke deep in his lungs and he stared up at the clear blue early October sky. Perfect fucking Fall day for a run, too. Not nut freezing cold or ball sweating hot.

He blew a long stream of smoke up toward the clouds.

Fuck.

He could use that run.

He was as tense as a motherfucker and a long ride might help. He'd been smoking weed every fucking day in a desperate attempt to keep his temper in check. But he was still on edge.

A very sharp one.

Most of it was due to him trying to talk to Red about her family. About her home. About her fucking life.

About anything which would give him some clues about her. About what happened to her.

She gave him dick.

She'd sleep, eat, watch TV, and clean. His apartment hadn't looked this fucking spanking clean since the day he'd moved in. He didn't ask her, she just did it. Stella said it was good for her since it kept her moving. Kept her mind busy.

It was good for him, too, since his place had been a shit pit.

Sometimes her eyes were glazed over like a fucking zombie and sometimes she was more coherent. Like when Red watched the news. She'd ask him about current events. Shit she'd probably missed in the months she was up on the fucking mountain.

But Sig couldn't give a flying fuck about current events. He wanted to know what happened to her.

Stella would take her on walks around the property and on those outings she'd also try to get Red talking. Trip's ol' lady failed every damn time. Red was more interested in learning about the town, about Stella and Trip and about the club.

She asked Stella a lot of questions.

Even about Sig.

He gave Stella permission to answer any questions about him honestly. He didn't give a fuck and Stella didn't know everything about him, anyway. What she did know, everybody else did, too. Including Trip. So, it wasn't like Red would hear any of his deepest, darkest secrets.

If he wanted her to know those, he'd tell her himself.

Sig made sure they were never out there walking alone. Someone was always following. Usually one of the prospects.

Just in case.

Trip had been handling all the repo jobs for the past week, but he was bitching about it. So, Sig had no choice but to get back to it. He'd just need someone to stay with Red while he was gone. Someone other than only Stella.

He also didn't want to lock Red into the apartment alone. That wouldn't be much different from being locked up on that fucking mountain.

In fact, the other day he caught her trying to open the door while he was grabbing some clothes from the bedroom. But he kept it locked from the inside so she wouldn't slip away when he was in the shower, or cooking, or whatever the fuck he was doing and not able to keep an eye on her.

What she said that day had cut him deep. "Not as bad. But a jail just the same." Then she had gone back to the bedroom, closed the door and he didn't see her for the rest of the day.

He'd heard her, instead. Crying softly. Probably muffling it into his pillow. Soaking it with her goddamn tears.

But he didn't know what else to fucking do.

Until she told him differently, she had nowhere to go and no way to get there.

And for some fucking reason he felt responsible to keep her safe.

To make sure the Shirleys never put their hands on her again.

To make sure they paid the price for what they did to her.

But he couldn't stop hearing her crying. Even when she wasn't. He'd tried covering his ears and grinding his teeth like he had when he was a kid to drown out Buck fucking his mother.

To stop hearing that headboard banging the wall.

To stop hearing his mother's cries.

To stop hearing the filthy fucking names Buck called her.

To stop hearing his father come home and do the same thing not a few hours later.

So, he locked Red in, went down into The Barn, grabbed a full bottle of Jack, went back up and sat outside the apartment door with his back against it, a hand-rolled in one hand and the whiskey bottle in the other.

Eventually he no longer heard the crying because he no longer heard anything.

He'd blacked out and only came to when Judge kicked him awake and helped him back into his own apartment so he could sleep on his own fucking couch.

When he woke up the next morning, the first thing he saw was Red standing in front of the picture window near the couch, her forehead and palms pressed to the glass. He had no idea what she was staring at, but he could imagine it was her freedom. Just out of reach.

He'd done it himself plenty of times along the razor-wire topped fence line of whatever prison he was in at the time.

His problem was, every time he got free, he'd do something within a few months to lose that freedom he wished for.

He doubted Red would do the same.

The minute she got free—from the Shirleys, from the burden she was carrying, from Sig—unlike him, he doubted she'd do anything to change that.

"Talk to me," he had urged her, trying to keep the desperation from his voice, which was rough from his all-night bender. His head throbbed as he watched her, hoping she'd finally talk. Just give him something.

Anything.

She didn't.

Not that morning.

Not this morning, either.

So, here he sat, smoking a fucking fatty and drinking a

beer, doing his best not to shatter into pieces he couldn't control.

The door next to his opened and the big man stepped out. Judge quickly hid his surprise at seeing Sig out there so early.

"Didn't think you'd fuckin' live after the other night," the deep, gravelly voice said.

"Was hopin' I didn't, but unfortunately, I did."

"Faster way to do it than drinkin' yourself to death."

"Will keep that in mind next time."

The dogs pushed past Judge and down the steps to do their thing. Judge grunted as he settled his bulk into the folding chair next to Sig.

"Thanks for pickin' up food for her from Dino's last night. Was stuck on that fuckin' repo over in Parsington."

Judge held out his hand and Sig passed him the joint. "You snag it?"

"Yeah, got chased with a fuckin' golf club, though. Fuckin' bitch was crazy."

Judge grinned and took a hit.

The two big dogs galloped back up the steps. Justice immediately laid down in front of them and began to lick his balls. The fucker was always licking his balls and dick.

"Life would be a lot easier if I could fuckin' do that," Judge grumbled, handing the joint back to Sig.

He took another hit and when he stifled a laugh, the smoke escaped. "Yeah, right?" That chuckle only hurt his ribs just a little this time. That was a good sign. "Why d'you have Justice?"

"Deke's outta town. Huntin' a bail jumper. Where he also happened to fall into some freshly divorced slit."

Sig knew what "freshly divorced," or even newly sepa-rated, meant. Those bitches' main goal was riding as much dick as possible, trying to catch up for all the time they wasted on the motherfucker they "mistakenly" married and was faithful to. At least the women who weren't cheating whores like his mother. And like Trip's first wife.

Hell, like most of them.

"When's he back? He missin' today's run?" Sig passed the joint, letting the smoke in his lungs roll out of his mouth and sucking it back up into his nostrils before allowing it to escape up into the sky.

"Yeah. He'll show back up when he either captures the asshole he's lookin' for or gets tired of fuckin' the same slit a few days straight. Or she rides his dick raw and his nuts dry."

Sig snorted.

Judge took a couple long drags on it before handing it back. He nudged the bottle at Sig's feet with his boot. "Early for beer."

"Yeah."

"We got a run later."

"Yep."

"Guess you ain't goin'," Judge concluded.

"Nope. Why I'm drinkin' that fuckin' beer and smokin' this dope." Sig shook his head. "'Bout ready to fuckin' snap, brother."

"Why?"

"Like Trip, got Buck's blood in me and it mostly runs hot."

"Yeah. You were takin' it out on that Amish piece of ass."

Sig blew out a long breath. "Yeah. She was into it."

"Bet she was."

"Know if any of the sweet butts or the bitches that hang around downstairs are into that?"

Judge's eyebrows rose. "Think I checked their fuckin' resumes?"

Sig grinned. "No, but guessin' a big guy like you likes it a little rough."

"A little rough ain't leavin' bloody welts on a woman's ass, Sig."

Sig's grinned flattened out. "Some are into it."

"Sure they are. Just haven't met any."

"Probably wouldn't know unless you asked."

"Pretty fuckin' sure they'd ask first," Judge grumbled.

"So, none of those patch whores are into rough?"

"Just said I'd lick my own dick and balls if I could. There's a reason for that." Judge held out his hand again and Sig passed him what remained of the joint. He pulled a roach clip out of the inside pocket of his cut and handed that over, too.

"Gotta ask 'em yourself, Sig," Judge finally said after smoking it down to almost nothing. He jerked his head back toward the apartment behind them. "Gonna whip and bust a nut in some other bitch while you got that one in your place? Or you gonna bring one up here for her to watch while you do it?" He crushed what little was left of the roach between his big fingers and flicked it over the railing.

"Don't know what I'm gonna do yet. Just thinkin' about my options. Gonna need to do somethin' soon, though. Can feel shit gettin' tight. Stickin' close to home ain't helpin', either. Makin' me more restless than ever. Today's run woulda helped somewhat, but not even gettin' that."

"So, go on the run and get Shady to stay with her like the other night. Those two can sit there not talkin' to each other for fuckin' hours." Judge snorted.

It bugged the shit out of Judge that Shady was so damn quiet. He was used to the Originals who were all loud-mouthed assholes and were drunk or fucked up more often than not.

"Ain't gonna be enough."

Judge frowned. "What won't?"

"The run. Wouldn't be enough, anyway."

Sig could feel Judge studying his profile, so he kept his eyes glued to the distant tree line and waited.

"You know, that one in there sticks, you ain't gonna ever be able to do that shit with her."

That wouldn't be a problem. "Wasn't plannin' on her stickin', brother."

"Good. It's clear she ain't what you need."

"Right."

"Her head space is nothin' but fucked up. Yours ain't much better."

That was something Sig didn't need to hear. He knew it already. It was hard to hide, so most of the time, he didn't.

He sucked on his teeth, then nabbed his beer off the floor, putting it to his lips as he said, "Goin' up there."

Judge shifted sharply in his chair. "Where?"

Sig took a long pull on the bottle, then sat it on his thigh. "Up there."

"The fuck you are. 'Specially alone."

"Yeah, brother. Just to see what I can find out."

"Don't be a stupid fuck, Sig."

"Easier to sneak in and out to grab some info doin' it alone."

"Get it from her," Judge ordered.

"She ain't talkin'."

Judge spit a hocker over the railing. "You blame 'er?"

"No."

"Try fuckin' harder."

"One of the reasons my patience is runnin' so fuckin' thin. Tired of waitin'. Tired of tryin'. Tryin' not to push her, but I gotta know."

Judge leaned forward, planted his elbows on his thighs and twisted his head toward Sig. "Why? Just said she ain't stickin'."

"Just need to know."

"Is it some sick fantasy for you, Sig, knowin' what happened?"

Was it? He twisted his neck to face Judge. "No. Wanna make 'em pay."

"Why?"

"'Cause they shouldn't get the fuck away with what they did to her."

"Like you did to that Amish girl?"

"Again, she wanted it. Asked for it. Was into it. Not gonna justify that shit again. Red didn't ask for any of what happened to her. She didn't beg for those bruises or to be knocked up."

"That you know of."

"I know."

"You wanted them to pay, shoulda dropped her off somewhere right away—the hospital, the pig pen—then let the law deal with 'em. Had two fuckin' easy choices right there to make them pay. It's more than that."

"They need to pay, Judge. Not in an easy choice type of way. But, yeah, it's more than that."

"Yeah." Judge turned to stare out over the back fields. "I hear you."

"Gonna help?"

"Go up on that mountain? Fuck no. I make a lot of money off those motherfuckers. Rather not fuck that up by havin' them catch me up there snoopin' the fuck around. Trip know about this stupid idea? 'Cause he tried ridin' up there like the Lone fuckin' Ranger one time."

"What d'you think?"

"Right. He don't know." Judge sat back in his chair and crossed his thick arms over his chest, tucking his bottom lip into his mouth and chewing on his beard.

Sig could see his mind churning. He was the club's enforcer. If Red was Fury property, he'd be the one out looking for blood. Responsible for planning revenge. Like his father, Ox.

"If it was Ox, he'd rush up that fuckin' mountain and plug a hole in every fuckin' one of 'em, includin' women and children. He wouldn't give a fuck. He'd want them all dead. Then torch that compound to the ground."

Judge's big chest, along with his crossed arms, rose and fell. "I ain't Ox."

"Right. Trip wants us to be smarter and stronger than them. Do shit right."

"You think goin' up there is doin' shit right?"

"It's a step to makin' shit right."

"For who? A woman none of us even fuckin' knew a week ago?" Judge combed his fingers through his long beard, then again. After a long minute, he shook his head. "Such a motherfuckin' asshole, you know that, Sig?"

"Yep."

"They got that mountain booby-trapped. Also probably got armed rednecks keepin' watch. Which is the reason the cops don't fuck with 'em unless they absolutely have to," Judge reminded him. "And when they do, they go well prepared and with a team."

"Yep."

"Jesus fuck," the Sergeant at Arms muttered, then released a resigned-sounding sigh. "You go up, get the layout, any deets, then get the fuck out with both nuts intact. Snag pics, too, if possible. You survive those inbred lunatics, we'll make a plan with whatever info you get."

Sig grinned.

"A brotherhood's gotta stick together after all," Judge murmured, though not sounding happy about it.

"Anyone should know that answer, we should. A lot of us witnessed what happened when it didn't."

"But the plan may not happen right away, Sig. Tellin'

you that. Not riskin' my bail bond license or my biz by goin' up there half-cocked. Hear me?"

"Yeah."

"If we gotta wait 'til Deke closes the deal on that crematorium, we wait."

Sig met Judge's eyes. "Might be the best biz this club buys."

"Thinkin' that may be true. Keeps everyone's ass outta jail if it's done right. That's why we need to think first and act carefully. Temper's gotta keep in check 'til then. Hear me?"

"Yeah."

"So, do whatya gotta do to keep it that way. Even after you go up that mountain. Better have somethin' or someone waitin' for you when you come back down to handle that inferno that's gonna be rippin' your gut apart. You snap 'cause of what you find? You'll fuck shit up. Shit'll go sideways if you don't keep it together."

Nothing new. Shit always went sideways.

The big man got to his feet and both dogs also jumped up, tails slowly wagging. "Gonna leave the dogs with you and Red durin' the run, yeah?" Judge headed toward his door.

"Whatever you need, brother."

Judge hesitated and glanced back at Sig over his shoulder. "Need you to stay off that fuckin' mountain."

Sig said nothing and Judge just muttered something under his breath that sounded similar to "stupid fuck," went into his apartment and slammed the door shut.

Chapter Nine

THE HUGE SPEAKERS hanging on the walls near the ceiling in all four corners of the common area of The Barn were cranked up. Open bottles of booze, kicked bottles of beer, and red plastic cups littered the bar top and almost every other flat surface, including some places on the wide wood-planked floors. The crack of pool balls could be heard almost in stereo from both occupied tables.

After making sure she ate plenty of the food the sweet butts had set up after the run, he settled Red into an old recliner near the center circular fireplace. A fire roared bright since the double barn doors facing the courtyard were both wide open and the October night had turned to blue ball temps.

Shady was now the only prospect at the party, since Dodge was working Crazy Pete's while Stella and Trip had gone on the run and were now hanging out with the rest of them.

Sig had told Shady to keep an eye on Red, this way she didn't disappear into the fucking night. He was not in the mood to track a woman—just about eight months pregnant—on the run in the dark.

He'd do it if he had to, but he preferred not to. It would piss him off and he was already fighting to keep from exploding.

One of Cage's friends, who had become a regular hang-around, had broken out an eight-ball of coke and a few of them were doing lines where Trip wouldn't notice.

Sig noticed.

And he was tempted.

But he knew how that shit got him wired as fuck and it might cause that volcano inside him, which was currently simmering dangerously, to erupt. So, he turned his back to that temptation and went to the bar instead to grab a couple of shots.

When he got there Mouse was behind the bar, pouring himself a beer from the tap into a plastic cup. But his eyes weren't on his beer, they were on Red.

"Yo, Mouse," Sig yelled, stepping into the former prospect's line of sight to block his view.

"It's Rev now. See?" He pointed to the new rectangular patch on the front of his cut.

Sig rolled his eyes. "Yeah, whatever, *Rev*. You into pregnant women?"

Rev sucked the head off the draft. The foam clung to his dark blond mustache for a second before he sucked it clean. "Nope, but I'm into redheads. Thinkin' that color's real, too. You saw her naked. Is it?"

Sig wasn't discussing Red's fiery-colored pubes. "She's got another man's kid in her belly."

"But it ain't yours. And she ain't gonna be knocked up forever. In fact, she'll be good like six weeks after poppin' out that kid."

Sig's eyebrows shot up and so did his blood pressure. "Oh yeah?"

Rev grinned. "Fuck yeah."

"Think she's gonna want dick from a dick like you?"

"Well, she's fuckin' sleepin' in *your* bed, ain't she?"

Sig slowly put his glass down on the bar before it shattered in his fingers.

Rev laughed. "Sig, brother, just fuckin' with you."

Sig stared at him. He didn't find any of that shit funny.

"Just a little payback for all the shit you put me through while I was a prospect."

Sig's eyes narrowed. "So, you ain't into redheads?"

"Fuck yeah. Love 'em. But ain't stupid enough to step on one of my brother's toes like that. 'Specially since I just earned my rockers. Don't wanna have to cancel my appointment with the ink slinger."

"Yeah? You gettin' the club colors on your back?"

"Of fuckin' course. Didn't you?"

Sig didn't want to admit he hadn't and why. Instead, he swallowed a mouthful of whiskey. He hadn't planned on sticking around long term. Having those colors inked into his skin meant *forever* and he wasn't ready to land anywhere permanently any time soon.

Maybe not ever.

Right now he was just rolling with the punches until he got the inheritance that was due him and then he could roll back out of town with a fat wad of scratch in his pocket.

His eyes landed on Red who was sipping on a can of ginger ale while talking to Stella. Shady was standing about six feet behind her like a fucking well-trained guard dog. Fucker didn't have to stick that close.

But whatever, at least he took the order seriously. He was one man he didn't mind leaving with Red when Sig couldn't be there. Shady hadn't shown any interest in any women that Sig had seen. No girlfriend, no sweet butts, no hangarounds, nothing with a pussy.

The man's hands were probably calloused. Either that or he swung a different way. Sig really didn't give a fuck as long as the prospect didn't have eyes for Red and could be trustworthy.

So far, he was proving to be the right man for the job.

With Stella and Shady keeping an eye on Red, Sig picked up his glass, let the whiskey slide down his throat and try to douse the fire burning in this gut. His gaze sliced through the large common area of the clubhouse.

It was noisy. It was busy. And like always, almost anything went.

Almost anything.

Sex out in the open, pool and dart games, drinking, smoking, snorting, wrestling, and constant ball-busting. But it was still nothing like the parties the Originals had at the warehouse.

Sig's fingers tightened on his glass. Tonight was not a night for him to go back down memory lane.

Luckily, something caught his eye to pull him back to the present.

Not something. Someone.

Short, dark hair. Dark eyes. Lots of dark "smoky" makeup around those eyes, reminding him of a goth look. A pierced eyebrow and both ears also full of piercings made him wonder if her nipples were pierced, too.

Her lips were painted a dark blood red. She had a tight black leather collar around her neck with short spikes with a ring on the front.

Her tits were so huge and the V neck of her tight top so low, Sig swore he could see the top of her areolas when she moved. And she was moving. She had a red Solo cup in one hand and was dancing by herself. Her short black leather skirt was working its way up her curvy thighs covered in fishnets, but on her feet weren't any kind of heels, she wore some sort of black combat boots.

Yeah, definitely reminded him of one of those goth

chicks. He'd had a couple of them in the past and they tended to like to play hard.

"Who's that?" Sig asked.

From behind the bar, Rev set his elbows on it, leaned forward, and looked in the direction Sig was. "Dunno. Must be a new sweet butt. Never saw her before tonight and she wasn't with us on the run."

That piqued his dick's interest and also made his fingers curl around an invisible belt. "Yeah?"

"Yeah."

Sig strode over to the corner where the sweet butt was still dancing, lost in the song. He stopped in front of her as she swayed her rounded hips back and forth with her eyes closed, the tips of her nipples pressing against the thin, almost see-through top. Yep. Pierced with barbells. Wearing no bra, it left him no doubt.

She was getting more promising by the second.

He waited and watched. Once her eyes slowly opened, she smiled at him and he gave her a chin lift. "What's your name?" Not that he cared, because he really fucking didn't.

Her smile became knowing. "Billie."

"Billy?" That was a guy's name. "You got a dick?" Because he needed to be sure she didn't, otherwise he was stopping the conversation right there.

Her eyelids got heavy as she ran her hand from her waist down the front of her short skirt. "Want to find out?"

"Just tell me." He needed facts, not bullshit flirting games.

"No."

"No, you don't got a dick? Or no, you ain't tellin' me?"

"No, I don't have a dick. I have a really wet pussy."

Jesus fuck. Just like her name, he didn't give a shit about her pussy. That wasn't what he needed tonight. "You drunk?"

"Not yet."

She didn't stop him when he dipped two fingers into her exposed cleavage. "Those real?" Her tits were way too big and perky without a bra to be natural.

"It matter?"

"Nope." Because he didn't really give a fuck about those, either. He just wanted to know whether he could whip her there. Women with implants didn't always appreciate it. "You got a load in your cunt right now?"

Her smile widened. "Sure do. You into that?"

Now, *that* shit might be important. "Whose?"

Her heated dark brown eyes slid past him and Sig glanced to where she was looking. Which was at one of the two new patched members. Whip. Before tonight, known as Sparky.

As a prospect, he wasn't allowed to fuck any of the sweet butts, but he must have popped that cherry as soon as he was handed his cut with all his new patches earlier. An unofficial celebration before the official one.

His gaze landed back on the woman who was still swaying to the music but now stood toe to toe with him, her bottom lip tucked her teeth. Time to get down to business. "You like it rough?"

Her eyes glittered. Fuck yeah, she liked it rough. But she played the game like a pro. One he had no time for.

"How rough?"

"Rough enough you'll remember it for fuckin' days no matter how many loads you take in that cunt afterward."

She pursed her dark red lips and a flush ran up her chest and her nipples were now rock hard. Those barbells were tempting him. But they weren't done with negotiations yet. Otherwise, he'd grab one and use it to pull her somewhere private.

"Depends."

Sig raised an eyebrow. "On?"

"On if you know what you're doing."

A corner of Sig's mouth lifted as he studied her parted lips, wondering how deep he could fuck her face before she'd gag. "Know what I'm doin'."

"And you stop when I tell you."

"Not a problem."

"You got a place to go?" She ran her tongue over her bottom lip, then stuck it out so he could see it was pierced. *Fuck.* That always made head better. He could already feel that barbell in her tongue sliding up the underside of his hard-on. His dick was starting to get more and more interested.

He and it were finally going to get what he needed badly. "Can find one."

"Find it," she whispered, an excited tremor in her voice, the flush now reaching her cheeks.

Even with Whip and Rev moving into their own rooms, two still remained empty in the bunkhouse. He could take her into one of those. They didn't need a bed, just privacy. And with the loud music playing in The Barn, no one would hear them unless they were listening on purpose.

Sig brushed his hand down his now throbbing hard-on and smiled when Billie's dark eyes followed the movement with another lick of her lips.

A hand on Billie's arm abruptly created space between her and Sig when she was jerked back. Whip's gaze, which wasn't holding a whole lot of happy, jumped from Billie to Sig. "Brother," he greeted, then dropped an arm around the woman's shoulders, pulling her into his side.

"Brother," Sig muttered back.

Whip pressed his lips to Billie's temple before saying, "See you met my girlfriend, Billie."

Sig's eyes closed. *Fuck.* When he opened them, he grunted, "Yeah."

"The answer to your question is a big fuck no."

Sig cocked a brow at him. "And what question would that be?"

"If I mind sharin'."

"Yeah, that question." Sig leaned in closer to Whip. "Don't think she minds it, brother. Offered me her pussy while it's full of your cum. Not all guys like to double dip like that, brother."

"You mustn't mind, then. Shot a big fuckin' load up there earlier."

"Wasn't plannin' on usin' her cunt." Sig straightened. "Maybe you should've attached a shorter fuckin' leash to that collar of hers. Because it came close to my cum leakin' out of her ass on your sheets tonight, *brother*. That woulda been one fuckin' uncomfortable wet spot to sleep in."

With a tight jaw, Sig spun on his boot heel, headed behind the bar, grabbed a half-kicked bottle of tequila, and shoved Trip out of his way when he tried to step into his line of escape. Then he headed out through the open double doors into the night.

HER HEART WAS POUNDING, her lungs struggling for oxygen, her bare feet cut up and in pain as she ran over sharp rocks and twigs. She slipped on damp leaves, barely catching herself in time to keep from crashing into a tree.

But she couldn't stop. Not even for a second. Not even to catch her breath.

She needed to ignore the sharp cramps in her back and stomach.

Needed to run faster.

Needed to get away.

Needed to escape.

She couldn't go back.

Not ever.

If she did, she'd no longer exist.

Hidden away, a sliver of her old self remained, that shard was what she needed to cling to. That was where she needed to run to. To the life she used to have, not the one she was living currently. That glimmer of hope was what she needed to focus on.

The woods were dark, the path dangerous. She quickly zig-zagged through the brush and trees, branches pulling at her, cutting her flesh, scraping her skin, grabbing at her like a monster's claws.

Trying to capture her and hold her until they could come find her.

Escape was her only chance for survival. If they found her, she would die.

Because, if they found her, she would make sure of it.

They couldn't have her. They couldn't have what they planted.

She refused to give it to them.

Fuck them.

Fuck them.

Fuck them.

She would take away what they thought belonged to them.

She would make sure they didn't get what they wanted, no matter how she had to do it.

They had broken her... *broken her... broken her...* Snapped her in two.

They wouldn't benefit from that. Not ever.

They thought she would submit. They thought she would willingly go along with their plans.

She would never.

Never.

Fuck them.

It wasn't a choice she'd ever make.

It wasn't a choice at all.

They had stolen her choice and she needed to steal it back.

Her belly was expanding more and more as she ran down that mountain, through those woods.

Expanding to the point it felt about to burst. Like whatever was growing inside her was also trying to escape.

Trying to be free.

A sharp pain shot through her like a lightning strike, making her gasp and stumble. The next one made her pause, pressing a palm against the rough bark of a nearby tree, using it to keep herself upright. To keep from doubling over.

She forced her feet to keep moving.

She needed to keep going no matter how much it hurt.

She looked for a path. There was none. She'd had to make her own.

Until she saw something. Ahead.

A pinpoint of light. Like the beam of a flashlight in the distance.

As she headed for it, it widened and got brighter, now like a single headlight from a vehicle.

And a silhouette standing in front of that light.

The shape of a man.

She needed to head toward him.

He was there to help her.

Not hurt her.

He would help her find her way out.

Then the light became blinding, making her shade her eyes with one hand.

She couldn't see his face, but she could see something else as she got closer...

An outstretched hand.

"Red..." A deep voice. A man's voice. "It's me or them."

He wanted her to take his offered hand. Accept his help.

She wasn't sure if she should.

It could be a trap. A trick.

Someone sent to capture her.

"Red," he said more firmly. "Me... Or them."

Oh God, oh God, oh God. Not them. Never them.

Once again her choice was taken from her.

She had *no* choice.

"You," she whispered and grabbed it tightly, hot tears rolling down her dirty cheeks. "You."

A gush of warm liquid rushed from her, covering her inner thighs, splashing on and around her feet.

She glanced down as she grabbed her stomach as everything inside her twisted in agony.

Drip.

Drip.

Drip.

Hot. Slippery.

Even in the limited light, she could clearly see what it was.

Blood.

Thick red blood.

She opened her mouth and screamed.

Chapter Ten

SIG JACKKNIFED STRAIGHT UP, almost tumbling to the floor. His brain spun a little but then slowed enough for him to realize he was on his couch in his dark apartment.

How the fuck he ended up back there, he had no fucking clue.

Last thing he remembered...

Yeah.

Fuck.

He pressed his arm to his bare ribs. What he'd done had aggravated them again.

Goddamn it.

He groaned as he tried to get to his feet. He needed to check on Red.

But fuck, his head...

He only wore his jeans, which were hanging open, his belt nowhere to be found.

Oh fuck.

Fuck.

He must have left it where it fell. He'd have to find it in the daylight.

He squeezed his eyes shut, trying to remember everything that had happened once he grabbed the tequila and escaped The Barn.

Where the fuck was his cut?

He opened his eyes, his temples throbbing, and scanned the dark room.

There. On the stool in front of the counter.

Thank fuck.

A belt, he could deny was his. A cut, not so much.

But, *Jesus fuck...*

He groaned again as he made his way down the short hallway to the back bedroom, doing his best to walk a straight line.

The tequila was still buzzing through his veins, but not as bad as earlier.

Maybe it was good that it was, otherwise he wasn't sure how he'd bear the pain of what he did.

Fuck. Fuck. Fuck.

He made it to the bedroom and opened the door. Even in the dark he could see Red asleep on her side.

He went over to the bed, squatted down and whispered, "Hey." He reached out and ran a knuckle down her cheek, finding it wet.

She was crying.

In her sleep.

Christ.

"Red," he tried again, afraid to scare her by shaking her. "Red." He found her hand tangled in the sheet and squeezed it.

Then her eyes opened and she blinked a couple times, her mouth open.

Her fingers intertwined with his, holding on tight. "You're here."

"Yeah."

"You came."

Of course he did. "Yeah, Red. You screamed."

"Sorry."

What the fuck was going on? "For what?"

She shifted but didn't sit up. She reached out and stroked her fingers down his beard. "Did I wake you?"

That soft touch made his heart seize. "What fuckin' happened?"

"I... I had a bad dream."

No shit. "Yeah, figured that. 'Bout what?"

"About the woods."

Sig said nothing. Just those three words took him back to that morning.

"When you found me."

The change she'd gone through the time between that morning and today... Only a week, but she was almost a different person.

Not completely because she still had a long road to travel.

"Can you go back to sleep?" he asked.

"I need to use the bathroom first."

No shit. He needed to piss like a racehorse, too. "Want me to help you up?"

"I'm very awkward now." She almost sounded embarrassed about it.

"There's a fuckin' reason for that, Red. You still don't have all your strength back and you're..."

"Lopsided."

"Yeah, that," he said softly. "Lopsided."

"Sometimes I feel like I'm going to tip over face first."

"Not a good idea," he said simply, helping her to get to her feet.

He was surprised to find that she was wearing only a long T-shirt and nothing else. *Nothing else.* And the T-shirt didn't cover her below the hips because the size of her belly wouldn't let it.

Jesus fuck. She was completely naked except for the shirt.

Maybe she was more comfortable like that since she probably lived without clothes for months.

Then he realized it was his shirt she wore. Why wasn't she wearing the maternity nightie Stella bought her instead?

"You're wearin' my shirt," he said, surprised. But for some fucking reason it also pleased him that she was. That was fucked up. It was only an old shirt.

She glanced down and plucked at it with her fingers. "I... I'm sorry... I'll put it back."

She reached for the hem and he stopped her by grabbing her hand and giving it a squeeze. "No, baby, that's fine. I don't mind."

Christ, he just called her "baby." He had to still be drunk.

"I'm sorry. I... It's comfortable. It's soft and it smells like you."

It smells like you.

He closed his eyes for a moment.

What the fuck.

What the fuck.

What the fuck!

"Probably needs washed, then," he quickly said. "Can wear whatever you want of mine, Red, don't worry about it."

Plenty of women had worn one of his T-shirts. Usually after sex. But there was something different about Red wearing one.

Totally fucking different.

What the fuck was going on? He had to be still pickled by all the tequila, that was all.

Or maybe he was still high from the pain. From...

Fuck.

Not now. Not now. Not now.

Never again. He needed to find another way.

He followed her to the bathroom, making sure she made it

okay. When he got there, he held onto the door jamb to keep himself steady. "Do your thing, then I'll help you back to bed." *Or at least, make sure you get there since I might not be much fuckin' help.*

Without closing the door, she practically waddled to the toilet and sat on it, not caring that he stood right there watching her take a piss.

She ripped some toilet paper off the roll and awkwardly wiped between her legs, before reaching behind her, again awkwardly, to flush. "You don't appreciate things like toilet paper until you don't have any."

"What'd they give you?" Her comment might be a good "in" to find out some info.

"Nothing."

He shouldn't be surprised. And even though the alcohol running through his system, along with what happened before he got totally fucking blitzed, should keep him on an even keel for a bit, hearing that made his temper wobble again.

He was tempted to help her off the toilet when she struggled, but she managed it on her own and washed her hands.

"Running water, sinks, toilets, I'll never take them for granted again."

He struggled to keep his voice even when he asked, "No water, Red?"

She didn't answer and he stepped backward into the dark hallway when she came his direction, her belly leading the way.

She stopped in front of him, practically toe to toe, tipping her face up to his. "Will you stay?"

His brow dropped low. "Stay? Yeah. I'll be right on the couch."

"No. With me. Until I fall asleep."

"You want that?"

He thought she was going to smile, but she didn't. It was like she tried but failed. "Yes."

"Red..."

"That's okay. You don't have to."

Christ. For most women, those words were an attempt at mental manipulation. It was anything but for her. She meant them and wasn't using them to make him feel fucking guilty.

For fuck's sake, it made him feel guilty, anyway.

"Lemme piss and then I'll come in for a bit, yeah?"

"If you're not comfortable..."

She was worried about him? *What the fuck.* "Red, worried about you not bein' comfortable."

"Then, I wouldn't have asked."

Yeah. That.

"'Kay, give me a sec to drain the snake."

Damn, did she snort?

He smiled and shook his head, moving to stand in front of the toilet and doing it in a way she wouldn't see his back. He flipped up the seat and dug his dick out of his jeans, pointing it.

"Don't miss. It's hard for me to clean around the toilet when you do."

Every day that she woke up in his apartment, more of what he assumed was her true personality was starting to emerge. Not the ghost of a human he rescued in the woods. "Don't want you on your knees cleanin' 'round the toilet, Red. I'll get a sweet butt to clean, if need be."

"What's a sweet butt?"

Oh fuck. "What we call the women who hang around the club." They did way more than that, but that was all she had to know for now.

"Like groupies."

"Yeah, sort of like that." He shook his dick off and tucked it away, his bladder thanking him for the relief.

"The ones who were... doing things... out in front of everyone... Them."

Shit. He had no fucking clue how much she witnessed after he left the party. If it was like most parties, it was plenty. He shouldn't have left her alone. *Stupid fuck.*

She probably didn't appreciate watching people getting sucked and fucked in front of her. Maybe that was what spurred the nightmare.

"Yeah, them. Most of them were, yeah. Not all, though." No, it seemed as word spread about the club, more and more women were interested in bagging a tattooed biker for their own. Even if it was only for a night.

Which was usually all it was.

He turned and saw her still standing in the doorway, her eyes on him. He guessed it was only fair she watched him piss like he did her. An audience didn't bother him, he'd had no privacy in prison. And most of the time when the club was partying in the courtyard, it was just as easy to whip it out and find a spot nearby to empty the tank.

"Wash your hands," she ordered.

He lifted his gaze to her, fighting his smirk, but he washed his hands.

He wondered just how fiery that redhead was before ending up in the Shirleys' hands.

After she was tucked back into bed, he stood there, undecided. He normally didn't sleep in his jeans unless he landed on the couch and passed out drunk, but he also normally didn't sleep in bed with her, either.

Usually if a woman was in his bed, they were both naked. Or women, since more often than not, he preferred more than one at a time. Especially the first few days after being released from being locked up. After a long dry spell, he was ready for pussy and lots of it.

But right now there was only one woman in his bed and

she was one he couldn't touch. "Gonna shuck my jeans. You okay with that?"

"I don't have any pants on, either."

That didn't need to be said. "That wasn't hard to miss, Red."

"Sorry."

"No reason to be sorry."

He heard her inhale. "I minded at first... being naked. Then one day I just... stopped caring."

Christ! She only gave him glimpses of what happened to her during her time on that mountain and every tiny piece she gave him pissed him the fuck off.

But that reveal gave him another opening. "Why didn't they give you any clothes?"

"They were afraid I'd do something with them."

"Like what? Wear 'em?" he half-joked, not that her situation had been any kind of funny.

"Like kill myself."

All air fled his lungs as he stared at her. "Would you have?" he whispered, an ache growing deep within his chest.

"Yes," she whispered back into the dark.

He quickly hooked his thumbs in his jeans and shoved them down his legs, stepping out of them and leaving them where they landed. He headed to his dresser and dug around in the dark until he found a pair of old boxers and tugged them on. Then he headed to the far side of the bed and climbed in.

Fuck, he had missed his mattress. It was like a cloud compared to that fucking couch.

He pulled the sheet over them both and turned to his side to avoid putting weight on his back. Since he had a king bed, he could leave a good-sized gap between them.

With a cute little grunt, she flopped to her back and then rolled to her other side so she was facing him, her belly only about two inches away.

He was once again tempted to touch it.

"You smell like alcohol."

"Yeah."

"And pot."

"Yep. Want me to shower?"

"No. It smells like you."

Fucking great.

"Are you still drunk?"

"Not like earlier," he answered honestly. Because he had to have been stupid drunk to do what he fucking did.

"When you left the party in a rush."

"Yeah. Sorry 'bout that."

"No reason to be sorry," she echoed him from earlier.

"Stella make sure you got back up here okay?"

"Shady."

It should have been Sig making sure she got upstairs okay. Not the prospect. *Goddamn it.*

"He's really nice."

"Wouldn't know, he hardly says a fuckin' word."

"He does to me."

What?

She continued, "He's quiet, but he's smart. He's got a lot going on."

Was he fucking chatting her up? What was his angle?

"What d'you mean?"

"In his head. Like me." Her fingers brushed over his cheek and along his beard. "Like you."

"Red, need to talk to me." Not Shady.

She said nothing, but her fingers kept stroking his beard, like she was petting a cat or something. Or like Judge petted Jury. But, *fuck*, that felt good. Now he knew why the dog fell asleep with her head in the man's lap while he was stroking her ears.

"If not to me, then Stella. If not her, then," *fuck it*, "Shady. Somebody, Red."

She still said nothing, and her fingertips traced lightly over his lips.

"Red..."

"Did you find what you need elsewhere?"

His heart began to pound. "What're you talkin' about?"

"What you wanted from that woman you were talking to downstairs."

Should he play dumb? No, that wasn't going to fucking work. Red was far from stupid. Unlike him. And he'd done it right in The Barn where she could see him doing it. "Billie."

"Is that her name?"

"Yeah."

"Yes, then Billie. Did you find elsewhere what you didn't get from Billie?"

Holy fuck. He should have left her upstairs and not brought her to the party. Another stupid move on his part.

He stilled her hand by capturing it in his, pulling it away from his beard and into his chest. "Go to sleep, Red."

"I was worried about you."

"Why?"

"You looked upset."

"Wasn't upset." He was a whole bunch of shit but upset wasn't one of them.

"Angry, then. When that other man came over and stopped you from talking to Billie." She paused but before he could respond, she asked, "Did you want to have sex with her?"

He was suddenly finding it hard to breathe. "Red," he forced out.

"There's nothing wrong with that, Sig. It's normal. Most people enjoy it. And as long as both parties agree—"

"Red... *Autumn,* fuckin' stop it." *For fuck's sake,* she was good at digging without even trying. Maybe he was wrong and she really was a master manipulator. He had no fucking clue as to what she was really like.

"Why?"

"Didn't just want sex with her." *Christ*, did he just admit that out loud? To Red of all people? *For fuck's sake!*

They needed to talk about her, not him.

"I didn't think so."

"What?" he choked out.

"I'm not deaf. I can hear conversations that are happening in front of me, Sig. Or even right outside your front door. And I'm also not stupid."

"Seriously, Red. Need to stop."

"You wanted me to talk to you."

"Not about that."

"Then let's change the subject," she suggested.

"How 'bout you just go to sleep." He released her hand but she didn't pull it away, instead she planted her palm on his chest. Her fingers were long and warm against his skin.

"I'm going back to that doctor, right?"

"Yeah. Tuesday."

"Are you going with me?"

"Want me to?" He couldn't keep the surprise out of his voice. This woman kept knocking him for a goddamn loop.

"Yes. Please."

"Stella was going to go with you." And now that he knew Stella had a baby at some point, she'd be best to help Red and would know what the fuck was going on during the appointment better than him.

"I want you."

I want you, too. But not in the way Red meant when she said it. Even so, he was too fucked up for her. Even after her ordeal with the baby was over, there was no way she could deal with his shit. She had dealt with enough. "Why?"

"I just do."

"Red, you'd be better off if Stella went with you. She

knows about... those things. I don't know shit about... that type of thing."

"The doctor will be checking to see how the seed is."

"Yeah. And you, too. She was worried about you."

"She wants the seed."

"Yeah, Red, she wants a seed of her very own."

Red needed to stop calling it a fucking seed and see the baby for what it really was. It was important that she realize what would happen to that kid after she gave birth to it. She needed to be really fucking sure about giving the kid up, if that's what she decided. Because once she signed those papers, he wasn't sure if the adoption could be reversed.

He didn't want her to regret giving up her flesh and blood down the road, even if the baby was a result of a rape, even if it was sired by one of those inbred goat fuckers.

"Why can't someone plant one in her?"

Sig frowned. Sometimes her questions sounded like one a child would ask. Other times, like while watching the news, she sounded super smart. She had two sides to her. Her real self that drew him and her broken self, which worried him.

Somehow her broken self needed to be healed so she could once again be whole. Maybe it would happen once she had the baby, once she was no longer tied mentally to the Shirleys.

He could only hope that for her.

It would also help her if she knew those assholes would never be a threat to her again. Or the baby.

And that was where he could do his part for her.

Knowing she was safe could help her heal and move forward.

But he also needed to know what the fuck went on up there. He needed to know who did what to her.

They couldn't just go up there and massacre them all,

though he'd fucking like to. They needed to do it quietly and be fucking precise. Pick off the ones who made her suffer.

They would never go to the pigs. Which meant, Sig could get away with doling out fucking justice to the few who deserved it. The PD might never know that the town had a couple less citizens. And being who they were, the pigs might not even care. They felt no love for those "sovereign citizens" who lived by their own laws and gave the pigs the middle finger salute.

But without her talking, he had no choice but to go up that goddamn mountain to see what he could find out on his own.

And nothing or no one was stopping him.

Chapter Eleven

Sig blinked. And blinked again. He winced as the light from the big picture window caused a knife to stab at his brain all Chucky-like. It didn't help that Red had tucked up the sheet covering that window so the morning—he assumed it was still morning—sunlight was blinding him.

Also proving he drank way too fucking much last night. Among other things.

He needed a little hair of the dog to help with this morning's hangover.

He groaned, closed his eyes and shoved his hand down his boxers, grabbing his morning hard-on and stroking it lazily.

Thank fuck Red wasn't in bed right now to witness how hard he was. Or maybe she had and bolted from the bed because of it.

He frowned when he heard the toilet flush and the shower start. With as big and awkward as she was getting, he worried about her slipping in the tub.

He tossed off the sheet and pursed his lips as he stared at the tent in his boxers.

Did he have time? And how would he get rid of the load? Sock? Shirt?

No shirt. She was wearing his shirts and probably wouldn't appreciate pulling one over her head and finding it stiff with his load.

His gaze slid to the bedroom door. It was closed, so he'd at least have time to let go of his dick before she walked in.

He squeezed and tugged at his balls, then fisted his cock again, his eyelids getting heavy, as the urge to pull one off quick made his hand slide up and down faster.

Keeping his eyes straight ahead on the door, he released himself long enough to spit in his palm before once again giving himself a good jerk.

Fuck yes.

He only got part of what he needed last night, but he didn't get everything.

He normally used the memory of fucking Rebecca's red-striped ass as jack off material, but for some reason, he was having a hard time concentrating on that. Instead, his mind kept going back to Red wearing his T-shirt. Then peeling it off slowly and touching and squeezing her own tits which were now a little bigger and heavier than when he first saw her naked.

They weren't huge because she was still way thinner than she should be, but they weren't anything to complain about. He imagined himself painting white lines of cum over them instead of creating red stripes on the ivory curves of her ass.

In his fantasy she smeared his cum all over her tits, wearing a wicked smile, and then licked her fingers clean.

Fuck yeah.

Fuck... those lips sucking on her own fingers, tasting his load. Moaning...

Then giving him an unspoken invitation as she moved to get into that shower. She waited, tossing her red hair, looking over her slender shoulder, beckoning, wanting him to follow her in.

But he didn't. He only wanted to watch.

She gave him a show as she soaped herself up, touching herself everywhere. Especially that dark red bush between her thighs. A couple of her fingers disappearing into that fiery patch.

Jesus.

"Red," he groaned, his eyes closing, his fist moving faster. He brushed his palm over the head, gathering the precum and using it as more lube along his throbbing dick. He jerked faster, harder, not being gentle at all. He didn't want it to be gentle, he wanted it to be quick.

But he needed to keep quiet, too.

Then he was back in that bathroom with her. Her long red hair now soaked and super dark as it stuck to her pale skin, water sliding down her tits and off her puckered nipples. The ones she twisted between her fingers. Her mouth opened and little whimpers escaped that got him all the way to his balls.

He squeezed the root of his dick, making a tight ring with two fingers, bringing out every vein, while his other hand pumped faster.

"Touch yourself," he whispered. "That's it, baby. Just like that. Fuck," he groaned. "Fuck yeah. Twist them harder. Yeah. Make it hurt. Show me how much you like that."

Red's head was thrown back and her lips were wide open as she panted, the water running into her mouth and then back out over her chin like a waterfall. He wanted to cum on her face, in her mouth. On her tits. In her pussy.

He wanted to fuck her ass and fill it with his cum.

He wanted to mark her everywhere.

Make it so she smelled like him.

Belonged to him.

His hips shot up, his head tilted back and he groaned

loudly as he milked his dick into his palm, catching all of the cum he wanted to give her.

But he couldn't.

Instead, it was his own hand.

His own palm.

His own bed.

By himself.

It could never happen with her.

He couldn't do what he wanted to do with her.

She couldn't be his.

Even if she wasn't broken, she could never handle him. Because he was broken, too.

There was sex. And then there was more.

He needed the "more" too often.

Unfortunately, Red could never give him that. Not with what she'd been through. He wouldn't even lie to himself by thinking she'd be able to down the road. It took the right woman.

Even with the small glimpses of her he'd caught—of her true self, of how she would be if she was whole—he couldn't see her ever doing anything he really needed.

Then he'd have to get it elsewhere.

Or get locked up like the animal he could be.

"Fuck," he whispered and opened his eyes.

He rolled out of bed, his palm full of his hot, sticky cum. Searching the floor, he found one of his dirty socks. He snagged it and was wiping off his hand when the door opened.

He froze.

So did she.

She was wearing one of his shirts again, but this time had on some sort of loose cotton pants underneath it. The kind Stella had bought her with a panel on the front that would stretch as her belly grew.

Her gaze fell to the sock in his hand and then she walked

right up to him, plucked it from his fingers, glanced at it for a second, went over to the overflowing laundry basket in the corner and tossed it on top.

He struggled to keep his expression blank.

"Is there somewhere I can do your laundry?"

What? *That* was the question she had? "No, baby, you ain't doin' my fuckin' laundry."

"Why? I have some of my own to do. Are there machines downstairs?"

"Red, you ain't carrying fuckin' laundry downstairs and you ain't doin' it. Gonna get one of the... Gonna get someone else to do it."

"But—"

"End of discussion."

"That basket stinks."

"Yeah."

"Like something died in it."

"Made your point. Gonna get it handled. Yeah?"

"Okay. You didn't have to hide what you did."

He stared at her.

"It's natural for a man."

"Jesus, Red."

"I'm just saying. I was sexually active before," she waved a hand around, "*that*. And I enjoyed it... a lot... I hope to enjoy it again... I hope they didn't destroy that for me."

He hoped not, either, but that didn't mean he wanted to picture her having sex with a bunch of different men and enjoying herself while she did it.

Though, he also hoped the men who were lucky enough to have Red didn't suck. For her benefit. Not theirs.

Still... He didn't want to think about it.

Fuck.

"So," she began.

"Not talkin' about it."

"I was just going to say I'm going to start breakfast."

"Oh...'Kay," he drew out in relief. "Gonna get dressed, take a piss and will be out to help."

"You should shower."

He lifted a brow.

She wrinkled her nose. "The basket isn't the only thing that stinks."

"Red, asked you before I got into bed—"

"I know. But—"

He lifted a hand. "Got it. Gonna shower."

She gave him a small smile.

For fuck's sake, he couldn't wait to see a bigger one than that pointed in his direction. To see some happy on her whole face and in those hazel eyes, too.

Even so, if it wasn't for that belly, he would think that woman who had been running through the woods was beginning to disappear.

He bent to grab the jeans off the floor next to the bed and Red made a sharp sound. When he looked up, she gave her head a little shake with another nose wrinkle.

It was cute as fuck. He wasn't into cute, he was into wicked.

But, *damn,* suddenly he wanted to kiss her.

He threw the jeans onto the dirty pile, hoping he had a clean pair somewhere. He couldn't remember the last time he'd done laundry.

"Breakfast, Red," he reminded her because if she kept standing there, she was going to find herself in a lip lock with him. And maybe even his tongue down her throat. And he wasn't sure how she'd handle that. Even if it was only a kiss.

He had no idea how long it had been since the Shirleys last violated her. Hopefully they had stopped after she'd gotten pregnant since that might have been their only goal. If so, then, besides the physical abuse, it had been at least six months since they'd touched her sexually. Possibly.

He could only fucking hope. But until she talked, he couldn't be sure.

"You have the stuff for pancakes?" she asked hopefully.

"Nope."

"Downstairs?"

"Probably. Know Trip gets maple syrup from the Amish. So figurin' there's a reason for it. If not downstairs, Stella probably got it. Want me to check?"

"I'm just in the mood for pancakes."

"Then you're gettin' fuckin' pancakes."

Again, her lips curved slightly. "With warm maple syrup."

"Yeah, Red, with warm maple syrup. Whatever you want."

"Whatever I want?"

He swallowed hard at the soft look she gave him. "Yeah." *For fuck's sake,* suddenly he wanted to hand her the fucking world if he could. Just to see more of that cuteness.

"I don't want you to lock me in anymore when you leave."

He blinked. "What?"

"Please don't lock me in."

"Red... Doin' it for your safety."

"Then let me have a key."

"Red..."

"I'm not going to run."

He didn't believe that. Not yet. "Can't keep you safe if you run," he whispered, his throat getting tight and a pressure building in his chest at the thought of her disappearing.

"I'm not going to run."

"Red," he breathed.

"Sig... I'm not going to run."

"You can't ever leave it unlocked."

"Okay."

"Not fuckin' ever."

"Okay."

"Promise me."

"I promise."

He didn't like it. Not one fucking bit. "Promise me."

"I just did."

"I need to hear it again."

"I'm not going to run. I promise. I have nowhere to go." With that she turned and walked out of the bedroom.

He quickly dug out his last clean pair of jeans and found a clean shirt. Then he went to take a shower so he didn't stink.

AUTUMN WALKED out of the bedroom and took a quick pit stop in the bathroom, which was becoming a too often thing. As she washed her hands, she studied her face in the small mirror over the sink.

Her eyes were brighter and her cheeks held a little color now, other than the bruises that had become difficult to see unless you looked for them. Her lips weren't as chapped and she was trying very hard not to chew nervously on her bottom lip until it healed completely.

Her thick hair was way too long. It was still duller than what it used to be and it hadn't been cut in ages, so it fell well past her shoulders. She liked the length but hated trying to keep it tangle-free and out of her face. It was also hot and heavy.

Her attention was pulled to Sig when he appeared in the doorway in only his boxers with a pair of jeans and a shirt in his hands.

"Gonna shower," he grumbled, studying her.

She nodded and turned to face him. "I'll give you your privacy."

"Not used to privacy, Red."

"Neither am I, anymore." She pushed past him. "The

bathroom's too small for both of us anyway, not with how lopsided I am right now."

With her eating more and actually getting some real sleep, the seed was growing more quickly than ever, like it was trying to catch up. Plus, her body was filling out, her bones not as noticeable, her cheeks not so hollow. But she still was nothing like she used to be.

She wasn't sure if she would ever go back to who she had been. Not just what she looked like, but how she saw others. She'd been badly betrayed, and would find it difficult to trust anyone so completely ever again.

However, for some reason, she trusted this biker who was full of tattoos, who drank, who smoked, who cursed and was rough on the outside and who, she suspected, was badly broken on the inside.

But then, he'd done nothing to make her distrust him. Except for locking her inside his apartment.

He said he'd stop. That he'd only done it because he believed it was for her own good.

She had no reason not to believe him.

Once he handed her a key.

In truth, she didn't understand why he was doing anything for her at all. They didn't know each other. They weren't related. They had no ties whatsoever. But he stepped up to help her when he didn't have to, when she had nothing and no one else.

Because if he hadn't found her when he did, running down that mountain, she had a feeling her escape would have failed.

And instead of being on that mountain in her prison, as Vernon waited for his seed to finish growing, she was now sleeping in a comfortable bed, temporarily living in a place with modern conveniences and about to make pancakes with warm maple syrup.

Her mouth watered and her stomach growled, making the seed shift restlessly inside her.

"Hey," he whispered, his voice low and thick, and she pulled herself from her thoughts to find she had stopped in front of him, and had planted a hand on his bare chest.

She blinked and shook away her wandering thoughts.

His skin was warm and smooth, and his heartbeat strong under her palm.

She let her hand drop and took a deep breath. "I'll go start the coffee and check to see what we need for pancakes."

"Yeah, you do that," he said softly, running a knuckle along her jaw. "I'll just be a few."

She nodded and he took a step back to let her pass.

She didn't hear the door close behind him, so the shower was easily heard when he started it.

She dug in his cabinets for the coffee, a filter and a couple of Harley mugs, got the coffeemaker set up and started, then looked around to see what else they'd need to make pancakes.

He had nothing but some sugar, a small container of hand churned butter and a half dozen brown eggs.

No flour, no vanilla. No baking ingredients at all.

But that shouldn't be surprising since he was a bachelor biker. She couldn't imagine him normally making meals from scratch.

He seemed to be an eggs, toast and bacon type of man. Or cereal and milk. Plus, coffee, of course.

Simple. Uncomplicated.

She mentally made a list of what they'd need, then headed around the counter dividing the kitchenette off from the rest of the open living space. She'd turn on the news, her way of catching up with everything she'd missed in the world for the past few months. The more she watched, the more she confirmed she'd been up there for about a year.

The doctor had said the seed had been growing inside her for about eight months. It only had eight weeks to go before it was done. And it had taken a few months for them to plant that seed. She had counted three periods before her monthly cycles stopped. And Vernon had bred her for a few more weeks after the last one, just to make sure it had taken.

Her periods stopping had been both a blessing and a curse. The blessing being, those breedings had stopped. The curse being, they succeeded in what they intended.

She grabbed the remote and turned to point it at the TV on the wall across the room and when she did, her gaze landed on the couch. Where Sig normally slept.

Her eyebrows pinned together and she wondered what he'd spilled on the worn fake leather. Whatever it was had dried to a brown, marking the tan cushions.

She turned again with the intent to get a wet paper towel and try to clean off whatever it was. But she froze as she spotted something else on the floor.

One of his T-shirts.

Sig dropped his clothes wherever he took them off, but that wasn't what bothered her about it.

No.

That wasn't it at all.

With a groan and her hand planted on the couch's armrest to keep from toppling over, she reached down and picked it up. She shook it out and turned it to see the back more clearly.

She pressed a hand to her mouth and struggled to breathe.

Why...

A noise escaped from between her lips just as she heard him enter the room, his normally loose and easy gait stuttering to a halt.

She lifted her gaze from the tee in her hand to him, a tightness in her chest and her thoughts spinning.

She didn't move but kept her eyes glued to his tight expression as he approached. She noticed the second his eyes slid across the couch first and landed on his shirt within her fingers.

"Red..."

"You're hurt."

"No."

Of course he was, no one bled that much who wasn't injured. "Then whose blood is that?"

"Red..." He yanked the bloody T-shirt from her fingers and balled it up in his fist. "Ain't nothin'."

"The hell it isn't." He was wearing a shirt now. Covering what she missed last night and again this morning. How had she not seen it? With the amount of blood...

He'd purposely kept his back to her, except for in the dark. That's how.

He'd hidden his injuries from her.

Why?

Was he afraid it would trigger something in her?

Would it trigger her?

She swallowed hard and moved to stand behind him, but he turned with her. "I want to see." She was not asking, but demanding.

"No."

"I need to see."

"No. Not a good fuckin' idea."

"For who? You? Or me?"

He shook his head, his brow furrowed. "Both of us."

"Sig..."

"Red..."

"I need to see it!" burst from her in a scream, surprising both of them. She slapped a hand over her mouth, shocked at her sudden loss of patience. Shocked at once again feeling something other than nothing. Of no longer being dead inside. Feeling a real emotion other than just despair.

He stared at her for the longest time, his face paler than usual, his mouth tight, his eyes troubled.

"Please," she finally whispered. Still not asking, because she was going to see it one way or another.

"Red, you can't tell anyone. Like the lock, you need to fuckin' promise me."

"Promise."

"I mean it. Not to Stella, not to Shady. To no one."

She nodded, dread beginning to fill her chest and make it tight.

"Need to hear it again."

"I promise."

He dropped his head for a minute and his chest surged as he sucked in a deep breath. Then he nodded and grabbed a handful of the worn cotton at the top of his back, tugging it up and over his head.

Her heart began to pound in her throat as he slowly turned and revealed his broad, muscular back to her.

She quickly covered her mouth to keep from crying out, but her heart broke for him. And she didn't think she had one left to break.

She tentatively reached out but only touched where the skin hadn't been broken. Where it hadn't been flailed to the point of splitting and bleeding.

The shower this morning had to be painful. His skin was still raw and swollen, and a few spots were shiny with fresh blood.

Somehow she managed to ask, "You... wanted this?" Who would want this? Ask for this? Take this kind of damage willingly?

"Red..."

She pulled her hand back and curled her fingers into her palm. "I need to know. I need to know you wanted this. You asked for this."

She almost didn't hear his quiet, "Yeah."

Autumn closed her eyes and just breathed for a moment, trying to wrap her head around what it all meant. Why he would want, or need, something like this.

Why he would feel the need to be struck over and over with something that would mutilate the skin of his back like that. To cause pain. To feel pain. To feel pain that wouldn't be just temporary. Discomfort that would last for days.

Like a reminder.

Was it some sort of punishment?

"Is this what you wanted Billie to do to you?"

"No."

"Then what?"

"Wanted to do it to her."

"Like that Amish girl your brother talked about?"

"Yeah."

"You like it."

"They like it."

They like it? But he was the one bearing the marks. He'd had it done to him, instead. Why? "You get off on that."

He stepped away and turned to face her, his Adam's apple jumping in his throat and every muscle tense. "Red, can't fuckin' discuss this with you." His voice was tight and almost pleading with her to let it go.

She couldn't. She needed to understand. "You want to know what happened to me. You want me to open myself up and tell you everything. But you can't share this with me?"

"No."

"Why?"

"'Cause I can't explain it."

That was an easy copout. "Yes, you can."

He shook his head. "Can't explain how it works."

"Works to do what?"

He went to step away, to head to the kitchen, to escape her questions, but she reached out and grabbed his arm. He could've easily pulled away. She didn't have the strength to hold him, but he stopped anyway and stared at her fingers wrapped around his forearm.

He didn't look at her when he said, "To curb my temper, to keep me from hurtin' someone. To keep me from spinnin' out of control. From seein' red. To keep me from goin' back to jail. To keep me from killin' someone 'cause they bumped into me or looked at me the wrong way or said somethin' that rubbed me the wrong fuckin' way. Any of it. All of it."

"You can't live without it."

"Wish I could. But no, not unless I find somethin' else."

"Another outlet for your anger."

"Yeah."

"Why are you so angry?"

He frowned. "That couldn't be explained in years of therapy, baby. Not even decades of it."

"But isn't it a good thing that you know how to control it?"

"Can't always control it."

"Why not?"

"'Cause no matter what, some things are outta our control, Red."

That she understood. "Like what happened to me."

He simply stared at her for a moment before saying, "Yeah, like what happened to you."

He pulled his shirt back over his head, covering what had been done to him. What *he* had done to him. She had no idea by who, though.

And what else had happened besides those marks being left on his body?

What else did Sig, or that other person, get out of it?

It wasn't her place to judge him. She didn't know him as well as he knew himself.

He did what he thought needed to be done.

Even so, she could understand doing something

someone else might not comprehend in an attempt to hang on to that last shred of sanity.

To do whatever was needed to survive.

She understood that only too well. So, she had no right to judge and, in truth, no right to question. "We can't always choose what happens to us, but we can choose how to handle it."

"That right there, Red, is an important thing you also need to remember."

"Yes," she murmured, heading toward the kitchen. "You're right. I need to remember that, too." She stopped in front of the coffeemaker and stared at it, but not seeing it. Her next words came out strangely flat. "I want to make pancakes."

Right now, that was one thing she could control in her life.

"Whatever you want, Red."

Whatever you want.

She wanted to heed her own advice, that was what she wanted. But she wasn't sure if it would ever be possible.

She hoped she was wrong.

Chapter Twelve

She could understand doing something someone else might not comprehend in an attempt to hang on to that last shred of sanity.

To do whatever was needed to survive.

The room was eerily quiet as Autumn kept her face turned away from the monitor, not wanting to see it. Sig stood by her side, next to the table, staring at it instead. She had to close her eyes when his face twisted for a moment before he caught his reaction and quickly hid it.

She wanted him there. When she had put out her hand, he'd grabbed it. He kept holding it tightly as the tech rolled the wand through the gel and over her belly.

"You still don't want to know the sex or hear the heartbeat, right?" Dr. Bryson asked gently.

"No," she answered, concentrating on Sig's belt. Was there a spot of dried blood on the bulky metal buckle?

"Well, it's doing well, surprisingly. Being undernourished like you were could cause a multitude of birth defects, like organ failure, brain damage, or even blindness. It's possible the baby could even die during childbirth. So, that's something you need to be aware of, Autumn. But fortunately, we still have time to turn this pregnancy around. From what I can see, you have maybe eight weeks to go, unless it's born prematurely. Which is also a risk. But both your weight and the baby's weight are up significantly. And I assume the baby has been active?"

Autumn didn't answer, she just tipped her eyes up to Sig. He nodded to the doctor.

"Good. Any spotting?"

"No," Autumn murmured. Not since those first couple of days after Sig found her.

"That's good, too."

The tech finished up and cleaned off Autumn's stomach before pulling her shirt down her to cover her up.

Dr. Bryson squeezed her knee. "You can sit up now." She moved over and powered the table until Autumn was sitting upright.

The doctor waited until the tech left and, once the door was shut, she said, "Like I told you last week, my husband and I are looking to adopt and we've been on a waiting list... To be honest, it took him a long time to get to this point. You mentioned you might be interested in letting us adopt this baby, but before I go to him, I need to make sure it's really what you'd want. You need to be sure. If you agree, my visits would be covered, we'd also pay for the birth and any medical expenses you incur." She paused. "Let me give you a little background before you seriously consider this..."

"He's a cop," Sig finished for her.

"Yes, but..." Dr. Bryson pushed her glasses up to the top of her head. "He's dealt with some bad PTSD due to his time in the Marines. He saw... things. And when we met, he never wanted kids... for reasons I'd prefer not to get into. While being a mother has been all I've ever wanted, fate made it so I couldn't have my own. However, with years of therapy and medication and with the help of his nieces and nephews, Matt's finally ready. But now that he's ready, we have to wait. If you're willing, we could take this baby. Love and protect him or her. And we'd be okay if you wanted an open adoption, Autumn. If you decided you'd want a relationship with him or her." Since Autumn didn't say anything, the doctor turned to Sig. "Since I'm still concerned with her and the baby's health, my recommendation remains that she come stay with us until the baby is born. We'll make sure she has everything she needs."

"No."

"Sig..."

"Will bring her here as often as you think she needs, but we'll keep her safe. No one else will keep her safer than us."

"Since Matt is a cop, he's quite capable of keeping her safe. His family is full of cops."

"No shit and he leaves for work. So do you. I got people who can watch her. Make sure she eats. Round the clock. Make sure she's safe. Round the clock. People who ain't afraid of doin' whatever's necessary to protect her. Bet you can't say that about your husband's family."

"If I tell him about what happened to her and how the baby was conceived, he'll want her with us."

"No," Sig said more firmly, the muscles in his jaw working. Autumn wasn't sure if he realized how tightly he was gripping her hand. She winced, squeezed his fingers and he dropped her hand.

"How am I going to explain where the baby comes from? He'll want to meet her. Being a police officer, he'll want to know the details. They're so damn detail oriented." She grimaced. "Believe me."

"Don't tell 'im. Keep it a secret. After the baby's born, just bring it home. Tell 'im the mother gave it to you at the hospital 'cause she couldn't take care of it. That's it."

"Autumn will need to sign legal paperwork. And he'll need to be on the birth certificate. Having both of our names on it will help protect the baby from... *them*."

"Draw up whatever paperwork you need. She signs, she signs. She don't?" Sig shrugged.

Autumn finally spoke, tired of this conversation. Tired of them negotiating over her and the seed like she was a used car. "I'll sign whatever you want, Dr. Bryson, as long as you don't tell anyone where it came from. If it gets back to them..."

Carly nodded. "No one will know but us. But, please, call me Carly."

"Not even your husband, Carly," Autumn said. Sig was right, the man was a cop. He'd be obligated to go up that mountain if he knew the truth and that could cause a huge problem. The Shirleys couldn't give a crap about her, they only wanted the seed. They only needed her to finish growing it since she hadn't submitted the way they had hoped when they first brought her there. They'd hoped for a submissive woman who was easily manipulated, and they didn't find that with her.

They had been lied to when she was traded to them. They assumed she'd be docile and obedient.

She wasn't. And Vernon had been angry when he discovered he got the wrong side of the deal.

Very angry.

"I'm not sure that's a secret I can keep," Carly admitted. "There was a crime..."

"Just tell him I'm a single mom who wants a loving family for the seed she can't raise. No one needs to know who planted it. No one."

Carly drew her hands over her face, then shook her head, her green eyes troubled. "I don't know."

"For its safety," Autumn pleaded. "Please. I'll meet your husband. You don't have to lie. I can do it for you."

Carly said nothing for the longest time. "Okay. I'll agree with this for now. But as much as I want a baby of my own, I also don't want to destroy my marriage. It's been a hell of a journey for us to get this far. I don't want to ruin every-thing we've worked for."

A muscle in Sig's jaw jumped. "You tell 'im how this baby came about and he'll have to do somethin' about it. By goin' up there and arrestin' 'em, they'll find out your baby's theirs and fight you for it. You know how those fucknuts like to sue, how they like to stick it to the legal system and the pigs, too. You could lose that fuckin' kid and it might end up being raised up on that mountain. You wanna risk that?"

Carly's face paled. "No."

"Then like Red said, she's just a single mom lookin' to give her kid to a lovin' family. That's you and your pig husband," Sig sneered the last part.

"She needs to be protected now, though," Carly insisted.

"You leave that to us."

The doctor moved closer to the table, concern etching her face.

Autumn was done with all this. It was exhausting and turning her stomach into knots. But before she made any final decision, she needed to know one important thing. "Carly, you mentioned possible defects. Will you love it if it has something wrong with it? Will you and your husband be able to deal with those problems? Or if it ends up with issues, will you no longer want it?"

If they didn't, then Autumn would have no choice but to go into hiding somewhere far away to keep that seed safe and out of the Shirleys' hands.

She couldn't stay with Sig forever. And why would he want to be burdened with her and a seed another man had planted?

He wouldn't.

He shouldn't.

They were not his responsibility. He'd done more than enough for her already.

"That's not a problem, Autumn. But let's get you strong.

Prepared. Give this kid a fighting chance. Give you one, too. It's why I want you to come stay with us." She looked from her to Sig, studying him for a moment before asking, "Is there something between you? You said you found her in the woods and you didn't know her at all. Has something developed since then? Why do you feel obligated for her to stay with you instead?"

"Ain't an obligation, Doc," he murmured, his dark brown eyes holding Autumn's. "Not a fuckin' obligation at all."

Tears began to well in her eyes, making the room and the man standing at her side become blurry. She blinked quickly to clear her vision.

He cleared his throat and finished with, "Let's let her decide."

When she could see him again, his hand was extended towards her.

"Red... it's me," he tipped his head toward his hand and paused, then jerked his chin toward Carly, "or them."

She stared at that hand. The hand which belonged to a man who had done nothing but help her and want to protect her, for whatever reason.

"Red," he said more firmly, when she didn't answer right away. "Me... Or them."

She reached out and grabbed his tightly, saying in a broken whisper, "You."

A look of relief flashed across his face. Quickly there, then gone. If she blinked, she would've missed it.

But she didn't miss the corners of his lips curl up just barely as he nodded and gave her fingers a squeeze.

———

Fuck, he hated the smell. Horses, hay, shit... All of it. But that wasn't why he was in the barn. It never was.

The reason was bent over the straw bales. The pale flesh becoming striped with each rise and fall of his arm.

And each strike, each slap of the narrow leather against her skin, filled his ears along with her encouraging words. She wanted him to keep doing it. Begged him to do it harder.

Make it hurt.

He had no problem giving her what she wanted.

Because he wanted it, too.

Not just wanted it, *needed* it.

It was sick.

Sick.

Goddamn sick.

Why the fuck did he need this?

Why the fuck couldn't he control his rage like a normal person?

Why was this the only way?

This needed to stop.

He needed to stop coming here.

He needed to find another way.

He just didn't know how.

When Rebecca's hands came around to grab her own ass, he knew she was done. That was the sign she'd had enough.

She spread her cheeks and whispered, "Now."

His dick was so fucking hard, her ass so fucking inviting. He'd missed how tight it was. How responsive she was.

What a horny slut she was, too.

He had ripped off her Kapp earlier and her long blonde hair fell over her back, her shoulders and her face, so he grabbed a fistful and yanked her head back until her neck couldn't bend any farther.

"Yes," she hissed. "Now."

He shoved his open jeans down just enough to free his dick, giving it a one-handed stroke, then another.

His fingers tightening painfully on her hair made her gasp. Opened that pretty little mouth that had sucked him earlier, never gagging once while he face-fucked her. Because sluts like that could take it.

They liked it hard. Rough. The harder, the rougher, the better.

She couldn't get enough of his belt, enough of his dick.

She couldn't resist texting him for more.

She'd missed it.

She'd begged him to come.

She said she'd been bad.

She said she deserved the punishment her daddy would give her. And promised to take it like a good girl.

But he wasn't taking her ass this time.

No, he was taking what she refused to give him. What she saved for someone else.

He was taking that for himself.

Because her future husband deserved to know what a dirty little slut he was marrying. What a whore the mother of his future children was.

That man needed to know the truth.

Rebecca would never admit it to him on her own. So, Sig needed to find a way to give him that message.

With a tight grip still on her hair, he ordered, "Spread those cheeks wider."

She did, her fingers digging into her own red and swollen flesh as she pulled them apart, showing him how shiny and pink her center was in that dark blonde bush.

He didn't dig into his front pocket this time. Fuck no. Instead, he moved forward and slid the tip of his dick through her slickness and then up to her tight anus.

He slid it over that hole, the one he'd used hard many times, and she relaxed it in preparation. "Now," she begged, "please."

"Bad girls don't get what they want," he growled, then shoved forward and down, plunging into her pussy instead.

And as he drove in and out, listening to her little mews, her driving her hips back with each thrust, he glanced down at her striped cheeks, watching them bounce.

Fuck yeah.

Fuck...

Oh fuck...

He'd missed this.

He gripped her hip with one hand and her hair with the other to keep her where he wanted her, as he rammed inside her as hard as he could, making that red ass ripple.

It didn't take long for his balls to pull up and get tight. For that pressure to build.

She was so fucking hot and wet.

He gritted his teeth and thrusted forward, burying himself deep as his load shot from him, filling her.

She ground against him, begging to come. But this was punishment for her being a naughty little slut and not a reward.

After a second of letting his breathing and heart rate slow, he pulled out and stared at his dick.

He wasn't wearing a wrap and he'd come deep inside her.

He never did that.

He never fucking did that. Ever.

"Why'd you do that?" Rebecca suddenly shrieked at him. "Now I'm going to get pregnant!"

"There's a pill for that," he said in a panic. She needed to take it right fucking now.

"Too late!" Rebecca screamed, her face twisted and ugly in anger. She straightened from the straw bales and as she spun on him, both her hands supported a huge pregnant belly.

"Look what you've done!" she screamed in his face, tears streaking her cheeks. "You've ruined me!"

Holy fuck!

His heart was racing as he raised his eyes to her face.

Only it was no longer Rebecca's.

It wasn't her at all.

It was Red.

Her face, her red hair. Her belly.

"What the fuck!" he shouted, his hand clawing at his chest because of the pressure. He couldn't breathe. Somebody was sitting on it, crushing him.

"They're coming," Red whispered, pulling out a large knife from the folds of the ugly, plain blue dress. "I can't let them have this baby."

She lifted the knife and instead of lunging at him, she plunged it into her own belly. Her stomach deflated like a popped balloon.

"What the fuck, Red!"

He needed to help her but there was no blood, there was nothing.

"Red," he tried to step forward, to grab her, but his feet were stuck to the ground. He couldn't move. "Need to get you away from them. Help me get free."

He tried to move again, but it was like his boots were soldered to metal.

"Free me so I can help you," he yelled, his rage building, heat rushing through his veins. She needed to choose him so he would no longer be stuck. "It's me or them, Red." Once he was unstuck, he could help her.

"You gotta choose!" he screamed, the fire inside him now burning white hot.

He reached out his hand to her and she only stared at it.

"Me... or them!"

She simply turned and walked away.

Chapter Thirteen

Sig shot straight up on the couch, gasping for air. Beads of sweat rolled down his temples and slid into his beard.

"Jesus fuck," Sig muttered on a pant. Either he needed to stop drinking or maybe the pot he'd smoked right before crashing had been laced with something. That nightmare was way too fucked up.

With his pulse still pounding in his ears, he drew his forearm across his brow to wipe off the sweat.

Movement heading his way caught his eye. The light over the stove in the corner lit her up enough so he could see her belly was still big. Thank fuck she hadn't stabbed it with a fucking knife.

He shuddered at the thought. *Fuck.*

He got to his feet and met her halfway so she didn't have to waddle all the way to the couch. "Hey," he said softly as she kept coming anyway until they were toe to toe.

She tipped her face up to him, her hair a mess, her expression full of concern. She didn't say a word, only studied his face, so he quickly masked his own worry.

For fuck's sake, her mouth called to him and he struggled

not to take it. Because if he started with her mouth, he wasn't sure if he'd be able to end it there.

So instead, he dug his fingers into her hair on both sides of her head and leaned down until their foreheads were pressed together. "You okay?"

Her hand pressed against his bare stomach, which was still damp from sweat and bellowing in and out more rapidly than normal. "I came out to ask you that question."

"I'm good," he whispered. "Fuck. I'm good. Long as you're good. You good?"

"Yes, I'm good. I'm having a hard time sleeping, though."

"'Cause of me yellin' in my sleep?" That had to be what woke her up. He can't imagine he was quiet through all that craziness.

"No, because of the baby."

Sig went solid. "The what?" That was the first time she acknowledged what was in her belly. Not a fucking seed, a baby. He wondered if the doctor's visit this morning had shaken something loose in her head.

"The baby. It's active. Here." She grabbed his hand and pressed it to the side of her stomach where it was shifting under his fingers.

He tipped his eyes up to hers, though he couldn't focus since their foreheads were still pinned together. "Yeah. It is."

"Hopefully that means it's happy now that it knows it'll have a family to love it."

"Red..."

She pulled away from him, dropped his hand and turned her back to him. "I'm going to get some water, use the bathroom and go back to bed. I just wanted to make sure you were okay."

"Yeah, baby, I'm okay."

She glanced over her shoulder at him. "It's your bed, Sig."

She was telling him something she didn't need to. "Yeah."

"You should be in it."

He knew that, too. "I got the couch." He hated the fucking couch. He'd rather be in his bed next to her.

"You should be in it," she repeated, this time much more firmly. Once again giving him a peek at what he guessed she used to be like and, hopefully, who she would be again one day.

It wasn't impossible. It just might take a while.

"It'll help me sleep."

He frowned. "You sure?"

"No. But it can't hurt, right?"

Oh fuck yeah, it could hurt. It could end up hurting a lot. "Red..."

"Only if you want to," she said softly.

At that moment, there was nothing he wanted more.

She headed into the kitchenette, grabbed a plastic cup off the stack he kept on the counter and filled it with tap water. While he was stuck where he was. Completely fucking stuck.

He watched her lift it and drink, then place the cup back down on the counter. Her eyes on him the whole time.

Watching him watching her.

But he still stood there frozen, his feet unable to move. Like in the nightmare.

"You need anything?"

She was asking *him* that? *Fuck*, he needed so goddamn much. Things he wanted from her she couldn't give him and never would be able to.

"I'm good," he lied.

She nodded, then headed back down the hall.

Still, he was stuck where he stood.

The toilet flushed, the water in the basin ran and the bathroom light clicked off.

He never heard the bedroom door close.

She left it open.

For him.

She wanted him in his own bed.

You should be in it.

Problem was, that was where she was, too.

When she called his name, his feet suddenly became unstuck and he rushed down the hall and into the dark bedroom.

"You okay?" he asked.

"Yes. I am now."

"Why?"

"You're here."

"Red," her name got caught in his throat. "I can't stay."

"Why not?"

"I just can't."

"I trust you."

Holy fuck. "You shouldn't."

"You haven't given me a reason not to."

"Haven't been around me long enough."

"Yes, I have."

"There's nothin' good about me, Red. Not one fuckin' thing. I swear it."

"I know that's not true," she said, her voice soft and gentle, her words swirling around him, touching him.

"It is."

"No," she insisted more firmly.

"You're not lookin' hard enough."

"I see you."

His body jolted. *I see you.*

"Can you hold me?"

This fucking woman was killing him. Taking her knife from the nightmare and driving it into his tiny black heart. "Red... that might not be a good idea."

"It's okay. Just hold me. Please."

"But—"

"It's okay. I'll be okay. You're just going to hold me. That's it."

That may not be it.

"Red..." Her name caught at the back of his throat. "I don't know how to be gentle."

"Yes, you do. You just forget."

What the fuck? Was he still stuck in his dream?

Sig closed his eyes and pressed the heels of his palms to them. To stem the unfamiliar sting. To tamp down the frustration of her not understanding.

He wanted to yell at her that she was crazy. That her mind was broken and still wasn't allowing her to see things clearly.

Like the baby inside her. Like him.

She wasn't recognizing the truth. She was ignoring it.

By her refusing to see him for who and what he really was could be dangerous.

She had only seen a very small part of him. She hadn't had a chance to see him completely. To see the real him. To see him when he spun out of control. When he went on a rampage.

When he became the monster who destroyed anything and everything in his path.

She hadn't seen that.

He hoped she never would.

Sometimes he couldn't stop the storm that raged inside him until he was pepper-sprayed or tased and bound hand and foot.

Until he was contained like an animal. In a cage, away from everyone else. Unable to hurt anyone else.

Removed from the rest of society because he was a danger.

Sometimes it only took the smallest thing to push him over the edge.

It was why he hadn't gone up that mountain yet. Because he knew once he did, he'd need an outlet.

And right now, he had none.

If he lost it, truly fucking lost it, he would end up back in a concrete box and then he'd have no way to keep Red safe.

None.

And he needed to keep her safe.

She needed him.

For a reason he couldn't understand, he also needed her. "Sig."

His name in her mouth always twisted something deep inside him. "Yeah."

"Come to bed."

This still had to be part of his dream. It couldn't be real.

A woman he had found naked, running for her life in the woods, a woman who he'd only known for not even two weeks, a woman he wanted to touch but couldn't... *That* woman wanted him next to her. In his bed.

The only time a woman was in his bed was when he was fucking her. Otherwise, there was no reason for her to be there. None.

Besides being forced to share a bed with his baby sister, he'd only slept with a female once without fucking her. And that was the other night with Red.

He wasn't sure if he was strong enough to do it a second night.

No, he knew he wasn't fucking strong enough.

But he'd do it for her.

Because he'd do anything for her.

He had no idea why a connection existed between them.

He knew nothing about her except for bits and pieces of what happened on that mountain. Even that wasn't much at all.

But then, she knew nothing about him, either. All she

knew was he was the man waiting at the bottom of that mountain for her. To help her survive.

Maybe nothing else mattered.

Only that. That single moment.

Maybe she came into his life to help him survive, too.

He scrubbed a hand over his eyes, wiping away that unfamiliar dampness.

Jesus Christ, someone must have slipped some good shit into his weed. Because all those crazy thoughts had to have come from some weird trip he was on.

"Sig," she called softly.

He didn't answer her this time. Instead, he moved. He slipped out of his jeans and let them drop to the floor, glad he thought ahead to wear boxers.

Then he moved to the bed and climbed in, tucking his legs under the cool sheets and biting back a groan at how fucking good his mattress felt.

This time she was already on her side, facing him. He tucked his arms under his head and stared up at the dark ceiling. And though he left a safe gap between them, she closed it, until her hard belly pressed into his side and her hand found his.

She didn't hold it, fuck no. She traced her fingers along his, from fingertips to wrist, up his forearm, over his bicep and his shoulder. Her touch light. Not sexual, just an exploration.

"I forget what it's like to be touched simply because you want to be touched or someone wants to touch you. Because they want to appreciate you, not hurt you. It's a different type of touch."

"Yeah, Red, it is. No fuckin' doubt." Did she want him to touch her, too? It was smarter to just keep his hands to himself.

"I miss it."

"What?"

"Being touched without it hurting."

Jesus Christ! "Red—"

She kept talking. "I miss that connection between two people. Touch can be a form of communication. Good, bad, even indifferent."

"Red..."

"But touch is important. *So* important. I saw it on a news segment once. Volunteers at a hospital holding preemies. It helps them. And I'm sure it helps the volunteers, too."

"Red..."

She pressed her fingers over his lips to quiet his growing anxiety at her starting something he couldn't finish. For her touch to cause a reaction that was way more than only communication.

He should get out of this bed right fucking now and head back to the couch. *Fuck that,* he needed to head out the door. To another fucking county, even another state.

But he couldn't move, the fingers that had stopped him from talking now explored his face. They traced his furrowed brow, around his eyes, across his cheeks. They skimmed over the side of his head where his hair was trimmed shorter, over his ear, down his jawline and his beard to his chin. Down his nose, across his lips again, along his throat, over his pounding pulse line, his jumping Adam's apple, the hollow of his neck. Landing on his chest which lifted and fell like he'd run a mile.

She lightly brushed over each of his nipples which were now beaded from not only her touch, but the goosebumps that had broken out everywhere.

He'd never been touched like this.

Not once.

Not in his whole fucking life.

Like he was breakable.

Or valuable.

Or... just because.

With his muscles tense, he blinked up at the ceiling, afraid to turn his head. Afraid of going face to face with her while she was still touching him.

She settled her palm over his heart. "Your heart is strong."

Its only function had ever been to keep the blood pumping through his body. Nothing else. Nothing more.

An organ that kept him alive.

But it was the blood rushing from his heart and down to somewhere he couldn't control, filling his cock, making it hard, lifting the sheet slightly.

He would need to stop her before she got that far.

"You have a lot of tattoos."

He couldn't answer her. He couldn't push any words out at all. He had somehow lost that capability.

"Right now, I can't see them in the dark, but maybe you can explain what each one means one day."

One day.

One day he could do that.

Right now he was struggling just to take his next breath.

With her hand still over his racing heart, she said, "In the meantime, tell me about this one. The angel wings over your heart. When I first saw it, I thought someone close to you had died. But then I noticed the script between the wings said 'die free.'"

He closed his eyes as she circled that tattoo lightly with her fingertips. The ink he'd gotten a few years ago during one of his longer prison terms.

"Shouldn't it say 'live free?'"

For anyone not fucked up, it probably would. He wasn't sure if he should share the meaning with her, but it wasn't exactly a secret. "The sayin's 'live free or die,' but spent more time livin' in a cage than livin' free, so when I die, I'll be forever free."

"Death frees us all."

What the fuck was she doing to him? She was digging up pieces of him he thought long buried.

And there was no way she was aware she was doing that.

She slid her palm down his sternum and to his stomach, letting it lay there as it rose and fell with each quick breath.

He would have to stop her if she tried to go lower. If she got closer to his throbbing dick which was screaming for her soft touch.

He blew out a relieved, but ragged, breath when her hand moved higher again, back to his chest, where it settled.

"Now me," she whispered.

What?

He had to say something now. He had to force the words from his throat. "No, Red."

"Yes, please."

"I can't."

"Is it because of... what happened to me? Because I'm... because of what's growing inside me?"

"Fuck no. It has nothin' to do with that." Unlike some other men, pregnancy had never been a turn off for him. He hadn't searched it out but he hadn't turned it away, either.

"Then what?"

"You would've kept goin', Red, would've figured out why."

She got quiet for a minute, then said, "I miss intimacy."

"Not your man for that, Red. Told you that."

"Intimacy doesn't have to be sex."

"Know sex, baby, not intimacy. Had the first, never the second, so I can't give you what I don't know."

"How do you know unless you try?"

"You're askin' too much."

"Does intimacy scare you?"

"Does sex scare you?" He squeezed his eyes shut at that stupid goddamn question. *Stupid fuck.*

"Not normally," she answered, unbothered by him being a complete motherfucking asshole.

He finally turned his head, and though his eyes had adjusted to the darkness, he couldn't read her face or her eyes.

Only the tone of her voice when she said, "What they did... what he did wasn't sex."

He turned to his side and her hand fell off his chest to the bed between them. He reached out to brush a lock of her hair off her cheek, then slipped his fingers into the thick of it by her ear.

He shifted enough to press his lips to her forehead. He kept them there for a few breaths, then as he began to pull away, she wrapped her fingers around his jaw and pulled him back, pressing her lips to his.

She didn't open her mouth and he didn't fucking dare open his because she was playing with fire right now.

And it seared his gut and burned hot in his chest.

He stayed still, letting her keep their mouths together for as long as she wanted. Which wasn't nearly long enough when she pulled away just slightly.

"Pot and alcohol."

He licked his lips hoping to taste her but tasted what she mentioned instead. "Yeah, baby. Nothin' new."

"Is it the only way?"

"Along with the other thing we talked about, yeah, it helps."

She grabbed his hand, pulled it from her hair and pressed the back of it to her lips. Then she turned it around and using her fingers to guide his, she drew them around her face just like she had done to him.

And when she got back to her mouth, she kissed the center of his palm before moving it to her throat.

He closed his eyes for a moment and remembered that

bruise on her neck when he first found her. Where someone had squeezed her neck so hard it left a mark.

Even though it was now gone, he'd never forget it.

He brushed his thumb back and forth over her pulse. She said his heart was strong, but so was hers, and her neck was delicate as he stroked it. So easily crushed if someone wanted this woman to stop breathing.

Her hand remained pressed to his as he slid it down to the collar of his shirt she wore.

He was rock hard and knew this would never lead to sex but he wanted to touch her everywhere. He wanted to feel the warmth of her skin against him.

He cleared the rough from his throat to ask, "Want me to touch you?"

"Yes."

"Where?"

Her breath caught. When she pushed herself up, she said, "Help me," as she reached for the hem of his tee.

"Red. Again, not sure this is smart." No, he was fucking sure it wasn't.

"I trust you."

But I don't fuckin' trust myself! screamed through his head.

She struggled to pull the shirt off but got it done without his help and tossed it to the floor. As she reached for the panties, he grabbed her hand. "No. Jesus fuck, no. Just don't..."

She left them on and laid back down, once again facing him.

He was being tested and he was afraid he was going to fail.

And if he failed, that meant he failed her.

He studied her silhouette in the dark and just breathed.

He might not be able to only do what she wanted. It might just break him.

It might take that last thread of his sanity and snap it.

But before he even attempted to do what she asked, he needed to know...

He needed to know how long ago they touched her last, the last time they hurt her, the last time they "bred" her.

He needed to know how fresh any and all of that was in her mind.

He wasn't sure how to ask it without taking her back to that place, without accidentally pushing her back into the thinking that the baby was just a seed someone planted inside her.

"Red, need to know what I'm dealin' with here. Tryin' to be careful. And not..."

"You don't have to."

Christ, it killed him when she gave up what she wanted too easily. He had seen flashes of her where she was a fighter. As fiery as her hair. But when she became submissive like that, it tore at him. Someone had done their best to beat that fight out of her.

"That ain't it, baby. I wanna. Fuck, how I wanna. But... But I'm fuckin' scared, Red. I'm fuckin' scared. Don't wanna do the wrong thing. Say the wrong thing. Break you more than you already are."

"You won't. It's just a touch. That's all."

That wasn't all. That wasn't fucking it at all.

"I'll be okay," she assured him.

"You tell me if..."

"Yes."

"Holdin' you to that, baby. Just fuckin' say the word and I'll stop."

She said nothing but grabbed his hand and placed it on her chest, above her tit and over her heart. "Okay."

Okay.

Okay, he could do this.

His dick was throbbing, his heart was pounding. His

mind was a goddamn tangled mess. But okay, yeah, he could do this.

He told her she could have whatever she wanted. And this was what she wanted.

A touch without pain.

A touch without worry.

A touch she could trust.

She wanted him to be that touch.

It might be the hardest motherfucking thing he did in his life. To touch her, to lay by her side and not to take her like he wanted to.

He was goddamn insane, that was what he was.

Because what Red wanted, he would make sure she got.

Chapter Fourteen

AUTUMN WAS surprised by the tremble of his fingers as his hand swept over her chest.

He was struggling. Struggling to remain gentle. Struggling to keep it just to a touch. She realized how hard it was for him. And she appreciated him all the more for trying.

But she needed this.

Oh, did she need this.

And she did trust him. Even if he didn't think she should.

His fingers were warm and long, but the pads rough, as he explored her face again, then her bare shoulders, her arms, skipping everything below her breasts.

But she wanted him to touch her everywhere. That touch reminded her of what she could have again in the future.

A man in her life. A lover who appreciated her and didn't hurt her.

A man who could fall in love with her, not simply use her as breeding stock. She was way more than a container to grow their seeds.

She refused to be reduced to that.

Tonight, she just needed that reminder. She just needed that connection. Even if it was only for a little while.

Good remained in the world. It hadn't all disappeared in the months she was in that compound on that mountain. She could find it again. She simply needed to look for it once she made sure this baby was safe and cared for. Protected and loved.

She could start over and find herself once again after the baby was born. She'd disappear, let Sig get back to his life instead of being saddled with a woman who was pregnant by someone else.

Sig shifting to his knees jerked her out of her thoughts and the relaxed zone she had fallen into.

She didn't know why she felt so safe with him. This tattooed biker who belonged to an MC. The party had been a bit wild. And while there had been some drugs and drinking, there had been no fighting or any violence. And, from what she could see, the women all encouraged the men when it came to the sex. Nobody was there against their will and everyone seemed to be enjoying themselves.

And if that was how they wanted to live their lives, who was she to judge?

None of it had bothered her.

Not until Sig approached that woman Billie.

She had studied their body language since she couldn't hear their words.

She also noticed the change when the other man had approached them, putting his arm around Billie in a way that spoke volumes. Billie was his and Sig was to back off.

When Sig had stormed out, she had wanted to follow. But Stella stopped her and had Shady take her back upstairs, locking the door behind him. Once again, locking her in.

For her safety.

The whole time she had worried about Sig and couldn't fall asleep until he returned.

But now, he was on his knees at her feet, rubbing them and running his hands up her calves, not going any higher than her knees. She groaned when he massaged her feet again for a few minutes and almost whimpered in protest when he stopped.

He moved to straddle her knees and he lightly touched her tight belly on both sides.

"Okay?"

"Yes," she whispered.

He touched every inch of her stomach—where it housed a baby she couldn't think of as her own—stopping right before he'd get to her aching breasts, her pebbled nipples.

This wasn't supposed to be sexual, just simply touch.

A human connection.

"Red..."

She raised her gaze to him as he towered over her. "Yes."

"Not sure how long I can do this."

"You can stop if you need to."

"Don't wanna stop," his voice cracked, "that's the problem."

She didn't want him to stop, either. But his fear was also hers. Even though it had been at least six months since Vernon last touched her in *that way*, she didn't trust her brain to separate what Sig wanted to do with what Vernon had done.

She didn't want to go backward when she was already moving forward. She didn't want Sig to feel guilty if he caused a reaction he really wouldn't be the cause of. It would be her memory, not his actions. She didn't want him to be hurt by her rejecting him if she needed him to stop.

Because she had no doubt he would stop if she asked.

Even so, she still needed his touch. It was another step forward.

And it gave her some hope that she'd find the woman she used to be.

"You want to have sex with me?" She found that hard to believe, not in the condition she was in, not after what she'd been through. Who would find any of that attractive?

"Baby, hard as a rock right now. I was before I even started touchin' you. That's a pretty fuckin' clear answer to your question."

"I don't understand why."

"Remember when you said you *see* me?"

"Yes."

"Well, I *see* you, Red. The second you took my hand at the bottom of that fuckin' mountain, I saw you. You're a fuckin' fighter. You weren't givin' up until you were free in one way or another. That right there, baby, is sexy as fuck. Right now, I can only guess what fuckin' happened, but you didn't let it break you completely. You did what you needed to do to survive. Just like I do. I do what I need to do to get to the next day and the next. You did what you needed to do 'til you got that chance to run. No matter what the fuck they did to you, you didn't give the fuck up. You gave them the goddamn finger is what you did. By givin' this kid up to the Brysons, and not lettin' those motherfuckers have it, you'll be doin' it again. By livin' a goddamn good life after this kid's born, you're givin' it to them a third time. That right there turns me the fuck on. Everythin' about you is sexy, Red. Every goddamn thing. You're a fighter but you also got moments where you're vulnerable. We all are. Every fuckin' one of us. Some of us just try to hide it."

Autumn swallowed, not expecting any of those words to come from him. He just said something that proved who he really was, too.

Maybe it was only to make her feel better, to help her

feel like a woman again, instead of an object. But by doing so, he revealed more about himself than he knew. Something he probably never shared.

But he had with her.

"Can you kiss me?"

His head jerked back, and it took him a second to answer, "Yeah, baby, I can kiss you."

"I can't do anything more than that. I just don't want... I'm afraid to go backward."

"Won't let you go backward."

"But after that little speech, I need to kiss you."

"Taste like pot and booze," he reminded her needlessly.

She smiled even though he might not be able to see it. "That's you."

"Yeah, baby, that's me. Will always be me. Can't see that ever changin'."

Was he warning her? She had already decided to leave after the baby was born, to no longer be his burden, to get back her own life, to not rely on anyone else. She also wanted to get as far away from the Shirleys as possible.

But right now, she had to get through the next eight weeks. She had plenty of time to make a plan. Luckily, every day her thoughts got clearer. And she remembered where she had been headed in life before she hit this huge speed bump. She needed to get back on that path.

He moved off her and to her side, helping her turn with a hand on her hip. And when they were face to face again, they stared at each other through the dark. "Gonna kiss you now."

"Okay."

"Just a warnin', kissin' you ain't gonna help the issue with my dick."

She pressed her lips together. "I understand."

"Gonna leave it to you how far you take it. Liked you touchin' me. Liked touchin' you. But this is all you, baby.

You saw my back. You know I can take whatever torture you give me."

"I don't want to torture you."

"My dick bein' hard and not fuckin' you is pure fuckin' torture."

At least he was being honest. "Sorry."

"It happens. Might get outta bed quick. If I do..." He let that hang but she got his meaning.

"Okay."

"Okay," he whispered, digging his hands into her hair again and pulling her face to his.

Then he kissed her. Not just the press of lips from earlier. No, this kiss was deeper, more thorough, with open mouths, mingled breaths and tongues touching. Exploration and discovery.

She searched her mind to see if anything was rushing forward.

There wasn't.

Nothing existed but Sig and his kiss.

It was gentle at first, until it wasn't.

He took complete possession of her mouth, making her breath catch. When he felt it, he tried to pull away, but she quickly wrapped her hand around the back of his head and kept him there.

He was trying to swallow her whole. Inhale her completely.

She couldn't remember the last time she had been kissed. Especially like this. It had been forever.

Actually, maybe even never.

This wasn't a kiss, it was much more.

She was surprised when her breasts began to ache for his touch and her pussy began to pulse and get wet.

She was pleased to find she could still react to the right touch, the right man.

But she wouldn't risk taking it much farther. Not tonight.

She also couldn't ignore how much she wanted this man. And it was so unexpected. With that hope was also worry that if she let this continue, it might be hard to leave in a couple of months.

Maybe she *should* go stay with the Brysons.

Because leaving would be so much harder, if in the next few weeks she fell in love with him. A man who came into her life so unexpectedly and for the wrong reasons. A man she never would have met under normal circumstances.

As he continued to kiss her, his hands stroked her back, her ribs, her hips, sometimes skimming just lightly over her ass before heading back up.

He twisted his head away, panting, "Can't, Red. At my limit. Wanna be inside you too fuckin' bad. Strugglin' not to flip you to your back and just fuckin' take you. Just wanna be honest. Let you know why I gotta stop. 'Cause if we don't stop now, ain't gonna be able to. Don't wanna become the animal they were. Wouldn't be able to live with myself if I did. Never wanna fuckin' hurt you."

"Okay," she breathed, doing a little panting of her own. She closed her eyes, wishing they could take it further, wishing she could be sure she wouldn't have a bad reaction. Maybe they could go slow. Eventually work their way toward that.

Because in truth, she wanted him to flip her onto her back and take her, too. But, again, she was afraid of taking that positive step and turning it into a negative. Sig deserved much better than that.

He suddenly put space between them and rolled out of bed.

"You're leaving?" Her heart began to pound.

"Gotta. Just for a bit."

He snagged his jeans off the floor, yanked them on but didn't fasten them, then grabbed one of his clean T-shirts she had folded and put away in his dresser. He pulled that over his head as he headed toward the door.

Then he walked through that door and a few minutes later the one leading outside.

She couldn't miss the sound of the deadbolt turning, of being locked inside once more.

Then he was gone.

And she couldn't go after him even if she tried.

———

SIG'S HEART was pounding so hard, it was like his whole body thumped along with it.

He was fighting to keep his shit together. But his brain was screaming at him to either break something or hurt someone.

The voice whispering through his mind encouraged him to take his frustration out physically, promised he'd feel so much better afterward.

Sig knew that was a lie.

He would feel better while he did it, then feel worse later when he crashed from the high. When his vision cleared, and he realized what he'd done. What damage he'd caused.

And, depending on what it was, when he discovered what he had to live with afterward.

He rushed down to The Barn in his search.

Not for booze. For something else.

For something that would help unravel the tight rubber band ball of pressure which was building. Something to give him even that short-term relief.

But the Fury's clubhouse was surprisingly quiet and regrettably empty.

His disappointment and irritation was also mixed with relief.

If he had found what he was looking for, he might regret

it later. Which would make him feel even worse than he did now.

With nothing there for him and no reason to stay, he strode out of the barn into the dark night, across the uneven grass to the long equipment shed where everyone parked their sleds.

He threw open the garage door, mounted his bike and turned the key, hoping the deep rumble echoing inside the large metal building didn't catch anyone's interest.

He eased his sled out and left the garage door open as he worked his way down the shitty lane that Trip hadn't fixed yet.

Maybe he needed to step up as VP and take some of the burden off his brother. That would be a start.

He needed to do his part or just fucking leave.

But he still wanted his half and until he got that...

He also needed to keep his shit together long enough to help put Red back together. That meant he needed to stay with this gig until that happened.

She had maybe two months until the baby was born. Until she handed him over to that pig and his doctor wife. Sig could do it. He could stay a couple more months for sure. He'd just have to work harder on convincing Trip to hand over what was owed him during that time.

Two months wasn't long, but hopefully long enough to get that done.

About twenty minutes later, he was riding down Copperhead Road and to the long dirt lane that headed up that fucking mountain. The lane with the warning signs posted everywhere. All of them basically saying: *you trespass, you die.*

Well, fuck those motherfuckers, tonight he was trespassing.

Because tonight he'd wanted Red and she wanted him but neither could have each other due to those inbred hillbillies up that lane, in those woods, on that mountain.

And, because of that, they needed to pay.

The way he was torqued right now, if he ran into any, he might use them as a way to relieve the barely-contained rage flowing through his veins.

The rage from them trying to destroy a woman like Red.

They had no goddamn right.

No fucking right at all.

He parked in a narrow dirt pull-off located right along the road near the entrance to their compound, where, at the end of the lane, the biggest sign of all was posted, hand painted in red and white. The one that stated: *VILATERS wud be shot on site.*

Yep, that's what it said. But then, Sig didn't speak inbred goat fucker, so he just ignored it as he took off on foot up the rutted, dirt road. He also passed a shitload of other signs he couldn't read in the dark. Didn't matter, he would've ignored those, too.

The higher he trekked, the harder it was to see the path as the moon began to disappear due to the thick of the trees. But there was no way he was hoofing it through the woods since everyone said it was booby-trapped.

And if it was, it was a miracle Red made it unscathed as she ran.

He also hoped the clan didn't have a guard posted with a weapon because Sig had nothing but a small knife in one pocket of his cut.

And any semi-sane man knew you didn't bring a knife to a gun fight.

It took about twenty minutes for him to reach the point where he could see a clearing ahead, where the moon was illuminating some metal roofs. That was when he slipped into the trees and carefully picked through the brush, circling around the clearing, trying to get his bearings, trying to get a good idea of the layout. The main clearing was huge and mostly leveled out. It had a few large buildings, some shacks and what looked like a barn. He could hear the low grunts of some pigs in a pen nearby. Maybe even the rustle of some other animals.

He was good as long as they weren't human. Calling the Shirleys human was pushing it.

Most of the sheds were built half-assed. Shitty cars and trucks, some with flat tires and rusted out fenders, were parked haphazardly around the open space. He noticed more lanes going higher up the mountain and deeper into the woods like spokes on a half wheel. He assumed they led to more clearings and buildings. Maybe those dirt lanes led to little "homesteads" where they raised their inbred snot monkeys.

Judge had suggested he take pictures of the layout but it was too dark for them to turn out decent enough to be of use. Instead, he saved it all to memory, figuring once he got back, he might be able to hand draw some sort of map.

Through the trees, he could see a bigger home with a few lights on in the second floor windows. He wondered if that was where the "leader" of their sovereign nation lived.

The Guardians of Freedom was what they called themselves. Which was a fucking joke since Red had hardly been free. If she had been, he had no doubt she would not have come up this mountain on her own. She would not have volunteered to subject herself to whatever happened.

Even if it wasn't the leader who hurt Red, the man knew it happened and most likely had a hand in it. Sig doubted anything happened on that mountain the leader of the Shirley Clan wasn't aware of.

He skirted around a few rusty, abandoned cars tucked within the trees and made his way to the run-down barn which looked like it had been built with a mix of materials. Wood planks, sheets of metal, whatever scrap they could repurpose. It had a fence around it and Sig heard a low bawl of a cow from somewhere close.

His nose wrinkled, reminding him of when Red did it, as the stench of piss and shit burned his nostrils.

He had one single focus tonight. That was to find where they had kept Red.

He needed to see for himself where she'd been locked up. Where she'd been forced to submit.

Where they tried to break her and bend her to their will.

Where they tried to make her theirs.

As he headed behind the barn, another shed was tucked along a tree line with the door hanging partially open. A stack of split firewood sat next to it, along with a crude homemade furnace with a pipe running from the top into the shed.

A fucking tiny shed with heat? That didn't make any sense. Unless it was a smokehouse, most sheds, even outhouses, weren't heated. Not that he knew much about homesteading or farming. He didn't know dick about it, but he had some sort of common sense. More than these uncle-daddy fuckers.

He carefully made his way closer, his head on a swivel to make sure none of them were up and about, making rounds or anything. Just waiting to plug some buckshot into his ass.

As he got closer, his stride stuttered as the stench that came from inside seemed a bit pungent.

That wasn't smoked meat inside that shed. Unless they were smoking rotten roadkill.

He pulled the collar of his long-sleeved T-shirt up and over his nose as he moved forward. The door had two metal hasps on it. One at the top, one closer to the bottom. And two open padlocks hung from each metal loop screwed to the outside wall. He grabbed the edge of the door and slowly opened it, the hair on the back of his neck now standing, the lump in his gut twisting, his mind racing.

Still holding the T-shirt over his nose, he pulled his cell

out of his back pocket and hit the power button, quickly found the flashlight app and turned it on.

He closed his eyes for a split moment, simply to brace himself. If he thought his heart was pounding before, it was now ready to escape his chest.

He lifted his cell phone, pointing it inside and opened his eyes.

It was nothing but an empty room. He should be relieved since it had nothing except a bucket in one corner.

He stepped inside and froze. The bucket was knocked over, and surrounding it was dried human waste.

Shit. Piss. What might be puke.

He tried to swallow but couldn't. *Hell*, he could hardly breathe. He took a step deeper into the tiny shed and moved his phone in a circle, lighting up the corners, the walls, the floors as he inspected it all.

The floor was concrete, so she had no chance to dig free.

No lights. No electricity. Nothing. No bed or bedding. No clothes. Not even a fucking goddamn blanket.

Nothing.

Not even a window.

Just a small hole up at the top of one wall, where they pumped in the heat. Probably just enough to keep her from freezing.

Heat rose. Didn't those motherfuckers know that? If she was on the floor, how was she supposed to benefit from that fucking heat?

Dark spots dotted the dirt-crusted concrete. Bloody fingerprints were along the wall in one corner. Two long tracks marked the filthy floor from the door to the center of the shed. Like she had been dragged and her heels had left a path in their wake.

He turned and glanced at the inside of the thick wood-planked door. Solid, handmade, too strong to kick in or kick open. With gaps between the boards just large enough to let in the wind, the cold and the sleet or rain.

He moved closer and held out his phone, lighting it up.

On the inside of the door, at the edges of those boards, were bloody gouges and scratches. Like someone had been clawing to get free.

Someone.

Red.

He wondered how many times she had pressed her face against those gaps and screamed for help, begged for her freedom, or hoped someone would come along and save her.

He had no idea how she got out of this sadistic jail. This cell no bigger than the ones he'd lived in for years. Though the concrete boxes he'd lived in were more humane than this.

He'd had a toilet, a sink, a mattress pad, even if it was shitty. He didn't have to sleep on the concrete floor. He had clothes and had a chance to shower, to work out, to get sunlight during his time in the yard. He could buy snacks and cigarettes if someone put money on his account. He could read a fucking book. He could take fucking classes.

He knew what day it was and how long he had left until he'd be free.

She had none of that!

FUCKING NONE OF THAT!

Their goddamn pigs had a better life than she'd had.

He needed to get out of there before he rushed up to that house and sliced everyone's throat. Or he choked the goddamn clan leader with his bare hands until he was dead. Then filleted him with his knife from nuts to neck.

Or cut off his fucking dick and shoved it down his throat until he suffocated.

Any one of those would do.

He didn't come prepared for that. To be able to do a hit and run.

He stepped out of the shed and walked a few steps away until he found some air that didn't burn as badly. Sucking in a breath through his nose, he held it for a count of five and blew it out of his mouth.

Then he did it again when it didn't work the first time.

When the second time didn't work, either, he circled the shed to get one more good look at the lay of the land and stopped dead.

"Holy fuckin' motherfucker."

He took two more steps and blinked to make sure he was actually seeing what he was seeing.

"Jesus fuckin' Christ." He hit the power button on the side of his phone and lifted it once it lit up.

What the fuck was that used for?

What. The. Fuck. Was. That. Used. For?

Whatever it was reminded him of a sawhorse. But it wasn't.

It wasn't used for construction.

Fuck no.

No.

He lifted his phone higher to see it more clearly. Then he moved the light along the object built out of plywood and two-by-fours using some nails and screws.

And four thick leather straps with metal buckles and holes punched into the wide leather.

Those straps were to keep someone in place. But where they were attached on the wood "bench" were at the very bottom of all four legs.

That meant whoever was strapped down was on their belly, spread out, all four wrists and ankles secured tightly.

She had been laid over it and tied down, her hands and feet stretched almost to the ground and her...

Her...

What they needed for easy access to "breed" her exposed.

Jesus Christ. It was some sort of breeding bench.

Being strapped on it, she couldn't fight. She couldn't escape.

She just had to lay there helpless.

He jammed his phone back in his pocket and slammed a hand over his mouth to muffle the roar that rushed up.

Falling to his knees, his forehead hit the dirt. Like someone had taken him down with a hard kick to the middle. Someone had sawed out his lungs and spooned out his gut.

He squeezed his eyes shut, but he couldn't erase what he saw.

Too late, too late, too late.

It was permanently etched into his memory.

He'd never forget that.

He'd never forget picturing Red being...

Being...

That roar he fought back, tried to muffle, escaped into the dead of the night. And it only fueled the flames, threw gas on the fire inside him.

He needed to get up, he needed to move. Get off his knees and get back down that mountain. And make a plan.

He needed a plan.

Because right now, he had no clear thoughts.

He had nothing but the urge for revenge running through him.

But he couldn't move, he found himself crippled. Frozen. The unstoppable fury surging through him, burning white hot.

He wanted to destroy everything in that compound.

All of them.

Every fucking single one.

No one there deserved to breathe the same air as she did.

Not one.

A noise in the distance, a creak of a door, a racking of a shotgun, sank into his spinning brain.

Forcing himself to his feet, he stumbled as he tried to move since he was blinded with his rage.

Move away from the sound.

Move away, not toward it.

You'll fuckin' get 'em.

You'll get 'em.

They will fuckin' pay.

Whoever did this will fuckin' pay.

He forced himself to ignore his instinct, to right the wrong the Shirleys had done and to go into the woods instead. He paused every few yards to try to hear past the rush of his own blood in his ears. To hear if anyone followed.

He kept moving through the dark and the shadows until he stumbled over a tree root and fell into a tree.

Then he held onto that tree because everything began to spin out of control. Like a tornado, ready to wipe out everything in its path.

He pressed his forehead to the rough bark and tried to catch his breath. Tried to regain control.

He was in the middle of nowhere and he needed to find somewhere.

But he couldn't.

He couldn't.

He was lost.

He was so goddamn lost.

His chest heaved and he doubled over, throwing up. Expelling everything from his churning gut onto the forest floor.

Again and again.

Until he was empty.

All but the anger. That was what remained.

The fury. That was all he had left.

He had nothing to destroy so it would destroy him instead.

From the inside.

It would rip through him until there was nothing left of him. Until nothing recognizable remained.

Just an empty shell.

No heart. No soul.

Nothing.

A keen escaped him before he could control it and he used the tree to push himself upright.

Then he funneled all that anger and pain into one part of him in an attempt to rid himself of it.

Because if he destroyed himself, he couldn't help Red.

She'd be alone.

Disappointed in him.

He held that ball of rage in his palm and curled his fingers around it, squeezing it tight.

It burned him, seared him.

So, he smashed it into the tree to put it out.

Again and again.

Over and over.

Until the anger was gone.

Until he almost had nothing left. Which was what he'd been afraid of.

He was nothing but that shell.

But like his brother always said, something was better than nothing.

An empty shell could be filled, while a broken shell would only leak.

He needed to keep that shell whole.

Because something was better than nothing.

And Red was that something.

Chapter Fifteen

SIG HEARD the door open and black heavy boots came into his line of vision.

"Jesus fuck, brother!" Trip yelled. "What the fuck happened?"

He was on his brother's porch, back at the farm. He couldn't remember how he got there.

His throat was dry and raw like he'd been screaming. His body was stiff from being curled up into a ball on the wood floor of the farmhouse's back porch. Most likely for hours since the sun was now up.

"Stella!" his brother screamed.

More footsteps and then an upset female's, "Christ, Sig."

Trip's ol' lady was on her knees next to his head, one hand on his cheek, cupping it gently. "Sig, where's Autumn? Is she okay?"

"His fuckin' hand. It's all busted the fuck up," Trip said, worry lacing his words.

"Holy shit. He needs to go to the hospital," Stella said next.

"No," Sig forced out, trying to get his brain working. Shake off the darkness and get it unstuck. "No. Red..."

"Is she okay? What did you do?" Stella was now sounding a bit panicked.

"Gettin' shit to clean that up," Trip announced.

"No," Sig said louder. He forced himself to sit up, his head throbbing, his hand pulsating, too.

"It might be broken," Stella insisted.

"No. Red."

"Where is she?"

"Need a key."

"D'you lose yours?" Trip asked, standing over him, and, for the first time since Pete and Buck had beat the shit out of him when he was fifteen, Sig saw fear on his face.

"No."

"What d'you need a key for?"

"My place."

"For what?" Trip yelled. "What the fuck's goin' on?"

"Need another key."

"We need to clean you up, Sig. Is Autumn all right?" Concern. Fear.

"Gotta check."

"You don't know?" Stella's voice again, a higher pitch than normal.

"Been gone."

"Gone where?" his brother demanded.

"Up there."

"Up where?" Trip shouted, his frustration only too clear. Then a long hesitation before his brother exploded with, "Up that mountain? By your fuckin' self? D'you go up there?"

"Saw it."

"Saw what?"

"Where they kept her, what they used..."

"Oh my God," Stella whispered.

"They're all gonna fuckin' die."

"Sig," Trip said more firmly.

But before his brother could continue, Sig repeated, "Need a key."

"Why?"

"Just get me a spare."

"Your hand," Stella started.

"Fuck my hand!" Sig yelled. "Fuck my fuckin' hand! Gimme a goddamn spare key."

"Trip," Stella whispered.

Trip nodded and headed into the house.

"Let me see your hand. Just to make sure it isn't broken."

"You a doctor?"

Her face got hard and her eyes narrowed. "I'm going to stomp on it if you don't let me see it."

Cursing under his breath, he lifted it and she carefully took it into her own hands.

"You can't go to her like that, Sig. It might freak her out. Does she know you went up there?"

"No."

"Let me at least clean it up and wrap it. It looks like ground meat." Her voice hitched as if she had swallowed a sob. "God, Sig. Why? Why are the two of you like this?"

"You know why," he mumbled.

"He ruled our lives then, don't let him rule our lives now, Sig. *Please.*"

"Why d'you care?"

"Because you're family," she whispered.

He lifted his face and stared at her. Tears ran down her cheeks as she held his bloody hand between hers, the knuckles split open, his fingers swollen.

He hadn't felt the pain of it.

Not until that moment.

When his pain had become someone else's.

And if what he did affected Stella like this, it might

bother Red worse. She was right. He couldn't go back to his apartment like that.

"Don't destroy this family like he did," she begged, sniffling.

He sucked in a breath and nodded.

She released his hand. "Can you get up on your own or do you need Trip to help?"

"I'm good," he mumbled, slowly getting to his feet.

Stella got him inside and over to the kitchen sink, holding his hand under the faucet. She gently rinsed away the oozing blood, removed any dirt and pieces of bark, and inspected just how bad it was.

"You'll live. You'll just have to use your left hand to jerk off for a little while," she said with complete seriousness.

His eyes hit hers which were full of sadness and regret, so he turned and stared at the running water instead. He didn't want to see that.

Trip came into the kitchen and placed a single key on the table. He moved over to them, carrying a bottle of peroxide, some gauze and an Ace bandage.

His brother and his woman patched him up while Sig stood there as helpless as a fucking baby.

And when they were done, Stella quietly disappeared, leaving him and Trip alone.

They sat down at the table together, and he told Trip what he discovered on that mountain. After he was done, when he'd stopped speaking, Sig saw what he'd felt up there reflected on Trip's face.

"We need a plan," Trip said, his words strained as if he was struggling to contain his own fury.

"Yeah, brother, we need a plan," Sig agreed.

"Shouldn't have went up there on your fuckin' own."

"Yeah. Needed to know."

"She's still not talkin'?" Trip didn't sound surprised but more disappointed.

"No. But that ends today."

Trip tilted his head and considered Sig for a moment. "Might break her to take her back."

Sig understood what he meant and he agreed it was a risk. But he also needed to know everything. "Yeah, gonna give her that key, then I'll just start talkin'. Open up to her about some of my own shit. Hopefully that'll get her talkin', too. Just need to hear it once. Just once. Then we can plan." In truth, he was hoping he was wrong about what happened up there. That the shed wasn't where they kept her and she hadn't been strapped down to that bench.

He hoped to fuck he was wrong.

He knew he wasn't.

"You need Stella up there with you?"

"No, brother. Gotta do it on my own. Gonna do this as easy on Red as possible."

Trip sat at the table, staring at it for the longest time. When he lifted his head, he asked, "Sig... You expectin' her to stick when this is all done?"

He knew what his brother was asking. "No." *Hell,* he wasn't even planning on sticking afterward but he couldn't tell Trip that.

"Then why the fuck you goin' through all this?" He jerked his chin toward Sig's now wrapped hand.

"Got no choice."

"Brother, you got a choice."

"No, Trip, you're wrong. I fuckin' don't."

———

AUTUMN HEARD the key turn in the lock, but she didn't bother to move.

He had locked her in when he'd promised not to do that anymore.

He'd done it anyway and disappeared.

Her trust of him was now a little shaky. Her disappointment in him now not shaky at all.

She kept her eyes glued to the TV, not really seeing the program. Not seeing anything as the door opened and Sig stepped into the apartment, closing it behind him. But not locking it.

The tension in her chest loosened a notch.

She kept her gaze straight ahead as he moved through her line of vision to the kitchenette, shrugged out of his cut and hung it over the back of one of the stools at the counter.

"You eat?" he asked in a hoarse voice.

She thought about not answering but didn't want to be rude. Not like he was when he had locked her in and disappeared. "Yes. You?"

He didn't answer. Instead, he came back to the couch where she was. As he sat, the cushions sank with his weight and, with a groan, he bent over and began to unlace his left boot.

That was when she noticed the bandaging on his right hand.

Had she caused that? "I shouldn't have pushed you last night. I'm sorry."

He lifted his wrapped hand for a second like he had to think about it, then went back to slowly unlacing his other boot. "Wasn't you, Red. Was nothin' you'd done. This was on me."

"Like your back?"

"Yeah. Like that."

Once his boots were unlaced, he kicked them off and yanked off his socks, dropping them onto the floor.

Then he simply sat there, staring straight ahead the same as her.

Neither of them said a word for a few stilted minutes.

However, she needed to say something. It was her fault if he'd lost control and hurt himself. "I shouldn't have asked you to touch me when I knew I couldn't let you do more than that."

"Wasn't it, Red. Liked touchin' you. But won't lie, wanted more." He turned his head toward her. "A lot more."

"Me, too," she whispered.

His lips became a slash and his nostrils flared slightly. He nodded. "Yeah. Maybe we'll get there. Maybe we won't."

"I don't want you to suffer. It's best I move in with the Brysons. I've been thinking about it all morning. I'm nothing to you, there's no reason you should be put out because of me. You shouldn't have to take care of me. I'm not your responsibility. And you should be sleeping in your own bed, not forced to sleep on the couch."

"Ain't movin' in with the Brysons, Red, and you ain't puttin' me out. Just get that outta your head."

"You said it was my decision."

"It is."

"Then that's what I want."

"No, it ain't."

She furrowed her brow. "I just said it was."

He leaned back to dig his hand into the front pocket of his jeans, pulled out something metal and held it out to her.

A key.

He was giving her a key. She would never be locked in again.

"You're safer here than there. But don't want you to feel like you have no choice. You already had too much choice taken away from you. Don't wanna be someone who did that to you, too."

"You said it was for my safety."

He nodded. "It is. So, you need to fuckin' promise me

that door," he pointed to it, "is locked at all fuckin' times when you're in here alone. Understood?"

"Yes."

He held out his uninjured hand, the key in the center of his open palm. "Now, you wanna go live with the Brysons for the next coupla months? Or you wanna stay with us?"

She didn't miss the tremor in that hand. She also didn't miss that he was handing her her freedom.

Her freedom of choice.

She reached out and, as she went to pluck the key from his palm, his fingers curled around hers. Using their clasped hands, he tugged her closer and his brown eyes were darker than normal as they held hers. "Want that key?"

Her voice trembled just slightly when she answered, "Yes."

Something moved behind his eyes at her answer. Relief, maybe. With a mix of something else she didn't recognize.

"Thank you," she whispered as he leaned in, his lips just a hairsbreadth from hers.

"Welcome, baby. Now... It all right to kiss you?"

"Yes," she breathed as his lips closed in, brushing lightly over hers.

She opened her mouth, letting him in to explore.

This morning he tasted of only tobacco and not of pot and alcohol.

When he broke the kiss, he released her hand and gripped her cheek, brushing his thumb back and forth over it. "Need to talk."

She dropped her hands into her lap because if it was up to her, they'd spend the rest of the morning kissing and not talking.

"Gonna explain some shit about me. Why I do some of the shit I do. Can't explain everything because it's way too much. Would take weeks to do it, anyway. But I'm gonna give you a bit of me so you can gimme a bit of you. Deal?"

She wasn't sure she liked that deal. "Sig..."

He kissed her again, his tongue sweeping through her mouth, then he said against her lips, "You listen, then you decide, 'kay?"

He twisted on the couch and, settling against one end, put one denim covered leg up and settled his other foot on the floor, then pulled her in between his spread thighs so her back was to his chest and she was nestled tightly between his legs.

She wondered if he did that on purpose so she couldn't see his face when he told the story he was about to tell.

But if that was what he needed, then that was what she'd give him to make it easier. And she didn't mind leaning back on him, the arm with the injured hand across the top of her chest, securing her there, his other arm snaked around the bottom curve of her belly, supporting it.

She let her head drop back to his shoulder and he pressed his cheek against the side of her head and began to talk.

He told her what happened that fatal day when his real father was killed. What it meant to the club, what it meant for two young best friends. What it meant to all of them.

How that day was the beginning of the end of the original Blood Fury MC. How it tore them all apart.

How they all scattered. Trip taken by his mother to Wisconsin. And Sig being left behind with his own mother.

"Didn't know Trip was my brother until a few days later. Not until we landed in West Virginia in some backwoods hole of a trailer park. My mother loved to party when she was Razor's ol' lady, but once both Buck and Razor were dead, she blamed herself and began to drink heavily."

"She pitted two men against each other."

"Basically, yeah. She was a cheatin' whore."

"Sig," she breathed. "She's your mother." She assumed the woman was still alive but he didn't say either way.

"Didn't have a choice to come outta her snatch. Just did and had to live with it."

Good lord, the bitterness he exuded when he talked about his mother was palpable. But she understood it. Her own would never be mother of the year, either. But her mother had been a good one while Autumn grew up, when her father was still alive...

"She was a lyin' whore, Red. No other way to put it. Many a night, she'd tell me stories. Stories I didn't wanna hear. Stories no son should ever fuckin' hear about his mother. But she'd be fuckin' stoned out of her fuckin' gourd and soaked all the way to her bones in booze. She drank vodka like it was water. Began to trade her cunt for a bottle or drugs. Some nights more than one dick would come into our trailer and use her. Had to listen to it all. Even had some sick motherfuckers offer her shit for me..."

Autumn's heart raced as she waited to see if Sig went any further with that, but he didn't.

"Late one night, drunk as fuck, with the cum from three dicks runnin' down the inside of her thighs, she cried and confessed how she'd only ever loved Buck. Said she only pretended to love Razor, who I always thought was my father. She only stayed with him to remain in the fuckin' club, so she could be close to Buck. If she'd lost her ol' lady status, her ass would've been kicked to the curb because there was no way Tammy—Trip's mom and Buck's ol' lady —would've shared her ol' man if she'd known. That salty bitch didn't take shit from no one. Her man was the fuckin' prez and she acted like she was his damn queen. Though, in truth, she held no power. She just thought she did."

She squeezed his thigh as he paused to take a couple of breaths. But this was his story so she tried not to interrupt.

"Another night, Silvia was so fuckin' blitzed she let it slip that Buck was my real daddy and not Razor. That she'd been fuckin' Buck even before Razor claimed her as his ol' lady. She had kept it quiet since she didn't want Tammy to find out. Because again, she woulda had her ass kicked and been tossed from the club, if not killed for sleepin' with Tammy's ol' man. Trip's mother was no fuckin' joke. Neither was Buck. Buck had a fuckin' temper that was unmatched. Never saw anyone who could fuckin' flip a switch in a second flat. He didn't like what you said...?" Sig shook his head. "Seen some bad shit, Red. A lot of bad fuckin' shit. That's why it surprised me Trip came home and wanted to do this shit all over again."

"But not like Buck."

"Fuck no, not like Buck."

On their walks, Stella had talked a lot about the club, past and present. And she was proud how her ol' man—the new president of an old MC—was building something great. Stella said she'd been skeptical at first, but now the woman backed him completely. Supported him one hundred percent.

Autumn had no doubt that Stella loved Trip and was completely loyal to him. It was easy to see it on her face when she talked about him.

Stella said their relationship wasn't perfect and probably never would be. But then, whose was? She had laughed and said, "Whoever says their relationship is perfect is lying."

Autumn had agreed.

"But still," Sig continued, "Trip lived through alotta the same shit I did. Judge, too. A few of us who are old enough to remember. All got scars from some of the shit we've seen and been through. But back then we knew no fuckin' different, all that shit was normal. My point of all this is, got my temper from my sperm donor. So does Trip. Somethin' we both share and struggle with. Thinkin' he fared a lot better 'cause of joinin' the Marines. Think that gave him some discipline and control. More than me, anyway."

"You just need to find the right outlet to focus that anger."

"Yeah, baby, just need to find the right outlet. Got no fuckin' clue what it is."

"Stella said Trip's temper sent him to prison."

"Yeah. His wife was a cheatin' whore like my mother."

"Have you been to prison?" Autumn held her breath as she waited for his answer. Knowing it before he even said it. Stella had warned her, even told her about some of the charges, but Sig had never mentioned what they were and she wanted to hear it from him.

"Ain't gonna lie. Spent more time in than out."

"That makes me sad." And that was what it was. Him being an ex-con didn't make her scared of him, it made her sad for him, instead.

"Point is, know what it's like to live in a small box, Red. Know what it's like to lose your freedom. Know what it's like to have choices taken away from you. Understand it better than you know."

Every muscle on her seized.

"Don't wish what happened to you on anyone. 'Cept for the people who did it to you. They need a taste of what they fuckin' did. No, more than a taste, a great big fuckin' servin'."

"Sig," she whispered, dread bubbling up her throat, beginning to choke her.

"Last night when I disappeared... I went up there."

Her breath caught. "Where?" *Oh God*, she knew where. "Why did you go up there?" She tried to pull away, but he held her fast. Her hands pulled at his arms but he just held on tighter.

"Hear me out, baby."

She yanked at his arms harder. "I can't."

"Yes, you can. You're fuckin' goddamn strong. Look at

you. In only two weeks look how far you've fuckin' come. Anybody else woulda been a quiverin' fuckin' mess. Hidin' in a corner, not lettin' me touch them like I'm touchin' you. They woulda given up. You didn't give the fuck up."

"I did."

"No, baby, you didn't."

"I did give up, Sig. I did. For the longest time, I wanted it all to end. I couldn't take the darkness anymore. The loneliness. The suffering became too much. My mind began to play tricks on me."

"But you did it. You survived. You found a way to escape."

"I survived because they took everything from me. Which meant, I had nothing to kill myself with. No clothes, no blanket, nothing. So I stopped eating. I decided a slow death was better than staying there forever. But they forced me to eat. They forced it down my throat."

"The bruise."

"Yes, she'd kick and hit me to get me to eat and toward the end, I was too weak to fight her off sometimes. So, I'd roll into a ball. Then she'd go get Vernon's son and he'd choke me until I opened my mouth and they shoved the food and water down my throat."

She didn't want to talk about this. Why was she telling him any of this?

"But it was when they began to do that, I knew they wouldn't let me die that way. So, my thinking changed. If they didn't let me escape that madness by dying, then I had no choice but to find another way to get out."

"How'd you do it?"

Autumn closed her eyes. He wanted to know everything. She wasn't sure if she could tell him everything. She told him too much already.

"Don't tell me that yet, then, if you can't. Tell me about

your family. You said you can't go back to 'em. That you got nowhere to go. Why?"

"My mother is my only family left."

"Can't be as bad as mine, Red. And haven't told you everything about her."

She squeezed his forearm. "I don't know if I want to hear anymore. Not now." It hurt her heart to hear about his childhood and that was only a small part of it.

"Then tell me about yours instead."

She pressed her fingertips to her forehead and rubbed it hard, gathering her scattered thoughts. If she started talking about her mother she might not stop. She might end up telling him everything.

She frowned when the truth hit her. "I was wrong."

"'Bout what?"

"About my mother being my only family left. In truth, I don't have any family left. I've got no one."

"Why?" he urged softly, his warm breath tickling her hair against her ear.

Yes, why? Why did any of this happen? How did she end up here in Manning Grove? How did she end up in the situation she was currently in?

How did she end up carrying a baby she did not want by a man she never wanted?

He thought he was asking about her family, her mother. Did he realize that by asking about her mother, it would lead her to what happened with the Shirleys, too?

Did he know there was a connection? Or was he just trying to get her to open up?

"Unlike you, I had a great childhood. My parents were loving. Comfortable financially. Average. I lived a normal life, I guess. Though, everyone's normal is different, right? But..."

"It was good."

"Yes. No complaints. When I was away at college, my

father died from a massive heart attack. It was unexpected since he didn't have any heart issues that we knew of... So, it devastated us. He was the breadwinner in the family and, really, the glue. I went home for the funeral, but afterward I needed to get back to school. My father had been excited when I got accepted into his alma mater and decided to major in accounting. However, after his funeral, my mother begged me not to go back, so I compromised by taking the rest of the semester off to stay with her. But it was important I honor my father by finishing what I started, by following in his footsteps and becoming an accountant like him, so I went back. While accounting isn't the most exciting career, it's solid, would give me a good future and job security. Accountants will always be needed, right?"

"Good with numbers."

"Yes. Well, that next summer break I didn't go home except for Fourth of July and a couple short visits because I had landed an internship in a pretty big firm not far from campus. It was an opportunity I couldn't pass up. But in the meantime, my mother was struggling. She was having a hard time dealing with the loss of my father, who had always been her rock. Add in the fact that I was no longer living at home and it all snowballed. I never wanted to settle in the town I grew up in and told my mother once I graduated and found a good position somewhere she could move closer to me, get rid of the big house and move into something smaller.

"She seemed to like that plan, but failed to mention that her loneliness had driven her to join some online dating site. If I would've known, I would've warned her to be careful."

"She get hurt?"

She frowned. "Not exactly. She met a man who she began a relationship with, then without me knowing, she just up and sold her home in Virginia and moved to Ohio." Autumn had been in shock that her mother hadn't even said a word about this man until she had already moved and they'd been married.

That right there had thrown some red flags. But her mother seemed giddy and content.

"Without tellin' you?"

"Yes. When she told me, I was kind of in shock. I mean, every time I talked to her, she sounded happier and happier on the phone than the previous months, but I just thought she was finally getting out of her funk."

"She was gettin' dick instead."

Autumn shifted in his arms. "Um. Yes. I guess so."

"Dick made her stupid."

"Sig..."

"Pussy makes men stupid, too, Red. Same shit. Keep goin'."

While she didn't know everything about this man, she knew he had no filter. Sig's comments shouldn't surprise her.

"Well, I later find out this guy was a recent widower who had six children of various ages. His wife died while giving birth to number seven. We're talking just a couple of months before he reached out to my mother online." Another red flag. Who lost their wife and child and then was ready to date right away? *Hell*, not even date, marry another woman he hardly knew. Crazy.

"Fuck," Sig muttered.

"Yes, well. He lives in a community which believes the more children you have the closer you get to God. At least, that's what Mom said."

"Your mom's not too old to have kids?"

"She was forty-five when she jmet Aaron. She ended up having one. A boy. She kept that pregnancy a secret from me, too, until she couldn't anymore."

"Fuck."

"Yes, fuck. Anyway, she struggled with not only the pregnancy but the birth, so she's done."

"Thank fuck."

"That's what I said. It's too risky for her to have babies at her age. I was upset when she finally told me she was pregnant. I'm not sure if that's what her new husband's plan was or if he just needed someone to take care of his kids."

"Or both."

Autumn nodded. "Or both."

"You got a brother."

"Half."

"He with them?"

"Yes. Ezrah's maybe two now?"

"When d'you see him last?"

"Right after graduation. She couldn't travel because she just had him."

"Who the fuck was at your graduation?"

"A couple of college friends. That's it. But she begged me to come 'home' to celebrate and check out this tight-knit, self-sufficient community to see if I'd be interested in moving there. She also wanted me to meet my new stepfather and my step-siblings. And her husband's extended family, which was a lot bigger than I expected. Everything on the surface sounded sort of okay and she sounded very happy, but something bugged me about the whole thing."

"Fuck," he muttered. "Soundin' way too familiar."

It should. "Since my internship had ended and I hadn't found a permanent job anywhere yet *and* I wanted to meet my new brother, plus visit with my mom to make sure they both were okay, I went."

"Fuck," he muttered again.

Fuck wasn't strong enough.

"When I got there, what I suspected was confirmed. My mother had fallen into the cult mentality of that community. A community that followed their own rules. Who claimed they were not government sheep, that they only answered to God and their community leaders. No one but their leaders made the rules for their sovereign nation. They were free citizens to do whatever they pleased however they decided to do it. My mother explained their distrust of the government was what made them break off from regular society. And they wanted to be independent as a whole."

"The Guardians of Freedom," Sig growled.

"Yes."

"Jesus fuck," he bit off.

"I didn't really want to leave my mother and baby brother there, so I decided to stick around long enough to try to convince her to leave with me. To try to get her to see things weren't what they seemed." It was a struggle she lost. "Every night at dinner, they'd invite a different man over and introduce me. They were trying to set me up. A couple of them already had wives, but my mother explained that if they held a high position within the community, their reward was to be allowed more than one wife. First off, no way would I marry any of them or live in that community. And, second, they were crazy to think I'd ever marry someone who had more than one wife. After being there a month, I realized convincing my mother was a losing battle. I packed my bags and told her I was leaving the next morning." She pressed her fingertips to her lips and whispered, "I never should have told her."

Sig went solid against her. "She fuckin' snitched."

"She was my mother." Someone she should be able to trust. Someone she trusted her whole life. Someone who was supposed to love her unconditionally. Someone who was supposed to protect her, her own daughter. Her child.

"Fuckin' cunt threw her own fuckin' daughter under the bus."

Autumn swallowed, trying to loosen the tightness in her throat. "I should've left that night. I went to bed not realizing..." Not realizing she was being betrayed. "I should've left."

"What the fuck happened?"

"When I finally woke up..."

"Red..." His arms tightened around her again. He tucked his nose into her hair by her ear. He was taking long inhales as if trying to keep himself together.

She mentally shook herself. "When I finally woke up, I found myself... Are you sure you want to hear this? I can feel you getting tense. I can hear how you're breathing. I can feel your heart racing, too, Sig."

"You can handle tellin' me, I can handle listenin'."

"I don't need you disappearing again and coming back injured because of something that has to do with me." Even though he wouldn't lock her in because she now had a key, she didn't want to be the reason he hurt himself again.

"Baby," he murmured close to her ear. "Asked you to tell me. Gonna keep my shit under control."

"You promise?"

"Promise."

"Promise me," she insisted, squeezing his thigh again.

"Just did."

"I need to hear it again," she echoed the same words he'd said to her when he wanted to be sure she wouldn't run.

With a grunt, he said, "Promise to keep my shit together."

"I need you to help me keep mine together, too." If he concentrated on that, maybe, just maybe, he'd try hard to keep himself together for her.

He swallowed so hard, she could hear it. She reached back and cupped his bearded jaw, which was tight and popping.

"Need you to help me keep mine together, too," she repeated in a whisper. A burn in both her eyes and her nose began, but he was right. She *was* strong. She had to look at everything that happened to her as making her stronger. That she could survive whatever life tossed at her.

She missed her father. She had to call on the strength that man had passed down to her.

She also missed her mother the way she used to be. Her mother had let herself be manipulated, enough so she let her own daughter be put into danger. And worse.

"Just gotta tell me once. Just once, Red. But need to hear it all."

For him to hear it all, she needed to tell it all. She'd told him a lot already, but wasn't sure how much more she could relive.

But maybe if she got it all out now while it was fresh, while the baby was still inside her, then once it was born, she could keep moving forward and never look back again.

Yes, that's what she needed to do.

Purge herself from the past, and look toward her future.

That's what she needed to cling to.

"When I showed no interest in any of their marriage prospects in Ohio, *they* decided to bring me here, hoping I'd change my mind." She frowned. "Why would they think that? What sane person would think you could kidnap someone and they'd just up and decide... 'Oh, yes, I see this would be a great life here. I'd be glad to marry one of your community members, have lots of children and raise them in this fucked up place.'"

She shook her head, wondering if it had ever happened before. If they'd ever kidnapped some woman, she woke up, smiled and married one of those fucked up men, popped out his babies and lived happily ever after. At least the community in Ohio wasn't like the one up on that mountain where most of the Shirleys lived in squalor.

From the outside, the Guardians of Freedom community in Ohio could appear normal. You only discovered it wasn't once you scratched below the surface. You didn't have to scratch at anything to know the Shirley branch of the Guardians of Freedom was not normal. There was no way for them to hide it. Autumn didn't even think they tried.

She took a deep breath and continued, "When I woke up, I had no idea where I was. A day or two later, I was told that I was in Pennsylvania and my 'family' sent me there as a trade. A trade! In exchange, one of their women went to Ohio to marry one of the men I had no interest in. Because I wasn't related to anyone on that mountain and they needed new blood, they considered it a great trade. Until they realized I'd never change my mind and I'd never willingly marry any of the men who 'courted' me in that dark, damn shed!" She blew out a harsh breath trying to keep her blood pressure from spiking.

"That where you woke up?"

"Yes."

"Jesus, Red."

"Since I refused to voluntarily pick a husband, the leader, Vernon, decided he would pick one for me. Funny how it just happened to be one of his younger sons, Tomlin. Vernon figured once I became pregnant, I'd change my mind and never want to leave."

Sig had already been tense behind her but the mention of Tomlin turned his body to stone. "How old was his fuckin' son?"

"I'm not sure, but a lot younger than me. He was awkward, gangly and built like a teenager. Maybe eighteen, which was when the Shirley 'men' were encouraged to find a wife and begin having babies.

"They moved me from the shed and into Tomlin's room at the main house. They," *inhale*, "strapped me to the bed after I fought to keep him from..." She squeezed her eyes shut. "They... he... Two months. Two whole months I spent in that room, in that bed, someone always watching me. After two months... They said if after two months I wasn't pregnant, then I was just a waste of food and resources, especially since I wasn't cooperating. In what damn world would I cooperate with any of that?"

No one in their right mind would.

"Vernon wasn't happy with his son when after those two months I wasn't pregnant and he wanted to see if it was me who was defective or his son. Because if it was me, I was no longer any use to them and they'd done a bad trade. I swear every day I thought I was caught in some nightmare and hoped I'd wake up, because these things didn't really happen in real life. They couldn't. How can they get away with something like they did?"

His voice sounded growly when he answered, "They stay to themselves, Red. That's how. And with your mother involved, no one was lookin' for you."

"I had a few friends in college who promised to keep in touch after graduation."

"The Ohio fuckers keep your cell phone?"

"Yes." Autumn closed her eyes. That was how no one would look for or worry about her. If any of her friends called, her mother could've made excuses.

That was so screwed up.

"Vernon already had three wives since he was the leader. I have no idea how many kids he has. At least a dozen since I heard a lot running around and screaming in that house. It was always noisy. He ordered one of his wives to take care of me. One day when they released me long enough to eat, shower and use the bathroom, I pushed her down. I ran through the house, trying to escape." *Breathe.* "Vernon's son caught me, knocked me out and when I woke up, I was locked in that damn shed again."

Sig jerked against her and his breathing sped up.

"Even after that, their fucked up minds still thought if I had a baby, I'd want to stay. They were so wrong, Sig. So wrong. The youngest wife, Anna, who wasn't much older than Tomlin, got beaten for letting me almost escape, so she *hated* me. And she was the one tasked with my care. She was also jealous of me, worried that if Vernon... if he planted his seed in me, he'd make me his fourth wife."

"Jesus," he growled.

"Eventually, I convinced her that was true. That once the... the... seed came, Vernon was moving me into the house and taking me as his wife since Anna had disappointed him. I told her that her husband came and visited me a lot late at night and we talked when he did. And he promised once the... the seed was here I would replace her since she didn't listen, he said she was stupid and ugly, and because of that he was giving her to his younger son, instead. By no longer being Vernon's wife, she'd lose her power in the clan because Tomlin had no power of his own."

"Did he?"

She blinked, bringing herself back to the apartment. "Did he what?"

"Visit you a lot?"

"No, I had lied about it all. Once Vernon was sure his seed had taken, he stopped... visiting. He never saw how much weight I lost. Never saw she had removed the little bedding I'd been given, never saw that I had no clothes... Never saw the bruises."

Vernon never saw the weight she had lost from her refusing to eat. The bruises from Anna kicking her when she wouldn't. The welts from the whip she'd sometimes use. The marks she got from Tomlin forcing her to eat.

Anna actually wanted Autumn to miscarry but wouldn't go that far and risk the wrath of her husband. If she caused Autumn to lose Vernon's seed, then she could very well be killed by him.

She eventually convinced the youngest wife that if she allowed Autumn to escape, she'd never see her or the baby again. That her position as Vernon's wife would be safe. She even convinced Anna that she should hurry up and get pregnant again to secure that spot.

Luckily, Anna's mental capacity had been limited so she was easy to manipulate. But it took time and patience. And being locked up in that shed, Autumn had the first, just not the last.

Chapter Sixteen

SHE JUST STOPPED TALKING. Like she had nothing left to say. Sig was pretty fucking sure there was a hell of a lot more to tell him.

He worried about pushing her, but he couldn't get that shed and that bench out of his fucking head. "He stopped comin'. How long did it take for him to stop the visits?"

"I don't know. I started losing track of time in the shed. For a while I tried to pay attention to when the sun came up and when the day turned dark, when the shed became pitch black. But there ended up being too many to count. Way too many. But Vernon visited almost every night for weeks, until..."

"Yeah." Until she was knocked up. "Then he stopped completely?"

"Yes. My guess was his three other wives weren't happy about his nightly visits."

So, it had been months since that motherfucker violated Red. But her nightmare didn't end there with those "breedings."

"Anyone else visit?

It took her way too fucking long to answer. "Just Anna and Tomlin."

Either that was a lie or she wasn't sure. But Sig's nostrils flared at that little bastard's name. "Did he..."

"No. He only came when Anna made him force me to eat. Once Vernon took me away from him, he was the only one who was allowed to... touch me."

So, unless she was unconscious during one of those "breedings," there was no doubt whose kid was in Red's belly.

It was that motherfucking clan leader who needed to die.

Tomlin, too.

And that fucking cunt, Anna.

Not to mention, a trip to Ohio might be in order. But right now his parole terms wouldn't let him leave the state. And crossing the border to commit murder might not be really fucking smart right now.

She moved to get up. "I'm going to make you something to eat. I'm sure you haven't eaten since yesterday."

"Red..." He kept her pinned against him. "Ain't done."

"I have nothing else to say."

"Saw where you were kept. Saw that fucking shed. Saw the blood on the door. On the floor. On the wall."

"I was desperate."

"Yeah."

"But Anna left the door open that last morning with the excuse I made up for her. She was supposed to tell Vernon I attacked her when she was bringing me my breakfast and I escaped."

"The mornin' I found you."

"Yes."

"Did she tell you about the booby traps?"

Red twisted in his arms and he loosened his hold so she

could do it. Her hazel eyes were wide and her face paler than normal. "No."

"Not sure what they got rigged through those woods, but word is, they got somethin'. You were fuckin' lucky."

"Maybe she was hoping I'd die escaping."

"Yeah, that would be best for her. 'Cause if you escaped and went to the pigs, those mountain goat fuckers would have a shitload of problems on their hands right now and it would all be 'cause of her bein' a jealous bitch."

Red shook her head. "Never in my life had I lied like I did to her. But I didn't care. I would have told her *anything* to get free."

"You were smart."

"I was desperate." She shifted again to get up and he tightened his hold. "I need to make you something to eat."

She wanted to be done talking about this and, though he didn't blame her, he needed to hear about one more thing. "Red... I saw the bench."

Her body jerked in his arms.

"When I found the shed, found that, too."

A sharp breath hissed out of her and her nails, which weren't as ragged as when he first found her, dug into his arms.

"Not wrong thinkin' that's what they used, right?"

She still said nothing. That right there confirmed it.

"Don't gotta say nothin', just needed you to know I saw it. Went up there 'cause I needed to wrap my head 'round it. What we're dealin' with. You'd told me nothin'. Had to assume too much shit. Not knowin' was eatin' at me."

"It isn't about you." Her voice was thin and it made a sharp pain shoot through his chest.

She was right but she was also very fucking wrong. "Yeah, baby, it is. The second you took my fuckin' hand at the bottom of that mountain and trusted me, it became about me, too."

That morning he couldn't walk away from her even if he'd wanted to. Her desperation had pulled at him, drew him in. And now he was unable to let go.

"I was treated like an animal," she said in a shaky whisper.

"Yeah, baby, I get it. Know how that feels."

She grabbed his right wrist and pulled it away from her, asking, "Is that what set you off?"

"That fuckin' bench finished me off."

"What did you hit?"

"Unfortunately, not one of those motherfuckers. A fuckin' tree."

"Sig," she whispered.

"It'll heal."

"I'm sorry you saw it."

For fuck's sake, she was sorry. "So am I, baby. Not 'cause I didn't wanna know. I did. But 'cause it happened to you. 'Cause they hurt you like that. 'Cause they treated you no better than one of their fuckin' livestock. 'Cause your fuckin' cunt of a mother betrayed you like that."

"I need to face you," she whispered.

He released her and slipped from behind her, off the couch and onto his knees on the floor between hers.

He lifted his face to her. "Sorry for callin' your mother a cunt, but she's a fuckin' cunt."

Red pressed her lips together.

Sig grinned. "My mother's a cunt, too. We got a lot in common."

Her lips pressed tighter but the corner of her eyes wrinkled.

He took a breath. "It's over, baby, you're done with them. They ain't ever touchin' you again. They ain't touchin' this kid. You're good."

"I hope you're right."

"I'm right. Brysons are gonna help with that. Once it's born, you can move on. Forget this shit ever happened."

"I don't think it'll be that easy."

"No, but it'll be *easier*."

"Again, I hope you're right."

"Until then, you're here. You got a key. A place to stay. Protection."

She reached out and brushed a knuckle down his cheek. "And you."

"Yeah, Red. And me." He stared at her lips, which had a slight upward curl to them. "Now... gonna kiss you again, yeah?"

That curl lifted. "Yes."

He leaned in, she leaned down and their lips met in the middle. She tasted so fucking good.

When she opened her mouth, he took it as a sign to take it further and he did, exploring every inch of her until she was gripping his shoulders tight. He wanted to pull her into the bedroom and get so much closer to her, but the tale she told was too fresh and they needed to go slow.

Not once in his fucking life had he ever taken anything slow.

Not fucking once.

For some reason, he didn't mind taking things slow with her. They had two more months before that kid was born.

Two months before she could start fresh somewhere else.

Like he said earlier, maybe they'd go there. Maybe they wouldn't.

Sex with a pregnant woman had never bothered him, but it wasn't up to him. It'd be her choice if and when it ever happened.

Giving her a key was the first step in her trusting him completely. He just needed to make sure to keep his temper in check so the steps they took forward didn't cause them to stumble back.

Just that thorough kiss between them and her digging her fingers into his shoulders made his dick hard.

He needed to end it.

So, he did.

And when he did, he pressed his forehead to the hard curve of her belly and simply breathed to get his pulse under control.

She combed her fingers through the longer hair at the top of his head and he closed his eyes at how good that simple touch felt.

At that attention, a feeling went through him he didn't recognize. It made a warmth start in his gut and expand out. He turned his head until his cheek rested against her baby bump, and he held onto both sides of it.

She didn't want any attachment to this baby for good reason. He didn't blame her one bit. He was the last person to judge anyone else's decisions. But he agreed giving up the baby was for the best.

Too many parents, who shouldn't be, raised fucked up kids. Like his mother.

It was one reason he had smuggled his baby sister out of the trailer one night when their mother was passed out. He gave her away to another family without Silvia knowing.

Because Sig had worried that when Syn was old enough, Silvia would pimp her young daughter out. Or even go as far as selling her outright for cash or booze, or a fucking hit of whatever her drug of the week was.

And if that had happened, Sig would've sliced her fucking throat.

Sig had been taking care of Syn only because no one else was.

He'd been pissed when Silvia had been careless and got knocked up, pissed when she had the baby, pissed when she brought the baby home when he damn well knew Silvia didn't give a fuck about having another kid.

And their mother had no idea who Syn's father was. Worse, the baby was just another monthly check and more food stamps for Silvia, which she traded for more booze. It had been up to Sig to make sure Syn ate and was kept somewhat clean.

Once Syn was gone, Silvia never asked where she was. Not fucking once. As long as those checks kept coming, that was all that mattered to her.

So, he did what was best for Syn. Just like Red was doing what was best for this kid, too.

He slid his hands over the curves of her stomach. "Do you want to know the sex yet?"

"Do you know?"

"I know."

"No, I still don't want to know. Are they happy about it?"

"Think they'd be happy either way. You're givin' them what they've been wantin' for a while now."

"But he's a cop."

Sig huffed out a, "Yeah."

"You don't like cops."

No, he fucking *hated* pigs. But Bryson being a pig might be a good thing in this case. "Not my decision, Red. It's yours and only yours. You gotta live with that decision. I'm good with whatever you decide. Even if you change your mind. Just want you to be safe."

"Keeping it wouldn't be safe."

"No." It would be too risky. Especially now that he knew there were more goat fuckers than just the Shirley Clan involved. That the actual grandmother of that kid was involved with what happened to Red.

Whether that woman knew all the details of what happened to her daughter or not didn't make a difference to Sig. She was still a goddamn cunt.

"Dr. Bryson said they had a big, loving family with grandparents and cousins..."

"Yeah, baby. The kid'll be loved and cared for."

Her fingers stilled in his hair. "I don't know if I could..."

"No one expects you to. Gotta do what's best for you and..." *Fuck*, he almost said *him*. "It. Maybe one day you'll want to meet him or her. Maybe not. Maybe you'll just want pictures and occasional updates to ease your mind. Or maybe you won't. Up to you. Think they'll be good either way. No one's gonna judge you for it."

Even though he got Syn away from his mother, he'd kept in touch with her whenever he could. It wasn't often, especially during his stints in the joint, but he just needed to know she was doing better than Silvia. Better than him. That he had done the right thing for once in his fucking life.

He didn't even know if Silvia ended up having any more kids. He hoped to fuck she didn't. Not long after he got Syn out of there, he left, too. And he never went back.

He lifted his cheek from her belly, then he rose to his feet.

"Now I can eat."

She held out her hand for him to help her from the couch and he shook his head. "I got it. Whatcha in the mood for?"

"Those loaded French fries Judge had brought me that night."

He grinned. "Yeah, they're fuckin' addictin', right?"

"Yes, but you don't have to go."

"No. You want fuckin' loaded fries from Dino's? Gettin' loaded fries from Dino's."

What Red wanted, Red got.

She held out her hand again. "Can I go with you?"

He hesitated. "Not sure that's a good idea." It was bad enough when he had to take her to her weekly doctor's appointment. He always worried she'd be spotted.

"I'll stay in the car, but it would be nice to get out of the apartment for a little bit."

"Maybe Stel will let me borrow the Jeep."

Her hazel eyes lit up, as did her face. "Yes! A ride and loaded French fries!"

"Whatever you want, baby."

Whatever she wanted. At least for the next two months.

—————

Autumn sat low in the passenger seat with the Jeep's doors locked, a baseball cap pulled low on her head and an oversized pair of sunglasses covering her eyes. She kept those eyes focused on the entrance to Dino's Diner, waiting for Sig to return with the huge order of food he had called in.

Because she was so focused on that front door, she jumped and squealed when a loud tap came from the passenger side window.

She swallowed her pounding heart from her throat back into her chest and turned her head to see a man standing right outside her door. He made a *wind-down-the-window* motion with his hand.

She frowned.

The man, who was tall and slender and had the most beautiful high cheek bones, squinted at her for a second, then his mouth formed an *O*. "Oh, sorry! Thought you were Stella and maybe that gorilla of hers was inside Dino's."

This man knew Stella and Trip. That meant he wasn't a Shirley. Since Sig had left the old Cherokee running, she powered down the window.

His high-pitched squeal and him reaching through the window to snag the cap off her head made her want to roll the window right back up.

As he tossed the hat to the floorboard and dug his fingers into her hair, he gushed, "Oh... my... God! Look at that color. And that is one hundred percent natural! You know how I know that?"

Autumn just stared at him as he fluffed her hair around her face.

"Oh my God, this needs some work and I know the perfect fella for that. You know who?" His question ended on a higher pitch than it should.

When she didn't answer, he yelled, "Me! I am such a lucky, lucky boy to get to do something with that fiery mane. You know why?"

Autumn blinked.

"Because you are my newest customer and you're lucky, too. All my new customers get their first cut for free!" He squealed the word "free," released her hair, leaving his right hand jutted towards her. "I'm Teddy and you must be new in town. I am *the* proprietor and head hottie of Manes on Main." He curved his left hand around the side of his mouth, leaned in and whispered, "That's on Main Street right here in town, so it's easy to find."

Autumn took his extended hand and before she could shake it, he gasped and yanked her hand out of the window, inspecting it with a look of horror. "What the hell happened to your nails? Oh... Em... Gee... This is not right, not right at all. A pretty sprite like you shouldn't have nails like this. I'm going to fix you right up."

"I—"

"Yep. You just tell me how soon you can sit your little fanny in my chair and I'll pencil you in. Again, first one's on the house."

"I—"

"What's your name?"

She blinked again. Not sure how she should answer that. "Uh... Red."

Teddy frowned. "Red? Red is the color of your beautiful, but badly damaged, locks." He again curved a hand around the side of his mouth and loudly whispered, "But we'll have those tresses shiny and those broken ends trimmed up in no time." He released the hand he'd been inspecting, slapped his hands on his narrow hips and tilted his head. "But Red is *not* a name for a pretty girl like you." He stepped closer to the door, glanced down, and frowned. "Wait... *Ooooh*, a baby. You're having a baby. No wonder your hair is dull and damaged. Those little monsters will suck the life right out of you, won't they? Like leeches. It took a while for my bestie's hair to come back to its glorious splendor after she popped those kids out. But I'll get you fixed right up."

"I can't—"

"No." He lifted a palm. "The word *can* is a part of *can't*. You *can*."

"I can't go to your salon," she said quickly before he interrupted her again. "But I thank you for the generous offer."

His head tilted sharply. "Why ever not?"

"Because... I... My doctor doesn't want me to be out and about too much."

His eye narrowed. "Your vagina doctor?"

Autumn's eyebrows shot up her forehead. "Uh... Yes... My OB/GYN. I need to stay home and rest," she lied, though it was somewhat true. Dr. Bryson didn't want her doing too much since the pregnancy was still high-risk because of the baby's underdevelopment.

"Your vagina doctor wouldn't happen to be Dr. Carly Bryson would it?"

"Y-yes."

Teddy squealed and bounced on his toes. "Well, I'll ask her if it's okay if I can come to you instead. I'm sure she'll be fine with it. She's practically my sister-in-law."

"She is?"

Teddy waved a hand round. "Yes. Close enough. It's

complicated. Just give me your address and a time and I'll be there."

"I don't think that's a good idea."

"Honey, doing a woman's hair and nails is *always* a good idea."

Not in her case. She doubted Sig wanted a stranger coming to his apartment. Or knowing the address where she was staying.

Though, this man knew Stella and also was related somehow to Carly Bryson. And it would be nice to feel a little more human by getting her hair trimmed and her nails done. Oh, even her toenails which she could no longer reach very well.

"I don't have any money."

Teddy leaned into the window and gave her a great big smile. "You don't need a dime. I can bring my stuff with me and we can get you fixed up lickety-split!"

"I... I would love that."

His smile got brighter.

She saw movement heading toward the Jeep. "But I would need to ask him."

"Him?" Teddy appeared confused and then looked in the same direction as Autumn was. "*Oooooh.* Him. Yes. Another handsome gorilla."

The man actually licked his lips as they both watched Sig, his expression holding all kinds of unhappy, walking quickly to the SUV.

"What the fuck?" was the first thing out of his mouth.

"Hi there, handsome!" Teddy greeted, fluttering his eyelashes at him. "*Ooo.* I could do your hair, too." He rushed over to Sig and when he reached up to touch his hair, Sig snagged his wrist and held it tight. "Ow. You're a strong one."

"Don't fuckin' touch me."

Teddy nodded and, as soon as Sig released him, he stepped back. "Not secure in your manhood?"

"Plenty secure. Just don't need you touchin' me." His dark eyes slid to Autumn and he moved to open the rear passenger-side door of the Jeep and put the bags of takeout inside. He slammed the door shut and spun on Teddy. "What's goin' on here?"

"I just offered to do her hair and nails, that's all."

"No."

Teddy ignored his answer and spoke quicker. "She said Carly doesn't want her out and about so I offered to come to her place."

"Her place is my place and that's a no."

Teddy frowned. "Don't be a jealous gorilla. I'm gay, if you haven't noticed. I just want to do her hair, not her."

"Hard to miss it."

Teddy smiled and wiggled his ass. "Oh, so you noticed." He winked at Sig who scowled.

"Why's your hat off?" Sig asked her.

"It fell onto the floor and I can't reach it." She had a hard time bending over now, especially in a tight spot like in the car.

"How'd it fall off?"

Her and Teddy's eyes met. His were much wider than hers. "I... knocked it off accidentally."

"So, *aaaaaanywaaaay*," Teddy started, "I'm coming out to your place and fixing her all up. She looks like she's been living in the woods like a wild child."

Sig stared at Teddy for a moment, then at Autumn. "That what you want?"

She gave him a little smile.

He frowned and faced Teddy. "You do Stella's?"

Teddy's face lit up. "Yes! She comes in regularly."

Sig pursed his lips. "How much is it gonna set me back?"

The hairdresser bounced on his toes. "Nothing. It's on the house!"

"When?"

"Whenever you want! Tomorrow?"

Sig turned to Autumn. "You sure?"

She smiled wider and nodded.

"Whatever you want, baby," Sig grumbled, not looking happy about it at all.

Teddy squealed and clapped his hands together. "Oh, it's a date! And I don't need the address, I know where all you leather-clad, motorcycle-riding gorillas live out on that farm." He dug out his wallet and pulled out a business card, handing it to Autumn. "I'll be out tomorrow around five after my other appointments." He clapped his hands in excitement again. "*Ooo*, I can't wait to get my hands on that mane. He won't be able to keep his hands off of you afterward. But by that big tummy of yours, seems like he already knows how to get the job done." Teddy gave her an exaggerated wink and an eyebrow wiggle.

A rattling behind the Jeep caught their attention, and Sig's eyes narrowed, then he muttered a, "Fuck."

Teddy saw what he was looking at and waved a hand around again. "Oh, those whack-a-doodles drive the shittiest cars and only come off that mountain once in a while. My fiancé hates dealing with them!" He shuddered.

Autumn's heart began a slow thump in her chest and she turned her head just in time to see a rusty Buick sedan creeping by behind them. She couldn't turn far enough but what she could see... *who* she could see behind the wheel looked like Vernon and in the passenger seat was Tomlin. And they were looking right at her.

"Sig," escaped her on a hitched breath.

"Fuckin' son of a bitch."

"Oh, don't worry," Teddy said, unaware of the problem. "They don't stick around town very long."

"We gotta go," Sig said quickly, rounding the Jeep and climbing into the vehicle without him even taking the time to turn his cut inside out. Something he always did when she'd been in the SUV with him going to the doctor.

He had explained anytime an MC member got into a cage, which is what he called a car, he turned it inside out because he was part of an MC and "an MC wasn't a car club." It was a sign of respect for the club's colors.

Sig took that seriously, so for him to jump in without removing his cut or flipping it inside out scared her even more.

"Tomorrow!" Teddy called, giving them a finger wave even though he now wore a worried look on his face.

Sig shoved the Jeep into reverse with his bandaged hand and jabbed the gas, making her head jerk back. He jammed it into first gear and hit the accelerator so hard the engine screamed as he raced out of the diner's lot and headed the opposite direction from where the Shirleys went.

"Fuck, fuck, fuck!" he shouted, his eyes bouncing back and forth between the windshield and the rearview mirror.

Autumn couldn't help mask the shake in her voice when she asked, "Do you think they saw me?"

"Yeah, they fuckin' saw you! Never shoulda taken that fuckin' hat off!" He was pissed.

"S-sorry."

His jaw got tight and his lips became an angry slash. "Told you to keep that fuckin' thing on."

"It fell."

"Yeah, baby, you said that."

"I couldn't reach it."

"Yeah, you said that, too. Only hope they have no fuckin' clue who I am and where we live. But if they saw my cut, they might."

He raced down some side streets in town, taking corners faster than he should. Then he turned onto County Line

Road. She had no idea what road the farm was on. She never asked and also never paid attention.

"Are they following us?" She couldn't get a good look in the passenger side mirror.

His eyes flipped up to the rearview mirror one more time. "No. Don't see those fuckin' assholes." A muscle in his jaw jumped. "Shoulda left you back at the farm."

"Now they know I'm still in the area."

"Yeah, baby, they know you're still in the area," he echoed flatly.

"I should leave..."

"Gonna get you back to where you're safe. That's all. We'll be good. It'll be good."

"Sig..."

He shoved the shifter into another gear, then reached over and snagged her hand, giving it a squeeze. "We got it covered, Red. We're gonna handle it. And once that kid's born, shit will be okay."

"But I have two more months to go!"

"We fuckin' got this. It'll be fine. Gonna make a plan."

"Who?"

"The club."

"To do what?"

"To handle shit."

"To handle the Shirleys?" Her voice went almost as high as Teddy's.

"Yeah, Red, just to make sure they don't ever touch you again."

"They only want the baby."

"Brysons will cover that."

"I mean before it's born."

"And *we'll* cover that." He pulled her hand over to his lap and pressed it against his thigh. "Baby, we got it. You'll be good."

She hoped he was right.
Because right now, she wasn't feeling so certain about it.

Chapter Seventeen

SHE ASKED. And whatever Red asked for, for some reason, Sig had a hard time saying no.

Maybe it was those big hazel eyes, maybe it was that girl-next-door face, maybe it was her situation, maybe it was the fiery attitude which became stronger every day, or maybe it was just everything about her.

So, when she wanted him to sleep in his own bed, when she wanted him sleeping next to her, he didn't say no.

He wanted to be there, anyway.

Most nights, when she wasn't too uncomfortable, she asked him to hold her.

He did.

And doing that made him question his sanity too many fucking times.

When the fuck had he ever wanted to sleep with a woman without fucking her? He asked himself that countless times. And the answer was always the same...

Never.

And the answer was still never since he wanted nothing more than to fuck Red, too.

Even though sleeping with her helped get him decent *zzz's* some nights, other nights, it put him on edge.

And that edge had been made sharper ever since the Shirleys took that slow drive past Stella's Jeep with Red's hair exposed like a red fucking beacon a month ago.

They needed to go up that mountain and deal with those motherfuckers and do it soon.

Judge and Trip both argued it was stupid to go up there since the clan was as heavily armed as any militia. They also had those woods booby-trapped and it was better to wait for Vernon to come off that mountain, snag his ass and get him to mysteriously disappear.

How, Sig didn't care, as long as he did. And hopefully that "disappearance" wasn't quick and easy.

But in reality, he knew that wouldn't happen until Deke finished closing on the pet crematorium so they had a clean way of disposing of any evidence. It was the plan they had put in place and the one Trip wanted them to stick to.

Sig was not happy with it but, as antsy as he was, he also knew better than to go back up that mountain alone. He wanted his revenge to be successful and to make sure it was, he needed his brothers at his back.

He'd feel better going in with an army than going into battle as a lone soldier.

He fucking hated it, but he waited.

Judge and Deacon were keeping an eye out and an ear close to the ground. His other brothers were, too, when they were out and about around town. Stella and Dodge listened for any gossip about the clan at Crazy Pete's.

Sig also took slow drives down Copperhead Road whenever he was out for a repo. And whenever he took his sled out and opened it up on the back roads just to try to blow off some steam.

But it was like they had hunkered down and were keeping low, just like Sig had Red doing.

Now, the only time she left the property was to go to her weekly doctor appointments.

Even that flaming hairdresser had stopped by twice to do Red's hair, give her a facial and do her fingernails and toes.

Red had asked if she could borrow some money with the promise to pay it back to give the gay guy. But Teddy refused the cash since Carly confided in him about her adopting Red's baby.

Sig wasn't happy about that info getting shared and said something to the doc at their next appointment. She insisted she'd sworn Teddy to secrecy and told him nothing was set in concrete until the baby was born and Red decided to put Carly and Matt Bryson on the birth certificate.

Even so, Sig had a hard time ignoring the man's over-the-top excitement about becoming the baby's "uncle," so, *of course*, Teddy didn't charge Sig a dime for all the shit he did for Red.

How that man was going to be the kid's "uncle," Sig didn't know or care. But what he did care about was the man's fiancé was another of those Bryson pigs. He swore the Brysons were a clan of their own.

However, Sig did make it known during that first visit Teddy was not to run his mouth about Red at all. And warned him, if he got loose lips, he'd regret it. Teddy had pinned his mouth closed, twisted his fingers in front of his lips like he was locking them and then tossed the invisible key over his shoulder.

Whatever.

As long as Red was happy and safe, that was all Sig fucking cared about.

In another effort to keep Red safe, whenever she and Stella went for a walk, they did not go far and at least two brothers, who were packing, were with them.

Also, not long after the Dino's Diner incident, a new

prospect had shown up named Easy. Since he was currently the lowest piece of dog shit in the club, Trip had him sit at the end of the lane by the road, stopping anyone from entering unless he got the okay from one of the more senior patched members.

But this waiting to deal with the Shirleys was bullshit.

Sig wanted to do shit now. Not later.

Red still had a month to go before she popped.

Sig was ready to pop now.

His temper had been simmering for the last month, since the day Red was outed to the Shirleys, and he had no fucking way to relieve it.

He didn't feel right about going downstairs, using a sweet butt to get off—and more, depending on her limits—and then climbing into bed with Red.

She didn't deserve that kind of filth. She'd had enough of it with what she had to deal with while on that mountain.

So, he suffered instead.

He suffered with his temper, he suffered with sleeping next to Red and he suffered with the hard-ons she gave him even though she didn't mean to.

She was now huge compared to what she was when he found her.

Because of that, her awkwardness was much worse. She waddled around the apartment like a fucking penguin, her hands always holding onto her belly as if she was afraid it would just drop to the ground.

And then she'd wince when either the kid kicked the shit out of her insides or when she had back spasms and stomach cramps, which the doc called Toni Braxtons or some such shit.

The doc said it was her body preparing to spit out that kid. Why they were named after some singer he had no fucking clue. Even so, Red said she couldn't wait. And though Sig kept it to himself, he couldn't wait, either.

Not that he wanted Red to leave, which would happen once she pushed the kid out, but because she looked completely uncomfortable. Miserable even.

However, the doc also said she and the kid were looking a lot healthier and hoped for a birth without too many complications.

In Sig's opinion, one complication was too many. Not that anyone asked him.

His eyes slid to the bedroom door as her belly entered the room before she did.

Fuck, it looked as though she'd swallowed a fucking basketball. Or a large pumpkin with a stem because her belly button was totally pushed out and visible against the maternity nightie that she now had no choice to wear since she no longer could squeeze into his shirts.

She'd tried. And she'd split one.

One night he caught her sitting on the bed in just her "boy shorts," what she called those panties she wore, crying about it with the ruined tee clutched in her hands.

"It's an old T-shirt, Red, nothing to fuckin' cry about."

She'd lifted her tear streaked face up to him and wailed, "I *knooooow*. But it's *your* T-shirt."

"Jesus fuck," he had muttered under his breath. She fucking cried about everything. A stupid commercial, her toast being too dark, the fact that he had to leave to actually do some repo jobs so he could buy her fucking groceries—since she now ate non-stop—and, worse, she cried over nothing.

She just cried.

It had been cute at first. Now it wasn't.

He worried about her sanity more than ever.

But that day she sat on the edge of the bed naked, except for those light blue boy shorts, had got him right in the fucking chest.

Why he had a thing for pregnant women, he had no fuckin' clue.

Or maybe it was just Red.

Her tits had gotten heavier, her nipples bigger and darker, her belly had blown up and her face had rounded out a little. Her hips had widened and her thighs had thickened. But fuck, when she sat there crying over his fucking ripped shirt, all he wanted to do was fuck her until she stopped crying.

He didn't.

Instead, he'd taken a fucking shower, whacked off and watched as his cum circled the drain and disappeared.

And when he opened his eyes, he'd noticed she was in the bathroom peeing, and watching him.

"It's only natural," she announced, wiped, washed her hands and waddled back out of the room.

She was whacked.

And, *for fuck's sake*, her being that whacked made him want her even more.

Fuck.

Fuck.

Fuck.

He was afraid he would start spinning out of control the day she left and never stop until something or someone had to force him to.

But for now, she had a month to go and had taken one of her countless trips to the bathroom and was headed back to the bed to climb back in with him.

And he was in no rush to get out of bed this morning, not when she was in it with him.

With cute little grunts and groans—which he was sure she didn't think were so cute—she got back into bed, rolled to her side, facing away from him, then backed her ass, which was also a lot fuller now, right into his hard-on.

"Oh," she squeaked.

"Yeah, shoulda known that might be an issue." Because it wasn't anything new with them sleeping together.

She giggled but didn't pull away.

"Probably be best to give it some space, Red."

"I'm okay."

"Yeah, well... It ain't always about you."

She giggled again which *again* shook her ass against his dick. That did not help.

It wouldn't take much for him to pull those boy shorts she now wore everyday down her thighs and slide deep inside her.

But he wasn't sure if she was ready for that mentally, and physically, he wasn't sure if that was allowed this late in the pregnancy. It wasn't anything they'd asked the doctor because Sig didn't think it would happen anyway.

They touched. They kissed. Sig disappeared and fucking whacked off elsewhere.

With another little grunt she reached behind her, grabbed his arm and drew it around her. Then she released a contented sigh like she always did when she wanted him to hold her.

She had no idea how much fucking willpower it took to just do simply that: hold her and not take it any further.

But it wasn't as bad as the times she explored his body with her touch or she encouraged him to explore hers. Those days almost fucking killed him.

He felt like he had a constant hard-on. His dick hated his guts and his nuts wanted to split up with him.

He never jerked off so much in his goddamn life. And it wasn't just that one time she'd caught him in the shower. He was doing it so fucking often, she didn't even blink an eye anymore when she saw him.

She never acted disgusted, never was embarrassed, she just acted like it was nothing out of the ordinary. Since she seemed to be okay with it, he stopped worrying about her catching him.

It was almost to the point where he hoped she did. Having her watch turned him the fuck on and he was hoping it turned her on a little bit, too.

He shifted his hips back and away from her soft ass, grumbling, "Gonna go shower."

She tightened her grip on his arm, holding it more securely across her body. "It's only four-thirty."

"Yeah."

"You have somewhere to go this early?"

"Nope, just the shower."

She wiggled back again, shoving her ass tightly against his dick.

"Red, baby," he warned.

"It's okay."

He lifted his head slightly but couldn't see her face because her back was to him. "What's okay?"

"You being hard."

"Okay for you, not okay for me. My dick hates me right now."

She laughed softly. "I'm sorry."

"No the fuck you're not 'cause you're fuckin' laughin'."

She smothered another little laugh, but ground her ass cheeks into his aching dick.

"Red... fuck. You're killin' me here."

She grabbed his hand and slid it to her tit.

"Red," he breathed.

What the fuck was she doing?

"Red," he said again, a lot more firmly this time as she squeezed his hand over her tit, which made him squeeze it.

"Touch me."

"Baby, a man can only take so much."

"A woman can only take so much, too."

"You want me to touch you there?"

"Not just touch."

"Red..."

"Sig... I trust you. I want you. I want this."

"What's 'this?'" Because if it was just a bunch of touching again where he ended up more frustrated and horny than anything, he wasn't in the mood for that this morning. He was already at a breaking point. If she kept grinding her ass against him, he wasn't going to make it to the fucking shower, he was going to blow his load in the boxers he forced himself to wear.

He pressed his face into her hair and squeezed his eyes shut. "Red," he whispered, "Seriously, you're playin' with fire right now."

"I'm over eight months pregnant."

No shit. "Hard to miss."

"And you're still getting hard."

"That's hard to miss, too."

"You want me..."

"Ain't hidden that fact."

"Like this."

"Yeah, baby. You're still you."

Her fingers tightened on his hand she held against her tit. He hadn't moved it at all, afraid if he gave in to temptation and began to play with them, he might take it farther than she was ready to.

"You sneak one of my joints when you went to pee or somethin'?"

She chuckled. "No. But the truth is, I never expected to be horny when I'm this big."

"You're horny." He'd kept his voice level, though it was difficult.

"Yes! I wanted to wait until after the... baby is born to have sex with you, but I don't think I can wait."

Sig lifted his head again, then shifted his weight so he could get a better look at her face. "Look at me."

She turned her head enough so they could see each other.

"You were plannin' on havin' sex with me after the kid was born?"

"Well, as soon as it was okay to have it."

"You wanna have sex with me."

"Yes. You couldn't tell?"

"How long after the kid's born can we have sex?"

"I don't know... I didn't ask Carly. But I don't want to wait."

"Hold up."

"Sig..."

"Red, you want to have sex with me now?"

"Yes. I pulled it up on the tablet you got me and read that it's okay to have sex up to the day of delivery."

Sig's lips twisted. "So, you got dick going in while the kid's comin' out?"

She laughed. "Not *during* delivery. Yikes. That would be unpleasant."

"Yeah. For everyone involved."

"So, it should be safe."

"You ask the doc?"

"I asked her, yes."

"When?"

"I texted her to make sure."

"You texted the doc to make sure it was okay for you to have sex with me." Was he awake? Or in some sort of fucking whacked-out dream? Because they both were still having those.

"Yes. She just said that it shouldn't be missionary or any position where there's pressure on the baby. Doggy-style and on my side would be fine."

Doggy-style and on my side would be fine.

"Jesus fuck," he muttered.

"If you don't want to..."

"Red, you seriously want this? I mean... I... *Fuck.*"

"You don't want to," she said, sounding disappointed.

He hated to disappoint her so he usually made sure she got whatever she wanted. But this wasn't like pancakes or loaded French fries. Or even a subscription to Netflix.

"Baby, want you so bad, you have no fuckin' idea. I can come up with plenty of positions that aren't gonna put pressure on your stomach. But are you *ready?*" Her wanting to have sex with him scared the shit out of him. He'd never been careful having sex before because he never had to.

He took what he wanted, how he wanted it and never worried about the bitch attached to the snatch. He'd always told them they were just getting his dick and usually some extra shit, whatever he was in the mood for.

He'd never asked a woman what the fuck she wanted because he'd never given a fuck before.

"I'm not going to let them control or destroy the rest of my life."

And that was fucking great, but... "Baby..."

"And by you not trusting my judgement, then you're letting them do that."

Damn. There was that fiery attitude that turned him the fuck on. "No, just wanna make sure. It's a big fuckin' step. Not just for you but for us."

One of her eyebrows rose sharply. "Oh, that's what you tell all the women beforehand who you have sex with? How many times do you ask them if they're sure? How many times do you tell them sex with them is a big step for you and her?"

Fuck. "Never."

"Right."

"But they..."

"Yes. I get it. Now can we not talk about that? In fact, I'd prefer not to talk at all and do other things instead. If you're worried, we'll go slow. If anything bothers me, I'll let you know."

"Not sure I can just shut shit down like that, Red. That's my fuckin' worry."

"I've been here for a month and a half. Not once, Sig... *Not once* have you done anything to me I haven't wanted. When we needed to stop, you stopped. Not once have I worried that you'd totally lose control and take it too far."

"I've lost control," he reminded her.

"Not with me."

She was right. He'd never once pushed her farther than she'd wanted to go or could handle. Not once.

He never treated any woman like he had her. Not fucking one.

But then he had never been given a reason to.

There had been only one reason for him to deal with a woman. Okay, two. One had been just to bust a nut, the other was to relieve his mounting temper.

Red had never been either of those.

She still wasn't. And never would be.

"Gonna take it really slow," he warned, more to himself than her.

"Not too slowly." She squeezed the hand that was cupping her tit again, then released it and he left it there. "My nipples are really sensitive right now."

He hesitated.

"I didn't tell you that so you'd stop."

He grinned and began to knead her tit and brush his fingers over her hard nipple through the fabric.

"Help me take this off," she said breathlessly, tugging at the loose nightie.

He helped her to a seat, yanked it over her head and tossed it to the floor.

She tucked her fingers into the top of her boy shorts. "These next and your boxers."

"Red..."

"Just do it."

He raised his brows but slowly helped peel her out of her panties and shucked his boxers, throwing them somewhere behind him.

"We gonna need a wrap?"

"A wrap?"

"Yeah, are we gonna..."

"A wrap... Oh... I hope so. So, yes?"

He didn't quite like the question mark on the end of that, but his dick twitched at that news, anyway. He scrambled to his knees, leaned over her and reached for the nightstand drawer on her side of the bed. When he did, he jerked when she grabbed his hard as fuck dick and began to stroke it.

"Red... might not wanna do that."

"Why?"

"Just... not now." Because her touching it right now was like pulling a pin on a grenade.

She released him. "I've been jealous of your fist."

"Yeah?"

"Yes," she whispered. "I've been wanting to touch you there for a while now."

"Wouldn't have stopped you."

"I know. But I know how hard," she released a soft snort, "it is for you to be left hanging."

He ripped the drawer open, grabbed a strip of wraps and moved back beside her.

He now had a string of precum hanging from the tip of his dick. Anticipation was a goddamn heady motherfucker.

And this had been a long time coming. That meant it wouldn't take him long to come. A wrap would help keep him from blowing his load in less than thirty seconds. Hopefully.

"Touch me," she moaned when he pressed himself

against her again, so he was behind her, both of them on their sides.

What Red wanted, Red got.

"Tell me if I get too rough, baby. If somethin's wrong, if you need to pause, stop, whatever, just say the word."

"This time I want you to touch me all over and then... have sex with me. If this goes well... next time I want to touch you all over and then have sex with you."

"Fuck, baby. While that sounds like a plan I can get the fuck on board with, let's just get through this time first and see how you feel."

What happened on that mountain could screw with her head, and even if it didn't, he wasn't sure how comfortable sex would be for her being that pregnant.

But they were both fucking naked, he was hard as a fucking rock, and she was asking for him to touch her.

So, he touched her. Everywhere. Starting with her face, her lips, moving down her throat and then stopping at her tits, a place he hadn't touched her before. All those nights, all those mornings they touched each other, he'd avoided them, waiting for her to give the go ahead. Now he had it.

He squeezed and kneaded, her hand wrapping around his to encourage him to continue. He brushed his thumb over the tight tips and twisted each one gently.

Her breathing became hitched, as did his. Since her head was laying on his extended right arm, he only had his left hand free. But he made good use of it. At least, according to Red's little moans and sighs. He stayed there awhile, showering her now heavy tits with all of the atten-tion, listening to her whimpers and words of encour-agement.

Burrowing his face into her hair, he swept his palm over the tight skin of her belly and lower, where he paused. "Red..."

"Please."

He closed his eyes for a second, inhaled deeply and then he touched her tentatively there. And though he couldn't see that fiery patch of hair, his fingers brushed through it, almost afraid to go any lower.

"Red." Her name got caught in his throat. He did not want this to go wrong. He did not. Not their first time together.

They should wait.

He could fucking wait. He'd already waited. There was no reason to rush it. Though, his dick disagreed.

As he pulled his hand away, she grabbed it and stopped him, putting it back where it had been. "Please," she said more firmly. "I know you're scared, I'm scared, too. But we can't let fear stop us, Sig. I can't. I trust you."

I trust you.

No one had ever fucking said that to him in his life. Not one fucking person. Only her. And this wasn't the first time she'd said it and he hoped to fuck it wouldn't be the last.

"Show me where you want me."

She pushed his hand lower, then singled out his middle finger, pressing it to her clit. "Just in case you're one of those who has trouble finding it."

He smothered his laugh in her hair. But that laugh quickly disappeared as she circled it, her hips tipping a little as she showed him what she wanted.

What Red wanted, Red got.

"Got it from here, baby."

She released his hand and reached behind them to cup the back of his head. "I want to kiss you."

"We can do that later." He had never appreciated kissing until Red. All those nights and all those mornings of kissing showed him just how fucking hot it could be. Just tongues and touches.

"Promise?"

"Whatever you want, Red."

"I don't know when was the last time I had an orgasm. Can you give me that?"

"I'll do my fuckin' best."

Her fingernails dug into his skull as he slipped two fingers through her slick folds, stroking her, making sure she didn't tense up. She didn't.

He unburied his face from her hair and pressed his cheek to hers, watching her body's reactions. She moaned and grabbed her own tits, squeezing them until he noticed a little liquid bead at the tips.

He was dying to lick them off for her. He didn't. That could wait, too. He didn't want to do anything out of the ordinary this morning. Not this time, not until they saw how she handled it.

If she enjoyed it and wanted more, he'd give her whatever she wanted and take what he needed.

He slowly slipped those two fingers inside her and he froze when she clamped around his fingers.

"Yes," she breathed. "Please..."

He relaxed and started slowly by fucking her with his fingers, whispering in her ear how hot she was, how wet. How he wanted to feel her come.

When he added his thumb to her clit, she cried out, her body arching slightly. And she got even wetter.

He wanted to suck her tits, eat her pussy, and come deep inside her without a wrap.

Instead, he closed his eyes and did what she wanted when she encouraged him to go faster.

And then she was coming, pulsating around his fingers, crying out his name, her nails from her left hand digging into his skull, the nails from her right hand digging into the soft flesh of her own tit and leaving little half-moons.

And, *fuck*, that was hot.

He slowed the pace of his hand until every last ripple was gone, then slid them out of her and right into his mouth, tasting her for the first time. "Fuck, want you to ride my face."

She sounded breathless when she said, "I'm not sure if—"

"Not now. Later." After the kid was born. When she wasn't so awkward. When he could eat her out, then throw her to the bed and fuck her hard, while she was on her belly, on her back, on her knees. When that pussy was all his to do with what he wanted. When that ass was, too.

When he wasn't worried about her having a possible setback, when he wasn't worried about her pregnancy. When it was just him and Red.

However long it took for all of that to happen.

"I want to come again. I missed... I forgot..." She took a big inhale and simply finished with, "I want you."

"Want you, too, baby." He grabbed the wraps, ripped one off the strip and then tore it open with his teeth before rolling it over his throbbing dick. "You sure?" This was her last chance to say no before he made her his.

"Yes."

"Tip your ass, baby... that's it, like that."

He slid the latex-covered head of his dick back and forth through her slick folds. He was so close to having her. So fucking close. "Don't know how long I've wanted this."

"I do, actually. I just wanted to make sure I wanted it as much as you."

"And you do?"

"I do."

She did. *Damn.* "Don't give a fuck who I am?"

"I said 'it,' not you. And I know who you are, Sig."

No, she didn't. She only thought she did. "Don't know everything." This was his last warning to her before he went further.

"I know enough."

"Hope you're not wrong." He hoped to fuck she wasn't wrong.

"I've been wrong a lot."

That made him almost smile. Not a lot of people admitted when they're wrong. "Yeah, baby, me too."

"But even so, I'll risk it."

He wasn't sure if she was trying to be funny, but funny or not, he was taking her at her word.

"Need me to stop, you say it." *But for fuck's sake, please don't say it. Let me have this. Let me have you. Let me show you I can be better. For you.* "All you gotta do is say it, Red."

"I want you."

He'd heard those words from plenty of other women through the years but they'd never had the same meaning as when Red just said them.

He slid his dick through her folds again until he found that spot. "Want you, too, baby." He pushed his hips forward and took her slowly, giving her plenty of time to change her mind.

Automatically, his eyes closed as her warm, slick sheath surrounded him, squeezed him and once he couldn't slide any deeper, he stilled. He could barely ask, "'Kay?"

"God, that feels good. I've missed this... This type of intimate connection between two people."

He didn't miss it because he never had it. Sex had always been sex for him, nothing more.

"Glad I can give it to you. Gonna move now."

"It's okay, Sig, I don't need a warning for everything you're about to do. Just do what you know how to do."

That was the problem. He didn't know how to do this. Not this.

He knew how to fuck hard and come harder.

This gentle shit, this "connection," was so fucking foreign to him.

So, he kept his mouth shut and fucked her as gently as

possible until she complained he was being a little too careful with her.

He gave it to her a little harder and she responded just as he hoped. And as she threw her head back against his shoulder, as she played with her own nipples, as her mouth gaped open and sounds escaped that drove him deeper and harder, he found her clit again and did what he knew women liked. What they craved. That touch there.

And for once, he cared how he did it.

For once he cared if she was enjoying it.

For once, the woman in his bed would remain there afterward.

This wasn't a bust a nut, then ghost situation.

This woman wasn't going anywhere. At least, not yet.

As long as she wanted to remain in his bed, he was keeping her there.

Even if they didn't have sex again until the kid was finished baking.

He could wait. Because she was worth that fucking wait.

He'd waited so long for this, he knew he wouldn't be able to last as long as he'd like. But he needed to last long enough to make it good for her.

If it was, maybe they'd do this again. If it was, she'd ask him to fuck her again.

While the kissing and touching had been great, this was better.

And all three would be perfect.

"Give me your mouth," he growled, his hips pistoning in and out of her.

She hadn't told him to stop or slow down, so unless she did...

She twisted her head enough so he could take it. He swallowed her groan, his fingers pressing and circling her clit, his tongue claiming her mouth, his dick so fucking hard inside her.

And then everything tensed on her, inside and out, and he almost stopped out of worry, but her climax exploded around him and she cried out inside his mouth, her fingers squeezing her tits harder, making them leak.

Fuck, he wanted to taste her there, too.

He pulled out and carefully rolled her onto her back before sliding inside her again, her eyes held his and he leaned over, careful not to put his weight on her, but he couldn't resist licking her tits clean and sucking her nipples.

Her fingers dug into his hair, not to stop him, but to hold him there. With one hand he squeezed and sucked.

Her head rolled back and her mouth opened but nothing escaped.

But he felt it. The squeeze and pull of her cunt as he drove deep, needing that connection she talked about.

And before her orgasm was finished, he drove his palms into the mattress and powered deep one more time, his balls pulling tight and his dick pulsating as he came hard.

Holding all his upper body weight on his arms, he dropped his head and closed his eyes, trying to catch his breath, trying to slow his racing pulse.

But her fingertips tracing over his damp face and then over his lips had him opening them again. "Okay?"

Her face was flushed and her eyes still unfocused, but her lips curled up just slightly. "Yes."

"Sure?"

"Yes," she whispered.

"Good." He shifted just slightly since his arms were beginning to shake a little bit. "Now gotta get rid of this wrap. Sure it's filled to the fuckin' brim."

"And I have to pee."

He shook his head. "Of course."

As he went to pull out, she stopped him. "Hey."

Their gazes met.

"Thank you."

"Should be thankin' you, baby."

"No. Most men wouldn't be interested in having sex with a woman who was almost nine months pregnant. Never mind with another man's baby."

"Didn't see any of that, Red."

"What did you see?"

"Only you."

"And I don't see your past, either, Sig. I only see you."

Jesus Christ.

He was fucking toast.

Chapter Eighteen

Sig watched Red waddle back to the bed for what he swore was the tenth time. He needed to get the fuck up and do the repo jobs Trip had assigned him, but it was getting harder to leave the bed every morning since they started having sex a week ago.

She wasn't always feeling up to him fucking her, but they found plenty of other ways to play when she was in the mood. They'd also found different positions to keep the pressure off her stomach and now he had tasted every fucking inch of her body and explored them, as well. She also knew every part of his body, too.

Two days ago, when she couldn't sleep and had taken her umpteenth pee break, Sig had woken up to her sucking his dick. Even though it was three in the morning, it was the best fucking wakeup he'd ever had. Even better, she didn't stop when he warned her he was about to blow.

Fuck no, she kept going until he shot his load down her throat. He'd handed her one of his dirty T-shirts to spit it out but by then she had already swallowed it and simply gave him a fucking smile.

He was pretty fucking sure if he could love someone, he fell in love with her at that very moment.

While things were good, sometimes she still had bad nightmares.

Sometimes he did, too. His were no longer about himself or his past, but were always about Red. Sometimes it was centered around the shed and bench. Sometimes it was about her running down that mountain. And sometimes it was fueled by him being scared to death something would happen to her while giving birth.

And, while he tried not to think about it, he was scared to death she would leave afterward.

In the end, starting fresh somewhere else was her choice, and he'd leave that decision to her. If she wanted to leave and get away as far as she could from that mountain and that incestuous clan, he'd do what he could to help her.

And if, for some reason, she wanted him to go with her, he'd do that, too.

He only came home to Manning Grove because he had nowhere to land after that last prison term. He found himself drifting and he knew if he didn't find something solid, at least for a short while, he'd end up right back behind bars.

Truth be told, he needed a fucking break from being caged.

A long one.

Plus, he still wanted his half of his grandfather's shit. It was his and Trip had no right to keep it all. Sig didn't give a fuck if a will said otherwise. A will was just a piece of paper while Trip and he were supposed to be blood.

Red slowly climbed into bed naked, rolled to her side with a cute little grunt and then awkwardly wiggled her ass backward until it was against him. He rolled to his side and spooned her, which was what she liked.

He hadn't said it out loud, but he liked it, too.

She always used his upper arm as a pillow until his arm fell asleep and he was forced to move it. But until then, he let her use it.

Draping his left arm around her, he let his hand drift lightly over her now enormous belly. This kid had to be coming soon. And at the last appointment, he had taken the doctor aside when Red was using the bathroom to ask her how soon after she popped the baby out that they could have sex.

Dr. Carly advised it was best to wait four to six weeks.

Four to six fucking weeks...

Fuck.

She might be gone way before then.

It wasn't as if he just wanted her to stick around for sex, he didn't...

He could get sex anywhere. Maybe not the kind of sex he *needed*, but he could also find that if he looked hard enough.

The point was, he didn't want to have sex with just anyone anymore. And, if Red stuck around, he was determined to find another outlet to handle the rest of what he needed.

She grabbed the hand he had laying on her belly and shifted it to where the baby was moving. It kind of fascinated him that she had a whole other person inside of her. Too bad that person was half Shirley.

"I'm ready for this to be over," she said softly.

"I bet," he murmured, wondering how deeply he should read into that statement. "Kid ain't fully cooked yet."

When she whispered, "I wish this was your baby," his chest got tight and his fingers flexed within hers.

And that would be a big fucking mistake if it was. He wouldn't fool himself or even Red about that. He hadn't been lying when he told her she didn't know everything about him. She didn't and probably never would. But there were some things she needed to know.

"Haven't loved anyone since I was twelve years old. Not sure I'm capable of it anymore. A kid deserves love. You givin'," he almost said *him*, but she didn't want to know the sex of the baby, so he respected that, "it... to the doc and her hubby is for the best. This kid's gonna be so fuckin' loved, Red. Unlike alotta babies born, they want this one desperately."

"I'm doing the right thing, right?"

She knew she was doing the right thing. And this wasn't the first time she'd asked him that. In fact, he'd lost fucking count. But he got it. It was a huge fucking decision. One, as a woman, that had to be difficult to make.

Women were "expected" to be mothers and sometimes they shouldn't be. He knew quite a few mothers who should've skipped that life decision, including his own.

He pulled his right arm from under her head since it was starting to tingle painfully, swept a lock of her hair off her cheek and pressed his nose into the rest of it. He had to admit that gay hairdresser had fixed her up, which had made her happy.

"You're doin' the right thing, Red. No fuckin' doubt. And when the time's right and you're ready, they said you can get to know," *him*, "it."

"I don't know if that would be good."

She didn't clarify for who, he assumed both the kid and her. But still... "You stay in Manning Grove," *he's*, "they're gonna be hard to avoid."

"I can't stay here. I can't risk them ever finding me."

He didn't want to hear that first part. He also planned on taking care of the second if Vernon Shirley and his cousin-son ever came off that fucking mountain. If it was up to Sig, he'd sneak up to their compound with a few containers of gas and a match.

"That's your decision. You got us, Red. Don't gotta go anywhere if you don't wanna. We gotta make a deal with 'em to keep you safe, we will." If they don't kill them all first, which was Sig's preference. "Then you can stay close to... it. Just in case you wanna get to know it. To make sure he's happy and loved." *Oh fuck.* He slipped. He was afraid it was going to happen and it did. He fucked up. "Fuck, Red. I'm sorry."

"It's a he?"

Shit. He could just lie and say he was speaking in general terms but he really didn't want to lie to her. He'd lied more times than he could remember in his life, so why he felt guilty about lying to Red, he didn't know. Yeah, he did. He didn't want to disappoint her if she found out he'd done it. And she *would* be disappointed because she said a few times now that she trusted him. And he didn't want to break that trust. To him, her trusting him was everything.

"Yeah."

"Why did you feel the need to know?" She almost sounded betrayed. And that right there killed him.

"The doc told me after that first appointment. You didn't wanna know and I stupidly asked. I shouldn't have. Wasn't my business. And I shoulda known I'd fuck up. And, of course, I fuckin' did. Sorry, baby."

"It's a boy," she whispered, her fingers tightening over his.

"Yeah. Is knowin' gonna make it harder for you?" He hoped to fuck it didn't.

"Are they happy about it?"

"My guess is they'd be happy with whatever the baby is, Red." As long as it didn't come out with three legs and one big cyclops eye, but he kept that to himself. "I don't think they give a shit whether it's a boy or a girl. It'll be a Bryson and that's all that matters."

"A Bryson," she repeated, like she was tasting the name.

"Yeah, baby, the more I ask around about 'em, the better I feel and so should you. Besides bein' a family full of pigs, which is the worst thing about 'em, they're a good, solid family. The kid's gonna want for nothin'. And that's how a kid should grow up."

"Yes, a good, solid family who doesn't trade her daughter off to some mountain clan to be used for breeding. A good, solid family who doesn't lie to her son about who his father is. Or who thinks about her kids first over herself. Who makes sure her kids are cared for before she drinks herself into oblivion."

Jesus. "Yeah, baby."

She got quiet for a moment, then said, "I don't know if I could love him as much as they could."

Being Red, she probably could. She was the type of woman who could look past how he was created. But it still might bother her some days more than others and would that be fair to the kid?

And if she decided to have more kids in the future, would she treat him differently than kids she actually chose to have? She might not mean to, but in reality, it was a risk.

Like Red, that baby was an unwilling participant in what the Shirleys decided was Red's and his fate. They forced her to become pregnant with him and by doing so, forced him to be born.

He just hoped the kid never found out his sperm donor was some inbred goat fucker. Sig hoped he took after his birth mother in looks and smarts but without the red hair. That might be a dead giveaway to any Shirleys who remained after the MC was done with them.

And they needed to be done with them. He needed to get on Trip and Judge about it. They couldn't wait much longer. They couldn't keep waiting to close on that fucking crematorium.

He was trying to keep his patience about it, but it was a

fucking struggle. And without any kind of outlet to relieve his tension he was ready to fucking snap.

———

Autumn groaned as she pushed herself up from the couch. Even though she couldn't be one hundred percent sure because the pregnancy wasn't typical, Dr. Carly was pretty confident she was now thirty-eight weeks along. That meant she only had to wait about two more weeks before he would be born. Hopefully.

She'd be fine if he decided to make an appearance today.

He.

At the last appointment, she'd asked the doctor if they had picked out a name.

She said she had, but she wasn't jinxing anything by saying it out loud. That made Autumn smile.

She had met Carly's husband, Matt, only once. He'd stopped in during last week's check-up to introduce himself. He had been in uniform at the time, which made Sig struggle to keep his mouth shut.

When Officer Matt Bryson extended his hand to Sig, assuming he was the father of the baby, Autumn thought Sig was going to spit on it instead of accept it.

He didn't, to Autumn's relief, but he didn't accept it, either.

It was sort of a compromise.

The pounding on the door sounded again and she cursed at Judge's impatience. He knew she was huge and was slower to get around.

But, hey, he was bringing her a whole bunch of food from Dino's Diner so she shouldn't bitch. She had given Sig a huge list before he left to do a repo. But just an hour ago, he texted her and said Judge would drop the food off, instead. Sig had to do a tow job for Dutch as a favor after he did the repo, so he'd be back later than expected and asked her to save him some of the loaded fries.

She made him no promises in that regard.

More pounding, even louder this time. "Okay, Judge, I'm coming! *Sheesh.*"

When she made it to the door, with one hand on the key she'd left in the lock, she leaned forward as best as she could with her big belly in the way and peeked through the peephole.

"Oh shit." Her heart began to race. "Oh shit!" With a hand griping her stomach, she spun and began to look for her phone.

That wasn't Judge outside her door.

Fuck! It wasn't any of the Fury members at all!

She frantically moved about the room. What the hell happened to her cell phone?

Then she heard it.

A noise that froze her in place. That seized her heart. That sucked every last molecule of oxygen from her lungs.

Even though the door was metal, the frame was not. And it couldn't withstand the force they were using on it. It gave way.

The lock had been useless all along.

She'd never been safe there. She'd been given a false sense of security.

That had been Sig's mistake.

She should have left town right away. She should've kept running at the bottom of that mountain and never stopped.

Not for Sig. Not for anyone.

And that had been her mistake.

"Oh shit." She was afraid to turn around.

The front door was her only avenue of escape.

And they were coming through it.

With burning eyes, she grabbed her stomach with both

hands, dropped her head and whispered, "I'm sorry, baby. I'm so sorry."

Because she would not survive going up that mountain again.

———

They didn't tell him.

They didn't fucking tell him.

They waited until he was done with that fucking tow for Dutch and had come back to the farm with the wrecker.

Because they didn't want him to go up there alone.

Because if he had known, he would have.

Instead, he had no idea how long Red had been up there.

No fucking idea because they could only guess.

Judge had told Trip what he found when he brought Red her food. Then Trip got everyone else together.

Everyone but him.

Trip said he didn't want Sig flipping the fuck out.

But that wasn't good enough.

It wasn't.

Trip should've told him immediately.

Trip should've told him that the Shirleys knocked out Easy who was guarding the end of the lane, then drove up to the bunkhouse without anyone to stop them.

Everybody had been gone.

Including Sig.

He'd left her alone, thinking she'd be safe.

She wasn't.

He'd been wrong.

So fucking wrong.

Judge said the only way they could've known where Red was at on the farm was by watching. And there were plenty of woods and buildings on the farm where they could hide and do so.

Those motherfuckers spied on them. On her.

They had planned for the right moment.

They had waited for the right time.

And when it came, when all his brothers were gone, doing the shit they needed to do, taking care of the responsibilities they had, those fuckers moved in.

And they fucking stole her.

They fucking stole her.

He promised her she'd be safe.

He fucked up.

Again.

There was no way she could run this time, not in the condition she was in. She needed them to get her free this time. She needed them to go up there and steal her back.

Because the Shirleys were not keeping her.

They were not taking that kid.

They weren't getting anything but dead.

As soon as he had parked the rollback, he received a text from Trip to come straight into The Barn.

And when he did, every fucking member of the Fury was there. Waiting.

His gut had twisted when he saw their faces.

What they couldn't hide.

And Stella's face was ravaged. Her eyes were red, her nose was swollen and tears slid unchecked down her face.

And that woman was tougher than any other woman he knew.

It was seeing her that almost made him fall to his knees right there. On the floor in that barn.

Somehow he'd kept himself on his feet and they circled him, blocked him from running to the nearest exit. Blocked him from jumping on his sled and riding to that compound as fast as it would take him.

Trip was talking, Judge was talking, all of them were talking.

They were talking and not doing a fucking thing.

But he heard none of it.

All he saw was Red.

That shed.

That breeding bench.

And the image on the ultrasound.

They were not getting her.

They were not getting that fucking kid.

"Everybody can't go," someone was saying. Maybe Trip.

Sig's head was spinning so hard, he had a hard time concentrating on the discussion.

"Need everybody available," someone else said. Judge. "Gotta go in quietly. They're heavily armed. And they'll be expectin' us."

He was tired of all the talk, they needed to act. And they needed to do it now.

"Someone's gotta stay back with Easy. He might have a fuckin' concussion." He had no idea who said that and he didn't care. His only concern right now was Red.

"Think they'd cut that kid outta her? Would they do some fucked up shit like that?"

"My guess is that they waited 'til she was almost due to get her back. Who knows, maybe they'll let her go once she has it."

Sig's brain exploded and he screamed, "We're not waitin' 'til then! We're doin' this now!"

"Yeah, brother, we're not waitin'," Trip said, way too fucking calmly.

Why the fuck wasn't he freaking out, too? If it was his woman, he'd be losing his shit. He wouldn't be standing around just jawing.

Sig scanned the circle of Fury members, beginning to focus. Starting to realize once they had a plan they could move. "The first one we're starting with is that inbred leader. That motherfucker Vernon."

"The leader would be good. Cut off the head of the serpent and let 'em scramble," Judge agreed.

"And his cousin-son, Tomlin," Sig added. "And that cunt Anna. Vernon's wife-sister. She's dead, too."

"Sure you wanna take out a woman, Sig?" someone asked behind him and he didn't care who.

"That fuckin' cunt deserves everythin' Red got. She's lucky I don't strap her down to that fuckin' bench and rip her a new goddamn asshole."

"Jesus, Sig," Trip whispered. "Ain't doin' that shit."

No, Trip would never let him do that shit but if it was up to Sig... That bitch would pay. Get the same thing done to her as was done to Red. "A fuckin' quick death is too good for 'em. And lettin' their spawn live means they might do shit like this again. Thinkin' they all need to die."

"Can't kill 'em all. Gotta do it quietly. Takin' out a couple will go unnoticed by the pigs. We wipe out that whole mountain and someone's gonna notice," Deacon said.

Judge nodded. "Agreed. We take two or three out, 'specially the leader, they'll think twice about fuckin' with us again. Give 'em a warnin' showin' that'll be what they'll deal with in the future if they don't."

"They fuck with us again, they're all goddamn dead," Dutch growled. "Ain't playin' a game of back and forth with those assholes. This is once and done. We show 'em a taste of the Fury and make sure it's a taste they don't like."

"Who's goin?" Ozzy asked.

"Me," Sig said. "I'm fuckin' goin'."

"Not if you don't keep your shit together, you ain't, brother. Can't go rippin' in there and gettin' us all killed," Judge said.

"Yeah, need to do this quick and quiet," Trip agreed.

"Who's got military trainin' besides Trip?" Deacon asked.

"Nobody needs fuckin' military trainin' to go up there and slice some goddamn throats!" Sig yelled. They needed to move now and stop all this fucking talking.

Red was up on that mountain and who the fuck knew what the Shirleys were doing to her while they were down there jerking on their dicks.

"Dutch, you stay with Easy. Get 'im to the hospital if it's needed," Trip ordered. "The rest of you are goin' up there. Dodge, you're stickin' with Stella. You got me?"

"Got it."

"Got one goal and three targets." Trip the biker was gone, a Marine in his place. "Goal's gettin' Autumn out of there alive and in one fuckin' piece. Targets are Vernon, Tomlin and Anna Shirley. Soon as one of us locates Autumn, that person's gettin' her the fuck outta there and to Stella and Dodge who'll be waiting down by the road in Stella's Jeep. Dodge, want you armed. Stel, you wait with him and need you to get Autumn the fuck away from there as soon as possible. You get her to the doc if you need to. Do not fuckin' wait for us to come back down that mountain. You just go. She's priority."

"Trip," she whispered, her face now pale.

"Gonna be okay, just need you to stick to your orders, yeah?"

Stella nodded. "Okay."

"The rest of us is gonna fan out and then close in like a noose. One of those fuckers shoots at you, take 'im out. They shoot, they die. Make sure you bring whatever weapons you got. Guns, knives, clubs, what-fuckin-ever. Don't give a shit if it's legal or not. You got shit I don't know about on this property that's illegal, grab it. Then after this is over, it's gone. You get me?"

A few grumbled *yeahs* were heard.

"Try not to shoot anyone if possible 'cause of ballistics. Unless you got a shotgun. Then it don't matter."

"We done talkin' 'bout this shit?" Sig yelled, his fingers curled into fists and pressed to his thighs. He was soon going to barrel through the circle of men surrounding him and head up that mountain on his own.

Trip grimaced. "Yeah, brother, we're done. Know you can't have weapons, but know you got some, go get 'em. You're ridin' with me." He began to walk toward the front of the barn. "No sleds. They're too loud. Gonna park the cages at the bottom where there's a pull-off, then hoof it up the mountain together. You hear me?"

This time a loud roar of *yeahs* went up and most of their brotherhood headed for the bunkhouse to get ready while Trip and Stella headed out the front.

"Everyone meet at the house in five. Then we roll," Trip shouted over his shoulder.

Thank fuck.

Sig headed out to one of the sheds where he kept Razor's Sig Sauer, an old Beretta, his oversized buck knife and a blackjack hidden. He hid everything on his person, then headed to the farmhouse to meet up with Trip.

He was ready to fucking roll.

Chapter Nineteen

SIG SNUCK AS QUIETLY AS he could through the woods near the shed, Judge on his heels. Trip probably put the big man with him to make sure he didn't go rogue and just take out everyone up there.

"Fuck," he muttered. The door was still hanging open like the last time he saw it, but he leaned inside anyway to check to make sure it was empty.

"What the fuck is this?" Judge asked in a low, quiet voice.

"Just what you think it is," Sig answered.

The club's enforcer pointed a small LED flashlight into the building and took a peek inside. "Get the fuck outta here. This was where she was kept?"

"That ain't the half of it, brother."

"Jesus fuck."

"Yeah."

"This whole fuckin' mountain needs to be dynamited."

"Fuckin' got any?" Sig asked. "'Cause I'm all fuckin' for that."

"Even if I did, blowin' this whole place up might catch unwanted attention."

"No shit. But might be worth it."

"You landin' in prison for fuckin' life won't help Autumn."

Sig shook his head. "Thought I was helpin' her. Them snaggin' her proved I wasn't. Shoulda took her elsewhere."

"Your goddamn self-fuckin-pity right now ain't helpin'. Just shut the fuck up about it and let's keep lookin'. Where else?"

"She said Vernon and Tomlin lived in the main house. Anna should be in there, too, unless they're all in hidin'. And if they are, we're fucked. They could be anywhere. Sure they got all kinds of hidey-holes up here and maybe even bunkers."

"Not thinkin' they're that smart. And their stupidity makes 'em think they're some kinda militia, which they ain't. They're just a bunch of inbred hillbillies with guns," Judge said, then added, "Which don't mean they ain't dangerous, they are. Stupidity will get you killed."

"Yeah." He was pretty sure the Shirleys had won their share of the Darwin Awards.

"Trip, Rook and that Shady motherfucker were headin' to the house."

"Yeah, with the shed empty, hope to fuck they got her in the house. For fuck's sake, she better still be breathin'."

"And if she ain't? Then we're findin' that dynamite," Judge told him.

"Yeah."

Fuck, after the Fury imploded and the survivors scattered, Sig never cared about anyone in his goddamn life except his baby sister, Syn. And only because he felt sorry she was born to their whore mother. Then he lost track of his sister the last few years during his last stint in that New York prison.

So, yeah, he'd cared about his sister and now Red.

He tried to protect both of them. He did his best for both of them.

But he failed Red for sure.

They never should've gotten their hands on her. Never.

And that was all his fault for letting his guard down.

If she survived this...

He would hand her his belt and she could beat him until he paid the fair price for failing her.

He would accept every strike no matter how hard it was because he'd deserve every fucking one. If she handed that belt off to someone else who could hit harder than her, someone like Judge, he'd be okay with that, too.

Whatever pain she endured during this, he needed to endure the same.

After clearing the barn and a couple other small outbuildings, Sig and Judge stuck to the edge of the woods —not out in the open and not where there may be booby-traps—and headed toward the main house.

They stopped when they saw a dark figure ahead of them hunkered down behind a junk car.

"That one of 'em?" Sig asked, having a hard time making out whoever it was. And it turned out, that person was bent over someone else.

"Looks like that Shady motherfucker," Judge muttered under his breath.

"As in the prospect?"

"Yeah." Judge moved forward and when they got to Shady, the man looked up from where he squatted beside another man.

A man with a dark gaping slit across his throat.

Even in the dark, Sig could see the Shirley was bleeding out as Shady had a tight grip on the back of the man's mullet.

"This one of the targets?" the younger biker asked.

"Hard to say," Sig said, kind of impressed with the

prospect. He never saw Tomlin except that one time in the vehicle when he and Vernon drove past Dino's Diner. But Sig hadn't gotten a good look.

Judge squatted down beside the body and turned on his flashlight, pointing it low and directly into the dead man's face.

"Fuck. Know I dealt with most of the leader's sons when they've been snagged by five-oh for one reason or the other, but they all fuckin' look alike to me. Can't tell if this is Tomlin. Bet we check his undies, his momma-auntie probably wrote his name in marker somewhere in them."

Shady snorted and got to his feet. "Think he shit himself before I sliced his fuckin' throat, so I ain't checkin' them." He wiped his knife off on the flannel shirt of the possible Tomlin.

Judge shot Shady a frown. Those were the most words Sig ever heard the prospect say.

Sig pulled out his cell and snapped a pick of the man's face to identify him later. Before this night was through, he wanted to make sure they got their intended targets. Any other fuckers who stopped breathing would be a bonus.

"Who else?" Shady asked, a huge buck knife in his hand.

"The leader and his bitch," Sig said, giving the body a good kick with his boot. Then he spat a hocker on the asshole's face. "Piece of motherfuckin' shit."

Judge tugged on his long beard. "Which bitch? He got three, I think."

"The youngest cunt, Anna. The one that hurt Red, took her clothes and treated her like a fuckin' animal."

"Let's go huntin', fuckers," Shady said and moved off, keeping low and to the edge of the woods as he headed toward the big house.

"What the fuck?" Judge asked Sig.

"Don't know. Don't fuckin' care. Kinda likin' the guy right now," Sig answered, then followed Shady.

"Hey, Shady," Judge whispered. "You take out anyone else?"

The younger brother paused, whispering over his shoulder, "Any males I came across. Don't know who's who, so just makin' sure we don't miss the targets."

"Damn," Sig whispered. He wanted to fucking grin *and* buy the guy a beer.

Sig's cell phone vibrated in his back pocket and he paused long enough to pull it out and read the text from Trip. "Trip found Red in the main house. Seems to be good. He's gettin' Dodge to bring up the Jeep 'bout halfway and Rook's helpin' her get down to meet them."

"Good fuckin' news, brother," Judge said, whacking him on the back.

Yeah, but a fucking nine-month pregnant woman shouldn't be hoofing it down the mountain even a hundred feet, forget over a half mile. But bringing the Jeep all the way up that rutted lane would tip off too many other Shirleys who might not be aware yet of what was going down.

Not only did they need to keep that element of surprise, they needed to get Red out of there before any of them saw her leaving. Her safety was priority number one.

However, even once she was safe, they were not done there.

Not even fucking close.

Sig quickly texted Trip back. *Want that fucker n his bitch alive.*

The answering message, *Think they scattered,* popped up on his phone.

Don't give a fuck. Need 2 find them. Save 4 me.

Sig didn't get an answer and he didn't like that at all.

A minute later, just as they were within feet of the dark house, another text popped up. *Found Anna locked in attic w/ rest of wives n kids.*

Sig texted, *Hold her 4 me.*

No clue where leader is. Mighta deserted his women n kids.

Figures. That pussy motherfucker. Having to strap a woman down to make her submit to him.

His blood pressure spiked again and he took a deep inhale to try to keep him from only seeing red and nothing else. Because if his world went red, he would be useless. He wouldn't be able to think straight or get the job done he needed to do.

So, he needed to keep himself from spiraling and concentrate on the revenge he was looking forward to tasting.

It was right there on the tip of his tongue.

Got him came in a mass text to everyone, not by Trip but Cage. *Was trailn Rook n Red.*

He alive? Sig texted quickly back.

Fuck yeah. Savn his ass 4 ya.

Sig smiled. *Location?*

Near barn.

He said to Judge and Shady, "One of you get the wifey from Trip. Bring her to me at that fuckin' shed. Tell Trip and the others to keep the rest of the Shirleys away from there. Take any of 'em out if you gotta. And make sure that dead one was Tomlin. If not, find that fucker, too." He spun on his heels and headed back to the area near the barn.

AUTUMN CRIED out when her foot got caught in a deep rut and her ankle twisted sharply as they made their way down the pitch dark lane, only using Rook's cell phone to guide their way.

Her heart was wildly thumping, her back cramping severely and so was her belly.

But she didn't stop, she kept going with Rook tightly gripping her elbow to help her stay on her feet.

But they were moving too slowly.

She wanted to race down that mountain and get as far away as she could as fast as she could. But she wasn't racing anywhere. She doubted she should even be walking as far as she was.

However, she had no choice, so she kept putting one foot in front of the other, hoping freedom wasn't too far away.

Rook promised her that Dodge and Stella would bring the Jeep up as far as they could. But the slow, agonizing downward trek seemed endless.

Her feet were bare and one eye was swollen shut from where Vernon backhanded her when she fought to keep him from strapping her to the bed in Tomlin's room. She was told that was where she was staying until the baby was born.

And after he was, they would then decide what to do with her.

She had spat in his face when Vernon leaned over her to buckle one of her wrists fast to the headboard. That got her another backhand and a hand gripping her throat until she thought she would pass out. Vernon had taken her right to the edge where she was seeing spots.

But before everything went black, he released her and said if she hadn't been carrying his baby, he would've finished what he started and then buried her in the woods where no one would ever find her.

She had also spat in Vernon's face and scratched Tomlin's cheek back at the apartment. She hadn't gone willingly when they busted in, but they'd tied her up and threw her into the back seat of the same rusty Buick they'd been seen driving the other week in town.

Every bump that car had hit caused another sharp, excruciating pain to shoot through her stomach. Because of that, she was afraid she might go into labor early.

No matter what, she somehow needed to prevent that.

She refused to have the baby while they held her captive. Because if she did, she worried they would take that baby and no one would ever be able to find it.

Screw them, they weren't getting him.

And they weren't taking either of them alive back up that mountain ever again. So, if Rook couldn't get her down to the Jeep in time...

"You have a knife?" she could barely ask since she was having a hard time catching her breath.

"Yeah."

"Give it to me."

Rook's fingers gripped her elbow tighter and he sounded suspicious when he asked, "For what?"

"I just need it. Please."

"For what, Red?" He continued to tug her along.

"In case we don't make it."

"What the fuck you talkin' about?"

"I won't let them take me or this baby again."

"What the fuck you gonna do with a knife that I can't?"

She didn't answer him, but cried out when she stumbled again. And when she did, a sharp pull shot through her stomach.

"Red, whatcha gonna do with the fuckin' knife?"

Again, she didn't answer him, instead she gasped at another sharp, almost crippling, pain.

"Ain't givin' you a goddamn knife," Rook growled. "Holy fuck."

"I can't go back up there."

"Ain't goin' back up there."

"That's what I thought before."

Rook said nothing and kept moving, his profile grim. He also sped up a little, just about dragging her along with him.

Between her huge belly and her bare feet, she struggled

to keep up. Plus, her closed, swollen eye made it even tougher to find her footing in the dark.

The next cramp was so excruciating, it made her double over and cry out.

"Fuck," Rook barked. "Gotta keep movin'."

She gasped as she tried to straighten and only doubled over again. Something was definitely wrong. Her insides felt like they were being clawed from the inside out.

She was not having that baby on that mountain. She was not!

Then warm fluid gushed from her, soaking her maternity pants and running down the insides of her thighs.

"Oh... no," she cried. "Oh no. No. No."

"What?" Rook asked, sounding a bit panicked himself.

"My water broke."

"What the fuck does that mean?" Yes, he was definitely panicked. He wasn't the only one.

She clenched her teeth and forced herself to straighten and keep moving, but he jerked her to a stop.

"Carryin' you the rest of the way."

"You can't," she said between gritted teeth as another wave of cramps or contractions, or whatever was happening, almost crippled her.

"The fuck I can't. You're still skinny as fuck. Most of your weight's at your center. Don't think we got much more to go."

"If you trip..." She gasped again and groaned, holding onto her belly with both hands and feeling it become rock hard.

Without another word, he squatted down low enough to scoop her up. She bit back a squeal from not only being lifted but him stumbling back a step in trying to balance her weight.

"If you fall..."

"Ain't gonna fall. Hang the fuck on. Gettin' you and this

kid outta here. They ain't takin' you and they ain't takin' him. Fuck those inbred hillbillies."

She hooked her arms around his neck as he held her tightly against his chest, struggling with her weight, but determined to keep going until he found the Jeep.

And besides the fluid still dripping from between her thighs, tears began to slide down her cheeks. She pressed her face into Rook's neck and just let them flow as she hung on tight.

Somehow she got out a shaky, "Thank you."

Rook said nothing, but his fingers flexed against her and he kept moving.

Somehow he managed to get them both to the Jeep.

Then he disappeared back up that mountain while Stella, trying to remain calm, got on her phone and Dodge drove way too fast to get them to the nearest hospital.

———

He stared at the piece of shit who was on his knees in front of Cage but was facing Sig.

Cage must have struck the fucker from behind with the bloody leather blackjack he was gripping in his hand.

Vernon—the leader of the Shirley Clan, the man in charge of the local branch of the Guardians of Freedom—didn't look so powerful now with his ankles and hands trussed together behind him and his head hanging forward.

He was about to learn a lesson he wouldn't be able to forget because he wouldn't live long enough to forget it.

"What're we doin' to him?" Cage asked.

"*We* ain't doin' nothin'. He's mine. So's that cunt wife of his. Grab an arm, gotta drag his ass over there." Sig jerked his chin toward the shed that was barely visible behind the barn.

But even that wasn't the final destination.

They both grabbed a side and dragged the fucker on his knees through the dirt and stones past the barn, around the shed and behind it.

"What the fuck is that?"

Sig didn't bother to answer that question. Cage could most likely figure it out on his own. "Help me throw him on that bench. Face down. Ass at the end."

"Fuckin' Sig, man..."

"Just fuckin' do it."

They heaved Shirley's heavy weight onto that bench and Cage held the man in place while Sig stopped, spun and walked away a few steps, taking a few deep, slow breaths, trying to fight the rage from blinding him.

He needed to stay in the here and now.

He needed to stay focused.

"Sig, brother..." Cage muttered.

As soon as his narrowed vision opened up enough for him to see clearly, he spun back around and went directly to the rear of the bench. "Untie his fuckin' ankles. Hold one while I strap the other."

Cage stared at him for a few seconds.

"Wanna know what the fuck they used this bench for?" Sig roared at him. "Wanna know? Maybe this fucker would be happy to fuckin' explain it."

With a slight nod, a tight jaw and without another word, Cage untied Vernon's ankles, keeping a secure hold of one while Sig strapped the other to the bottom of the bench leg. Then he moved around and strapped the other ankle tight.

Exactly how that motherfucker had strapped Red to it.

Fucking Karma was a goddamn evil bitch.

And right now, Sig's name was Karma.

"Now his hands," Sig ordered Cage.

Sig strapped down one and then the other. He back-handed Vernon in the face. "You awake, motherfucker? Need to be awake for this."

Vernon's head flopped to the side and his eyes slowly blinked open.

That motherfucker was awake. And once Sig started doling out his revenge, it would wake the fucker up even more.

He pulled his knife from his boot, sliced Vernon's thermal shirt down the center of his back, then tore it off him, wrapping the torn cotton tightly around the man's head and making sure he was gagged.

He didn't want Vernon yelling out to his cousins-brothers-uncles once Sig started.

Then he tucked the knife into the waistband of Vernon's jeans and sawed at the denim until both the man's ass and back of his thighs were exposed.

Sig ignored the muttering behind him. "Can't watch that goddamn shit."

As soon as Cage was gone, Sig heard someone else approach.

"Fuck, Sig." Deacon.

He also heard a muffled female voice.

He glanced over his shoulder to see Deacon had brought a woman with him. "That her?"

"Yeah."

"You sure?"

"Yeah. When we asked the women in that attic, they all pointed at her. Have a fuckin' feelin' she ain't well liked."

"What're they doin' with the rest of the bitches?"

"Using the women and older kids as shields. Judge and Trip figured if they start shootin' at us, they'd sacrifice their own first. They're settin' up a perimeter to give you time to do what you need to do. But Trip said do it quick."

Sig nodded. "Hold her there and let 'er watch to see what's gonna happen to her next. Make sure she watches. Don't fuckin' let her look away. You got me?"

"Uh... yeah. Okay," Deke answered, worry starting to

creep into his face. And when Sig unbuckled his belt, the man yelled out, "What the fuck, Sig!"

"Ain't gonna fuck 'im. Though he deserves his fuckin' asshole to be violated just like what he did to Red."

Sig finished slipping it from the loops and took the worn leather into his hands. His belt had touched a lot of flesh over the years, including his own. But this may be the last time he used it for anything other than to hold up his jeans.

He snapped the narrow leather together, the sharp crack that usually got his blood humming filling the air.

Right now, his blood was boiling, not humming.

He moved around to the front of the bench, grabbed Vernon's hair and jerked his head up, holding the folded belt in front of his face. "Normally get off on this shit. You'll be lucky I ain't shovin' my dick up your ass when I'm done. Can't guarantee I still won't, but can guarantee this bench will be the last fuckin' place you take a breath. Also ain't promisin' how you get there's gonna be fast and easy. It ain't. Gonna suffer like you made Red suffer and while you are, want you to think about all those fuckin' times you had her strapped to this same goddamn bench."

Vernon made a muffled sound behind the cotton stuffed into his mouth. Sig didn't want to hear what he had to say.

He just didn't give a fuck.

Not fucking one.

He dropped the fucker's head and moved to the back of the bench, then glanced over at the leader's young wife.

Sig trailed his fingers down Vernon's back and then over the man's ass, making sure she was watching his every move. "See all that white flesh? Watch what happens to it." He lifted his eyes to Deacon. "Make sure she watches it all, Deke."

He turned back to the bench, planted his boots apart, and lifted his arm. For the first time ever, he gripped the end without the buckle.

He began counting. One strike for every month Red endured being on that mountain and held captive against her will. Then he gave one strike for every day. And if he needed to, he'd do every hour, every minute, every fucking second.

But he lost count.

One blurred into the other and he no longer knew what was happening around him. His focus had narrowed solely on the man in front of him. The red, swollen, bloody, ripped open flesh that used to be whole.

Like Red used to be whole.

His arm lifted and dropped over and over in a mindless, endless rhythm, until blood began to spatter him. On his clothes, his arm, his face.

And still... he didn't stop. Couldn't stop.

He wouldn't stop until the need for revenge was gone, until the rage had disappeared.

Until he could think clearly again.

The leather became slippery from the sweat of his palm and Vernon's blood, but he only adjusted his grip and continued.

Until his arm felt like lead, his fingers were cramped, his heartbeat had slowed and his breathing had steadied, following the cadence of the never-ending strikes.

And still... he didn't stop.

He wasn't going to stop until he couldn't lift his arm any more.

Until he could see clearly, until he could hear clearly.

But right now his vision was nothing but a pinpoint, his ears still ringing.

Nothing else existed but him, his belt and the flesh before him.

Chapter Twenty

"Sig!"

Sig's arm raised.

"Brother!"

His arm fell and a warm spray splattered him.

"Sig!"

It raised again.

"Jesus fuck!"

The belt was yanked from his fingers and he didn't have the strength to fight whoever it was.

Then someone was grabbing him and yanking him away from his target.

He wasn't done.

Not yet.

Not fucking yet.

Why was someone stopping him?

He blinked when hands grabbed his face and another appeared within his narrowed vision.

Trip.

"Sig!" His brother's face was pale, his eyes holding a deep worry, maybe even a little fear.

Maybe something was wrong with Red.

"Fuckin' Sig, breathe. Breathe, brother."

He was breathing, wasn't he?

Trip's face remained in his and Sig concentrated on his brother's moving mouth. "Sig, breathe, damn it!"

Sig forced out, "Not done."

"Jesus Christ, you're done. You broke your belt. You sliced him to the bone, Sig. You've filleted the fucker open a few times over."

Sig breathed.

And breathed again.

He concentrated hard on his brother's face.

The brother who he'd thought was his best friend so long ago and would be forever. The brother who'd offered him a place to land. A place to keep his shit together and his ass out of jail. A family.

He frowned, then turned his head to look at the bench. What used to be whole no longer was. Nothing but bloody and shredded flesh remained.

But he hoped Vernon Shirley was still breathing.

He hoped that fucker felt every strike.

"He breathin'?" Sig asked, his voice sounding strangely flat and as if coming from a distance.

"Don't know. If you're worried 'bout that, slice his fuckin' throat and let's go. We need to get the fuck outta here." Trip dropped the grip on Sig's face, dug a knife out of his cut and offered it to him.

Sig watched his own fingers wrap around it like they belonged to someone else.

He wasn't slicing that motherfucker's throat. Fuck no.

Sig tightened his blood-covered fingers around the hilt of the large knife and frowned as he stared at it in his hands.

No, he wasn't slicing that fucker's throat.

He blinked and turned to where Deacon still stood with

a tight hold on Anna. His arm was hooked around her throat and one hand had a tight hold in her hair, forcing her to keep her head up. Forcing her to watch.

Deke had done what he'd asked.

He'd done it and didn't pussy out.

He gave Deke a slight nod and the club's treasurer gave him one back.

Even if the man wasn't comfortable with it, he did it.

For Sig.

For Red.

That right there earned him a fuck-ton of respect. And Sig would never forget it.

He stepped closer to the back of the bench and dug his hand into what was left of Vernon's gaping blood-soaked jeans. He found the fucker's dick and balls with his left hand and, with a yank, exposed them, then sawed them the fuck off with the serrated buck knife in his right.

"Let the fucker bleed out if he's still breathin'," he said softly.

"We gotta get the fuck out of here, brother. Need to let the rest of the women and children go and Autumn had to go to the hospital. Think she went into labor."

Sig heard him, and he tried to process the words, but he wasn't done there yet. "Need to make sure Red and that kid's safe first."

"Thinkin' we made a clear statement."

"No. We didn't. Not yet."

"Fuck, Sig," his brother muttered, closing his eyes and shaking his head.

Sig handed Trip his knife back and went to where Deacon stood with the wide-eyed, pale Anna.

A strangled sound came from behind the bandana that had been tied over her mouth.

"Give her to me. You can all go. Go to Red."

"No fuckin' way, Sig. Not leavin' you here. Our brothers are lined up with their shields, makin' sure no other Shirleys approach. But that doesn't mean those fuckers might not set up and start shootin' at us, anyway. Not sure how many of them are out there in the woods. Can't waste any more time."

"Not done, brother," Sig said.

"You're done," Trip said more firmly. "We gotta go."

"Need a minute."

"Fuck," Trip muttered and blew out a loud breath.

Sig snagged Anna's throat within his fingers. "Let 'er go, brother."

Deke's mouth got tight. "Sig..."

"Let. Her. Go."

Deacon reluctantly released her and Sig immediately swung the bitch away from him. His lip curled in a snarl as he stared at the woman who hurt Red. The woman who made her live naked, cold and filthy in that shed for fucking months. The woman who treated Red worse than their livestock.

And if it wasn't for being a jealous cunt, never would've let Red go.

He snorted a thick wad of phlegm into his mouth and spat the hocker right into her face. And as it slid down her cheek, which was wet from crying, Sig began the statement he had went up there to make. He leaned in and tightened his fingers around the front of her throat until he knew it cut off the flow of air. "How you like havin' your fuckin' throat squeezed like that, huh? How does a dumb twat like you like bein' choked hard enough to leave a mark? How the fuck do you like havin' somethin' forced down your throat?" He lifted his fistful of Vernon's severed genitals. "Like your husband's dick. Would you like that? How you like the feelin' you might pass the fuck out? You beggin' for air yet?"

He turned his head and put his ear near her gagged mouth. "Can't hear you if you are."

He sneered and loosened his fingers just enough so she could suck in a breath through her flaring nostrils and then he tightened them again. He wanted her to stay conscious until he had his say.

"We ever see you off this mountain," he growled, "those fuckin' inbred hillbilly kids of yours? Dead. You? Dead. You'll join that motherfuckin' uncle-husband of yours in hell. You get me?" he roared. "Nobody... No-fuckin-body's gonna be lookin' for some missin' Shirleys. In fact, the world would be a better goddamn place without any of you. 'Cause you give us a reason to come back up this mountain? We ain't stoppin' with just a few of you. You forget she *ever* existed. You forget that baby *ever* existed. To you all, they don't. Any of you Shirleys see her in town, you go the opposite way. Any of you take one step toward her? You all die. Any of you try talkin' to her? You stop breathin' and all your snot monkeys do, too. You get me, you fuckin' cunt?"

He waited for a sign she heard him. He loosened his fingers again slightly because her face had turned an unhealthy shade of purple, just like the color of Red's bruises when he found her. "That a nod? Not fuckin' sure it was. But it don't matter. Only one correct answer. Incorrect one will cost you. Won't be a Shirley left breathin'." He jabbed his finger into her temple hard and her cry was muffled. "Remember that, bitch."

He shoved her and she fell backward. Not able to catch herself since her hands were bound behind her back, she landed on her ass. While she was down, he threw her husband's bloody dick and balls into her lap.

"My brother learned a hard lesson once about not puttin' his hands on a woman in anger. I watched that fuckin' lesson and never forgot it. But you ain't a woman. You're a piece of fuckin' shit that should be grateful you're still breathin'. Because if it was up to me, you wouldn't be." He spat once more on her face, wiped his mouth and strode away.

He paused in front of Deacon, whose expression he couldn't read. But the man had done what Sig asked once already, so he was pretty sure the man would do it again. "Take those cords and tie her down to that bench on top of her uncle-husband. Let 'er think about the shit she's done. Make sure she's naked when you do it. Take her clothes away like she took Red's." Without waiting for Deke's answer, he stopped in front of Trip. "Make sure that's done. Headin' to the hospital." As he spun on his heel to head back down that mountain—one he hoped to fuck he never saw again—his brother grabbed his arm, stopping him.

Sig stared down at the hand keeping him from getting to Red.

"Need to clean up, brother. Can't go in there lookin' like that. It'll raise a fuckload of red flags."

Sig's nostrils flared but he nodded after he took a glance down at himself. He was covered with blood and dirt. Trip was right. He needed to go to Red without the Shirley filth covering him.

"Need a ride back to the farm and my sled."

"Rev and Whip both have their cages parked at the bottom. I'll get one of them to take you back while we finish up and get outta here without all gettin' shot in the fuckin' backs." Trip pulled his cell out of his cut and texted one of them. And after he did so, his brother lifted his head and held Sig's eyes for the longest time.

Sig didn't like seeing what he saw in them.

But he got it.

He fucking got it.

Trip and him had gotten the demon inside them honestly.

"Let us know if you want us all at the hospital. Up to

you. Up to Red. Stella and Dodge are stayin' at least 'til you get there."

Sig inhaled the night air, trying to settle his roaring blood. But that air stank.

It stank really fucking bad right now.

He needed to get the fuck off that mountain and get to Red. That's what he needed to focus on right now. Not about what he'd done and what he still wanted to do.

Red needed him.

He needed her.

And he hoped to fuck she'd forgive him for letting the Shirleys steal her away.

He'd pay whatever price for that she wanted from him.

Whatever Red wanted, Red would get.

Even if it was a pound of flesh. Even if it was a ton.

His brother kept talking even though Sig was so done with it all. "Even in the dark, can see the tendons in your neck and jaw still poppin' and the veins at your temple poundin'. After Autumn's done at the hospital and every-thin's under control there, gonna need to have a discussion."

He wouldn't disagree with it because Trip was right. They did. "Yeah," he muttered. "Need to have a discussion."

The temporary gig with the club might be over sooner than expected. It was what it was and, if necessary, as soon as Red was good to go, so was he.

———

SIG WAS READING Stella's last text to him as the elevator doors whooshed open. The one where she told him to hurry.

Her previous texts had given him Red's room number at the New Beginnings Birthing Center that was attached to the hospital. This was after she had been checked out in the ER while waiting for Dr. Carly to show up.

As he stepped off the elevator, he lifted his head in time to see the doc's husband, Matt Bryson, heading his way like a freight train, his face holding a whole bunch of unhappy.

Oh fuck.

Sig braced as the pig in street clothes yanked him by his shirt and flung him into what looked like an empty waiting area.

Sig stumbled into one of the chairs and before he hit the floor, Bryson yanked him back to his feet with a fistful of cotton and got in his face. "No fucking wonder she doesn't want this kid. You hurt her like that, what would you do to the fucking baby?"

Dodge, who had been slouched in a chair in the corner, jumped to his feet. "Yo, dude, it wasn't him."

Bryson ignored him, his icy blue eyes pinned on Sig. "Wasn't you what? Who got her pregnant or beat her the fuck up?"

Sig's jaw shifted, his lip curled into a sneer and he barely refrained from spitting in the guy's face. "Didn't do fuckin' either. Now lemme the fuck go before shit gets real."

"She has a black fucking eye, a swollen face and a bruise on her neck. I can drag your ass in for that. All I have to do is see the marks and I have every right."

She had what?

What the fuck! No one told him she'd been hurt like that.

He needed to get to Red but this fucking turd was blocking him, so he had to deal with him first.

His fingers coiled into tight fists, but he kept them pinned to his thighs, reminding himself if he hit this badge-wearing motherfucker it was agg assault. "Won't be the first time I'd be accused of doin' shit I didn't do. Also won't be the first time gettin' my ass hauled in. Won't be the fuckin' last for either. Spent more time in a concrete box than out of it, so you threatenin' me with that shit ain't nothin'. Can do time with one hand tied behind my back, so do what you fuckin' need to do, pig. But you'll be wastin' your fuckin' time. Now, lemme the fuck go so I can check on Red."

Feet rushing towards them had them both pinning their lips together and Bryson released Sig's cut when his wife in blue scrubs not-so-gently wedged herself between them, her expression not giving anyone any doubt she was pissed off.

That was when Sig noticed Stella standing not far behind Bryson and Dodge looking a bit antsy, like he was ready to jump in at any time.

Problem was, that fucker got out of prison not long ago, too. Sig was sure Dodge wasn't anxious to go back any time soon. And fighting a pig would land them back behind bars especially since they were both on parole.

He wouldn't be any use to Red if he ended locked up again.

"What the fuck is wrong with you two?" Carly, her eyebrows pinned together, pushed her husband back another step and jabbed a finger toward a closed door down the hall. "You think she needs to hear this shit right now?"

Carly's head twisted and they realized hospital security was headed in their direction. She lifted up her palm and called out, "It's okay, Sam. Everything's okay here. Just a couple nervous fathers-to-be."

Sig's head jerked back and so did Bryson's.

Sam the security guard gave her a raised eyebrow as if he didn't believe her.

"It's all good, Sam. I swear. I have it under control."

"Okay, Doc, just call if you need us."

Carly muttered under her breath to Bryson, "The day I need to call a security guard on my cop husband is the day I..." She shook her head. "Good lord, just don't test me like that, Matt. Not today."

"Baby," Bryson started.

"Uh uh. No. Mouths shut. Ears open." She turned to Sig and jabbed a finger at him. "You." She then jabbed it at the closed door again. "You go in there and hold her damn hand and act like you've got a lick of sense. You." She jabbed it at her husband, then at one of the chairs in the corner. "You go sit the hell down over there until I tell you otherwise."

"Carly—"

She lifted a palm, her mouth tight and her blue eyes sharp. "No. Not another word. That woman in there has dealt with enough shit already without you two boneheads causing more issues. And, dear husband, you screw this adoption up for me... Remember that fucking tent you used to sleep in? You better find it because it'll be a long time before you're sleeping in my bed again."

"Baby—"

"Oh no. Nope. Today it's Doctor to you. I'm in charge here. Not you." She spun on Sig. "Not you, either." She clapped her hands sharply. "Go."

Sig gave the Bryson pig a scowl but before he moved toward the door, the doc stopped him cold.

"Sig... Was it them?" she asked him quietly. "I didn't ask her since she needs to concentrate on other things right now." Her head twisted sharply to Bryson. "Like giving birth to our son. And I don't want to upset her more than she already is."

"Them who?" Matt asked, shooting out of his chair and back to his feet. "Who fucking did that to her, if not him?"

Sig ignored the pig and met his wife's eyes. "Yeah. They took her because they wanted that kid. Thought I could protect her better than you. They proved me wrong. She shoulda stayed with you."

"I'm pretty sure it was her choice to stay with you," Carly said softly.

"Yeah, but it was the wrong one."

"It isn't wrong for her to stay with someone who cares deeply about her. Every week I saw how she flourished by being with you. That's why I stopped pushing for her to come stay with us. Her ordeal up there could've destroyed her. It didn't. You treated her like... Like she was your queen, Sig. You treated her like none of what happened to her happened. You didn't treat her as if she was different or broken, you treated her with love and respect. I witnessed it and it was the best thing for her. She was dealt a really horrible and shitty hand, but Sig... everything you did helped her move forward and not stay in that past. You get that, right?"

Sig's jaw got tight.

The elevator doors opened and Trip stepped out. But it was the pig's words that drew his attention. "What the fuck are you talking about, Carly? You said she was just a single mother who couldn't handle having a baby right now."

"And that's true."

"The fuck it is. Sounds like there's a lot more to this than you've told me. I'm a fucking cop. If shit happened to her that I need to know about, someone better start talking. If we're taking this kid, I need to know the circumstances around this pregnancy. I need to know everything."

"The fuck you need to know everything," Sig growled. "All you gotta know is she's givin' you this kid out of the kindness of her fuckin' heart. That's all you gotta know."

"Not good enough."

Carly chewed on her bottom lip as she glanced from her husband to Sig. "He needs to know."

"The fuck he does!" Sig yelled, feeling his temper begin to rise dangerously.

She placed a hand on Bryson's stomach and told him, "I don't know all the details either, Matt. I only know some of them. And the little I know is bad... But..." She looked at Sig. "I should at least tell him who's involved. Just in case."

Bryson's eyes narrowed and his body tensed. "Who?" When no one answered, he spun toward Sig. "Who the fuck is she to you anyway? She isn't your wife. She probably isn't even your girlfriend. Who gave you the right to make decisions for her?"

Sig's jaw got so tight, it popped.

Trip was at his side in a second. "If he's adoptin' this baby, he's got a right to know, Sig. He needs to know this baby might need protection."

"What the fuck is going on?" Bryson bellowed. "Protection from who?"

"The Shirleys," Trip answered.

Bryson's head snapped back. "Holy fuck. That kid's fathered by a Shirley?"

"Honey…" Carly started. "It's an ugly tale we're not discussing here. Not now."

"Willingly or unwillingly?"

"Think about it," Trip said.

"Fuck," Bryson muttered after a second. "Fuck! Our kid's going to be a product of rape. You okay with that?" he asked his wife.

"Yes. He'll never know and it's the reason she's putting him up for adoption. Our names will be on the birth certificate and no one will know but us."

"Carly."

"Matt, no. It'll be fine. I promise. This baby will grow up healthy and whole, and very loved by us and your whole family. This baby's an innocent in all of this. So was Autumn."

Bryson's nostrils flared and he stared at his wife for a few seconds, then nodded. Then he spun again toward Sig. "Want to know names. Every single Shirley involved so we can go up there and charge them, get them to pay for the shit they did."

"No," Sig said.

"Yes," Bryson insisted. "It wasn't a request. It was a lawful order."

"They were handled. No names left to give," Sig said.

"What the fuck does that mean?"

Was he fucking dense? "Means what the fuck I said. We handled it."

"Christ," Bryson muttered. He shook his head. "How was it *handled?*"

"Want that fuckin' baby? Your woman want that baby?" Sig growled. "Then all you gotta know is it's been handled."

"That's not your decision. I've got a legal oblig—"

Trip interrupted him. "Heard you're a fellow jarhead. All your brothers are, too."

Frowning, Matt's narrowed gaze swung to Trip. "Yeah."

"You see combat?"

Something flashed behind the pig's eyes and his brow dropped low. "Yeah."

"See some ugly fuckin' things like I did?"

Bryson's chest rose and fell sharply, but he didn't say anything.

Trip kept at him. "Do things you never thought you'd fuckin' do?"

Matt's nostrils flared and his eyes became unfocused.

"Thinkin' you did. That shit scar you?"

Again, no answer.

"Scarred a lot of us. We did shit we had to do. We did shit we needed to do to survive. Sometimes to survive you can't play by the fuckin' rules. If you done time over there, you know that. Especially durin' combat."

"Last I checked we're on American soil and this isn't a war."

Trip's eyebrows rose. "Ain't it?"

"We had to fight to get Red and that baby back. Seemed like a fuckin' war to me." Sig then added, "One I was determined to fuckin' win. Because of it, you'll get the baby your wife wants so badly and we get Red."

"Shirleys lost this battle and there were some casualties." Trip shrugged. "None of those losses should come to light 'cause I doubt they're gonna be callin' anyone to report 'em. If they do, then you can deal with whatever *legal obligation* you gotta. But doubt you're gonna hear a peep from any of those clan members."

The Bryson pig still wasn't looking any kind of satisfied with what Trip said. But before anything else could be addressed, a nurse came hurrying out of what Sig assumed was Red's room.

"Dr. Bryson! Contractions are now about a minute long. She's fully dilated and feels the need to push."

Carly gripped Bryson's arm and gave him a big smile, a total one-eighty of her earlier bossy, pissed-off self. "If you feel the need to discuss this further with these gentlemen, honey, you do it another time. Now it's time for what we've been waiting for. Both of you stay here and I'll see if she wants either of you in there with her. I'll be leaving it up to her, since she probably heard you fighting like damn children."

"It's not my kid," Sig muttered. He jerked a thumb toward the pig standing next to him. "It's his. *If* he agrees to forget everything he heard about what happened on that mountain."

Carly's gaze slid to her husband.

Bryson muttered, "Fuck," scraped a hand through his dark hair and nodded. "My memory sucks."

With a nod and an excited smile, Carly rushed down the hallway and into the room.

Stella followed her and waited in the doorway. A few seconds later she turned and called out, "She wants both of you. Hurry up."

"You fuckin' go. Like I said, ain't my kid."

Bryson's jaw shifted. "She wants you in there. Or are you going to let her down again?"

Damn, that was just a dick thing to say. But then, pigs were nothing but tiny dicks with big badges.

Even so, the fucker was right. He didn't want to disappoint Red. If she wanted him with her, he was going to be with her.

What Red wanted, Red got.

He was such a motherfucking sucker.

Chapter Twenty-One

Autumn swallowed hard as she stared up at Sig's concerned eyes staring back at her.

She hadn't watched when Matt Bryson, with that last hard push, caught his son and then cut the cord. She hadn't looked when she heard their son's first soft cry.

But it made her breasts ache.

And her heart ache more.

Sig hadn't let go of her hand the whole time she'd been in the last stages of labor. From the second he and Matt had walked in the room together, he'd grabbed it and stood by her head, talking to her, encouraging her. While Matt had moved to the end of the bed where Carly was. His face didn't show excitement but more of a bit of panic at first, which he quickly hid.

Autumn wondered what that was about, but then, the thought of having a new baby had to be nerve-wracking. Especially since this one would be their first.

But no matter how hard she squeezed Sig's hand, he never let go. Not once. And he didn't complain about his crushed fingers, either.

He'd wiped her brow like Carly suggested. Again,

without a complaint. He talked to her low and quietly, telling her this day would be the first day of her new beginning. She no longer had to think about what happened in the past and all she had to do was think about her future.

If only it was that easy.

And she had no idea where she'd go from here. None.

A sob caught her attention and she twisted her head to see Carly holding her new son and crying.

Autumn pressed her lips together and felt the burn in her own eyes.

She wasn't sad. She was happy.

She was happy that with all that had happened to her, out of all the ugliness came something so beautiful.

Not only a healthy baby boy, but a loving family for him.

"He's normal, right?" she whispered to Sig. "All his fingers and toes?"

"Think so. Neither of them has made a shocked face or ran screamin'."

Autumn's lips twitched. "Well, that's promising."

"Yeah, baby, he's good. Looks like they love 'im already."

She nodded and blinked a few times, trying not to cry.

"You sad?"

"Tired."

"No shit. I'm tired for you." He leaned over and kissed her forehead, then pressed a light one to her lips. "That was some crazy fuckin' shit. 'Specially when that other thing came out. Thought you were havin' twins no one knew about."

"The afterbirth?"

He grimaced. "Yeah, whatever."

Carly stepped closer to the bed, the now swaddled baby in her arms and a little light blue beanie on his tiny head. "Do you want to nurse him? At least for the first time? It would probably be best for him with how he was malnourished during most of the pregnancy and also with him being two weeks early."

She squeezed Sig's hand, but not as tightly as during the contractions. "I don't know if... I can."

"Nursing will not only be good for him, but good for you, too."

She could barely make out the baby's face, but she could hear his soft sounds. Matt moved up behind his wife and put a hand on her shoulder in what looked like a silent message.

Maybe he was worried Autumn would change her mind if she nursed the baby. She still had time to decide to keep him. But not once during the pregnancy or even during the birth had she thought she should.

For the longest time it wasn't a child inside her, it was just a thing she didn't want to get attached to. Something that had been forced on her.

And then after deciding to let Carly and Matt adopt him, she began to let herself see him as a baby, not just that seed anymore.

"If it'll be too much for you, don't worry about it. I was hoping you would, at least for the first few days—"

"First few days?" Sig asked sharply.

"Well, until Autumn is allowed to go home and then afterward, if she wants to pump... And we can pick up the milk. With how she was malnourished when you found her, I'd like to give our son a fighting chance by having him get the colostrum she produces in the first few days. It might help with his development. Then after that it would be up to you, Autumn, how long you'd like to pump. As long as you're willing, we'd be willing... A mother's..." Carly grimaced. "Shit. Sorry."

"So, you want her to be like a fuckin' milk cow. Treat her like livestock just like—"

Autumn squeezed his hand, stopping him. "It's okay. I don't mind. What do I need to do?" She wanted to do whatever was best for the baby. It wasn't about her. It wasn't about the Brysons. It was all about that unplanned life brought into this world. It was all about him.

Carly helped get the baby settled in Autumn's arms and after a bit of encouragement, he finally latched on and began to nurse. The pull at her breast was as strong as the pull on her heart as she glanced down and watched his little mouth suckle against her.

She squeezed her eyes shut and tried to stop the memories of how he was conceived. Tried to forget the other half of his DNA.

Tried to forget the reason why he even existed.

One day. One day, when she was ready, when her life had some semblance of order and normalcy, she'd do this again. On her own terms.

One day...

Just not today.

Today wasn't for her. Today was for the new Bryson baby.

She didn't even know his name.

"What will you call him?"

Carly and Matt glanced at each other, then the doctor gave Autumn a smile. "Levi. Levi Matthew Bryson."

"Levi," Autumn said softly, going back to watching him nurse. "I like it."

"We'll give you two a few minutes while he nurses, okay? This way," Carly's voice hitched, "this way if you two change your minds... if you're even thinking... I'd like you to do it now before we take him home. I'm not sure if... I'm..."

Matt wrapped his arm around his wife and turned her toward the door. "We'll give you a few minutes, Autumn, just to make sure this is what you want before we put our names on the birth certificate."

Then they were gone.

Autumn slipped the beanie off Levi's head. "He doesn't have a lot of hair."

"Nope," Sig said, sitting on the edge of the bed by her hip. "And it ain't red."

"It's dark like Matt's. That's a good thing."

Sig just tilted his head like he sort of agreed but also didn't.

She put the beanie back in place, checked for all ten fingers and then glanced up at Sig.

Matt and Carly wanted to make sure she was certain. But if Autumn changed her mind, it would break Carly's heart. It was amazing how fast humans could bond with each other and fall in love. In just the little bit of time the doctor had held the baby, she saw both of Levi's new parents fall deeply in love with him.

But she still needed to hear it. To make sure she wasn't the only one who saw it. To make sure she was doing what was best for Levi.

Because he was all that mattered right now.

She sucked in a shaky breath. "They'll love him forever, right?"

Sig ran his fingertips down her jawline and then tugged up her chin. "Yeah, baby."

Suddenly, Sig was just a blur and her voice trembled when she asked, "They'll care for him forever, right?"

He nodded. "Yeah."

"They'll protect him until their dying breath, right?"

Sig touched the beanie lightly. And for a second, Autumn thought she saw a little bit of regret in his dark eyes. "Yeah, Red. They'll love 'im more than anyone. You're doin' right. This is the best thing for 'im."

"Are you sure?"

"Ain't you?"

She dropped her gaze down to the baby and said, "Yes.

I'm sure I'm giving him the best life possible. It's not about anybody but him."

"Yeah, baby," he agreed as they heard a light tap on the door.

It opened and the Brysons stepped back into the room. It looked like Carly had been crying. She had probably been worried Autumn would change her mind.

Autumn wiped away her own tears. "What do we need to do now to put your names on the birth certificate?"

Carly smiled and began to cry again. "I'm sorry. I'm usually not like this."

"Jesus, baby, you need to keep your shit together," Matt said, squeezing her shoulders but there was a little bit of a shine to his eyes, too.

"Your parents are going to freak," his wife said to him.

Matt groaned. "Oh yeah. Totally fucking freak since we didn't tell anyone this might happen."

"We didn't want to disappoint any of our family if this didn't work out," Carly quickly told her.

The baby released her nipple and as soon as he did, Carly rushed in and took him, throwing a small towel over her shoulder, and began to burp him, the doctor's expression soft and her eyes full of love.

That look of awe in the doctor's face made Autumn's decision so much easier. "I'll pump for as long as you need me to."

Carly's red-rimmed eyes went wide. "You mean even after the first few days?"

"Yes. For as long as what's best for him." Because that was what she wanted. Whatever was best for the baby.

"But..." Carly's eyes slid to Sig. "Does that mean you're staying in town?"

Before she could answer, Sig said, "Yeah. She's stayin' out at the farm as long as she wants."

They hadn't discussed that.

Carly frowned. "But the Shirleys..."

"Ain't comin' near her ever again. Like we said out there, got things straight with them. They ain't gonna touch Red or Levi. They're both safe."

"We are?" Autumn asked, surprised. Did he do something to the Shirleys that would get him in trouble? Or possibly thrown in jail?

She had no idea what went on after Stella and Dodge drove her away.

"Yeah, baby, we got it all handled. Your decision whether to stay or go. You stay? They ain't gonna bother you."

That was good news for both her and the baby, though how he got the Shirleys to agree worried her. But, still... She and Sig hadn't discussed her staying at the farm past the baby's birth. And they definitely didn't discuss where she'd stay on the farm. Did he expect her to remain in his apartment with him?

Was that what he wanted?

Was that what *she* wanted?

She was too exhausted to think about it right now. She wanted a clear head when they discussed it.

She was just happy she'd never be forced to go back up that mountain ever again. And she wouldn't have to worry about that clan stealing Levi from the Brysons. They could all breathe easier.

"Autumn, I'll have them send in something to eat and then you can get some rest. I'll check back later to make sure everything's okay with you. We'll take Levi down to the nursery for now and I'll monitor him closely."

"I'll feed him whenever he's hungry."

Carly smiled softly. "Thank you."

Matt squeezed Autumn's blanket-covered knee, his expression serious like he was having some heavy thoughts. "You don't know how long she's wanted this. Long before she got stuck with me. She's only ever wanted to be a mother and had to put that dream off when I came into her life because I struggled with it." He paused and took a couple of breaths before continuing. "I'd seen things... Things hard to shake. But I can promise you our son will want for nothing. He'll be extremely loved and will be a part of a family with so much love to give, sometimes it's smothering. He'll have cousins to grow up with, family traditions and unity, too. I promise you won't regret your decision." Matt grabbed her hand and ignored Sig's scowl. "When you're ready, anytime... *anytime* you want to see him, spend time with him... We'll leave that up to you. And if you decide to be a part of his life, you'll also have a seat at our family's table since there's always room for one more. I'm sure Levi's grandparents would love to get to know you. The door will always be open."

"There's never a dull moment at the Bryson family meals and holidays," Carly assured her.

"Thank you. We'll... I'll see." She wasn't sure that would be good for Levi. She wasn't sure if it would be good for her.

"And if it's too much, we'll understand that, too. Whatever you decide," Matt finished.

"When can she go home?" Sig asked Carly. Probably more than done with Matt's speech.

"I don't want to release her for at least twenty-four hours. I'll monitor her periodically and then tomorrow, I'll reevaluate. If you want... I can have someone bring in a cot. If you want to stay with her tonight, that is."

"Yeah. Not leavin' her alone."

He didn't need to stay since he stated the Shirleys were no longer a threat. And if that clan was no longer a worry, then him staying meant he wanted to be with her. Not to protect her but to simply be near her.

Carly smiled and shot Autumn a knowing look. "Okay,

that's not a problem. I'll get that set up for you." She put Levi in the rolling bassinet tucked in the corner and began to push it out of the room.

"Doc," Sig called out, making Carly pause in the doorway and glance over her shoulder. "Thanks."

"No, Sig. Thank *you* for taking care of them."

———

Sig knocked back half the beer in the bottle as he stared with a frown at Red on the couch. He was going to need a lot more than that to bring up what he needed to discuss with Red.

He tipped the bottle to his lips again and downed the rest, tossed the empty into the trash, and then went for a fresh one. He stared at the contents of the fridge. He'd never seen such a full refrigerator in his fucking life.

Not just because it was full of titty milk, but because ever since he had brought Red home that morning months ago, Stella, Trip and Red had made sure it had been full.

And again, except for the titty milk stored in both the fridge and freezer, it was probably what most people's fridge normally looked like.

Growing up, he'd always had to scrounge for food. His mother had never made an effort to keep a good house. Or take care of her kids.

Or keep her legs together.

He twisted off the cap, tossed it into the sink and took another mouthful.

His blood was pumping and he wasn't sure how to start the fucking conversation they needed to have.

Which was Red's future and his possible future with Red.

She sat there on the couch reading something on her

tablet as the double milking gadgets were sucking her titties dry.

Like a fucking dairy cow.

Each session lasted about twenty minutes and occurred almost every three fucking hours since she came home yesterday from the hospital. If she was going to do that for months, he might lose his fucking mind.

He wanted it to be his mouth on those nipples. His mouth showing her pleasure instead of those two gadgets only giving her full tits some "relief."

But her milk was supposed to be good for the kid. And that kid needed all the help he could get since he was half Shirley.

Good thing he was half Red, too.

His frown turned into a grimace.

She'd signed the adoption papers with a soft smile and only a few tears shed. And when Carly and Matt Bryson showed her the birth certificate with their names on it, with nowhere on it showing Red had done all the fucking work to make that kid, it made something inside him twist.

But she seemed happy. That was all that mattered.

Wasn't his kid.

Now Levi wasn't hers.

She could now start fresh. He just hoped she didn't want to do that elsewhere. And if she did, he only hoped she'd let him start fresh with her.

If she didn't want to stay in Manning Grove, he'd consider going anywhere she wanted. As long as it was with her.

Trip might not like it. But it wasn't up to Trip.

No, it was all up to Red.

But Sig couldn't imagine she was in a rush to go anywhere. She needed to heal a bit and she told the Brysons she'd provide that titty milk for Levi for a while.

Sig wondered how long "a while" was. And if it would

be long enough for him to talk Trip into giving him his half. If he got that, he'd have enough money to set Red up wherever she wanted.

Once everything was settled, he might just take a fucking trip out to Ohio. Or with some of the money, hire someone else to make that trip.

Because, while he was done up on the mountain for now, that whole thing wasn't done. Not yet. Two people still lived and breathed who had caused Red a lot of hurt. And that didn't seem fair to him.

Not fucking fair at all.

He sucked air in through his nostrils and deep into his lungs, held it for a few seconds and blew it out before taking another long pull on his beer. He then headed around the counter to where Red sat.

"Hey," he said softly, putting his beer down on the scratched side table. He noticed he'd left a half of a joint in the ashtray. Maybe he should go smoke that before talking to her. It might soften any sharp blows.

She lifted her gaze from the tablet and gave him a smile. "Hey." *Fuck*, he loved her smile, it got him in the gut every fucking time. "You okay?"

"Not sure," he answered honestly.

Her smile faltered.

"Don't you get tired of doin' that shit so often?"

She glanced down at the machine sucking on her tits. "Doesn't bother me. Carly said eventually I won't have to do it so often."

Thank fuck. "That means I get to..."

"Nothing is stopping you from them now, Sig. I mean, now that I'm home. Not right this second, of course."

Home.

That's what he needed to talk to her about.

"I just... don't..." He'd never been with a woman who'd actually been nursing. He wasn't sure...

"It won't bother me if it doesn't bother you."

Well, damn. "You want me to?"

"Don't you?"

"Fuck yeah," he whispered.

"We can't do everything right now, but we can still be intimate in other ways."

"Fuck yeah," he repeated in another whisper, her words giving him some hope.

Her lips twitched.

"Red..."

"What's wrong?"

Just as he was getting ready to sit, they heard a knock on the door.

"Fuck," he muttered. He was trying to gather the courage to have a serious conversation with her and then, *fucking figures*, someone fucks it all up.

With a sigh, he headed toward the door, checked the peephole and then warned her, "Trip," in case she wanted to cover up. He unlocked the door and yanked it open to see his brother standing with his hands on his hips and a serious expression on his face.

And he smelled like he'd just smoked a fatty.

Fuck.

That meant he had geared up to have a discussion of his own with Sig, who knew it would be coming sooner than later.

And now that Red was home...

"Brother," he greeted, his face grim. He looked past Sig and gave Red a chin lift and a, "Hey, Autumn, you good?"

"Yes. Not bad, all things considering. Everything okay?"

Trip was staring and didn't answer, so Sig twisted his head to see Red hadn't covered up. He moved to block Trip's view. "Brother," he growled.

Trip's dark gaze moved to his and he seemed to shake himself loose. "Yeah. Need to have that discussion."

Fuck. "Now?"

"Got somethin' else pressin'?" Trip asked sharply with a raised brow.

Sig's lips flattened and his jaw tightened as he considered his brother. The brother who'd done nothing but give to Sig and Sig took whatever Trip had given.

Sig realized he hadn't thanked his brother once. Not fucking once. And the man had even let Red stay when he didn't have to.

He also went up that mountain with the rest of their brothers when he didn't have to. When he was at risk to end up behind bars again for taking part in that whole thing. A place Trip had sworn he'd never go again. But he went up there anyway.

Trip went to the hospital to check on him and Red, too, when he didn't have to.

Sig was an ungrateful bastard. He needed to be better than that.

He dug his key out of his front pocket and tossed over his shoulder, "Trip and I gotta talk, baby. Lockin' the door, 'kay?"

"Okay. You two aren't going to fight, right?"

Trip dropped his head, stared at his boots and shook it. When he lifted it, he was grinning. "No."

"Promise?"

"Promise," Trip answered her.

"Sig."

"Promise me and Trip ain't gonna fight," Sig assured her, hoping that was true.

"Okay. I'll be done here in about ten."

Sig gave his brother a look, then said, "You got ten."

Trip, fighting a smile, nodded and turned to head down the stairs.

Sig locked the door and followed. "Where we headed?"

"Somewhere we ain't gonna be interrupted."

Chapter Twenty-Two

THEY ENDED up in the executive meeting room and sitting at the table. Trip took the prez's normal spot and Sig sat a couple chairs away, staring at the carved Fury insignia in the center of the wood table.

"We talkin' as Prez to VP or as brothers?" Sig asked.

"Both."

Sig's attention caught on the old gavel that laid near Trip's hand. The one Buck used to wield with the power of a goddamn dictator.

So far, he hadn't seen any of that in Trip.

Sig lifted his eyes to his brother's. Same color eyes, same color hair, same temper. All from the same father neither knew they shared until too late. "Jealous of those fuckin' pumps, brother."

"I bet. Long wait to get back in there."

"Yeah." The doc said maybe six weeks. It depended on how soon Red healed up. *If* she stuck around that long.

"That where you're headed?"

"Thinkin' so," Sig murmured.

"She on the same page?"

"Hopin' so. Me and her need to have that conversation. Was bracin' for it when you came up."

"Shit. Sorry. Didn't know."

"She didn't, either. Figured when she's stuck in place with those things stuck to her tits, it's a good time to have her complete attention."

"She dealin' with givin' up the baby okay?"

"Think so. Haven't seen otherwise. They gave her plenty of chances to back out."

"You okay with it?"

"Wasn't my decision. If it was my kid, then no. Wasn't my kid, so had no say."

"Sure if you had stepped up, she mighta considered keepin' him."

Sig frowned. "Should I have stepped up?"

"Truth? No. Think she did the best thing for that kid. She went through a lot of shit. She's handlin' it well but woulda been reminded of it every fuckin' day with that baby."

"Why it worries me about her supplyin' that milk. That's gotta be a reminder."

"Thinkin' maybe it's one way she can live with her decision," Trip said.

"Yeah, maybe. She wants the best for that kid. It ain't me." Unlike the Brysons, he might never be able to get over how that baby came to be. It might bother him for the kid's whole life and that wouldn't be fair to Levi.

He might always see that goddamn shed and bench. He might always see the way Red looked when she was running down that mountain, dirty, bruised, naked and pregnant.

Trip didn't say anything for a few seconds, he just tapped his index finger on the table a couple times, staring at it. He lifted his head. "You want her to stick."

"Like the kid, up to her."

"But you want her to stick."

Sig sat back and considered his brother. "Yeah, brother, want her to stick."

"She gonna be able to deal with your shit?"

"That I don't fuckin' know."

"You worried about it?"

Fuck yeah, he worried about it. He worried about hurting her by accident. He worried about scaring her away when he couldn't control his shit. He worried about betraying her if he had no choice but to find an outlet for his anger elsewhere. He'd never want to be a cheating whore like his mother.

So, fuck yeah, he worried.

"Were you with Stella?"

"Not really. She was part of the Fury when we were kids, Sig. Autumn wasn't. She don't know any of the shit we went through, what we dealt with. She don't know anythin' about the club life. Don't want to say she's not as strong as Stella, but right now? She's not as strong. Whether that'll change down the road?" Trip shrugged. "Remains to be seen. And not for nothin', you ain't easy to deal with. You got a past that'll keep fuckin' with your head. Though, in truth... we all do. You're just a little more fucked up than the rest of us."

Sig needed to make that clear to her. But Trip was right, Red wasn't as strong as Stella. Not yet. But it didn't mean she wouldn't be in the future. It was just getting to that future that worried him. "Seen bits and pieces of the real her, brother."

"Yeah, and you like what you saw."

"Yeah." He liked what he saw even in the beginning when she was mostly a shell of who she was now. He saw past it. He also figured their two broken pieces could make a whole if she was willing to try.

"Stella keeps me sane, brother. Just her touch sometimes keeps me from spinning. That the same with Autumn?"

"Not yet." He hadn't had the opportunity to try it with

her yet. At this point, if he felt himself begin to spin or the darkness start to set in, he would go as far from her as possible. He didn't want her seeing it or even being touched by it in any way. He didn't want to be the reason she retreated into her own darkness. He didn't want her hiding inside herself to escape his violence.

"Fact is, you got fuckin' issues. So does she. Might be a while before she's back to bein' whole, if ever. She worth that wait?" He scraped a hand down his beard. "When you first came back you told me nothin' worth havin' is easy."

"Yeah."

"Ain't gonna be easy with her."

"Nope. Ain't gonna be easy with me, either."

"Gotta talk about that, too."

Sig muttered, "Great," under his breath.

"The shit that happened up there. That dark place you went to with that belt in your hand. Been there. Recognized it. Know it's dangerous as fuck."

"Can mostly control it if I got the right place to focus it." But "mostly" might not be good enough.

"And like I said before, that woman in your place..." Trip hooked a thumb toward the apartments on the other side of the wall. "She ain't ever gonna let you do that shit to her."

"Know that, brother, but also don't know what to do about it. Know she won't be open to that shit. That she won't be able to handle me when I'm like that or need that..." He raked his fingers through the longer hair on the top of his head. "Fuck! Also don't wanna lose her. Don't know what to fuckin' do 'cause when I find someone to do that shit, it's more than just usin' the belt... It's just... more. The belt... the whips... whatever I use beats the fuckin' fire back but it's the sex that finishes smotherin' it. And there's no way she's gonna let me do that with another fuckin' woman and then come home and get into bed with her. Even if she let me get the first part elsewhere and then do the second part with her..." He shook his head. "Even the second part's rough. Gotta be someone who gets the fuck off on pain. Doubt that will ever be her."

"Don't fuckin' blame her."

"Right. So, don't know what to fuckin' do about it. Need somethin' but don't know what."

"Got an idea."

Sig's brow furrowed.

"Called a buddy, a guy I served in the Marines with. He's a fuckin' expert with his fists. Teaches people to fight, box, kick box, even a little bit of MMA. He's also a fellow biker, a part of the Dirty Angels down south. He's willin' to come up for a few days and get the two of us squared away with that shit. Give us the outlet we both need. My breathin' exercise only does so much. Stella ain't around all the time where I can reach out and touch her when I need to. This would help me, too. Anyone else who wants in on it, can get in on it. Gonna set somethin' up in one of the sheds. Turn it into a place where we all can take our fuckin' shit out on a heavy bag or one of those life-like body punching bags. He can set us up with everythin' we fuckin' need. Thinkin' we can also set somethin' up for you to beat the fuck outta with whatever you need to use. Belt, whip, whatever. Just ain't gonna be able to fuck it." His lips twitched. "Unless you put a hole in it, I guess." He snorted. "Almost like a rage room but more like a place we can punch and kick shit."

"Think it'll work?"

Trip shrugged. "Can't hurt, right? Sure there's plenty of us who'll use it. Hey, if it fuckin' keeps even one of us out of a concrete box, whether above ground or below it, then it'll be worth it."

"We got the scratch for it?"

Trip studied him for a split minute. "Yeah, gonna find it. Think this is important enough. Want you to stick, Sig. Want us all to stick. Gonna do whatever we need to do to make that happen. So far, we got the fuckin' booze, money comin' into our pockets, roofs over our heads, full bellies and empty nuts. This will just be one more thing to keep our brotherhood solid." Trip sat back and crossed his thick arms over his chest, drawing Sig's eyes to the president's patch on his brother's cut. "Hopin' you stick, brother. Nothin' I want more, 'cept maybe Stella givin' me sons."

"She thinkin' 'bout it?"

"Yeah, she's thinkin' about it. Not sure she's ready yet. Just like it'll be a long time before Autumn's ready. They both have good fuckin' reasons." Trip took an audible breath and grabbed the gavel, turning it within his fingers and studying it. "Again, want you to stick, brother, but if you don't wanna stick... You wanna take Autumn and start elsewhere... If that's what she wants... Gonna help you do that."

Sig's spine snapped straight. "How? Money's tied up in all these businesses and shit."

"Can sell a part of the farm to get you started elsewhere."

"You'd give me my half?" Did Sig just hear that right?

His brother wasn't any kind of happy about that offer, though. And he wasn't hiding that fact. "Not sure it'll be half but there's a piece on the other side of the tree line a developer approached me about when I first came back to town. Said offer would remain open. Whatever he'd pay is what would go into your pocket. Set you and Autumn up so you two could start fresh." He paused. "If that's what you want."

"That's not what you want," Sig murmured watching his brother's face closely.

"Used to be best friends, Sig. Closer than brothers. Now we know we're real brothers, we ain't even friends." Trip swallowed hard. "Miss that, brother. Want you to stay and wanna work on rebuildin' what we had. But you gotta want it, too."

Sig dropped his head and studied the table. The table that their father used to sit at. The table both of them had hidden under a few times. The table where they witnessed shit no boys should witness. The table that held both their past and their future.

The table that could build a strong brotherhood.

The table he might claim Red at.

If she wanted that.

If she stayed. If he stayed.

He had it good there. He probably wouldn't have it this good anywhere else. He had brothers at his back and a woman in his bed. In truth, he wanted for nothing.

He also had more than he ever had in his whole fucking life.

But he needed to talk to Red. See where her head was at before he made any decisions. Because if she didn't stick, he wasn't sure he could, either.

He fucking needed her more than she knew. More than anyone knew.

It was fucked up, but it was true.

He hoped to fuck she would stick with him. Whether there as a part of the MC or elsewhere. That would be her choice.

Because what Red wanted, Red got.

And he didn't give a shit if that was true for the rest of his life. He would break every goddamn finger trying to give her what she wanted. Just to keep what he needed.

Which was Red.

Fuck, he wanted her so goddamn bad, it hurt. And never in his life had he wanted anything so badly.

Except for his sister Syn to be safe.

"Gonna leave it up to Red," he finally said to Trip. "She needs to agree to stick with me. If she does, she needs to wanna stick here. She does, gonna do my best to repair what's broken. Me. Her. And you and me."

"Then I hope she sticks," Trip said softly.

"Yeah, me too, brother."

"Now, one more thing..."

Sig groaned. But what Trip said next surprised him.

"Need to fuckin' apologize. To you and to her. You're sittin' here, so gonna start with you. We made a bad call with the Shirleys. We shouldn't've waited. Wanted those fuckers to come off that mountain so we could snag 'em one at a time and dispose of them properly. And by dispose, you know I mean the pet crematorium. Was waitin' for that paperwork to all be settled. We waited too long. I'll take the blame for that. Wanted shit to be fuckin' neat. Sometimes life ain't neat. Sometimes we gotta get our hands bloody to protect ourselves. Promise you, won't make that mistake again. We need to handle shit? We're gonna handle shit."

That sounded promising, but Sig hoped shit like what happened up on that mountain never happened again. Even so... "Havin' that fuckin' crematorium's gonna make handlin' that type of shit a fuck of a lot easier, Trip."

"Yeah. Not only a perfect way to keep shit neat, but it's profitable, too. Hope we don't need it in the future to clean up messes, but if we do?" Trip shrugged and smiled. "We do."

"Ain't gonna hurt to have it. Will also keep any future prospects busy and makin' scratch for the club."

"Yeah," Trip answered.

"That it?" Sig needed to get back to Red. It had been over ten minutes and he needed to get this conversation over with. And the one with Red over with, too.

Trip rapped his knuckles on the table. "Talk to Autumn."

"Doin' that next." Sig pushed to his feet.

When he began to head toward the stairs, Trip stopped him. "Sig..."

He paused and turned his head to look at his older brother.

"You stay? Gonna need to get our colors inked onto your back. Wanna know you're all in. Think it's time for you to plant some roots. It'll help keep you on solid ground and out of those fuckin' concrete boxes. Because I know it only too well, bein' in one of those ain't a way to live, brother."

Sig only gave him a nod and then jogged down the stairs. Red was waiting.

———

AUTUMN CHEWED her bottom lip as she heard a key turning in the lock and then held her breath as Sig came through the door. She let her gaze slide over him from head to toe to make sure he was okay.

He looked fine on the outside and hoped that was true on the inside as well. Even though Trip and Sig were brothers, there always seemed to be some tension between them.

Neither were responsible for the sins of their father, so why their relationship was rocky, she didn't know.

"Everything good?" she asked him as he closed the door and locked it behind him.

"Should you be up like that?"

She stood at the sink, filling a glass with water. She wasn't doing anything taxing. "Yes, I'm fine. Moving around is good, running a marathon is not." Though, she couldn't wait to get back to her walks around the farm with Stella. She missed their chats, too. The bar owner had quickly become the sister Autumn never had.

His brow furrowed. "You ever run a marathon?"

Only down that mountain the day you found me. "No. Never. You?" she asked, teasing.

"Baby, we need to talk."

Crap. "I figured. The baby's been born, there's no reason for me—"

"No. Not about that. Well... Yeah, about that... Fuck. Sorta." He dragged a hand down his bearded face on one side, the other, then he scrubbed at his forehead. "You need to sit."

Her pulse began to speed up. "Is it that serious?"

"No. Well... Yeah. Fuck. Sorta. Goddamn it."

Oh boy. "Where do you want me to sit?"

"Truth? On my fuckin' face, but that ain't happenin' any time soon."

Well, she knew the man had no filter so she shouldn't be surprised by his answer. At least he was honest. "Yes, well... I wouldn't suggest that right now. But I'll keep it in mind for the future."

"That's what we need to talk about."

"Me sitting on your face?" she teased. She didn't like how heavy the room had become, but her teasing him wasn't helping relieve any of that tension.

"The future."

Oh shit. She had nowhere to go. She wanted to stay close for now to provide her milk for Levi. She could find a place in town, she guessed, but she had no money, no job. Nothing.

And even if she had all those things, she didn't want to go anywhere. She wanted to be with Sig no matter how screwed up he was. Because, in truth, so was she.

They both had bad nightmares and always might. And while she didn't really know everything that caused his or made him the way he was, he knew what caused hers.

From the second they met, he seemed to accept her the way she was. And not once had he looked at her like she was only a victim. Even with some of the things he told her about himself—and also with what Stella had warned her about—he'd never done anything to hurt her. She'd never been on the receiving end of his temper or violence. He'd been nothing but loving.

And that was the only way she'd describe it. Loving.

From the second he held out his hand to her in those woods.

Whether he'd admit to it or not.

For someone with such a short temper, he'd been nothing but patient with her. So, no matter what he said, she saw him for who he was now. Not who he used to be.

He came around the counter, grabbed her hand and guided her to the couch, making sure she was settled comfortably before he joined her. He didn't face her, instead he propped his elbows on his spread knees, dropped his hands between his thighs and stared at the floor.

Holy crap, this was not settling her nerves.

"Now that the baby's born, you're free to do what's best for you, Red. No reason to stay here anymore."

Oh, this wasn't starting out well.

"If you wanna go, not stoppin' you from goin'."

If you wanna go... If. "Maybe I don't want to go."

Autumn wasn't sure if he heard her because he kept talking like he hadn't.

"Not sure I can be what you need. You need someone who's soft and understandin'. That's never been me. I'm hard, got issues, got nothin' inside me." He pressed a palm to his chest. "Nothin'. It's cold and empty. Nothin' in there to give you. And you need more than just nothin'."

"That's not true. You have plenty to give. You just won't let yourself see it. You've got it tucked away so you don't get hurt. But I've seen it, Sig."

"Spent most of my life behind bars."

Good lord, he was coming up with every excuse to push her away.

"I know." Stella had told her all about his extensive record back in the beginning. She had wanted Autumn to know who she was staying with and offered to have her move into the house if she wasn't comfortable with the things he'd done in the past. At least the things he'd been caught doing.

Autumn imagined that list wasn't everything.

"Never cared about anyone but my baby sister."

"You cared about Trip once..."

"You need someone to love you as you fuckin' deserve to be loved, Red."

"Sig—"

"Never thought a woman would come into my life the way you did. Knew we were the same that very fuckin' second you took my hand, when you put all your trust in me. Never thought my life would change the way it had because of that one fuckin' moment."

She swallowed, remembering that moment, the moment where her thoughts had been spinning and she took that leap of faith and trusted him.

That moment changed her life, too. Not just his.

"I'm far from fuckin' perfect. Will never be perfect. Got issues I gotta deal with and so do you. Wanna deal with them together. But that'll be up to you. You don't wanna be with me, you can stay however long you wanna stay and go when you're ready. Ain't gonna stop you. You wanna be with me, then you decide where that happens. You wanna stay here, we can stay here. You wanna go far the fuck away, I'll go wherever you want. Don't fuckin' care. Got no roots here yet, so I'll plant 'em wherever you wanna plant 'em. Just want you to plant 'em with me. That's all I'm askin'."

What she thought was him pushing her away wasn't. Not quite. She now realized he'd been laying out all his bad points so she could make the right decision. "You want me to stay with you."

"Yeah, wherever you want that to be."

"You want to be with me."

He frowned at the floor. "Yeah, said that."

"Sig," she said softly. "Look at me." She reached out, took his chin within her fingers and turned his face toward her.

His brown eyes were troubled. Even apprehensive.

He was worried she'd say no. That she didn't want him.

But this man, the tattooed biker who talked rough and acted even rougher, had never hidden the fact he wanted her. He'd shown it in so many different ways. Even despite knowing what happened to her on that mountain.

He knew almost everything.

And some men might not be able to handle it.

But he had looked past it to who she was. Or would hopefully be again soon.

She was getting there. Every day was a step forward. And he had a lot to do with that.

Not just him. All of them.

In the short time she'd known them, the club had become more her family than her own. She now understood the appeal of the MC and the brotherhood. It wasn't orthodox but it was real.

"Sig, you saved me. I'm not just talking about the day you found me. But every day I've spent with you since. Every single day you helped me move forward and stop looking behind... It wasn't just you, it was Stella, Trip, Judge, Shady, all of the MC. All of you accepted me, took me in, treated me like one of your own, when I was far from it."

"You didn't make it hard, Red."

"You didn't make it hard for me to fall in love with you, either."

He closed his eyes and his jaw shifted. It was something he wanted but he still struggled with it. Hearing it. He believed he was unlovable.

His mother and father, whether Razor or Buck, never

showed him any. He probably didn't even know what it felt like. So, she wanted to show him.

Whether he knew it or not, he'd shown her love, too. He probably just didn't recognize it.

"Sig..."

"'Cause of you I've changed."

"No, you haven't changed. You're still you. You're still who you've always been. Like me, you still have issues to work on. And if I stay, you need to find a way to direct your temper when it starts to overwhelm you."

"Trip's workin' on that."

"Good. He loves you, too, you know. And you need to let him."

Sig said nothing.

One step at a time.

"Just wanna make shit clear—"

"Hold out your hand," she ordered, cutting him off.

Without hesitating, he did. He held it out to her, waiting, until it started to tremor just slightly. His dark brown eyes searched her face.

She searched his.

He hadn't ridden in to save her like a knight on his white horse. Instead he rode a black and chrome horse with loud exhaust pipes. He wasn't a typical savior, but he was hers.

And she'd keep him.

He was beginning to curl his fingers into his palm when she stopped him by putting hers in his and gripping it tight.

"You," she whispered, her voice trembling as much as their hands. "You. The choice has always been you."

Epilogue

RE-AWAKENING

AUTUMN GLANCED up from her laptop as Sig walked into the apartment, unwrapping the tape from his hands.

Today had been a bad day for him. He'd struggled after almost being clubbed with a bat when doing a repo earlier. He managed to grab the bat out of the man's hands and had broken it over a charcoal grill instead of over the man's head.

So, he was improving.

Somewhat.

But as soon as he'd dumped the vehicle in the new secured storage yard that Trip had built on the farm, Sig had come up to the apartment, changed and disappeared without a word to her.

She recognized the signs when he needed to be left alone, when his temper was flaring and she let him work it out as he saw fit.

Well, all except for the way he used to.

She had two strict rules. No spanking and fucking other women and no going back to prison.

While he agreed with both of those, he still had moments where she worried he'd break their agreement.

"Is it helping?"

He was covered in sweat, his hair was damp and his shirt gone, showing off his many tattoos and the defined muscles he'd developed since one of the sheds had been converted to the club's "rage room."

Those bigger muscles meant he used that room a lot. Most likely due to the fact that since they'd been together, they'd only had actual intercourse a few times before her going into labor. And, of course, zero since the baby had been born. Though, they had done a few other things. Especially since Sig couldn't keep his hands off her bigger boobs.

"You tell me," he said, throwing the wraps onto the counter next to her.

"After the incident earlier, did you have the urge to... do what you used to do?"

"Not really," he grunted.

Not really wasn't a no. But she knew he was doing his best and that was all she could ask for.

He was also taking the advice and training he'd been given to heart.

One of Trip's Marine buddies named Slade had come up not long after Levi was born. The biker, who belonged to another MC in southwest Pennsylvania, had brought along his wife, Diamond, their son, Hudson, and new baby boy, Sawyer, who was absolutely adorable.

In fact, she and Diamond had hung out a few times as the woman nursed Sawyer and Autumn pumped breast milk for Levi. The woman was a trip and told her some interesting stories about her "family." She'd been born into the Dirty Angels MC just like Stella had been born into the Fury.

Diamond had told Autumn, even though life hadn't always been perfect growing up in an MC, she wouldn't have it any other way. That gave Autumn hope for the future. For her future children, *if* she and Sig decided to have any.

They hadn't talked about it and were in no rush to do so. Unlike Trip, who kept saying he wanted two sons, Sig never mentioned children. Not once.

But if, down the road, she asked, she was sure Sig would be fine with it. He always tried to make her happy, no matter what.

She loved that about him.

And it was why she tried to make him happy, too.

It was also the reason why she was sitting at the kitchen counter completely naked.

Though, he acted like he hadn't noticed.

It wouldn't take much for him to be naked, either, since he was only wearing those long, loose nylon shorts he wore when he needed to go out and burn off some energy when either his nerves were shot or he was completely wired and ready to split in two.

Sometimes she wondered if she should also use the equipment in the shed. On those days where things could get overwhelming and dark. Especially after a restless night of nightmares.

Diamond had told her if she and Stella wanted to learn to kick box, she'd be glad to drive up for a few days and teach them. Or they could come down to Shadow Valley to her gym where she taught it. She just needed a couple more weeks to recover from Sawyer's birth and she'd be ready to get back to business.

Sig moved behind the counter, grabbed a glass out of the cabinet and filled it under the faucet. He downed most of it before lowering the glass, a few dribbles of water sliding into the wiry hairs on his chin. "Whatcha doin'?"

"Working on the motel's spreadsheet. The books are a freaking mess and it's going to take me weeks to straighten it all out. I haven't even touched the repo business's books yet.

And Dutch wants me to start handling the garage's books, too. He said, quote, *goddamn numbers are the fuckin' devil*. I told him I don't agree, but he just flapped a hand in my direction." Dutch could be a grumpy old man but had a good heart.

"You gonna do 'em?"

"Yes. It's money for us. But... I need a place to work, Sig. The counter isn't working now that I'm responsible for *all* the books from *all* the club businesses. Well, except for Justice Bail Bonds. But Deacon's been talking about handing them over to me also. If I get a little office somewhere, maybe I can do the bookkeeping for some outside businesses, too." She raised her eyebrows. "Make some money to help pay for things?"

Sig finished gulping down the rest of the water in the glass, then he just left it on the counter. Which was typical Sig. "Not in town."

"No," she murmured. "Maybe not in town. Not yet."

"Will talk to Trip 'bout it."

"I already did."

His chin jerked back. Autumn was learning to read his non-verbal expressions like an expert. The chin jerk pretty much meant, "What the fuck?"

So, she responded to it just as though he'd said it out loud. "Well, he's the one who gave me this job, Sig."

"Yeah, but I'm your fuckin' man."

"Wait. I need to go through you?" She jerked her eyebrows up in a non-verbal reaction of her own.

Sig's lips flattened out.

"I didn't think so." She pressed her own lips together to smother her grin. She had always been a bit on the bossy side and as the weeks went on, Sig was starting to get a taste of the real her.

She wondered if he was starting to regret wanting her to stay.

She never thought her path would lead her here. To this place. This family. This man.

But it had.

It was not the best or easiest path to find him, to find her place in life, but she did.

When she thought of Levi, she was always amazed with how something so beautiful had come from something so ugly.

That didn't only apply to Levi.

It applied to her relationship with Sig, too.

Ugliness had led her to him.

And he'd turned around and handed her beautiful.

Maybe beautifully broken, but beautiful nonetheless.

"Are you going to ask me why I'm naked?"

"Have I asked the five million other times you've walked around here naked? It's nothin' new, Red. Used to you torturin' me and thinkin' it's fun."

"I don't do it to torture you. I just got used to being naked and then coming here I was comfortable with it since no matter how big my belly got and how awkward I became you made me feel beautiful." She shut the laptop and turned on the stool. "But that's not why I'm naked right now."

"No?" He stepped up to her and in between her thighs. His nylon shorts did nothing to hide the fact that he had a full-blown erection.

He cupped her face and leaned in to give her a long, deep kiss that took her breath away.

When he was done, he pressed his forehead to hers and said, "You are beautiful, baby. Most beautiful fuckin' woman I've ever seen."

"Ever seen naked, you mean."

"Ever seen, period."

She smiled even though he was too close to see it. He dropped one hand to her breast and thumbed her nipple.

When he did, a little bit of milk dribbled out and he caught it on the pad of this thumb and licked it off.

"You due to pump?"

"Soon."

"How soon?"

"It can wait. I have other plans first."

He straightened, his eyes getting dark as he cupped both of her full breasts. "Yeah?"

She caught her bottom lip in between her teeth and nodded. "Umm hmm."

His brow dropped low and he studied her, looking a bit suspicious. "Some of your plans get a little whacked, baby."

She giggled at the fact he called *her* plans whacked. He should talk. "Well, I was just trying to get creative while we waited."

He grabbed his hard cock through the nylon and squeezed it. "How much longer we gotta wait?"

"We don't."

He stepped back and frowned. "What?"

"It's been almost six weeks. I double-checked with Carly. She said if I feel ready... she gave me... *us* the green light."

"What?"

She said it more slowly this time. "It's. Been. Almost. Six. Weeks. C—"

R ED SQUEALED as Sig grabbed her, threw her over his shoulder and hoofed it down the hallway as fast as he could. As soon as he hit the end of the bed, he tossed her. All he saw was a cloud of red hair and whole bunch of white flesh bouncing.

Along with hearing another high-pitched squeal as she landed, of fucking course.

Wasting no time, he shucked his damp shorts and boxers, threw them somewhere over his shoulder and dove for the bed, all his weight almost landing on her. He caught himself just in time.

"Sig!" she screamed in fake outrage.

"No time for talkin'."

She laughed and, *for fuck's sake*, did that sound good. But her moans were going to sound a fuck of a lot better.

In the months since she came into his life, he'd only been inside her a few times. Definitely not enough. They fooled around, sure, but he couldn't wait to fuck her and claim her as his, now he knew she was staying.

But, *fuck him*, he also couldn't go unwrapped. In anticipation of this very day, he'd been tested and she had been tested, too, during one of her prenatal appointments, but she wasn't on any kind of birth control yet.

He growled with impatience as he rolled close enough to the nightstand to grab a strip of wraps from the drawer, rolled back, then up and over her onto his hands and knees.

Her hazel eyes, more green than gold, sparkled up at him.

"Fuck, you're so fuckin' beautiful."

"You said no time for talking."

Right.

He took her mouth deep and hard, tasting every inch of it like it was the first time. Even though, he'd already had that mouth more times than he could count.

When her hands grabbed her own tits and squeezed them together, he abandoned her mouth for what she was offering. He latched onto one and sucked hard, tasting her sweet milk on his tongue for a second before moving back up to her lips and sharing that taste with her, causing them both to groan into each other's mouths.

Her body had changed a lot since that first morning he saw her. It had filled out, produced another life and now produced sustenance for another human. Her fiery hair fell around her shoulders long, thick and shiny. Her nails were longer and no longer ragged. Her eyes clear. Her mind sharp. Her attitude full of fucking sass.

And sometimes her bossiness turned him the fuck on.

Sometimes.

Sometimes his bossiness turned her the fuck on.

Though, not as much.

Whatever. It worked.

"Get up," he ordered her.

"Why?"

"First, gonna have you sit on my face 'til you come. Then gonna put you on your hands and knees and fuck you 'til you come. Then gonna put you on your back and fuck you while I suck those fuckin' tits 'til you come. Then gonna have you ride my dick 'til you come and *then* I come. Sound like a plan?"

"Sounds better than my plan. Are you going to last that long?" she asked with a straight face.

"Fuck no. Gonna be an all-nighter."

"We're going to make up for all those weeks in one night?"

"Fuckin' gonna try."

"I'm going to have to pump sometimes during this marathon."

He tilted his head. "Mmm. We'll see."

"Sig!"

He grinned. "They ain't gonna fuckin' miss it. You give 'em way too much, anyway."

She rolled her eyes.

"Don't act like you mind, you fuckin' don't."

"No talking, remember?" she scolded him, a blush coloring her cheeks.

It was fucking cute.

But then, she was fucking cute.

She'd be even cuter when her mouth was screaming his name and his dick was deep inside her.

"Gotta say one more thing."

"What?"

"I get too rough, things get too dark, or somethin' ain't right for you, tell me to stop. Yeah?" When she only blinked up at him, he said, "Need to hear it, Red."

"Okay."

"Been a while for us and been wantin' you so long, I might get rougher than I mean to. So, do what you gotta do to fuckin' let me know."

"Okay," she whispered.

"Okay," he whispered back. He gave her a quick kiss, then rolled away from her to his back, tucked a pillow under his head and held out his hand to her. "Get on board. Tongue train's gettin' ready to depart."

She gave him an answering smile, but didn't hesitate to straddle his face, and then she rode it like a wild pony instead of a train. He licked and sucked her clit while he squeezed her ass, spread her cheeks and played with her tight hole. Which he already knew she liked because he'd done it before. And he'd definitely do it more in the future.

But it was her moans which were the best thing he ever heard, besides the moment she told him she'd fallen in love with him.

That moment he'd never forget. It had scared the fuck out of him, but made him realize how much he loved her, too.

He never thought he'd love anyone. Didn't think he'd ever be capable of it.

But Red had proved him wrong.

He loved the fuck out of her but hadn't told her yet. If she ever left him, he didn't think he'd survive it.

So, when she came once, then a second time while riding his face, he didn't immediately put her on her hands and knees. Fuck no. Instead, he flipped her onto her back because he wanted to see her face when he slid inside her, when he made her come and when she made him come, too. Because he definitely wouldn't last long enough to do all the ways he wanted to do her. At least, this time. But they had all night.

Once she was on her back, giving him a heated look of anticipation, her lips parted, her breathing ragged, her face flushed, her long, red hair surrounding her head and draped over his pillow, he told her the absolute fucking truth.

"When I'm not with you, I'm in fuckin' pieces. When I'm with you, you make me whole. It's the only time I feel complete. That thought rocks me to my fuckin' boots, Red. It tears me apart in a whole different way, thinkin' that if somethin' ever happens to you or you ever leave me, I'll never fuckin' recover. That it'll shatter me beyond repair."

"Sig," she whispered, tears welling up in her hazel eyes.

"Just wanted you to know that, baby." He settled between her thighs, and dragged the head of his wrapped dick through her wetness, finding where he needed to be.

Home.

And as he drove home, he finally let what was building inside him go... "Love you, Autumn."

As tears slid from the corners of her eyes and disappeared into all that fiery hair, her fingers dug hard into his ass as she encouraged him to go even deeper.

What Red wanted, Red got.

As her hips rocked and his rolled, he did his best to keep it gentle, hoping one day she'd be on board to take it rougher sometimes. If she wasn't, he'd be fine with that, too.

Being inside her, feeling how slick she was because she wanted *him*, how she rippled around him, how she encouraged him with words and little noises, how she looked up into his eyes and saw *him*...

Fuck him, that was the best thing in the whole fucking world.

Her legs wrapped tightly around his hips and she tipped

hers sharply so he'd hit all the right spots, and then he began to suck on her nipples.

One of her hands clamped around the back of his head, her nails digging painfully into his scalp and her back arched. The motion of her hips drove him deeper, and her head rolled back as she called out his name.

His name.

Maybe *his* name on her lips was the best thing in the whole fucking world.

That exact moment was when he realized he didn't only give her everything she wanted, but she gave him everything he wanted, too.

Not once had she ever denied him anything he'd asked for.

Not fucking once.

Now knowing that, he sucked harder and drove deeper.

And when he felt it... when he heard it...

He flexed his hips and powered deep one more time.

And let go...

A few minutes later, once they caught their breath, their hearts weren't pounding so out of control, once they came off that high... He still wasn't ready to move.

But he needed to for now and he knew they had all night to continue what they began.

Hell, not just all night, but hopefully forever.

As he began to shift, to pull out, she tightened her arms around him, pulling him down to her to the point he was afraid of crushing her with his weight. She put her mouth to his ear and whispered, "I love you, too, Sig. But you don't call me Autumn."

He grinned. She was right.

He pulled his head back and looked down into her face. She was wearing her own grin.

He kissed that grin away, brushed the hair away from her face then whispered, "Love you, Red."

Her next smile was bigger. "That's better."

What Red wanted, Red got.

His lips twitched. "Gotta go get rid of this wrap and get somethin' to clean you up. Gonna need to talk to the doc about gettin' on somethin' so we don't have to use 'em anymore."

"Are you asking or you telling?"

He frowned. "Tellin'. This is one thing I'm puttin' my boot down about. Want nothin' between us. And wraps fuckin' suck. We ain't gonna be fuckin' anyone else, so no reason to use 'em."

"Well, I'm ahead of you."

He slid from her and slipped off the full wrap, rolling off the bed. He glanced back at her, where she looked perfect. Freshly fucked and in his bed. "Yeah?"

"Yes. Carly's going to put one of those birth control implants in my arm at my next appointment. She said it's a *set-it-and-forget-it* type of birth control."

He grinned and shook his head, relieved she'd been thinking ahead. "Sounds like a good plan, baby."

Because it sure fucking did and he couldn't wait, especially now that she got the green light to fuck. He headed to the bathroom to get rid of the wrap, take a piss, and grab a wet washcloth.

As he walked back into the bedroom, he was saying, "Could get used to comin' home to you naked. Ready to sit on my face and my dick." When he glanced up, he froze and his fingers clutched the washcloth tighter. And he might have even forgotten to breathe.

No *might have*. He did.

Holy shit.

Red was sitting on the bed still naked except for one thing.

"Jesus fuck," he whispered.

She sat cross-legged on the mattress, her back to him

and, when she heard him, she glanced over her shoulder, shot him a wicked smile and pulled her thick red hair out of the way.

It was the last thing he ever expected her to fucking wear. He never would have asked it of her, either.

Sig's gaze dropped from her face to the black leather cut she wore. The one with the rockers stating, without a fucking doubt, she was "Property of Sig."

He blinked to make sure he was reading it right. "You wear that, you know what that means?"

"Yes. Stella showed me hers, explained what it meant and when I asked, she had it made for me."

Holy fuckin' shit. "You don't got a clue about the MC life, baby. Sure you wanna be a part of it?"

"I'm getting a clue, Sig. I've been here long enough now. But me getting this didn't have anything to do with the MC life. It had to do with you. If you're a part of it, then I am, too."

Christ, this woman kept blowing his fucking mind. Just when he thought she couldn't get any fucking better, she did. "Can't wear it 'til I claim you as my ol' lady at the table."

"I know."

"You want me to do that?"

"Would I have gotten this vest if I didn't?" she answered all sassy-like. He needed to kiss that sassiness right out of her mouth.

"First lesson, it's called a cut." He approached the bed, the washcloth forgotten in his hand. As he got closer, she turned to face him and that's when he spotted it. Her name patch.

Red. Not Autumn.

He wasn't sure he liked that. It was his name for her and he might want it to only ever be his.

He'd give it some thought. But not right now. Because

right now his dick was getting hard again seeing her naked in his bed, wearing his name on her back.

She wanted him to claim her at the table.

And, *hell yeah,* he wanted to claim her at the table, too. He wanted his ol' lady on the back of his sled come their first Spring run, wearing his cut for everyone to see.

"You gonna be on the back of my sled for the next run and wear it?"

"Do you want me to be?"

"Really need an answer?"

Her lips curled up at the ends. And, *fuck,* he wanted to kiss her. Then he wanted to shove his dick between them as she sucked him off while wearing it.

"Might be a few months, but for now, you can wear it when I fuck you again."

"When I'm on my hands and knees like you said I would be?"

"Yeah, then. And while on your back, when you're ridin' my dick, straddlin' my face, or suckin' my dick. All of it." He wasn't asking for much.

"Won't that get it dirty?"

"Gotta break in that leather, baby. Might even come on it a couple times. Mark it to make sure everyone knows you're mine."

"Sig..."

"Just fuckin' kiddin'." He lifted his brows. "Or am I?"

She rolled her eyes as he climbed back into bed with her. Again with the sass.

He had a way of ridding her of it that they'd both enjoy.

He fucked her a few times with his cut on her back, which claimed she was his.

But in truth, she was claiming him.

What Red wanted, Red got.

And he was happy to give it to her because he wanted to give her everything. Just like she gave him.

That mountain.

That morning.

That moment when their hands first touched.

Maybe it was that moment when both of their lives began again.

Sig would do his fucking best to make sure for Red that life was a good one.

Sign up for Jeanne's newsletter to learn about her upcoming releases, sales and more! http://www. jeannestjames.com/newslettersignup

---

SOME RISKS ARE MORE dangerous than others...

Judd "Judge" Scott lives a simple life running a successful business with his cousin, Deacon. As a bail bondsman and bounty hunter, he's good at what he does.

He never expected Trip to come home and resurrect the Blood Fury MC, reopening old wounds. Being asked by the new prez to fill his late father's boots as the Sergeant at

Arms should be a hard no for Judge. Not only are they some pretty big boots to fill, but he also has too much to lose if things go sideways. Besides it risking his bail bonds business, he's worried history will repeat itself and Judge wants to avoid ending up in prison, or dead, exactly like his father did. Even so, he reluctantly takes the spot as the club's enforcer and wears his old man's colors on his back.

Despite having no interest in a woman complicating his life, he's intrigued by the young mother who shows up in town with her little girl. However, once Judge learns why she's come to Manning Grove, he finds he has no choice but to get involved. And that could create more complications than they're worth.

Turn the page to read the prologue of
Blood & Bones: Judge

Blood & Bones: Judge

BLOOD FURY MC, BOOK 3

Prologue
The End

JUDD CREPT through the used car lot, keeping low and to the shadows, ducking behind each car he came to until he spotted the one he was looking for.

He grinned and his dick was already hard in anticipation.

At sixteen and not yet a member of the Blood Fury MC, he wasn't allowed to touch any of the club's sweet butts, unless his pop gave his permission. Like Buck had done for Trip when he was fourteen and got his cherry popped by one of them. In front of everyone.

Judd didn't want his first time to be in front of the club members because he didn't need them heckling him as they watched. Just like they did Trip.

Fuck that.

Instead, he found a way to pop a nut on his own. At least in a snatch and not his own palm. *That* he'd done more times than he could count. Sometimes him and the other boys would hide under the exec committee table during parties and watch when one or more of the brothers used that table to bang one out with any female they could find.

His fist had gotten some good workouts while watching some of that.

He'd tuck that shit away and remember it when he was in his bed at night, too. It gave him plenty of spank bank material.

It was his time. Trip lost his cherry at fourteen. And Judd was now sixteen. It wasn't fucking fair and none of the girls at school would let him down their pants.

It wasn't like he hadn't tried.

He was too tall and gangly, and they called him a loser. They also called him dirty, even though he wasn't.

The girls would say nobody wanted to let white trash like him touch them. Because if they did, no other boy would ever want to touch them afterward.

Well, fuck them.

He didn't want one of those snobby-ass bitches, anyway. All he wanted to do was blow a load deep in their cunt, not marry them. Or even date them.

They probably preferred to take it up the ass anyway, so they could say they were still virgins.

Right.

He blew out a breath and slid his hand down the hard-on under his jeans. He'd stolen some wraps from the pharmacy in town and had a couple tucked into his front pocket.

He was ready.

He had also stolen some money from the cash register when the clerk was distracted by Sig tripping and knocking over a display of sunglasses.

Judd slipped him a five for doing it. Then Sig had demanded more. But Judd told the twelve-year-old he could fuck off. It hadn't been worth any more than five since he only had to knock something over while Judd did the crime.

Sig threatened to tell the clerk if Judd didn't give him a twenty. So, he popped Sig in the mouth, making him bleed. The kid accepted the five and shut the fuck up after that.

Judd needed the rest of the money since tonight was the night he was going to get what he'd been waiting for.

He popped his head up from behind a Chevy and glanced around the dark sales lot. At midnight, no one was around. He just wanted to make sure the pigs didn't roll by and see him, fucking up his plans.

He moved closer to the old Dodge Caravan and peeked through the side window.

His heart pounded so hard, he could feel it all the way to his dick.

She was in there. Waiting like she said she would.

Because the cunt wanted the cash.

And he wanted the cunt.

With his blood racing through him, he jerked on the handle to the sliding side door of the minivan and carefully pulled it open, trying to be as quiet as possible.

"Got the scratch?" Molly asked.

He could hardly breathe enough to answer, "Yeah."

She held out her hand with her long nails and lots of dumb bracelets on her wrist. "Let's see it."

"I got it," he told her, worried she'd snatch it right out of his hand and go tell his pop. Then he'd get busted right across the mouth—if not worse—for trying to fuck a sweet butt when he knew he wasn't allowed to.

But fuck Ox. All he had to do was tell one of those patch whores to fuck Judd and they'd do it. And he wouldn't have to pay them shit.

"How much do you have?"

"What you wanted." He was getting annoyed. She let any of the brothers fuck her for free and now she was getting picky?

He would be a future Fury member. She needed to learn a little fucking respect.

"You'll get it after."

She held out her hand again. "Least show it to me."

"Fuck you, Molly."

"No, kid, you want me to fuck *you*. So, scratch or no snatch."

"You're a fuckin' whore, you know that?"

"If I wasn't, you wouldn't be getting ready to lose your virginity."

Heat rushed into his cheeks. "Ain't a virgin."

"That's not what your fist says." Molly laughed.

Fucking laughed.

Fuck her.

"Show me what I'm payin' for first."

"I'm sitting right here."

"You know what I fuckin' mean."

Molly sighed loudly, like this was a chore for her. She shoved up her short denim skirt, opened her legs and spread her pussy with her long-nailed fingers. "There you go, kid."

He couldn't see shit since it was so damn dark in that minivan, even with the vehicle's interior light. But it was a free place to go and Molly had access to all the car keys on the lot since she worked there as a receptionist during the day.

Judd climbed into the van and slid the door almost closed. He left it open just enough for the overhead light to remain on. He pulled out the money, waved it in the air and then shoved it back deep into his pocket.

"Shut it all the way so the cops don't spot us in here."

He frowned and shut it, engulfing the whole van in darkness.

"How do you want me, kid?"

He wanted her to stop calling him a fucking kid, that

was what he wanted! He was fucking sixteen. He wasn't a kid anymore.

But he had no fucking clue on which way would be best in the back of a minivan. He'd seen a lot of fucking in his life. And he'd seen women getting it in all kinds of positions. But he knew this would be once and done for the fifty bucks he was paying, so he wanted to pick the position he'd last the longest.

Trip hadn't lasted long his first time, which was one reason he was ribbed so hard afterward by all the brothers. Judge didn't want that happening to him.

"Just pull your fucking pants down and sit on the seat. Christ, kid. It's not rocket science."

Judd quickly undid his belt buckle and his jeans, shoving them all the way to his boots.

"God, you're just a gangly thing, aren't you? Nothing like your pop."

"You seen my pop naked?" Judd wondered if his mother knew. Or if Trixie even cared.

Not answering, Molly moved off the seat, waited for him to get settled, and then she shoved her skirt up even higher.

A smell wafted to him that made his nose wrinkle. Is that what they all stank like?

So fucking gross.

But fuck it. They were there. He had the scratch and wraps. He was doing this.

He pulled a wrap from the front pocket of his jeans and handed it to her. With an annoyed sigh, she took it, ripped it open and rolled it down his dick.

He almost lost it when she did. That did not give him confidence in his staying power with what was coming next.

Maybe if he concentrated on the smell, he'd last longer. Yeah, that's what he needed to do. He inhaled deeply and almost puked.

Maybe that wasn't a good idea.

With that rot, maybe this whole thing wasn't a good fucking idea.

Fuck it. He was doing this. He could be pickier later.

"Wanna see your tits," he demanded as she began to climb on his lap.

"Not for a fifty."

"How much more?"

"'Nother twenty."

She was fucking crazy. He'd seen them before at the warehouse. They weren't worth a fucking twenty. *Fuck it.*

He held his breath as she wiggled herself into place, grabbed his dick, holding it where it needed to be and...

And...

Fuck. Fuck. Fuck!

He groaned as his load shot out of his balls and into the wrap before he was even able to stick it in. "Fuck!"

The bitch snorted.

Judd didn't find any of it funny.

"Wanna eat me out, instead, for that fifty?"

He tried not to gag. "No."

Molly shrugged, climbed off him and yanked her skirt down. "Better luck next time, kid." Then she dug into his jeans and yanked out the money he had tucked in the pocket. She slid open the door and disappeared into the dark.

He dropped his head back onto the seat, closed his eyes and blew out a breath. He just paid fifty bucks for something he could've done himself.

He yanked off the full wrap and tossed it onto the van floor with a curse. Then he yanked up his jeans and climbed out.

He was still a goddamn virgin.

He had already told Trip and Sig he was getting some tonight with Molly. Now he was going to have to lie.

He cautiously made his way out of the car lot, crossed the railroad tracks and hoofed it two more blocks home.

When a pig mobile raced past him, he hid behind a bush. His night had already gone to shit and him getting caught out after curfew would just be the fucking cherry on the...

Yeah, cherry on the virgin.

He blew out a frustrated breath and kept going. His pop wouldn't care if he was out after curfew, but he'd care if 5-0 brought him home.

Last time the pigs dropped Judd off, his pop beat him with a belt. Not for being out late, but for getting caught.

So now Judd was more careful. *Way* more careful.

As he turned the corner, he froze.

Their whole street was full of pigs. Not just local 5-0, but ones who were heavily armed, wearing all kinds of protective gear and hunkered down behind their vehicles and facing the old, run-down duplex they lived in. They looked like they were headed to war.

What the fuck was going on?

Did the neighbor in the other half of the house beat the shit out of his wife again? Even in all the times they'd shown up next door, he'd never seen a response like this before. Maybe this time he'd killed her instead of just giving her a black eye or a broken arm.

Judd ducked behind an overgrown bush and peeked through it.

What the fuck? The pigs were all focused on *their* front door, not the neighbor's, who shared the same porch.

Judd's heart began to thump. The pigs had their lights off, no sirens, no radios, and weren't saying a word.

Holy shit. Maybe they were arresting his pop for killing Razor and Tin Man.

His mom told him that Ox had shot Razor between the eyes in retaliation for killing the club prez, Buck. And then

Tin Man tried to take Ox out for killing the man's brother. Judd's pop blasted Tinny right in the chest, dropping him right where he stood.

So, yeah, maybe all the 5-0 out front had something to do with that since it only happened a few days ago.

Maybe somebody snitched.

And if somebody snitched...

He needed to sneak around back, get into the house and warn his pop.

But as he made his way through the dark, sticking behind the shrubbery, he came out behind the house, only to see the same shit as out front. Too many pigs, wearing vests and carrying high-powered weapons. Plus, a couple more local cops.

There was no way to get to the back door. They'd stop him first.

Something huge was going down.

Glass breaking at the back of the house, and a flash bang that scared the shit out of him, had him hitting the ground hard. A whole bunch of shouting quickly followed, the sound of doors being busted in at the front and back, shouts that included the words "arrest warrant," and pigs moving everywhere.

Holy fuck!

Judd was afraid to move, and he couldn't follow them in, anyway, because some of the pigs remained standing guard outside. Probably to make sure his pop didn't escape out the back. He watched the pigs, who had their guns drawn, enter the house, shouting to one another as they cleared each room.

Almost all the windows were propped open since it was ball-sweating hot out and the fucking piece of shit house they lived in didn't have air conditioning. Because of that, he heard everything like he was right inside along with them.

He crawled forward, the dead shrub scratching his arms, his fingers digging into the dirt, so he could get a better view of the back of the house. But he wanted to stay where the local oinkers wouldn't see him. Because if they saw him, they'd probably nab him.

Where the fuck were his parents?

Where the fuck was Jemma?

Had they left town and not told him?

Had they left town and left him behind because he was in some damn minivan trying to get his cherry popped and they couldn't find him?

Maybe they left town and just didn't want him anymore.

Through the open windows, he heard a scramble of feet, more shouts, then boots rushing up the steps.

"Gun! Gun! Gun!"

"Put the gun down!"

"Put it down."

Holy fuck!

Judd couldn't breathe and was frozen to the ground.

"PUT THE FUCKING GUN DOWN!"

"Fuck you!"

"Let her go, Scott. You don't want to do that."

"Fuck you, pigs!"

"Let her go."

"Put the fucking gun down and let her go."

Who? Who was *her*? His mother?

"She's just a baby, you won't be able to live with yourself if something happens to her."

Jemma.

His fucking pop had Jemma.

Judd forced himself to keep his mouth shut and keep from shouting out to his pop.

"Let her go, Scott. We can do this without any of you getting hurt."

What was Ox doing?

"Will let 'er go when you get the fuck outta my house."

"Let her mom take her. We'll get them both out of here safely."

That motherfucker was using Jemma!

"This isn't going to end well if you don't let her go."

Judd needed to get upstairs. He needed to get Jemma.

"You really want us to shoot you in front of your kid? Is that what you want? To show them how much of a hero you are? Scar her for life?"

"Fuck you! Ain't takin' any of us."

"We don't want anyone but you, Scott. Wife and kid can stay here. But we have a warrant for your arrest and we're not just going away. Let's do this without getting anyone hurt. Including your little girl."

"How come you gotta bring a pig army to deal with one fuckin' man? You all pussies?"

Judd didn't hear the answer or even if there was one, but he knew why. His pop killed people and didn't think twice about it. He'd kill all those pigs without even blinking.

But it pissed him the fuck off that he was using Jemma. His baby sister was only five.

Worse, Judd could hear her crying even from where he was lying on his belly in the dirt.

He could also hear his mom throwing out pot shots at the pigs. He wondered if Trixie had encouraged Ox to use Jemma as a shield.

If she did...

Judd's jaw shifted and his fingers curled into his palms, his dirty nails digging in painfully. If she allowed her own daughter to be used, Judd was running the fuck away and taking Jem with him.

"Ma'am, take your daughter from your husband."

"No, you fuckin' don't, Trix. Stay where you're at. It's a fuckin' trick. You know how these fuckin' pigs are."

"Get the fuck out of our house," Judd heard his mother

shriek. "Get out! This is our property! You got no fucking right to be here!"

"We're here to serve a warrant, ma'am, and we're not leaving until we do." The pig sounded pretty fucking calm for the situation. "So, let's make this quick and painless and stop scaring your daughter."

"You're the ones fuckin' scaring her with all those fuckin' guns drawn."

"Scott, this isn't going to end well."

"Yeah, it ain't, no matter what fuckin' happens."

When a sharp crack was heard, Judd's heart leapt out of his chest. "NO!" He jumped to his feet and began to sprint toward the back door.

Someone hooked him around the waist and pulled him to a halt. He began to struggle but was put in a hold that was not only painful, but made it impossible to break free.

"Lemme go!"

"Calm down, kid. You can't go in there."

"That's my sister!"

"She'll be fine."

"No, she won't!"

More shouts and boots stomping on the bare floors were heard. His mother was shrieking and his father bellowing out non-stop curses.

It sounded like a cluster-fuck.

But somehow through all that craziness and even through the pounding in his ears, he heard it.

Jemma screaming. Crying. Calling out Judd's name.

Judd lost all his strength and went limp in the pig's hold. His head dropped and he blinked back the tears that threatened to escape. "Jemma," he whispered.

The pig's radio squawked, and a voice announced Ox was in custody with just minor injuries. The woman and child were unharmed. Hearing that made him breathe a little easier.

"Lemme go!" Judd yelled, pulling on the arms preventing him from getting to his sister.

"You need to stay out of the way. If you don't, I'm taking you into custody."

Judd bit back his, "Fuck you," and nodded his head instead.

The pig slowly released him and as soon as he did, Judd ran toward the front of the house. The pig ordered him to stop.

He only slid to a stop when he saw a bunch of the military-like 5-0 surge from the house with his father in cuffs. However, it took a few of them to handle him because Ox wasn't going without a fight.

As Judd went to move toward them, an arm hooked him around the neck, cutting off his air. "Don't get any closer or you're going to end up just like your old man."

Judd forced a "Fuck you" past his crushed windpipe.

"Got a great future ahead of you, asshole. Just like him. Just give yourself a few years, if you live that long."

Fuck you. Fuck you. Fuck you, you scum-suckin' pig!

As they tried to drag Ox down the porch steps, his pop did a reverse head-butt and slammed the pig behind him in the nose. Blood gushed from the oinker's face and there were a bunch of yells, a raised metal baton and then it cracked his pop alongside his already bleeding head.

Ox dropped to his knees with his head hanging. The only thing keeping him from collapsing all the way to the concrete was the pigs hauling him back up. When they did, he spat a big, bloody hocker in one of their faces.

Judd shouted as everything became a blur. His father was shoved to the ground, a shin was pinned to his throat, and someone yelled, "Get a hood," as they shoved his face into the concrete.

Another one yelled, "Seems like someone earned himself a spit tax."

And then several of them began kicking his pop's ribs and stomping on him with their boots.

Judd's "No!" only came out as a squeak because of the arm pressing on his throat.

A flash caught his attention and he saw his mother, Trixie, rushing out of the house, screaming like a wild woman, her blonde hair flying behind her and her face twisted as she launched herself at one of the 5-0 beating up his father.

Another pig grabbed her, threw her to the ground and tried to pin her down, but she kept fighting. She was snapping with her teeth, clawing and spitting, too. Local 5-0 quickly jumped in and got her cuffed.

When the dust settled, his parents were both detained with their wrists and ankles bound, and screened hoods pulled over their heads. 5-0 dragged his father to a car, while a couple of them carried his mother.

She was still screaming but his pop was quiet as fuck, which was so unlike him.

Had they killed him?

One of the uniformed oinkers was yelling at Ox, "Double murder charge, resisting arrest, agg assault on several police officers, enough drugs in plain sight for a possession and intent to distribute charge. Illegal firearms. The list is fucking endless, Scott. You aren't ever seeing your kids again. Probably better for them, anyway. It'll give them a better future than an animal like you would ever give them."

The pig loosened his grip just enough for Judd to catch his breath. "Lemme go!" he cried. "Lemme go!"

"Who can come get you and your sister?"

"No one!"

"If you don't have anyone, Child Services will take both of you and most likely split you two up."

That couldn't happen. They'd run away first. He was

not letting Jemma go anywhere without him. "No! I'm sixteen and old enough to take care of her 'til they come home."

"No, you're not. And your parents aren't coming home any time soon. Both will be going away for a long time."

What? "Even my mom?"

"She's getting charged with agg assault on a police officer, and there were enough drugs in the house to be charged for that, too. You probably won't see her for the next five to seven years."

Holy shit. That can't be true! He couldn't raise Jemma by himself for that long. He didn't have money. He didn't even have a damn job. He didn't have shit. The only thing he had was what his parents had provided. Which wasn't much but it was something.

Now he'd have nothing. How was he going to take care of his baby sister?

"Got family close by we can call?" another pig asked as he approached with a pad and pen.

Judd blinked. Who the hell would want to take him and Jemma in?

The only person he could think of was his pop's sister.

But before he could tell the pig that, another oinker came out of the house carrying Jemma, whose face was ravaged from crying.

Holy shit.

Judd ripped from the pig's grasp and as he got closer, Jem spotted him and screamed, "Judd!" extending out her arms to him.

He snatched his sister out of the pig's arms, and she clung to him, snot running out of her nose and tears an endless stream down her cheeks. "It's okay, Jem. It's okay. Promise. Gonna take care of you. Don't worry."

The slam of car doors had him turning and watching

the pig mobiles tear down the street, one carrying their mother, the other their father.

He squeezed Jemma tighter. He had no fucking clue how he would do it, but he'd do everything he could to take care of her.

He just hoped he didn't fail.

Get Judge's story here:
https://books2read.com/BFMC-Judge

If You Enjoyed This Book

Thank you for reading Blood & Bones: Sig. If you enjoyed Sig and Autumn's story, please consider leaving a review at your favorite retailer and/or Goodreads to let other readers know. Reviews are always appreciated and just a few words can help an independent author like me tremendously!

Want to read a sample of my work? Download a sampler book here: BookHip.com/MTQQKK

Also by Jeanne St. James

Find my complete reading order here:

https://www.jeannestjames.com/reading-order

Standalone Books:

Made Maleen: A Modern Twist on a Fairy Tale

Damaged

Rip Cord: The Complete Trilogy

Everything About You (A Second Chance Gay Romance)

Reigniting Chase (An M/M Standalone)

Brothers in Blue Series

A four-book series based around three brothers who are small-town
cops and former Marines

The Dare Ménage Series

A six-book MMF, interracial ménage series

The Obsessed Novellas

A collection of five standalone BDSM novellas

Down & Dirty: Dirty Angels MC®

A ten-book motorcycle club series

Guts & Glory: In the Shadows Security

A six-book former special forces series

(A spin-off of the Dirty Angels MC)

Blood & Bones: Blood Fury MC®

A twelve-book motorcycle club series

<u>**Motorcycle Club Crossovers:**</u>

<u>Crossing the Line: A DAMC/Blue Avengers MC Crossover</u>

<u>Magnum: A Dark Knights MC/Dirty Angels MC Crossover</u>

Crash: A Dirty Angels MC/Blood Fury MC Crossover

Beyond the Badge: Blue Avengers MC™

A six-book law enforcement/motorcycle club series

<u>**COMING SOON!**</u>

Double D Ranch (An MMF Ménage Series)

Dirty Angels MC®: The Next Generation

WRITING AS J.J. MASTERS:

The Royal Alpha Series

A five-book gay mpreg shifter series

About the Author

JEANNE ST. JAMES is a USA Today and international bestselling romance author who loves an alpha male (or two). She was only thirteen when she started writing. Her first romance novel was published in 2009. She is happily owned by farting French bulldogs. She writes M/F, M/M, and M/M/F ménages.

Want to read a sample of her work? Download a sampler book here: BookHip.com/MTQQKK

To keep up with her busy release schedule check her website at www.jeannestjames.com or sign up for her newsletter: http://www.jeannestjames.com/newslettersignup

www.jeannestjames.com
jeanne@jeannestjames.com

Newsletter: http://www.jeannestjames.com/newsletter signup
Jeanne's Down & Dirty Book Crew: https://www.facebook.com/groups/JeannesReviewCrew/

facebook.com/JeanneStJamesAuthor
instagram.com/JeanneStJames
bookbub.com/authors/jeanne-st-james
goodreads.com/JeanneStJames
pinterest.com/JeanneStJames

Get a FREE Sampler Book

This book contains the first chapter of a variety of my books. This will give you a taste of the type of books I write and if you enjoy the first chapter, I hope you'll be interested in reading the rest of the book.

Each book I list in the sampler will include the description of the book, the genre, and the first chapter, along with links to find out more. I hope you find a book you will enjoy curling up with!

Get it here: BookHip.com/MTQQKK